Helen Glynn Jones is an author, blogger and freelance writer. Born in the UK, she has lived in both Australia and Canada. A few years ago, she returned to her native England where, when she's not writing stories, she likes to hunt for vintage treasures, explore stone circles and watch the sky change colour. She currently lives in Hertfordshire.

tiktok.com/@helenglynnjones

instagram.com/helenglynnjones

x.com/authorhelenj

facebook.com/AuthorHelenGlynnJones

threads.net/@helenglynnjones

T0274342

# THE LAST RAVEN

HELEN GLYNN JONES

One More Chapter
a division of HarperCollins*Publishers* Ltd
1 London Bridge Street
London SE1 9GF
www.harpercollins.co.uk

HarperCollins*Publishers*
Macken House, 39/40 Mayor Street Upper,
Dublin 1, D01 C9W8, Ireland
This paperback edition 2024
24 25 26 27 28  LBC  6 5 4 3 2
First published in Great Britain in ebook format
by HarperCollins*Publishers* 2024

A catalogue record of this book is available from the British Library
ISBN: 978-0-00-869540-8

*For my daughter*

# *Playlist*

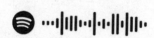

**Is Your Love Strong Enough?** - Bryan Ferry 🖤
**ZITTI E BUONI** - Måneskin 🖤
**Babe I'm Gonna Leave You** - Led Zeppelin 🖤
**Far From Home** - Sam Tinnesz 🖤
**Bring Me To Life** - Evanescence 🖤
**Gunman** - Them Crooked Vultures 🖤
**Hysteria** - Muse 🖤
**Ever Fallen in Love** - Buzzcocks 🖤
**Love Like Blood -** Killing Joke 🖤
**I Want You** - Savage Garden 🖤
**Nothing Breaks Like a Heart** - Miley Cyrus 🖤
**Spark** - Tori Amos 🖤
**Stockholm Syndrome** - Muse 🖤
**Love Song for a Vampire** - Annie Lennox 🖤
**The Air That I Breathe** - k.d. lang 🖤
**Evolution  Revolution Love** - Tricky 🖤
**Velociraptor!** - Kasabian 🖤
**I Knew You Were Trouble** - Taylor Swift 🖤
**Hella Good** - No Doubt 🖤
**Sober** - Tom Grennan 🖤
**Linger** - The Cranberries 🖤
**Fly On the Windscreen** - Depeche Mode 🖤
**Soul Asylum** - The Cult 🖤

# Chapter One

## CHANGING OF THE GUARD

W hen I was born, my father tried to kill me. No one would have been bothered if he had – it was the way of things for babies like me. But my mother fought him, or so I've been told. Still weak from my birth, blood on her legs, on her gown, spattered in her shining dark hair. And she won, as I screamed in the cot by the bed. She won. And so it has always been, her fighting for me. I love her like fire, like water, like something born of this earth that is bigger and stronger and deeper than words. When I was younger, she was my whole world.

Now she is my only regret.

'Come, Emelia, we are waiting for you.'

My father stands at the double doors to the sitting room, his arms folded. Tall and lean, the high collar of his black jacket stark against his angular pale face, the glitter of gold on the cuffs echoed in his eyes.

I pick up the pace, wishing I was faster, hating that I'm not. I keep my emotions locked inside, though, my pace gliding, my movements controlled, so I'm just like the rest of them. Hide my anxiety away, bank my anger to a low roar. Bertrand, one of my personal guards, takes up a position to one side of the doors. His massive arms are folded, the silver details on his uniform glinting in the faint light from the candle-lamps. My father ushers me inside.

'How are you, my gorgeous girl? All ready for Halloween?' My mother comes to hug me, linking her arm with mine, her long hair rippling like black satin around her perfect oval face. She's the one who's Raven, not my father, though he's taken her name.

'I'm fine,' I say, as she leads me to the sofa. Even though I'm not. Silk cushions slide against our gowns, soft like her cool touch. The room is warm, a fire burning in the fireplace, candle-lamps lit. The light and the heat are for me. They don't need it.

'So, Emelia', my father says. 'Your mother and I have been discussing the duties that come with your inheritance. We feel it is time for you to take on more.'

Oh darkness. Anxiety swirls in my stomach. My inheritance. A huge weight of responsibility looming ever closer, like a distant storm just over the horizon I hope won't ever arrive. When I turn eighteen next year, I'll be officially declared ruler of Raven, like every other Raven heir throughout the centuries. However, unlike those other

Ravens, I don't feel remotely ready to take on the role. Nor do I want it.

My father frowns, pinching the bridge of his nose with his long fingers. 'You're old enough now to be going out alone. You *should* be. There are certain expectations, despite your, er—'

'Alone?' I'm never allowed to go anywhere alone.

'With a guard, of course.' My mother glances at my father. 'But what your father is trying to say, is that we don't like to see you shut in, the way you are.'

'We realise that we've kept you... cloistered. And we have had our reasons for doing so.' My father paces, his hands together with the fingertips touching. 'So, we've arranged an outing. An opportunity to represent your house.' His golden gaze comes to me. 'Your cousin, Stella, is visiting Dark Haven to host a full moon party for Halloween. Usually your mother and I would make an appearance, but we felt you'd be better suited to the task.'

'I don't want to go.'

My mother's hand tightens briefly on my arm. 'There's nothing to be frightened of,' she says.

I open my mouth to protest, to tell her she's mistaken. I'm not frightened. I just don't want to go. Don't want to shame them any more than I already do. But before I can say anything there are footsteps.

Another guard enters the room, tall and muscular in the silver and black livery of Raven Guard. But oh, it doesn't really matter what he's wearing.

He's beautiful.

Ridiculously so. His smooth skin is pale, but there's a gold flush to it, as though he's swallowed sunlight. His cheekbones are high, his eyes a shimmer of silver grey, startling against dark lashes and glossy black hair like my own. He bows to my parents, then to me, and I swear he winks at me. His heels come together and he stands to attention, staring straight ahead.

I turn to my mother, a question in my eyes. She sees it, of course.

'This is Kyle. We thought if you had your own personal guard, perhaps you would feel better about going out.' Her voice rises on the end, like a question.

'What?' A blush heats my skin. My control is slipping, despite my best efforts. 'I have a personal guard! What about Bertrand?'

'Bertrand is needed elsewhere on the estate, and can't always be with you.'

'The heir to Raven needs a dedicated personal guard, especially now.' My father moves closer, firelight gleaming on his high cheekbones.

'So you're making me go with… him?' I gesture towards the new guard.

'We thought it might be nice for you to be with someone closer to your own age. You won't have to do anything – just be there in our name.' There's sympathy in my mother's onyx eyes. My father turns away, his nostrils pinched.

My frown deepens. My own age? Sure, Kyle might *look* eighteen, but that's no guarantee of anything. I glance at him again. He's not looking at me, but I know he's aware of me. Everyone in the room, as well as the hallways outside, is aware of me.

I try to break free of my mother's grasp but she won't let me, her long fingers cool. 'You can't make me do this.' I let anger curl through the words, just a hint, hoping it hides the pleading.

'We're not *making* you do anything.' My father's tones are clipped. 'It's a simple outing to a local club. Something you should be more than capable of handling. As Raven, far more will be expected of you.'

'Please, Emelia,' my mother says. 'You are the future of this house, after all.'

And I snap.

'How can I be the future when I'll be dead before you?' I hiss.

My mother flinches. 'How can you say—'

'*I will not have it!*' My father's voice thunders into the room. Everyone is silent. The new guard stares straight ahead. My father advances on me. 'How *dare* you speak so? You are the heir to this family, to our great name, and it's time you start acting like it!' He looms over me, all cold fury, like an iron statue.

My breath hitches in my chest, hot anger in my cheeks, choking my throat. I want to scream at them for what they've done, how they've made me. Unable to bear any more, I turn away, heading for the door. I hear the rustle of my mother's skirts, then her voice.

'Let her go, Aleks.'

I run across the foyer, taking the stairs that spill like molten gold from above. I race along the upstairs hallway as though trying to outrun my emotions, my fists clenched. Moonlight streams through long windows, painting silver squares on the dark carpet. I flash through them, light to dark, to light again, past the tall arched doors of the library where I used to take my lessons, beneath the huge gleaming map of the world on the wall. South America, coloured copper for Jaguar, Asia, jade green for Scorpion. Africa, golden like Lion. North America and Europe coloured silver for Raven, our major cities marked with stars. Places I've never been to, but that I'm expected to rule one day.

Except how can I?

I can't even go to a party without a fancy new guard.

Yet I'll be forced to take the crown when I'm eighteen, simply because of who my parents are. Never mind that my skin, my eyes, the way I move, *everything* will give me away for what I am.

Human.

In a world ruled by vampires.

A throwback, a reminder of our human DNA. And a liability, especially in one of the great families like Raven.

Blood borne, because my parents are both vampires, yet not a vampire at all.

Rage flares through me, fury at my parents, at the life they're forcing me to lead. I speed up, feeling as though I might burst into flames. How the hell do they expect me to suddenly become Raven? To go to parties, lead Gatherings, take my place on the global stage. I've barely even left the estate. I pause at one of the windows, gazing out into the darkness. Faint moonlight gleams from the distant boundary fence.

There's a whole world out there. A world I've never seen. But I *want* to. I want to see it, all of it. Not as Raven, but as I really am.

I've never even met another human, apart from the dancers who work for my parents. I bang my fist against the cold glass as though I can smash through it, break free of the walls that confine me, unleash my rage and fear. But all that happens is the window rattles. I lean my head against it, breathing hard.

My senses prickle as though someone is nearby, waiting in the darkness, even though I know there's no one in my parents' house who would hurt me. I push off from the window and start running again, letting my anger carry me.

A body slams into mine. I would fall, if not for an arm catching me around the waist.

'My lady?'

My breath catches. It's Kyle, the new guard. His face is close to mine, his violet scent all around me. His eyes widen.

'Forgive me.' He releases me and steps back, his hands clasped behind him. Moonlight carves his face into angles and shadow, catching the silver glitter of his eyes. 'I just thought that, as your new guard…' He pauses. 'Can I escort you to where you need to go?'

I wipe my cheeks and stand straight, imagining myself

pale and cool like my mother, despite my pounding heart, my rapid breath. 'I'm going to my room.'

He bows. 'Of course.'

I don't really want to go to my room, but it's the one place that's mine. But when we get there, he stops me from entering.

'Let me check,' he says. Which is ridiculous. Who would be in my room? They'd have to get over the perimeter fence, through the acres of grounds, scale the walls and break through the bars on my window. Not difficult for a vampire, except for all the Raven guards they'd have to get past first. Anyone who made it this far deserves to get me, as far as I'm concerned. Plus, I doubt my pretty companion would be much defence. But I let him look while I wait at the door.

'It's all fine.' He stands to attention. 'Do you… will you need to feed later?'

'I beg your pardon?' If and when I want to feed, I'll tell him. Not before.

His brows draw together. 'I have to ask.'

'No, you don't.'

His frown deepens, a ripple in his smooth brow. 'Fine.' He snaps the word out, then takes up a position to the left of my door, his back to the wall. 'I have to stay here,' he says, with a fierce glance at me. 'Unless that's wrong too?'

What the hell? He won't last long as my guard if he thinks he can act like that. I huff out a breath and stalk into my room, slamming the door shut and dropping the bolt. Like it would make a difference to him, or to anyone.

I flick the light switch on. Golden light pools along my bed, highlighting the tapestry cover, the cushions, the carved wooden panels lining the fortified stone walls. It slides along the velvet curves of the sofa by the window, the mahogany gleam of my dressing table and chair, reflecting in the black mirror of my television. My room is a calm place, somewhere I can relax. Usually. But not tonight.

I cannot do this. Even though it's just an outing to a local club, it's a step closer to who I'm supposed to be. But not who I want to be.

All I'll do is embarrass my family name, my parents. A human, thinking they can lead Raven. It would be funny if it wasn't so ridiculous.

Plus, I have to go with Kyle, who seems to hate me already. Who does he think he is, speaking to me like that? I pace back and forth, trying not to think about his body against mine, the cool violet of his breath on my skin. I don't know why I can't just keep Bertrand as my guard.

I flick on the TV, trying not to scream. It's mid-stream, one of my favourite shows. A boy and a girl, both about my age, sit at a table together outside, talking. Light gleams from the planes of his face, from her bright eyes, dancing through the leaves of trees. My anger slides away, replaced by sorrow.

I used to try and ignore the fact I was going to be Raven, as though it might go away if I didn't think about it too much. When it became clear it wasn't going anywhere, I knew I had to act.

I have everything I could ask for, except the one thing I

truly want. A human life lived in sunlight and warmth, instead of cool shadows. Like the lives I see in the old movies I watch, alone in my room. Somewhere I fit in, rather than being a liability, a monstrous throwback. An impossible dream, I used to think.

But now I have a plan.

I will *not* be the next Raven.

# Chapter Two

## DATE NIGHT

'What will you wear?'

My mother, her hands clasped together, surveys the contents of my wardrobe. She turns, her long skirts swirling, deep red like her lips. They look even darker in the dim light of my room, the electric candle-lamp on its lowest setting. Vampires can't really tolerate anything stronger.

'I don't know.' And I don't care, either. When I was small I used to like getting dressed up for events with my parents, putting on the small coronet, blurring my eyes in the mirror to pretend I looked like my mother. Now I'd rather be almost anywhere else.

*What is the point?* I want to scream the words, but instead I sit there, rage churning in my stomach, as my mother keeps rummaging through my cupboard.

'You don't know? How about this? Or this one?' The hangers rattle as she tosses dresses towards the bed. I wrap my arms around my knees, wishing I could burst into flames or disappear somehow. I may not have a choice about going out. But I refuse to pretend I'm happy about it.

'I feel like some things are missing,' my mother says, rifling through the hangers. 'Didn't I get you a black velvet shirt last month? Where is it?'

'In the laundry, I think?' I'm lying. I hope she can't tell.

'How about this, then?' She holds up a dress I never wear. It's short and tight and dark green. 'You'll look great in it.'

'Mother!' The word comes out as a snarl.

Her face falls. She comes to sit on the bed, putting the dress carefully on top of the others. She reaches for my hand, her fingers cool and satin smooth.

'I don't want to do this,' I say, trying to remain calm. 'I won't know anyone, other than Stella.'

'Which is why you should go.'

Sadness descends on me, smothering my anger. 'Am I the only one?'

The question that haunts me, through my lonely days. The idea of someone else like me out there, blood borne but not vampire. Someone who cannot be changed, even if they wanted to be, the blood magic already in their veins. Someone who doesn't belong anywhere. It's why they kill babies like me. Because we're useless. My fingers rub across the scars on my wrist. Their counterpart is etched into my soul.

'What?' A wrinkle appears on my mother's smooth brow, like a fold in silk.

I raise my eyebrows. 'The only human? You know, that isn't, um, food? Like, have any of the other families—'

My mother doesn't look at me. 'There might be.'

'There *might* be?'

When I was small I used to ask about it a lot, until I got old enough to realise it upset my mother. This is the first time I've mentioned it in a while.

Mother reaches to smooth my hair. Her perfect face is like a cameo, creamy white and sharp-edged in the soft light. 'I don't know for sure,' she says, 'but I did hear there might be one other.' I frown, my head down. 'Emelia, I swear, if there was another like you that I knew of, I would bring them here for you. But you are Raven,' her hand cups my face, 'and that brings you privilege beyond the norm. Don't be so quick to assume other vampires wouldn't want to befriend you.'

'We tried that before. Remember? It didn't go well.'

My mother's hand clenches. Yeah. She remembers. There's a reason I'm not supposed to go anywhere, not even to the kitchen, without an escort. Not that it stops me. The vampires on the estate are trained to resist my human scent, but it doesn't always work. I try not to think of the snap of bone in my old tutor's arm as she was dragged away by the guards after attacking me. She was sent to the pits, my mother taking over my lessons, my world shrinking further.

'But you're Raven,' she says again. Like it makes a difference. Like I haven't spent almost my entire life aware of how different I am, how I shouldn't even be alive. Like I've ever had a choice, in anything I've done.

'Oh, that's great.' I twist away from her touch. 'So I can expect people to befriend me because of my family name. It's going to be really fun when they want to eat me, but realise they can't!'

'Not every vampire is bloodthirsty.' My mother sounds disapproving. 'Once you go out more, you'll see.' Her tone turns pleading. 'Emelia, just try. For me.'

I sigh. I can't say no to her. Despite the fact I see absolutely no point to doing this, and don't want to shame my family any more than I already do.

'Fine,' I say, through gritted teeth. 'But not the green dress. The blue one, instead.'

Her face lights up. I'll miss her, so much. She jumps up from the bed, pulling me to my feet and dancing, like we used to when I was small. I play along for a few moments, my chest aching, then dance her towards the door. 'Let me get changed.'

She laughs, and I think I hear relief in it. She opens the door. 'I'll see you soon.' Then it closes, and she's gone.

I resist the urge to scream.

---

A short while later there's a knock at my door. I stand, smoothing my hands down my skirt. My anger is mostly gone, but I wish it wasn't – I can hide behind rage. Fear is a more difficult thing altogether.

Because I am scared, no matter how I try to deny it. This is the third reason I think tonight will be a disaster. The knock comes again, sharper this time. Wonderful. Maybe it won't be that hard to find my anger again.

I open the door. Kyle is standing there, dressed in black – jeans, T-shirt and leather jacket. I try not to roll my eyes. He's also wearing a small silver badge. Our house insignia, a silver raven with wings spread inside a silver circle, against a black background.

'You ready?'

Charmed, I'm sure. 'Don't I look ready?' I don't mind the dress I'm wearing, I suppose. It's short, and deep blue like my eyes, with a low V-neck and flared skirt. I add an extra spritz of anti-feed, the violet scent masking my natural perfume so I smell like a vampire, of velvet purple petals. Kyle wrinkles his nose. I hide a smile, tucking the small vial of spray in the pocket of my leather jacket.

'I suppose.' Kyle bows and holds out his arm, the elbow bent.

*Whatever, pretty boy.* I ignore his arm, starting along the hallway. After a moment, he falls into step beside me. When we reach the stairs to the main foyer my parents are waiting, their expectant faces turned up to us. 'Seriously?' I mutter. This evening is just getting better and better. Kyle glances at me. Annoyance digs its claws into the fear roiling in my gut. It helps with the nerves, but not much.

My mother comes over in a flurry of silk and kisses. 'You look lovely. Call me if you need me.'

'We are trusting you with our daughter tonight. Stella Ravenna is hosting, but you will have been briefed already.' This is my father, talking to Kyle. God. He sounds every one of his 547 years. I'm surprised he hasn't got his sword out.

'Of course, sir. I'm honoured.' Kyle bows. 'I promise to take good care of her.' My father smiles, his handsome face lighting up.

Oh *god*. I stare straight ahead, my arms folded, wishing once again that I could call the whole thing off. My fear and the fact that this is completely pointless aside, I feel stupid, think this idea is stupid, know that I'm going to look stupid compared to all the vampires, Raven or not.

The guard standing by the front door opens it.

'Your car is here.'

Gravel crunches outside. The black Mercedes pulls up to the bottom of the steps, Raven insignia on the doors silvered by the bright moon. My stomach lurches.

'Please convey our regards to Stella,' my father says, his hand on my back propelling me gently forward. 'And remember, you're representing Raven.'

How can I forget?

My mother frowns at him. 'But have fun! It's almost Halloween, after all.'

I go outside because I have no choice. At least Kyle isn't trying to take my arm anymore. But my stomach won't stop churning as we head down the steps. The driver opens the door and I get in, sliding across the seat, dark leather soft under my thighs. Kyle gets in next to me, folding his tall frame into the space.

'This is pretty nice.' He rubs his hand on the upholstery.

I watch it, distracted momentarily by the long fingers, his smooth skin.

'Is it?' My mouth twists and I turn away, watching night stream past the tinted windows, black upon black. I can hardly breathe.

'Who's Stella Ravenna?' I turn to see that Kyle has moved closer, one arm sliding along the back of the seat, and all at once it's oh-so-intimate to be enclosed with him in this space of leather and metal, the smoked glass panel separating us from the driver as though we're speeding along in our own little bubble. It's an uncomfortable feeling. I know I need a personal guard, but why did my parents have to choose someone so annoying? I clear my throat.

'Er, she's a cousin. Sort of.' I move away from him.

He huffs out a sigh, folding his arms. 'So, it's just going to be a party with all your rich Raven friends tonight?'

*My rich Raven friends?* How dare he. 'They're not my friends.'

'No? Not fancy enough for you?'

I don't say anything. First, because I need to control myself. And second, because he couldn't be more wrong. I have no friends. How could I? My mind shies away from the recollection of small hands grasping, needle-sharp teeth biting, blood trickling from a graze on my knee. These are not fun memories. I blink back tears.

'Sorry,' he mutters.

Oh no. That's the last thing I need. Pretty boy vampire pity. No thank you. I turn away, staring into the endless night. The landscape flashes past, dark humps of trees, the occasional building. I wonder how far we are from the nearest Safe Zone.

Safe Zones were set up two years after the Rising, during the Famine. Humans were dying, everywhere. And vampires realised that, if they wanted to feed, they had to take care of their food. So the four families got together and created the Safe Zones. Vampires were forbidden from hunting in them, their borders guarded, sun and wind powering silver lights to bind them in glittering strands of safety, keeping out the night, so that humans could live how they used to. I've never visited one. But I'm desperate to.

On impulse I lean forward, tapping on the glass partition. It slides down, the driver glancing back at me. 'My lady?' he says.

'How far is the Safe Zone?' I ask.

'About a twenty-minute drive,' he says.

'Really?' I bite my lip. 'Is it along this road? Can we go there, on the way?'

The driver shakes his head. 'I'm sorry, my lady. I'm under strict instructions from your parents. Perhaps you should speak with them.'

I sit back, disappointed. Something makes me glance at Kyle. He's looking at me, frowning. I return the frown, then turn away.

We reach the outskirts of Dark Haven, the closest town to our estate. It was a human town once, before the Red Rising when the great families came to power. The shops are decorated for Halloween, the streets full of people, some already in costume despite the fact it's still weeks away, everything painted silver and grey by the moon.

I spot a group of people dressed in black moving through the crowd, walking in formation. As we get closer, I realise they're Raven guards, moonlight catching the silver details on their uniforms. I sigh. Does my mother not think… My mouth drops open as I spot another group of guards, marching in the opposite direction. What the hell? Have my parents actually sent a battalion of guards to watch out for me? Even by their standards this seems excessive. I turn to see yet another group of guards on the other side of the road, moving quickly through the crowds. And I realise Kyle is still staring at me. His arm has returned to the back of the seat, his fingers tapping on the leather behind me.

Already this night seems far too long.

As we turn the corner we pass a building I recognise. It's a restaurant – well, at least it used to be, an old-fashioned soda place, they called it. I remember being taken there when I was younger, the colours muted by darkness, the smooth surfaces and mirrored wall fascinating.

Now it's derelict, the walls half collapsed, beams like blackened shards against the moonlit sky. The damage looks recent, too. I knock on the driver's partition and he lowers it again. 'What happened to the restaurant, on the corner there?'

'It burned down, my lady. A few weeks ago.'

'Oh.' I sit back, frustrated. It's obvious it burned down. As the car slides past, the crowds parting, I glimpse writing on the wall, scrawled on the soot-stained white paint. It says 'The North Wind will blow'.

I'm about to ask what that means when the car slows. We've arrived. My stomach drops. We're pulling up outside a nightclub, the Dome. There's a queue of waiting patrons, the doors blocked by several huge vampires. They're Ravenna guards, their silver-grey livery banded with black signifying their status as a branch of the Raven family.

As we pull up, all eyes turn to us. Vampires tend not to use cars. Petrol is scarce and they're expensive to maintain, so only the wealthiest families have them. Our sleek black Mercedes is going to turn heads. I practise smiling, but my lips are dry and stick to my teeth. I consider telling the driver to keep going, to take me away from here, safe behind metal and smoked glass.

The car door on my side opens. Kyle is standing there, his hand out.

'Get out,' he hisses.

I stare at him. He widens his eyes at me.

*Right. Pull yourself together, Emelia.* The waiting line of people are craning their heads and chattering excitedly, some of them holding up their phones. But when I take Kyle's hand and step from the car, their tone changes from excited to questioning.

My stomach sinks even further.

Heir to half the planet, and these people don't even know who I am.

## Chapter Three

UNDER THE DOME

The guards hold the club doors open. At least they seem to recognise me. I realise that, maybe, this is going to be even more difficult than I thought. I lift my chin as I walk past the waiting line of people, clutching Kyle's hand as though it's stopping me from floating away. My legs feel as though they don't belong to me, my stomach an endless sea of rolling waves. I've never been anywhere without at least one of my parents. I've never been to a nightclub, either. And now I'm about to do both with someone who's basically a stranger. But if I want my plan to work, I have to get used to being alone. To being out in the world. Things will be different when I'm living with humans. There will be no guards, no Raven emblems, nothing to tie me to who I was. So I fight the urge to pull away, to run back to the safety of the car. As we enter the club the guards bow their heads, saying, 'My lady.'

The doors close behind us, leaving us in a dark hallway.

Kyle lets go of my hand, his lip curled. I rub my palm on my skirt.

'Come on,' he says, impatient.

All at once, I'm angry. Who in darkness does he think he is? 'Just a minute,' I snap.

He sighs. 'Do you think I want to be here, either?'

'What?'

'I know you don't like me. I also don't care. But we can't stand in here all night. So let's just get it over with.'

My mouth opens, then closes. But before I can think of anything smart to say, Kyle opens another door, going through. I blink, then follow him into the nightclub.

Candles flicker at intervals along the walls, gold and black garlands hanging from their metal sconces. There's a large chandelier set high in the glittering domed roof, candlelight sparking from the mirror fragments embedded in the dark curves. People are everywhere, swaying on the dance floor, packed into lush red leather booths at the edges of the room.

'Well, if it isn't the heir to Raven.' I turn to see a blonde vampire approaching. She's dressed in silver, tattered lace wrapped tight around her lean form. I vaguely recognise her.

'Stella?' It's a shot in the dark, but hits true. She smiles, her green eyes lighting up.

'You remembered! I'm so glad you could come. We don't see you that often. Still, I suppose that's not surprising.' Her head tilts to one side, the green eyes less warm, more calculating.

Oh, so this is how it's going to be, is it? 'I don't go to many things. I choose my parties carefully.' I smile, not showing my teeth. Kyle coughs, though it sounds more like a laugh.

Stella narrows her eyes. 'Well, we're *honoured* you decided to come to this one. You and your... friend.' Her gaze flicks to Kyle, then back to me. 'Let me greet you properly, *cousin*.'

She takes me in her arms, cold and hard, her hug crushing. I can't breathe, and my legs buckle. Her face is buried in my hair, her nose moving across my neck, sniffing me. This is beyond the pale, even for family. 'Stop,' I gasp.

'Let her go, please.' The words are polite, softly spoken, but I feel Stella flinch, her grasp loosening. I take a deep breath, the muscles around my ribs protesting. Kyle has a hand at the back of my waist, the other still on Stella's shoulder. She's glaring at him.

'How dare you!'

'You were hurting her. Perhaps you forget?'

I'm still trying to catch my breath. Bitch. She did that on purpose. I shoot her a glare. 'Nice to see you again, Stella.'

'Sure, it's been a blast.' She curls her lip, then turns away.

'Are you all right?' Kyle is close to me, his voice low.

'What do you care? I'm fine.' I'm not fine. I'm furious. Stella and her friends are all staring at us. Kyle angles his body so they can't see me anymore. I can smell his violet scent, remember how his body felt against mine in the dark hallway. He's even more flawless close up, silver eyes a shimmer between dark lashes.

'I care,' he breathes, 'because it's my job. So don't give them the satisfaction.' He inclines his head slightly, eyes darting to one side.

'*What?*'

'You're Emelia Raven. You're royalty. The heir to—'

'I don't need you to tell me what I am,' I hiss.

'Good.' He grins, a flash of brightness in the dim light. He has dimples. Of course he does. 'So start acting like it. I know this is a drag, you don't want to be here—'

'You don't know *anything*,' I grind out the word, 'about me.'

'I know what I see,' he says. 'So, we have a choice here.'

'We do?' Part of me, despite the fact I can't stand him, feels drawn in. Beneath his violet vampire smell is something else, a fresh scent like green leaves. I consider holding my breath. Damn.

'Yeah. You can smile, pretend you're enjoying yourself, and forget about them—' he grabs a glass from a passing waiter with a tray, giving it to me '—or we call the car and go home.'

I stare at him.

'Make your choice. I have a job to do, and so do you. But we can't do it if you're going to spend the evening hiding in a corner.'

My mouth drops open in outrage. The drink is cold against my fingers, bubbles in the liquid popping like tiny sparks. I don't want to go home, I realise. Despite the fact I

24

didn't want to come here, going home feels, somehow, like failure. I take a sip, cool sting at my throat, warmth spreading in my stomach. Then I smile. It's forced, at first. I grit my teeth. I'm not sure who I'm angry with anymore. I take another sip. More bubbles, more warmth. Screw them. I'm Emelia Raven. I'm—

'I think we should dance.'

My heart sinks.

Vampires, as in everything else they do, are beautiful when they dance. Their movements flow, their bodies undulating like serpents. There's a legend of a woman, Salome, who danced for a king long ago. Allegedly she was from one of the original families, of the Scorpion line. She did end up taking someone's head, if I remember right, so there might be something to the story. The dance floor here is no different, vampires swaying and twisting to the beat, human blood dancers dressed to thrill, necks and inner thighs and wrists exposed, the veins over their hearts highlighted with glitter, an invitation to drink. They're beautiful too, their exposed flesh taut and muscled.

And then there's me. 'Dance? I'd rather sit down.' I scan the packed booths doubtfully.

Kyle shakes his head. 'No. If I have to be here, we can at least try and have fun. We dance, we have a drink, and then we go. Or are you scared?' He says it like a challenge, scornfully, but something else flickers in his silver eyes.

Is he insane? I am *raging*. I down the rest of my drink. I shrug his hand off my arm and follow him into the writhing throng.

The music is fast, a human song from before the Rising. Stella is still watching me, whispering to her friends, all of them laughing. Screw them. I start to dance, trying to twist my body the way vampires do, my anger fading as the songs change, enjoying the strangeness of dancing in a crowd, rather than alone in the library at home. Then the beat slows. Vampires start swaying, some moving fast, in a blur, as though listening to music no one else can hear, while others are wrapped around each other. Blood dancers move through the crowd, trailing scented wrists past potential customers. A slender dark-skinned woman is pulled into a vampire's embrace, his fangs dropping as his mouth closes on her neck. Kyle moves closer, leaning in. I hold my breath.

'Ready for a drink?'

I nod, annoyed that I'm disappointed, that part of me wanted him to pull me close. What the hell is wrong with me? It must just be a reaction to being out alone, to being vulnerable. Because I can't stand him. Yet I shiver when he takes my hand, pulling me through the crowd towards the bar area.

I stop walking.

He doesn't.

Oh gods. In several cages behind the long leather bar, there are humans. Men, women, all different sizes and colours. Mostly naked, other than scraps of fabric covering their most private areas. Their skin glistens in the candlelight, their eyes staring dreamily into the distance. I've never seen anything like this.

Kyle leans on the polished wooden counter. I swallow, then go to stand next to him, trying to act as though this is all normal. But inside I'm shaking. I dart a glance at the caged humans, my heart pounding. Our Raven blood dancers, lithe and healthy, many from families who've worked for us for generations, seem a long way from these humans curled up behind metal bars. I wonder what they've done to be punished so.

One of the cages swings out, the young man inside sliding his arm through a metal hole. A vampire grabs it, biting down hard. Blood spatters onto the bar, close to us. I try not to flinch. The boy pulls his arm back, his cage rattling. The vampire lets go, gesturing and shouting. There's blood on his mouth, and I smell sweat and violets. A huge vampire, twining tattoos along both exposed muscular arms, stands up from behind the bar. He gives something to the caged boy then turns to the customer, swinging out another cage with an older man in it, whose arm slides through the hole in the bars. The boy in the cage puts whatever the huge vampire gave him in his mouth, his eyes closing as he swallows.

'Ira!' calls Kyle.

The huge vampire turns. He grins, a curving scar up his cheek carving a white line in one dark eyebrow as he reaches to clasp Kyle's hand. 'Kyle! You made it out of the pits, then?' His glacier-blue eyes come to rest on me. They widen, then flick back to Kyle. 'Who is this you bring me?'

Kyle laughs. 'She's not for you. This is Emelia Raven.' At

this the dark eyebrows go way up, and Ira's expression changes from avid to respectful.

'Raven? Is that so?'

I nod, still shaken. 'Yes.'

'But you are – forgive me—'

'I'm the heir.' Yeah, I know I don't want to be. But still… I hold his gaze, daring him to challenge me, to say what I really am. Useless. Human.

Ira blinks. 'Of course,' he says. 'Tell me, do you like wine?'

'Yes, I do.' *Though I usually drink alone.* Ira bends down under the bar. I hear clinking and rummaging. The cage closest to me holds the young man who refused the vampire. He's watching me. I meet his gaze, then wish I hadn't. His eyes are dark brown and filled with endless pain. There are puncture wounds on his neck, scratches under the hair on his chest, blood running from the wound in his arm. His genitals are barely covered with a suede loincloth. He holds my gaze briefly before looking down.

Ira emerges, a dusty bottle in one hand and a glass in the other. He opens the bottle and pours the wine. It's dark red, like old blood, the candlelight waking ruby glints in its depths. I pick up the glass and take a sip. It's sour at first, then I taste the sweetness of grapes, the heat of the sun. 'It's very good. Thank you.'

Ira visibly relaxes. 'I'm pleased,' he says. 'Raven is always welcome here.'

*Well, we would be,* I think. *This is our realm, after all.* I drink more, finding I need it.

'What can I get you?' Ira turns to Kyle, indicating the caged humans. 'We have all blood types, plus these two—' he points to a stocky man who is staring and laughing, and an older woman, her blue eyes glazed '—have a little extra added, if you know what I mean.' He tops up my glass, looking expectantly at Kyle. 'We have blood dancers, too, if you prefer,' he continues. 'The Ravenna group brought their own, plus there's a few regulars. They cost a bit more, but free range always costs extra.' He nods conspiratorially. I avoid looking at the cages.

'Yeah. I might have something later. What do we owe you?' Kyle nods towards my wine. Ira steps back, hands up, looking scandalised.

'Nothing, nothing at all. It's an honour to see you here, really it is. Let me know if you need anything else.' He leans in close, jerking his head towards a darkened corridor to the left of the bar. 'There are human facilities down there, if you have need. And we're well guarded tonight, my lady – you need have no fear of any unrest in here.'

'Unrest?'

Ira seems about to say something more, but Kyle beats him to it. 'She's with me, Ira – what more protection could she need?'

# Chapter Four

### FEELS LIKE FLYING

I ra raises one scarred eyebrow, then his expression relaxes into a grin. There's something else in his icy gaze, though, when it flicks briefly to me. 'Of course. I mean no disrespect.'

Kyle laughs, clapping him on the shoulder. 'None taken, old friend. I know we have nothing to worry about.'

Kyle can speak for himself. My brows draw together and I open my mouth.

But Ira is already gone, moving along to another customer. Kyle leans over the bar, reaching for the bottle of wine. 'What?' He raises an eyebrow. 'Seems a shame to open the bottle and not drink it all.'

I'm not that easily distracted. 'What did Ira mean, about unrest?'

Kyle tops up my glass. 'Do you really think your parents would send you anywhere dangerous?' His voice is heavy with scorn.

'No, but—'

'And,' he leans in closer, a glint in his silver eyes, 'don't you think I'd look after you? It's what I'm paid to do, after all.'

I narrow my eyes. 'Stop.'

'Stop what?'

'Treating me like an idiot.'

'Fine,' he says. 'I'll stop treating you like one when you stop acting like one.'

'*What?*'

'Look around,' he says, still close to me. 'What do you see?'

I glance around the bar. People are dancing, blood dancers plying their trade. It's dark, and the air smells of violets and perfume. 'I see people having a good time. And I don't know what your problem is.'

'*People* having a good time? Or just vampires?'

I look around again. A woman is pressed against one wall, a vampire drinking from her throat. Her eyes are wide, staring at the ceiling, even as she caresses his back. A young man, clad only in tight black trousers, is bent back over a table. Stella and several of her friends are feeding from him at the same time, along his outstretched arms, another girl bent over his stomach, giggling, her mouth red with blood. He's not laughing.

There are also a lot of Ravenna guards, stationed around the perimeter of the room.

'Do you see?' Kyle's voice is close to my ear.

'But they're—'

'They're what?' I swear his lips touch my ear, shivers running down my spine. Stella glances over and smirks, nudging her friend. I glare at her. I've heard about her exploits, what she does with her guards. She has no call to judge me.

'No one would dare try anything while I'm here,' I say, sounding more confident than I feel. 'The guards would take them out instantly. It's why there are so many here.' But I'm aware, all of a sudden, of the world beyond, a vast unknown darkness. My parents' realm. I long for the light.

'Get over yourself. Nobody knows who you are, except for those pampered idiots over there. No, the guards are here because it's almost Halloween.'

*Get over myself*? I pull away, folding my arms. 'Fine. Tell me what's so significant about Halloween.'

'It's a sensitive time for humans.'

'Because…?'

'It's the anniversary of the Red Rising.'

Well, yeah. That's another reason we like to celebrate Halloween. I don't get the connection, though.

'So, there's always the chance they might try something,' he says.

'*Humans* might?' He must be joking. I know how weak we are.

'Yeah.' A line appears between his dark brows. 'So there are extra guards, just in case.'

'In case of a… human uprising.' I find this difficult to believe. 'Are you messing with me?' He has to be, surely.

'I swear on moon and darkness, I'm not.' He's still

frowning, though. 'Look around, Emelia. Why is it so hard to believe that humans might not be happy?'

'But it's just—'

'How things are? Is that what you were about to say?' His voice is hard, his expression tight. I don't know why he's so angry. He's being completely ridiculous. I don't know what else to say, though, so I watch the room instead, the ebb and flow of the crowd.

After a few minutes, Kyle speaks again. 'So, I guess we should dance again. Or something.' He sounds about as enthusiastic as I feel. All at once I'm tired of it, of him, of the evening, the way it's anything but a good time. I'm sick of feeling like a burden, somebody else's problem. It's exactly why I don't want to be Raven, and why I'm planning to run away. And I'm sick of Kyle's attitude.

I finish my wine, putting the glass down. 'Why don't you like me?'

'Why don't you like me?'

God and darkness, he is the most irritating person I have ever met. I hold back my temper, with an effort. 'I asked you first. And you've been rude to me since we met.'

He shrugs. 'I never said I don't like *you*. I don't like what you stand for, though.'

'Oh, and what's—'

'Here's a fresh one.' A hand grabs my arm, a voice harsh in my ear. Before I can protest I'm pulled into an iron embrace, cool breath on my neck. Then, just as suddenly, I'm free, spinning across the room. 'Anti-feed! Hey, what sort of establishment is th—'

There's a crash. Kyle's hand is around another vampire's throat, slamming him into a table. People are turning to look, and I realise I'm alone in the middle of the dance floor. My heart is pounding. Someone, probably Stella, laughs. Heat rises in my neck, my cheeks.

'Keep your hands to yourself. She is not for feeding!' Kyle sounds furious. I'm furious too. How *dare* someone lay hands on me. I step forward but Kyle motions me back with his free arm.

'Who says?' The other vampire sneers, pushing against Kyle, who slams him back again, muscles flexing under his leather jacket.

'Raven says, that's who!' he snarls in the other vampire's face, shoving him one more time. His head hits the table with a cracking sound and I wince. 'As do I.'

The vampire raises both hands, the skin of his neck cracked and reddened where Kyle is holding him.

'So we're fine?' Kyle's face is close to the other vampire's.

'Yes, fine. I want no trouble with Raven.' The vampire slants his gaze to me. I see the question in his eyes. I put my shoulders back, raising my chin. Kyle lets go of him and, with a whoosh, is in front of me, his shoulders curved forward, so close my nose almost touches the black fabric of his shirt. He sniffs.

'You need to top up.'

I smell my wrist. The anti-feed is wearing off, the violet scent faint. I reach into my pocket for the little vial, but my hand is trembling too much to open it. The vampire who attacked me is being escorted out, two Ravenna guards helping him on his way. Stella is smirking, and one of her friends rolls her eyes at me.

'C'mon.' Kyle takes my arm, his grip rough, heading for the hallway leading to the bathrooms. I let him, only because I'm shaking so much. I'm about to open the bathroom door when Kyle stops me, his arm coming up. His fangs are dropped, white points glimpsed in the half-dark. His hand is gentle, though, as it comes to my throat, brushing my hair aside. His fingers trace along my neck, and he exhales. 'There are no marks. He didn't get you. You need to remember to top up.'

My face prickles with embarrassment. I'm not five. But I should have remembered. 'Fine,' I mutter. 'And, thanks.'

'Just doing my job,' he says. His gaze moves over my shoulder. He frowns.

I don't want to turn around. I'm sure everyone is watching me. 'I want to go home,' I say, the words falling from me like seeds, bitter with shame.

'Stay here,' he says, moving around me. His back is against mine for a moment, then he's gone. I lean on the wall, my legs unsteady. And I wonder at his strength, the way he took on the other vampire so easily. What did Ira say? Something about the pits?

The pits are where vampires fight. But not just any vampires. Criminals, prisoners, those who fall foul of the Raven regime. All trotted out in the underground rings to meet their fates, either triumphing or being ripped apart by the gladiators. Kyle must be pretty strong to have been one of the champions, chosen to fight and trained from when he was changed, a life of blood and darkness. I blush, remembering how I'd thought he wouldn't be much protection. I suppose there's no way my parents would have sent me out here with someone who couldn't look after me. I still don't know why they haven't just had another child, though. Someone who isn't weak, who doesn't need constant protection, who isn't such a worry. I suppose when I leave they might consider it. They'll need another heir, after all.

I sigh, picking at a loose piece of paint with my fingernail, trying to ignore the ache in my chest. I wonder what Kyle is doing, and why it's taking so long.

'My lady?'

I turn. It's Ira. His bulk almost fills the hallway, his hands twisting together.

'Are you all right?' he asks. 'I'm so sorry. He had no right to touch you. All our stock is clearly marked.' His dark brows lower over his icy eyes and I step back.

'She's fine.' Kyle appears in a whoosh of speed. His arm slides around my waist, his body hard against mine.

I catch my breath. 'I am fine,' I say. 'I hope he'll be dealt with.' I try to sound like my mother, calm and cool. But it comes out half-strangled. I clear my throat, pushing on Kyle's arm until he lets me go. Why the hell is he holding on to me?

Ira lets out a sigh. 'He will,' he says. 'You won't see him again. I do hope this means you'll be staying for another drink?'

'We have to go.' Kyle doesn't sound impressed. 'Is there another way out?'

'Of course. The door behind you leads outside. Please, allow me.' Ira pushes past with a rattle of keys, the door opening with a cracking sound, letting in cool air. I start forward. Kyle comes around me, fast. 'I go first.' He shoots me a glare over his shoulder before stepping through the doorway. I follow, squeezing past our host. He's still frowning, his huge shoulders slumped forward. Something in his icy gaze touches me and I pause.

'Thank you,' I say, 'for the wine.'

Ira puts his hand on my shoulder. 'You're welcome. Safe travels home, my lady. I hope to see you again.'

I nod, not sure what to say. I doubt I'll be back. The door closes, leaving Kyle and me alone in the darkness. It's quieter outside, which is a relief, the pounding bass reduced to a dull thud. The cold air hits me like a shock, and I'm tired and weepy, despite my best efforts. All my walls, all the barriers I put up, are down. Such a stupid night.

Kyle puts his hands in his pockets, his head slightly tilted. 'You ready?'

'Ready?' My mouth twists against the tears I'm holding back. God and darkness, I want this night to be *over*. 'When is the car coming?'

'It's not,' he says. 'Not yet, anyway. So it's faster if I just take you.'

'What?' My stomach lurches. 'What, like, walking?'

'I'm pretty fast. And you don't look like you weigh much. We could be home in fifteen minutes, tops.'

'But what if we see any other—'

'We won't.' He grins. Damn those dimples. 'I told you, I'm fast. Besides, if we do, I'll tell them you're a nice takeaway, and I won't be sharing.'

My mouth drops open. 'Ass!' He can joke all he wants, but this is madness. 'I'll just call my mother.' I fumble in my pocket for my phone, but before I can get it he scoops me up, one arm under my legs and the other around my shoulders. His palm rests on my cheek, holding me tight to the contours of his chest. 'Hang on,' I hear him say. Then he starts to run.

'Are you insane?' I shriek, as we speed into the darkness. 'Put me down!'

'Sorry, can't. And don't think about being carried on my back, either. I've seen humans torn from vampire backs before. Don't worry, we'll be home soon.'

'What?' Fear thrums through me and I curl into him, my hand twisting in the leather of his jacket. Darkness is all around us and it's like flying, a dream of gliding above the earth, stars streaking into light overhead.

Both my parents have carried me, when I was younger, playing games on the long lawns and rolling fields of our estate. When my father ran with me it was part terrifying, part exhilarating, and I used to laugh and cry in turn, tears leaking from my closed eyes. When my mother ran with me I felt safe, held in a net of love strong and soft as her long hair, which wrapped around me like living tendrils.

And with Kyle, it's different again. The night is a blur of velvety dark, and it's as though we're the only two people on earth. All I hear is the wind rushing past, the pad of his feet on the road. I slip into a trance, feeling suspended in space and time, wrapped in his arms. When we finally come to a stop, I lift my head.

And blink.

'Kyle?'

'Emelia?'

'Where are we?'

'I wanted to show you something.' He tilts his head to one side, his silver eyes catching the moonlight. 'Don't you trust me?'

Trust him? Fear is like a knife inside me.

I have no idea where we are.

There's no light, other than the moon, but we seem to be in a meadow. The grass is cool with frost, stars sprinkled above us like silver glitter. There are trees, a wall of shadow. I realise we're on the edge of a forest. The Great Forest. Fuck.

The Great Forest covers a large swathe of land, extending almost to the Safe Zone. A portion of it runs on our own land, and we keep it tamed. But this, this is the wild wood, home to darkness knows what. Kyle is waiting, hands in his pockets, moonlight catching the silver Raven crest on his badge. I remember that he's pledged to my family, that death would be swift if he ever put me in harm's way. Not that it would help me much, of course.

I swallow, my heart beating fast. Then I realise Kyle's gone, leaving me in the meadow.

Alone.

# Chapter Five

## WATERFALL

'**K**yle?'

No answer. I strain to see into the darkness beneath the creaking trees. There are no landmarks, nothing I can orient myself by except the moon. My fists clench, tears in my eyes. When I pull out my phone, there's no coverage.

I'm stuck out here.

Anger rises, cutting into my fear. Kyle is *so* fired when I get home. *If* I get home. I chew my lip, considering my options. Perhaps if I keep to the edge of the forest, I'll make it back that way. I hope.

Before I reach the trees arms come around me, teeth grazing my ear.

'Let me go!' I push at the arms holding me like iron bands, even though I know it's useless. I have no strength against vampires. But to my surprise I'm released, and a dark figure appears in front of me.

It's Kyle.

'What the fuck!' I shriek. 'Take me home, now!'

He leans in fast, like a striking snake, his hand tight on my arm. 'No, and keep your voice down. It's not safe out here.'

'Keep my voice down?' I am going to kill him. 'I wouldn't *be* in danger if it wasn't for you, asshole!'

'Asshole?' One corner of his mouth curves up. Is he *laughing* at me? 'And here I am, thinking I'm doing you a favour.'

'How is bringing me to the middle of nowhere and disappearing doing me a favour?' I want to shriek so loudly the treetops sway, but I keep my voice to a sharp whisper.

'I brought you out here because I thought you needed it.'

'I *needed* to be put in danger? That is literally the opposite of what a guard is supposed to do!'

'You're not in danger. As long as you're with me, anyway.' He draws back from me, his silver gaze narrowing slightly. 'And I will take you home.'

'And then you'll be fired, when I tell my parents what you did!' Okay. Probably not the wisest thing to say to the person who holds my safety in his hands. He could disappear again, and then I'd be screwed. Still, it's done now. I fold my arms and wait, hoping he hasn't noticed how much my legs are trembling.

'You won't tell them.'

'I won't?' Fear, now, clenching around my insides like a fist. 'Why?'

'Because, like I say, I'm doing you a favour. I'm going to show you something wonderful.' He steps back, stretching his arms out and turning his face to the moon. 'Can't you feel it? Step outside your narrow world for a moment.'

'Feel what?' A couple of tears trickle down my cheek. I wipe them away, quickly. The last thing I need to do is tempt him.

'Just think about where you are right now.' His silver gaze softens, slightly. 'Come on, Emelia. I can tell you need this.'

I frown, looking around. What in darkness is he on about? What, about any of this, could I possibly need? Then, as I stand in the cold meadow, frost forming on my boots, something inside me shifts. And I realise. There's no one here to judge me. No family name. No need to pretend. Just me. And Kyle. Who, I realise, has done me a favour after all.

This is how things will be, once I escape my destiny. How it will feel to be alone, and free. It's an extraordinary revelation. I tingle all over, turning slowly, breathing in the night, the open space, the fresh air.

'Good,' he says, in a self-satisfied sort of way, and I want to smack him again. But instead, I meet his gaze.

'All right then,' I say, feeling as though I'm about to step off a cliff. 'What do you want to show me?'

Water tumbles past us, phosphorescent foam spattering against the dark flow. I can see more now we're out from under the trees, the moon's light unhindered.

It's beautiful.

The waterfall thunders into the gorge, the stream rushing through the forest to throw itself over the cliff. My toes are at the edge, stone slick beneath my feet. Kyle's arm is around my waist. I know it's to stop me from falling, but wonder whether it's just the waterfall that's making my heart beat so fast.

'This is amazing!' My voice is lost in the roar of falling water. I lean forward, the drop sheer below me to a moonlit pool churned silver and black.

'Careful!' He pulls me back. 'If you fall in I'll be in trouble.'

I try to imagine what this place will look like in daylight, how sunlight will dance off the water, blue and green and white and gold. I want to stay longer, feel the power surging in the water, droplets misting my skin. But the pressure on my waist increases, Kyle pulling me back towards the trees.

The Great Forest is a place of mysteries, of dark stories, the black mass of it glimpsed from my bedroom window just another thing to fear. But now, walking through it with Kyle, moonlight painting the trees with silver and picking out the details on his jacket, it feels more like a fairy tale. I'm transfixed by it, stopping to examine delicate lichen on a branch, frost patterns on a leaf, my breath puffing clouds into the air. Moon-silvered trees surround us, their branches tangled like lace against the sky, roots lost in shadow.

I should be afraid, out here alone in the middle of nowhere. It's what I've been guarded against my whole life, a wall of silver and black between me and the world, my parents keeping me safe. But as I stop again, my fingers tracing the velvet curves of a small mossy nest tucked into a low branch, all I feel is wonder.

The land falls away to one side of us, shimmers of golden light in the distance. I can still faintly hear the roar of the waterfall. It's as though there's a fluttering bird in my chest, and I can't quite place the feeling. But, as we head deeper among the tangled trees, I realise what it is. Freedom. Out here, I'm not Raven. I'm no one. My walls are completely gone. I have no idea who I am without them. It's terrifying and exhilarating at the same time.

Kyle was right. It's exactly what I need.

'Keep moving.' Kyle's tone is brusque, crashing into my reverie.

'But it's so beautiful. The moonlight. The forest. Everything.' I feel almost drunk. Maybe I am drunk, though I only had one glass of wine at the bar.

'Is it?'

I frown. 'Yes. Isn't that why you brought me here? To see this?'

He stops and turns, coming back to me. He stares down at me, his face shadowed. 'I brought you here because I could. Because that's the reality of your world.' He pauses. 'And also because you looked like you wanted out.'

'Wh-what?' My voice is a whisper. Something passes between us, as though a ribbon is binding us together, tightening. His body is close to mine, his violet scent all around me.

He leans in.

I swallow. My eyes close.

Cool breath mists across my lips.

There's a screeching noise, the flap of wings, the clatter of branches. I tense, my eyes coming open, and take a step back. 'What's that?' I gasp.

'Nothing,' he says. 'Probably an owl, hunting.'

*Hunting.*

The spell breaks and I remember I'm alone in the woods. With a vampire. This is everything my parents have ever warned me against. He leans in again and I panic. What the hell is he doing? One minute he seems to hate me, and now he's trying to *kiss me*? My heart is pounding, thunder in my ears. I force myself to calm down, using the control I've been practising since I was a child, the ways of making myself less tempting, less human, less vulnerable. I turn my head, stepping back.

'What was that writing I saw tonight?' I say, hoping it will break the tension.

'What writing?' Kyle also steps back. It's a relief, but at the same time part of me feels bereft. I squash that part down, stamping on it.

'The North Wind will blow. What's that? A new band I don't know about?'

'Where'd you see that?' There's a subtle tension in his

voice that wasn't there before.

'In Dark Haven. On the wall of the burned building. So, what is it?'

Kyle doesn't say anything for a moment. I start to feel nervous, like I've said something wrong. Finally, he speaks.

'You remember earlier tonight, when Ira mentioned unrest? And what I told you?'

My eyebrows shoot up. 'What? You're saying the North Wind is... the human uprising?'

He nods.

I laugh, because it's ridiculous. 'They can't imagine they can beat us, can they?'

Kyle raises his eyebrows. 'You'd be surprised.'

He's right. I'd be totally fucking surprised if humans thought they had any chance rebelling against vampires. But I don't know what else to say so I change the subject, hoping to hang onto the faint thread of connection still hanging between us.

'Is that the Safe Zone? It looks beautiful from here.' I point at the faint glow, just visible through the trees.

'A lot of things do from a distance.'

'What?'

'Nothing.' His tone is curt. The thread breaks.

I frown. 'I've heard it's a pretty nice place.'

'Have you? Because the way I see it, it's your family farm. One of many.'

Something about the way Kyle describes it as a farm makes me uncomfortable. 'But it's a good place to live, right?'

This is literally the basis of my plan to get away, so I hope it is. I silently curse my sheltered life, the way I've been kept in the dark, both literally and figuratively. Yet I know what I've seen, watching videos in the library alone. What a human life, lived in the light, is like. It's what I want, more than anything.

He huffs out a laugh. 'What makes you think that?'

'Well, because it's safe? And I know we take care of... um.' My discomfort increases, something about the night stripping the layers away, the gauze from my eyes.

He snorts. 'Would you like it?'

The woods feel darker, endless. Branches stab at the sky. Anger sparks inside me. *What* is his problem? Why bother bringing me out here, if he's just going to act like he can't stand me the whole time? 'I don't understand.' My voice is higher than usual. 'It's a safe place for humans, where they can live their lives.'

Where I can live *my* life.

'You think being farmed for blood is living your life?'

It's like a slap.

'Farmed? But isn't it only if h-humans want—'

Before I can finish he moves, faster than I can see. I'm pressed against him, bending back, his arm around my waist holding me up. His other hand moves my hair away so my neck is exposed. Fuck.

'*You're* human. Doesn't that mean I can eat *you*, whenever I want?'

'You know you can't!' I push at him, but it's like pushing against a statue. Fear sits sour in my throat.

47

Because he can. Of course he can. I have no way to stop him.

'Tell me.' His voice is a whisper, deep in the night. 'Why is that?' He traces his finger down my throat, cool on my skin.

I close my eyes, rage pulsing red behind my eyelids. But with it comes a deeper twisting, also red, from his closeness, his breath on my neck, the hardness of his body against mine. I try to swallow, my mouth dry. 'B-because I'm the heir to Raven.'

'You're still human, though. No different to any of them.'

I can't breathe.

His mouth is on my throat.

I stare up at the night sky, at the distant stars. So this is it. Relief, strangely welcome, overcomes me, and I relax in his iron embrace. Fine. Put an end to it, then. Drain me dry.

A strange whooping noise, like a bird call, echoes from the woods. Kyle's mouth stops moving on my skin, and he becomes very still. 'Don't. Move.' Cold prickles at the base of my neck, the dark woods seeming full of black shadows, moving things.

Then, without warning, Kyle scoops me into his arms and starts to run. He's going so fast it's dangerous. I curl myself into him as much as I can, wondering what the hell is going on. More of the strange whooping noises surround us, an eerie rise and fall of sound. Kyle, if it's even possible, speeds up. I can't see anything at all, the air rushing past my face.

'Hold on,' he says. I tighten my grip. There's a feeling of weightlessness, then another, and I realise he's jumping. He jumps one more time, grunting with exertion. We land and he comes to a stop, skidding on the damp undergrowth, just missing a couple of large trees. He lets go but momentum still has me and I stumble, then fall. I lie there, my senses swirling as I try to catch my breath. Kyle drops down next to me and I hear him laugh. Of all things, he's laughing. What the hell? The strange whooping calls move further away, voices shouting a warning. I turn my head and realise we're just inside the high black fence topped with silver that borders our lands. Thank darkness, we're home.

'Emelia, I'm sorry.' Kyle rolls towards me, briefly resting his hand on my waist. 'Gods.' He rolls on his back again, his arms over his head.

He's *sorry*? I sit up, running a hand through my hair, which feels stretched and windblown. 'What the hell was that?'

Kyle tilts his head towards me, moonlight catching silver in his eyes. 'That, my lady, was a Reaper gang.'

'*What?*' It wasn't what I was asking. But still... 'Are you serious?'

He nods. 'I couldn't warn you, I just had to get you out of there.'

I feel faint. Reaper gangs are wild vampires, who don't consider themselves subjects of any of the realms. If they'd caught us we'd have both been dead, me drained dry and Kyle ripped apart, trying to defend me. I understand his laughter, now. Relief. I feel it myself.

Along with rage.

'What is *wrong* with you?' I hiss. He is genuinely the worst guard I've ever met, like he has no idea how to act. 'How *dare* you take me into the woods like that, and-and…' I can't say it. Can't say the worst thing of all, the worst thing about this stupid evening.

'Nothing is wrong with me.' He gets to his feet and offers me his hand. I bat it away.

'I can stand up by myself, thank you.' I scramble to my feet, tugging my skirt down.

'What are you so angry about?' He's frowning. 'I just saved you.'

'*Saved* me?' I can't even speak for a moment.

'Is everything all right, my lady?'

Raven guards are the best in the land. Of course they heard us. Heard me, anyway. Half a dozen surround us, appearing almost from thin air. And, oh god and darkness, Bertrand is among them, his kindly face creased with disapproval.

'I'm fine.'

'Did something happen?' Bertrand has his arms folded. 'The car was just getting ready to leave. We weren't expecting you home yet.'

I sigh. Kyle is standing to attention next to me. I can almost feel his desperation. I have a choice again, it seems. I can drop him in it, or I can save him.

For some reason, I go with option two. 'I didn't feel well, so Kyle offered to bring me home.'

Bertrand's frown deepens. 'Through the Great Forest?'

I glance at Kyle. He can deal with this.

'We were on the road,' he said. 'Then we ran into a Reaper gang, so I took my lady into the woods, hoping to outrun them. That's why we came over the fence.'

Bertrand's suspicious gaze comes to me. I nod, my eyes wide. 'That's it,' I said. 'That's what happened. I'm lucky Kyle is so fast, I guess.'

'Emelia?'

All the guards, including Kyle and Bertrand, bow and step back.

Great. It's my mother.

## Chapter Six

### A GOLDEN CAGE

'What's happening? Why didn't you call?'

My mother comes to me in a rustle of silk. There's worry in her voice. I find mine.

'I'm fine. I was just tired, that's all.' But, before I can say any more she's hugging me, her hands stroking my hair. I cling to her for a moment, then push at her, feeling comforted and smothered all at the same time, love like a crackle in my chest. 'I'm fine.'

She releases me, a crinkle in her perfect pale brow. 'Are you sure? You do feel a little warm.'

'Honestly, I'm all right. It's just been a long night.'

'Come then, lovely girl. There is tea for you, and you can tell me all about it.' She turns to Kyle. Her gaze narrows. 'As for you,' she says, her tones suddenly glacial, 'I hope you have a very good explanation as to why you thought running my daughter home through the Great Forest was a good idea.'

Kyle's silver gaze flicks to me. I do nothing.

'My lady.' He bows. 'It is as Emelia says. She was tired and, rather than wait for the car, she wanted to come home. I thought to run with her, as the road to the house is usually safe. However, we ran into a Reaper gang and so I had to take her into the forest to evade them.'

I close my eyes.

'A Reaper gang?' My mother's voice rises. 'Are you mad? How could you put her in harm's way like that?'

Well, at least I'm not the only one who thinks Kyle has problems. But then I feel bad. I remember silver trees, rushing water, the wild flicker of freedom.

'I made him bring me home,' I say, opening my eyes.

Just in time, it seems.

Kyle is kneeling, his head down, my mother bending over him with her arm raised, like some sort of avenging angel. She turns, her face a pale oval in the darkness. 'What?'

'He's not at fault. I er, I ordered him to bring me home. And it's really not his fault we ran into the Reaper gang. In a way, he saved me.'

She straightens up. 'Is that so?'

'Truly, it is.'

She looks from me to Kyle. 'Rise,' she says.

He gets up and stands to attention, his heels together.

'Very well,' she says. 'I accept you had no choice in the matter. Go now. There is a meal for you, downstairs.'

'Thank you, my lady.' He bows again. His glance flicks

to me then he's gone, a darker blur against the night, the other guards following.

All except for Bertrand. He escorts me and my mother to the house, my mother matching her pace to mine. I'm fine with that. I've had enough of being carried for one evening.

I lean against her as we ascend the steps to the front door, the tall pillars either side pale lines in the darkness. I'm cold, despite the warmth of the house once we go inside. I'm also buzzing, adrenaline at our close call, at the evening I've had, still running through me. In the sitting room the fire is burning, electric candle-lamps lit. I sit on the sofa. My mother sits in the chair opposite, leaning forward to the small table to pour me a cup of tea. I smell peppermint, steaming and fragrant.

'What happened?' There's a faint line in the skin between her eyebrows.

I pick up the cup, holding it to me as I think. 'It was just how we said. I was tired, and my head ached. I wanted to come home, so I made Kyle bring me.'

'You did? Because our forces are stretched thin at the moment, and I'm not sure I can find a suitable replacement. Mistral sent him to us, actually, very highly recommended. That's why I thought I could trust him with you.'

Mistral? He heads the most powerful Raven subset, and is my mother's lieutenant, so he's almost family, I guess. That doesn't change the fact I think he's a dick. He and Mother were an item once, long ago, but then she met Father and everything changed. Mistral doesn't seem to have got the message, though, sniffing around Mother whenever he comes to visit. I wouldn't touch anything he recommended with a ten-foot pole, but Mother, and sometimes Father, seem to think he's all right.

In a way, it makes sense that Mistral recommended Kyle, seeing as he is also completely irritating. But, though I hate to admit it, he might have done me a favour after all. An idea is forming. I just need to make sure Kyle isn't fired first. I know, just an hour or so ago I would have fired him myself, if I could have. But now I see... potential.

'Well, you can,' I say. 'I know now it wasn't a great idea, but running seemed faster than waiting for the car. Really, I'm fine.'

It's not totally a lie. The adrenaline rush is wearing off, though, and I'm starting to feel tired. I cradle my teacup, the warmth comforting like the crackle of the fire, like my mother's love. I gather it to me like a blanket, as though I can hang onto it somehow. I'll miss her, more than anything, when I leave, and I know she'll be the same. I wonder whether my father will miss me.

'So how was the evening, apart from feeling unwell? Did you have fun at the party?' She's smiling now, a perfect pale beauty in the dimly lit room. When I don't say anything, her smile fades.

'Um.' I have to say something. 'Well, I had a good time.' More lies.

My mother's face lights up. 'You did? And how was Stella?'

I blink. 'I mean, it was strange at first, when I saw Stella.'

I pause. Stella was unforgivably rude. I decide to drop her in it.

'Well, she wasn't, um, that nice. She grabbed me. Tight.' I emphasise the last word. My mother's eyes widen. 'But Kyle, you know, he sort of…' I pause again. 'Well, he let her know, he reminded her, that I was, that she shouldn't, er…'

My mother looks pained. 'Do I need to speak to her father?'

'No! I mean, don't bother. The important thing is that Kyle looked after me, the whole night. Like he's supposed to.' I nod at this last bit. There's no way I'm going to tell her about being mistaken for a blood dancer – she'd probably have the club torn down. Humiliation washes over me again, at the memory of the vampire's rough hands on me, Stella and her friends laughing, people waiting outside the club turning to each other, frowning, as I got out of the car. If anything has shown me I'm in no way cut out to be the next Raven, it's that.

She narrows her eyes. 'Emelia?'

Damn. 'Yes?'

'Is there anything else you want to tell me?'

I fold my lips tight, breathing through my nose and blinking.

'Tell me,' she says, her voice gentle.

'Er.' I don't know how to say it. 'When we got there, I mean, we were in the Raven car, and I was with Kyle, but… no one seems to know who I am.'

'The Ravenna group—'

'Oh, they knew. Stella just wasn't nice. It was… everyone else.'

My mother looks away. She's silent for a moment. When her onyx gaze returns to me, I swear there's a tinge of blood tears.

'This is why we want you to go out more. Why we regret—'

'I'm not ready for this. For any of it,' I say, cutting her off. 'I don't know if I'll ever be.' It's a relief to finally say it. 'Maybe you and Father should wait, have another child or something—'

'I don't *want* another child.'

'But I'm so useless.' The words slip out before I can stop them.

'You are Raven!' My mother becomes fierce, baring her teeth, her hair flying silken strands of black, eyes glittering as she leans closer. 'You hold every power that name carries. Never let anyone tell you otherwise.' She calms down, sitting back, very still, the blood tinge in her eyes more obvious. 'Please, Emelia,' she whispers. 'Both your father and I believe in you. Please, try again. For me.'

*For her.* What about what I want? The teacup is burning my fingers.

'I think I need to sleep,' I say. I put the cup down and stand up.

Mother stands as well and, quick as a flash, is hugging me, her cool lips soft on my cheek. 'Go and rest, my darling – I'm so very proud of you.' She squeezes me briefly before letting go.

A guard waits in the hallway outside. He follows me in silence to my room. Once inside I climb into bed, the linen sheets cool. Dawn comes, and with it the rumble as the shutters drop, the house shutting out daylight once more. I can't sleep. No matter how exhausted my body is, my mind is racing.

I'm both exhilarated and furious about what we did, at how close we came to disaster. Lace-like branches, the rush of water, his silver eyes – a kaleidoscope of silver and black turns in my mind.

And a boy in a cage.

My mood changes. I try to find the feeling again, the flutter of freedom in my chest, when the night seemed full of beauty. Kyle gave me that, at least.

Then ruined it, when he reminded me what I was.

*Human.*

I roll over, punching my pillow, trying to get comfortable. I don't care what my mother says, or how much my parents believe in me. Becoming Raven, taking control of a huge realm – I'm just not ready. I don't know if I ever will be. My parents are going to insist on me going through with it though, despite my pleas, despite my ignorance.

I'm trapped, as surely as that boy in the cage in the bar. My bars might be golden, but they're a prison all the same. Which is why I have to leave. Why I've been planning it, for a while now.

I want a different life.

A human life. One where I have more choices than just

what to eat, or which movie to watch, or which velvet gown to put on in the evening. One where my existence isn't bound by guards and fences and darkness, by the weight of responsibility. One where I can be with others like me.

The walls feel as though they're closing in. I can't breathe. I sit up, pushing the covers back. There's a pile of folded clothes on a chair. I go over to them, picking them up. They smell fresh, like the forest, with a faint tinge of violets. I wonder for the first time who launders my things, who washes away the vestiges of my human frailty. Shame rushes through me again at my weakness, at my constant need to be guarded, to be washed and fed like an animal in a zoo. I want it to be over. I want to live my own life, among my own kind. I don't care what Kyle says about the Safe Zones. They have to be better than this.

I pull two T-shirts from the pile and go over to the fireplace. It's huge, the stone mantle carved with intricate leaves and vines. I press one of the carved leaves. A panel in the wall next to the fireplace swings back, revealing a stone passageway, a small packed bag leaning against the wall. I unzip it, and add the T-shirts. There's a pouch of gold in there, several refill vials of anti-feed, and some folded clothes. Not much, but I'm hoping I won't need more.

My plan. My way out.

I hope.

But to make the second half of my plan work, I have to do something I really don't want to do. I have to be nice to Kyle.

# Chapter Seven

## THE DANCE

My feet pound the grass, my breath coming fast. My lungs feel about to burst, but I keep going. A vampire keeps pace with me, easily, and I speed up, a pulse of adrenaline carrying me along. I slam into the high fence, my hands gripping it before I slide down, panting.

'Not too bad.' Kyle, barely a hair out of place, drops down to sit next to me. He hands me my phone. I look at it. Three minutes, twenty-six seconds. Almost a personal best time. 'Not too bad at all,' he says, sounding almost approving.

But the unspoken words are there, hanging in the air. *For a human.*

I've been practising for a while. Running around the estate, keeping track of my time and distance. I know I'm getting faster, but I'm not fast enough, not yet. There's absolutely nothing stopping me from leaving the estate during the day, once I get past my parents and the guards inside. None of them could follow me, even if they wanted to. I could walk along the curving drive, open the huge gates, and step out into freedom. The problems, however, start there. This is the part of my plan I need help with.

I have to reach the Safe Zone by nightfall, or else I'm dead, stranded in vampire territory with nothing but a few vials of anti-feed between me and who knows what lurking out there. But I'm too far away. The driver all but confirmed it, last night. The drive to Dark Haven took about ten minutes, but the Safe Zone was another twenty-five minutes away. At the speed we were driving it's a good forty miles or so. No way I can cover that before sundown, especially now as the days get shorter, the long nights of winter drawing in. But time is ticking, and my birthday is in April. If I don't do it soon, I never will. I'll get caught up in the Raven machine, what little choice I have left taken from me as I'm marched towards the throne. There's the final Gathering, where I'll be anointed and choose my lieutenant, plus tours of the realm, ceremonies and rehearsals, the heir roll-out taking over my life. The night out at the Dome was just the start of it. And I couldn't even do that without being mistaken for food.

'Thanks, by the way.' Kyle bumps me with his shoulder.

I glance at him. He's looking down, his long legs bent, hands hanging slack between them.

'For what?' I know, of course, but a small petty part of me wants to hear him say it. I'm trying to be nice, even though he infuriates me beyond measure. I'd opened my bedroom door with a smile, knowing he'd be waiting outside. It had been hard to maintain, though, when he'd frowned at me, scoffing, when I asked him to help me time my running. He'd done it, eventually, though I'd basically had to order him to do it, all the while trying to be sweet, to be nice. So he can give me this.

'For not telling your parents about what I did.' He still won't look at me.

I start to get annoyed, despite myself. 'What did you do?'

He snorts. 'Come on. That was a pretty close call last night.'

*Last night.* Anger escapes me, despite my efforts, the sting of his words in the woods biting at me again. 'Yes, it was! What the *hell* were you thinking, taking me into the Great Forest?! And a *Reaper gang*?'

'I didn't think there would be anyone there.' He looks at me then, moonlight catching the faint glitter of his eyes. 'The waterfall is one of my favourite places. I... wanted to share it with you.'

'Why?'

'Does it matter?' He shakes his head. 'Forget it. Forget I said anything.' He looks into the distance, his jaw tight.

I want to scream, but I hold myself back, pulling my anger back inside. 'Thank you for taking me there,' I say, trying to smile. I *have* to make this work. He might be the most infuriating person I've ever met, but something became very clear to me last night. If I'm going to get to the Safe Zone in one piece, Kyle is the only one who can help me. He got me over the fence last night, brought me through the forest safely. And I need him to do it again.

I know. He is completely irritating. But he's also the one chance I have, the only person on the estate who might actually be able to do this for me. I've thought about it ten different ways, but I can't see any other option. Kyle takes me over the fence, keeps running until we reach the Safe Zone. It'll take him forty minutes, an hour tops, even carrying me and my bag. And then he can either return to the house and swear up and down he doesn't know where I am, or take my bag of gold and start a new life. A fighter like him won't have any problem finding work.

So I try and think of something else to say, but he beats me to it.

'I think maybe we got off on the wrong foot.' The words are stilted, as though he's having trouble saying them. He still won't look at me.

I frown. 'We did?' Of course we did. It's obvious we can't stand each other.

He snorts again. 'I don't know why you're pretending we didn't. I get it, okay? I'm just another guard, and you're the big fancy heir to Raven. I don't know why you saved me last night, or why you're being nice now. But it makes my job easier, so I'm trying to be more reasonable.'

'Not trying very hard,' I mutter, getting to my feet.

I start back towards the house, not caring whether or not he follows. He does, of course. I ignore him.

*Makes his job easier.* What an ass.

He clears his throat. He's obviously trying to get my attention. 'I have something for you.'

'What?'

He grabs my arm, pulling me to a stop at the foot of the steps.

'Let go!' I shake my arm, but his fingers remain around it, though he isn't hurting me.

Quite the opposite.

He digs in his pocket, then pulls out a small glass vial filled with pale liquid. 'Here.' He holds it out.

I take it with my free hand. 'Why are you giving me anti-feed? Are you saying I *smell*, now?'

'You smell fine.' His mouth curves. 'I just want you to be safe. When we go out again.'

His eyes are a silver gleam, his dark lashes casting shadows on his high cheekbones. He is ridiculously hot. I stare at him, a thousand retorts rising to my lips then disappearing.

'How did you get this?' All the anti-feed in the house, including my own supply, is held under lock and key, doled out in small batches when needed. It's expensive, for starters. And not easy to come by. The spare vials I have took me ages to gather, filched from careless blood dancers.

'I have my ways.' His smile deepens. He's released my arm, but is closer to me. I take a step back, reminding myself how completely annoying he is.

'Thanks.'

'Like I said, I appreciate you not getting me fired. Or worse.'

'Fine,' I say. Like my heart isn't dancing in my chest. *He wants me to be safe. Because it's his job*, my mind adds, helpfully. I take another step back.

'So, why didn't you say anything? I'm just curious.'

Oh, I cannot do this. I need to find another way out of here. Maybe I can steal the car. Except I can't drive. I march up the steps to the front door, continuing across the foyer towards the stairs, conscious of the fact that I'm sweaty and emotional, feeling as though I'm glowing red. Absolute vampire catnip. I wouldn't last a minute outside the gates after nightfall, especially if I'd been running all day. I take the stairs, heading across the landing and down the hallway, Kyle still following. I'm trying not to stamp. 'You don't have to follow me everywhere,' I hiss.

'Actually, I do,' he says, a thread of laughter in his voice. I feel as though I might burst into flames with rage. 'It's literally my job.'

'Oh, your *job*.'

'Yes, my job. And you still haven't answered me.'

I stop dead. He does too. I glance at him. He has one dark eyebrow raised, a smirk playing around his perfect lips.

'I guess, I appreciated what you did,' I mutter. 'Taking me somewhere I could just be…'

'Emelia? Not Raven?' There's a softness to his voice that wasn't there before. He comes closer. 'Is that it?'

My heart is pounding, and I'm reminded again of our closeness in a darkened hallway. And then of another embrace, in frozen woods.

65

'Yes,' I say. 'So why did you have to ruin it?'

'Ruin it?' Still soft, his scent of violets and fresh leaves twining around me.

'When you said I was... when you...' It's like I'm possessed. Why am I telling him this? I just need to be nice, get him on my side, then get him to take me over the fence and leave me at the Safe Zone. That's it. No need for anything else.

'What is it?' He's even closer, leaning in, his broad shoulders blotting out what little light there is.

'Human.' I spit the word. 'You said I was just a human.'

'Is that why you're mad? Emelia, I think you're—' He stops talking, straightening up as two guards appear at the end of the hallway. They nod as they pass us. 'My lady.'

I'm going to scream.

'I need to shower.' I start along the hallway once more, before he can say anything else, move any closer. I need to keep focus.

But as I stand under needles of hot water a few minutes later, it's as though I can almost feel his presence through the walls, as though he's in the room with me, instead of waiting outside my door. I blush and blush some more, imagining his silver gaze on me as I twist under the water. I can't deny my response to him, despite how he infuriates me. But there is no way in hell I'm telling him, or acting on it. I need to stick to my plan.

He's waiting, of course, when I open my bedroom door a short while later. And if I took extra care to make sure my hair was smooth and shining, wore one of my favourite dresses, it was for my parents' benefit, that's all.

I don't say anything as I start down the hallway, because I don't know what to say. I feel like a stranger in my own home, the place more familiar to me than anywhere else on the planet feeling strange and new, the way the candle-lamps gild the velvet and heavy red carpets, the carved wood, the silver glimpse of moon through the unshuttered windows.

'So, where are we going?'

I have no idea. I should see my parents, but I don't want to, the strangeness running through me like quicksilver making me feel as though I want to run outside and dance beneath the stars, screaming at the moon like a wild creature of the woods.

'Are you still mad about the human thing?'

I am seriously going to deck him in a moment. But it also seems rude to keep staying silent, even though my throat feels choked by something huge, welling from my chest. I swallow. 'No.' Lies.

'You sure? Because being human isn't a bad thing, you know.'

I glance at him. 'Really?' I hiss. 'Tell me what's so good about it, then.'

But Kyle has stopped. I do, too. We're standing in front of a pair of double doors, carved with the Raven crest and gilded with silver.

'What's in here?' he says.

'Shouldn't you know? I thought you would have seen the entire house.'

'I've been told to follow you. I didn't get a tour, apart from the entrances, exits and weak spots.'

'Weak spots?'

'Nothing to worry about,' he says. 'We used one of them last night though, when I brought you over the fence.' He grins.

I realise I'm watching his mouth as he talks. 'We did?' This is useful information.

'We did. So.' He jerks his head towards the closed doors. 'Will you take me inside?' Then he winks at me, his hand brushing against mine.

Damn him to blood and darkness. Seriously. I can barely breathe as I turn the handle, pushing the door open. He's in like a flash, a streak of darkness in the shadowy room. But instead of completing the circuit he stops dead centre, his mouth dropping open.

'Wow. What is this place?'

I enter the room, floorboards creaking underfoot. It *is* pretty amazing. The room is large, with a vaulted ceiling. Long windows at one end let in pale moonlight. But there's no furniture in here. Instead, faceless black mannequins stand all around the room, dressed in gowns and armour, chain mail and satin, styles from the distant past. Our family archive, clothes belonging to Ravens throughout history. The castle we live in passes to the youngest in the family as soon as they take a mate, with whoever's in residence moving to one of the other Raven properties scattered across the realm. It's also how the other branches of the family, like Mistral and Ravenna, came to be, the deposed Ravens starting new dynasties. But this is the ancient seat of our family, so it's where our history is preserved. And the Costume Room is part of it.

I walk over to a small dial set into the wall. 'Do you mind?' I say. 'It'll be very dim, candle strength.'

Kyle is still looking around. 'No, go for it.'

I turn the dial and the bulbs in the wall sconces start to glow, casting a shimmer across the objects in the room, glancing off jet and ruby and steel, off swords arranged like fans on the stone walls. I've spent a lot of time in this room. Whenever I come in here, it's as though I connect to the energy of those past Ravens, and my heritage feels like something wonderful, rather than a weight to be borne. It feels like power. Like they're… encouraging me. When you spend a lot of time alone you look for friendship wherever you can find it. And here, among the silk and metal of my ancestors, I feel something close to capable.

'This is… amazing.' Kyle is still in the centre of the room, hands on hips, his head slightly back, turning as he takes it all in. 'Whose clothes are these?'

'Um, they belong to my family. My ancestors.' I try not to stare at his lean muscular frame, his gilded and shadowed beauty.

'Really?' His face lights up with a grin. He goes over to a suit of armour made from gleaming embossed silver, with the Raven crest in ebony on the breastplate. 'Man, if this were mine…' His long fingers run over the crest, tracing our motto. 'Raven claw, blood and stone. Whose was this?'

'My great-grandfather's.' I know all the pieces in here. Spent hours in the library researching their history, who they belonged to, the stories of my illustrious ancestors. Ravens fought in all the great vampire wars of history, including the Rising.

'And this one?'

I don't answer him. There's another beautiful garment, draped over its mannequin. Except this one is unworn. Because it's mine. I bite my lip as I touch the intricate jet beading, the stiff white satin dress embroidered with silver, the high collared cape with the Raven insignia on the back. My coronation robes. They're terrifying and beautiful at the same time. I can't imagine wearing them. It's a good thing I'm not going to.

'Shall we dance?'

'What?' I turn to see Kyle standing in the space at the centre of the room, one arm outstretched. He's taken a cape from one of the mannequins and looks so hilarious I can't help but laugh.

He frowns. 'What? I thought I looked pretty good in this.' He swishes the cape with one hand. It's black with silver filigree stitched along the hem, the collar tall around his face. He does look good in it – he'd look good in anything – but at the same time it's completely ridiculous.

'You know I don't like dancing,' I say. I'm blushing, despite my best efforts.

'Could have fooled me,' he says, swishing the cape again

as he comes closer. He twirls and I giggle, the wildness rising in me again. There's no one to see me here, no smirking Stella or hungry vampires. I pull a long red silk scarf from a nearby mannequin, the jet beads making a sound like rainfall, drape it around me and walk over to him. He bows. I curtsey, then laugh again.

'What's so funny?' He sounds injured, so I try to keep a straight face as I take his hand. His other hand comes to my waist and all at once the desire to laugh is gone from me, replaced by a different kind of desire.

'Nothing,' I say. 'Let's dance.'

'As you wish, my lady.' He sounds completely serious, so I resist the urge to snap at him. He pulls me closer, taking my hand, his other hand at the back of my waist. We spin beneath the long windows, my beads clicking and clacking like rain, his cloak swishing, silver filigree catching the dim light, the lawn outside silvered by the moon. He is effortlessly strong, the way he holds me against him, secure, protected. I'm tingling all over, my breath getting shorter. It's like twirling through a dream, and I give myself up to it, my feet leaving the floor, my whole body entwined with his.

'See, we can get on if we try,' he murmurs.

'What?' His lips are so close to my ear. I'm acutely aware of his body against mine, the cool hardness. I struggle to focus.

Our spinning slows, his head moving closer to mine. 'I think we could be friends. If you want. Or even more.' His hand at my waist slides lower, his other arm wrapping around me.

My heart is pounding, but I can't control it. Can't control anything, including my response to him.

There's a clapping sound and I jump. Kyle lets me go, stepping back. I stagger, but manage to right myself, feeling as though I'm on fire.

'Emelia! And Kyle. Just who I've been looking for.'

My mother comes towards us, her long skirts trailing like flickers of flame. She's smiling, her arms held out, red velvet sleeves tapering to points over her delicate fingers. I avoid her embrace, hoping she won't notice how flushed I am, how rapid my breathing.

'My lady.' Kyle bows neatly from the waist.

'Kyle.' My mother nods. 'I thought you were to bring Emelia to us this evening.'

'I am, my lady. However, she wanted to come here on the way and—'

'Of course,' she says. 'Emelia's wishes, and her safety, are of paramount importance.'

Except my wish to not be Raven, of course. The thought cools my rushing head and heart, dampens the fire in my veins.

Kyle undoes the cloak, going to drape it carefully back on the mannequin where he found it.

My mother tilts her head. 'That belonged to my father,' she says. 'He used to wear it to dances. Probably not his style these days.'

'My lady, I apologise if—'

'That's not what I meant. It's nice to see it being worn again.' She smiles at him, then at me. 'That red is lovely on you, Emelia.'

'Oh!' I pull at the scarf, trying not to damage the delicate fabric. My mother stops me, her hands soft on mine.

'You should keep it. I used to love wearing it.' She embraces me. 'Now, come,' she says. 'Let us go to your father. Kyle, report to Bertrand. He may need you elsewhere on the estate, and Emelia can stay with me.'

'My lady.' Kyle bows, then heads to the door. I go to follow him, as though we're connected by an invisible string.

My mother stops me. Her grip is gentle, though she's strong as iron. 'So,' she says once Kyle is gone, a smile in her voice. 'You're getting along well with the new guard?'

I blush. 'I suppose,' I say, not looking at her.

'He's nice to you?'

'Nice enough,' I say.

'That is good,' my mother says, though the softness has gone from her tone. 'You do, however, need to remember who you are.'

I look at her. Then around the room with its layers of history, its weight of robes and responsibility that I have to carry. 'How can I forget,' I say.

It's not a question.

## Chapter Eight

BLOOD MOON

'Emelia, the silver garland, please.'

My mother is at the top of a ladder. She could get someone else to do this, of course, but it's important to her to get every detail right. The great Halloween tree stretches to the ceiling of the main foyer, twisted branches devoid of leaves, blackened with age. It's been in our family for centuries, once a living tree upon the estate. Now it lives again each Halloween, garlanded with lights and sparkling streamers, cloudy cobwebs and glittering jet spiders.

I rummage in the chest on the table next to me. 'Here.' I reach up, but I'm not quite tall enough.

'Let me, my lady.' Kyle takes it from me, his hand lingering slightly longer than it should, then hands it to my mother. My fingers tingle, my breath shorter.

'Thank you,' she says. 'And some of those red moons, I think, Emelia.'

I pick several little red glass globes hanging from silver

thread, delicate as bubbles. They're a symbol of the Red Rising, our great triumph, when the four great vampire families worked together to take over the world in a single night. Destroying all power sources, overthrowing governments, decimating armies. I hand the globes to my mother who suspends them, carefully, from a cluster of slender branches. I pick up another, staring at it as I remember what Kyle said, about what Halloween means to humans. And how he felt, pressed against me in the costume room, how we almost—

'Emelia?' My mother frowns down at me. 'Are you all right? You've been distracted all evening.'

I usually love this time of year. My mother insists on me helping her with the final Halloween decorations, making sure each of the guest rooms are prepared, the hallways garlanded, carved and gilded skulls placed in alcoves, tiny twinkling pale lights strung through the trees outside. When I was younger, Halloween meant waking to piles of silk-wrapped presents, soft with velvet bows, and being allowed to attend the ball my parents hold every year, inviting friends and family from across the realm. It still holds magic, the long night of ghosts and costumes, a sense of the history of our kind.

But this year all I can think about is dancing and Kyle; I'm trying to remember how much he infuriates me even as I'm increasingly drawn to him. I need to remain focused on my plan to leave. Our dance the other night keeps playing through my mind, a swirl of silver and violets, the feel of his hands on me. It's not helping that he's still being nice. I suppose I have no one but myself to blame, my overtures obviously working too well. What I didn't expect was my own response to him. But my mother is right. I am distracted. 'Sorry. Guess I'm tired.' I pass her the bauble.

'And the red garland,' she says. I look in the chest again, but can't find it. I rummage around, tinsel slithering through my fingers.

'It's not there. I must have left it upstairs. I'll get it.'

'I'll come with you,' says Kyle. He winks at me. I look away.

'I think we also left a box of decorations up there,' my mother says. 'Will you bring it for me?'

'Of course, my lady.'

Kyle falls into step with me as I head up the stairs. I daren't look at him. We find the box of decorations, left in an alcove, the ornate moulded arch curving above us like a wing. I bend to gather up the red garland. Kyle does so at the same time. Our hands touch, and our eyes meet.

I wait for him to pull away. But he doesn't. His hands close over mine as we straighten up, his fingers tracing circles on my skin. I can't stop my sharp intake of breath.

'I enjoyed our dance yesterday,' he murmurs. 'I was hoping, perhaps we could do it again, later? Just the two of us.' His voice deepens, sex sliding across every syllable.

I'm strangled. Unable to form words.

'What?' I finally manage to say. It's a sliver of sound, a breath. Not going to win any prizes for eloquence. It feels like a last defence, a flimsy wall thrown up against whatever happens next.

He moves closer, backing me towards the wall of the alcove. 'I know you enjoyed it. I could feel your heart beating, you know.' His hand comes to my chest, resting lightly over the bird flutter of my heart.

'Could you?' I say, trying to be cool as a cucumber, as his smooth skin. But I'm blushing like a hot coal. I'm anything *but* cool.

'A shame your mother came in when she did.' The promise in his voice is unmistakeable.

I lean against the wall, an ache at the top of my thighs, the soft slither of tinsel in my hands.

His hand leaves my chest and he tucks a lock of my hair behind my ear, his silver eyes on me, his full generous mouth relaxed. My lips part, my whole body tingling.

'You have no idea who you could be,' he murmurs, the words a caress. 'A human, as ruler of Raven. Do you not realise what a difference you could make?'

We stare at each other. I can hardly breathe.

Then he leans in and kisses me.

I tense, surprise jolting me, the garland dropping from my slack fingers. 'What in *darkness* do you think you're doing?' I hiss in one last pathetic defence, even though my entire being is responding to his touch, demanding more more more.

He says nothing. Just leans in and kisses me again.

This time, I kiss him back.

My arms around his neck, his hands in my hair. Freedom flickers in my chest, wild like the night. I taste blood and violets, heat and darkness. I'm drowning in it.

Then it's over. Kyle lifts his head, his hands held up. 'I... I'm sorry.'

'Sorry?' The word is a whisper, faint on the air.

'I shouldn't have... I'm not supposed to—'

My face crumples and I try to hide my reaction, even though I have no chance. A predator sees every nuance, every movement, of its prey.

'It's not that I don't want to.' He says it fast, like he knows I need to hear it. 'God, you have no idea how much... since I first saw you.' His hands cup my face, his lips so close to mine. 'But you know we shouldn't do this – your parents...'

I don't care what my parents think. He's right, of course he is. My mother even warned me, in the Costume Room. The only daughter of Raven with a household guard. But my body is tingling, every nerve ending alive. I stare at him, and he at me.

Then he kisses me again. I press against him, my fingers in his satin hair, his hands roaming across my body. I don't care if anyone sees us. It feels inevitable, like I cannot resist the pull towards him.

The sound of the front door banging reverberates from below, and I hear my father's voice as though from a distance.

'... needs to be brought under control. We cannot risk another uprising like the one at Oxford – there's too much breeding stock at stake!'

Kyle and I come apart. I'm breathing hard, my mind a tangled snarl of lust and confusion. Kyle's hand moves across my hair, traces the curve of my cheek. Then he bends and picks up the garland, handing it to me. His fingers linger on mine.

'Emelia, I—'

'Shh.' I hold up my hand, wanting to hear what my father is saying. I think I glimpse hurt in Kyle's silver eyes.

'We've increased our guard presence throughout the entire country,' Father continues, 'and the North Wind are still getting through.'

'Surely more violence is not the answer.' My mother's soft tones.

God, what am I thinking, kissing Kyle like that? My cheeks redden with shame. I'm just supposed to be making him like me, so I can rope him into my plan to escape. Kissing isn't part of the plan, despite how he makes me feel. I move away from him, trying to focus on what my parents are saying.

My father's voice grows louder. 'I thought Mistral was supposed to be managing things.'

'He is, last I heard. I've asked him to go to London, too, acting on our behalf.'

I roll my eyes. Mistral. Of *course* he's getting involved. He usually lives in France, but it sounds as though he's in England to manage… whatever's going on. I guess that's why he sent Kyle to us, as well.

I'm acutely aware of him next to me, a darker presence in the shadows. Wanting some space, I go towards the top of the stairs, hugging the garland to me as though I'm naked and it's my only cover. I'm still blushing, still hardly able to believe what just happened. Then Kyle's arms come around me, his lips brushing against my ear, travelling down the side of my throat. Oh, darkness.

'Oh, so you've been talking to him, have you?' My father's voice becomes sharper. 'I suppose he's still angling for your hand, despite the fact you've been mine for a century.'

I lean against Kyle, finding it tough to breathe as he kisses my neck. I fight to stay focused. I know I should walk away from him, but I don't seem to be able to. 'You came from Mistral, right?' I whisper, my voice trembling. 'Do you know what my father is talking about? Is it the rebels?'

The kisses stop. 'I did.' Kyle's voice is a murmur against my skin. 'And yes, he's talking about the rebellion.'

I squirm in his embrace, half-turning to face him. 'Did Mistral say anything to you about it?'

Kyle snorts. 'Do you think Mistral discusses his plans with me?' He softens the words with another kiss. My arms wind around his neck, seemingly of their own volition. Maybe kissing *could* be part of the plan, after all. Again I feel the wildness Kyle inspires in me, the awakening at my core.

'I don't know how he does things.' We're still whispering, our mouths so close together.

'Badly. The guy is a dick. I'm glad he sent me here.'

Something Kyle and I have in common, then. I muffle my giggle, not wanting to give us away. Kyle kisses me again. My father's voice drifts up from below.

'Maybe if Mistral spent less time sniffing around here

and more time actually trying to find the root of this rebellion, it would be less of a problem. Because believe me, it is becoming one.'

'I know it is, Aleks.' My mother's voice is uncharacteristically sharp. 'I do govern my own realm.'

'I thought you said the North Wind were nothing to worry about,' I whisper.

'I never said that,' whispers Kyle. Another kiss.

'Emelia! Come downstairs.'

Damn. Kyle releases me. My shoulders back, I start down the stairs, trying to look as though I wasn't eavesdropping. Or kissing. My father is standing in the foyer, his arms folded, his eyes glittering gold slits. Mother is still up her ladder, looking annoyed.

'Um, we have the garland,' I say, holding it out. 'And the decorations.'

'Leave them there,' says my father, his tone dismissive. 'Your mother and I are talking.'

'Go and rest,' my mother says, sounding distracted. 'Or perhaps spend some time in the library. I think there are new books.'

'But—'

'Kyle, escort her.' My father is already half-turned away, his focus on my mother. She descends her ladder, graceful as though she were floating.

'Come, my lady.' Kyle, his hand on my elbow, moves me towards the stairs. I catch a smile curving his mouth.

'Just a minute,' I say, throwing his hand off my arm. 'What are—'

'Emelia! Do as you are asked!' My father's voice thunders through the foyer. I freeze, as does everyone else in earshot. Kyle takes my arm again. I let him. I'm fighting tears, though, as he guides me up the stairs once more. There's no hint of a smile on his face now.

# Chapter Nine

## HALLOWEEN

I lie on my bed, staring up at the carved and painted ceiling. I know every mark, every shape on it, the shadows it creates as the night passes. I know them like I know how my skin feels, or the sound of my breath in the morning.

I can't stop thinking about Kyle.

Despite the fact that I know I shouldn't, despite the fact that I'm crossing a dangerous line, I haven't been able to stay away from him.

I know I should remember who I am. But that's just the problem. Every single night that I wake, that I join the rest of the house, none of whom need to sleep or eat breakfast or have candle-lamps to light their way, I remember who I am. I'm the heir to Raven, and I'm human.

But with Kyle it's different. I can't believe he used to annoy me so much, or that he seemed to dislike me. Now I can't wait to see him. He just makes me feel like... Emelia.

A girl he likes. And he's just a boy I like. With him, unlike with anyone else I've ever met, I can forget who I'm supposed to be. And focus on who I want to be.

The bonus is that, despite his initial protests, he doesn't seem to be able to stay away from me either.

Except he's gone.

The week following the Halloween decorations was a haze of stolen, violet-scented kisses, hidden in alcoves and darkened rooms, trying to avoid the watchful eyes of both Bertrand and my parents. Of running across the estate, his arms around me, of getting to know each other. I was waiting for the perfect moment to tell him about my plan, to put things in motion, but it was hard to remember anything much when his hands, his mouth, were on me.

Then I woke up one morning and he wasn't outside my room. 'Called away, Mistral's orders,' was all Bertrand had said when I asked him, his gaze so kindly and wise. I'd panicked, going to my mother, asking for assurances that they hadn't got rid of him, while trying to hide my own desperation. But the fact he didn't tell me he was leaving pulls at me, like a scar beneath my skin. Him leaving means my plans are on hold. And I miss him, so much.

I need to get past this. He's a guard, and I'm Raven. I've been alone before, so I don't understand why it hurts so badly this time. If he doesn't return I'll figure out another way to get to the Safe Zone. The hot prickle beneath my eyelids tells me I'm lying to myself. I laugh, but it turns into a sob. I roll onto my side, pulling my blanket over me, the hum of soft velvet under my fingers comforting.

I wish I could stay here.

But tonight is the Halloween ball. The shutters have already risen, guests are arriving, all the most powerful vampires of Raven under one roof for the biggest party of the year. Bigger than the annual Gatherings, when all the clans loyal to Raven meet for three nights under the moon, loyalties pledged and matches made, the great dynasty ensuring its future. My parents will expect me to be there, just like they do every year. One of the very few spaces where I can be in public yet still be safe, flanked by guards and the walls of my home. I used to love going when I was younger, thought it was a special treat. Now the thought of it is exhausting. Because this is the last year I will attend as just Emelia. I know everyone will be thinking about it, as soon as they see me. And about how unsuitable I am to be Raven. Politeness, I suppose, will stop them from gossiping about it under my parents' roof. But the way Stella and her friends reacted to me at the Dome tells me everything I need to know about what vampires really think of me.

My dress is hanging on the door of my wardrobe, the silvery silk like ripples on water. Ready for me, the next Raven, to wear. I sit up, then flop back down again.

There's a knock at the door. 'Emelia?'

Damn.

I slide from my bed, rubbing my face and yawning. I pull on my robe, tying it tight. 'Come in.'

The door opens to admit my mother. She's wearing a long full robe, deep red and embroidered, her hair rippling loose down her back. Her face lights up when she sees me.

'Gorgeous girl! Happy Halloween!' She holds out her arms. I go to her, reaching for her hug. She kisses me, her spicy perfume mingling with her violet scent. I hang onto her for a moment, wanting to remember this, remember her.

'Here.' She pulls back, taking something from one of the pockets of her voluminous robe. It's a small square package wrapped in black silk and tied with a silver bow. 'From your father and me.' Her dark eyes are shining, a faint flush to her pale cheeks. I suppose she's just fed.

'Where's Father?'

'Oh—' she flaps her hand '—supervising something in the ballroom, I think. He's obsessed with every detail.'

Hurt blooms. He can't even come and see me for Halloween. I don't say anything.

'Emelia.' My mother takes my hands in hers, the laughter gone from her voice. 'He loves you, so much. It's just, there's a lot going on at the moment. And you know how important the ball is. He's looking forward to seeing you later.'

'Sure.' More important than me, I guess.

'Come on.' She tilts her head so she's looking up at me. 'Open your gift. Please?'

I take the parcel from her, undoing the silk to reveal a square wooden box, my initials carved into the top and inlaid with silver. There's a card as well, written in dark red ink.

'It's gorgeous,' I say, turning it in my hands. 'Thank you.'

She shakes her head. 'No, no, open it!'

I open the small box. Nestled on black velvet is a pendant on a long silver chain, delicate links interspersed with tiny silver beads. The pendant is silver, too, ebony enamel and diamonds making up the Raven crest. It's beautiful. I lift it from the box, the candle-lamp making it sparkle.

'Do you like it?' My mother puts her arm around me and I lean into her.

'I love it,' I say. 'Thank you.'

'I'm so glad.' She pauses. 'Is there something else troubling you, dear one?'

'I'm fine,' I say. 'Looking forward to the party.' Lies.

'Hmmm.' She regards me a moment longer, her eyes narrowed. Then she tilts her head, glancing back as though she hears something. She smiles. 'Come now, you must get ready. Guests are arriving, the celebration's starting soon.' There's a wildness to her voice and I take in a breath, caught in the magic of it, of Halloween. Maybe tonight won't be so bad.

She hugs me once more. 'Will you wear your necklace?'

'I will, I love it.'

'I love you, too.' I feel her kiss on my brow and then she's gone, the door closing.

---

The hallway is wide and high-ceilinged, gold carvings like lace decorating the rust-coloured walls. Music, sinuous and sweet, emanates from beyond the double doors up ahead.

Guards stand at intervals, two more following me. I smooth my hands down my skirt, waiting for the ballroom doors to open, the scent of my anti-feed curling in my nostrils. I know I'll never be as beautiful as any of the vampires in there, all chiselled perfection, but I like my dress, at least. The fitted bodice is held up by thin silk straps, the long skirt flaring from my hips to swirl around my feet. There's a tasselled belt at my waist, twisted silver and black silk threads fastened with the house crest, matching my new necklace. My shoes are silver as well, straps wrapping my feet fastened by wickedly pointed buckles studded with small diamonds. If I blur my eyes, I even look like my mother – same dark hair, same pale slender limbs.

I make my entrance, brushing aside the guards as they try to announce me. I'm not ready to be noticed yet. The ballroom is lit with candles, flames dancing in the huge chandeliers, the glow of electric candle-lamps picking up the glitter of gold-painted wall panels, the shimmer of diamonds and silk. There are also guards, lots of them, more than I ever recall seeing at a party, standing at intervals along the walls. Kyle isn't among them. The air smells of violets and smoke and perfume, is filled with laughter and conversation. Blood dancers in scraps of black chiffon and lace work the room, their veins marked with silver glitter.

*Would you like it?*

I look at our blood dancers, smiling and healthy, laughing and dancing, and try to imagine how it would feel to be one of them. When I was small I thought they were beautiful, complained when I wasn't allowed to wear glitter like they did. Now, for the first time, I wonder at their lives beyond our walls, whether they know about the rebellion brewing out there, while the Raven elite dance and drink and celebrate their great victory.

For a moment, everything seems strange and different. Like I've wandered into a world I've never seen before, the whirling vampires grotesque, the contortions of the blood dancers like pain, rather than ecstasy. It's as though something has ignited inside me, burning through old walls, my old way of thinking.

I look around, wondering if Kyle is here, then spot my mother across the room. She's changed from her robe into a fitted dress of crimson silk, strapless, her alabaster shoulders bare. She's wearing the Raven insignia on her choker, jet and diamonds around her slender neck, glittering chains of silver in her dark hair. A tall blond vampire is talking to her, his head bent close. I recognise him. Mistral. Of *course* he's hanging around Mother. I change direction but she sees me, beckoning me over. Damn. I paste a smile on my face and head over, curtseying when I reach them.

'No need for that.' Mistral takes my hand, raising it to his lips. 'It is I who should bow to you, Emelia Raven, heir to our throne. She's more like you every day.' He turns to my mother, who smiles, her onyx eyes flicking to me.

'She is, isn't she?'

'And yet...' Mistral tilts his head. I frown. My mother raises her eyebrows.

'And yet…?'

'Well, she has something of your husband as well, especially around the cheekbones.'

Heat rises to my face, more from annoyance than anything else. I'm standing right here, for fuck's sake! Mistral's eyes widen, and he licks his lips. My mother twines her arm with mine, bringing me close.

Mistral touches my cheek, then cups my chin. 'A real beauty,' he murmurs, his iridescent blue eyes on me. I take in a breath. He's beautiful, all smooth skin and cheekbones, his hair like spun gold. I try to slide my arm free but my mother clutches it tightly, so much that it hurts.

Mistral smiles. 'A shame you're human. Though, a very special one. You know, my youngest son is a similar age.' He turns his attention to my mother. 'Perhaps we need to talk, Penelope?'

I take a step back, shaken. A shame I'm human? He really is a dick. I feel a hand on my shoulder.

It's my father. His cool lips brush my cheek. 'Halloween greetings, Emelia.'

'And to you,' I say, but he's already turned his attention elsewhere.

'Any such discussion can wait, Mistral. Surely we have other things to manage at this point.'

Mistral grins, all white teeth and cheekbones. 'Is he always this boring?' He winks at my mother, who looks outraged.

'Friedrich, you know better than this—'

'Oh, I'm joking.' He laughs, then bows to my father. 'My

apologies.' He bows to me, too. 'And to you as well, beautiful one. Come, Aleksandr, let's talk business then, shall we?'

My mother watches them go, her perfect crimson lips half open. My mouth is tight.

'There will be dancing soon,' my mother says, still holding my arm. 'You'll stay for that, won't you?'

'Er, sure.' She knows me too well. I've been at this party for ten minutes and I already want to leave. 'I'll just get a drink.'

My mother kisses my cheek and releases me. I head to a table at one side of the room, set with refreshments for the blood dancers, and me. Fruit spills from silver gilt baskets, meats curled into succulent morsels nestle among gleaming olives and soft cheeses, hunks of fresh bread like soft pillows. A novelty, or so I've been told, among vampires. We've always fed our blood dancers well, wanting to keep them in top condition. But when I was born my mother had no idea how to feed me, vampire children needing only the blood of their parent to survive until they're old enough to hunt. A wet nurse was brought in, then apparently a human chef was found in one of the Safe Zones, and brought to the house with instructions to teach my mother how to cook. She fed me until I was old enough to insist on doing it myself, spending hours alone in the kitchens with the lights on, listening to music while I experimented, my mother happy to indulge my whims. But the presence of real food, well-prepared, at a vampire function, is seen as an eccentricity. I suppose it's also a reminder of the disappointment of their human heir. Again, I feel that flame inside me, flickering. It feels like defiance.

Glasses stand in orderly rows next to the food, some full of wine, blood red and sunshine gold, more with water, sparkling silver bubbles. I pass on the wine, despite how I usually enjoy it, another way I while away my days. Something about the room seems off and, even though I'm in my own home, I feel the need to stay sharp. I fill a small plate with food and pick up a glass of water, nodding to a blood dancer standing nearby, holding a jug of what is probably more wine. The air is filled with the scent of violets, and I wonder why he isn't dancing. Perhaps he's tired. He seems tense, though, his gaze darting around the room. I don't recognise him. When I smile at him, he doesn't smile back.

I find a seat near the long windows, eating while I watch shadowy trees dance under the moon. My thoughts shift to the humans out there, living in the Safe Zones. I wonder whether they're celebrating Halloween too.

*Your family farm.*

Kyle's words sit uncomfortably with me, like a prickle in my chest. I'm desperate to go, to live a life in the light with them, free from the weight of my family name. To live in a place where I belong, where I can do as I wish without worrying about being attacked, rather than being under guard the entire time. A place where I fit in, rather than standing out. But doubt now blooms inside me, along with my desire to leave, to forge my own path. My plan *has* to work. I don't know what I'll do if it doesn't.

*Do you not realise what a difference you could make?*

More words, spoken in a darkened hallway. They sit strangely with me as well, but for a different reason. No one has ever suggested that to me before. That *I* could make a difference. I can't imagine how. And I don't plan on sticking around long enough to find out. Panic twists, low in my stomach, at the thought of my impending coronation, as I stare into the darkness. Along with it is yearning. I wonder whether Kyle is somewhere out there, what he could be doing that has taken him from my side.

'… The North Wind will blow…' My ears prick up and I turn, scanning the room. There's a small group near me, three blood dancers. I think it was one of them who spoke.

'It's a nursery rhyme,' says another, leaning in close. 'But they've changed it.'

Who? Who changed it? Are they talking about the *rebels*? I lean in as well but one of them notices me and nudges the others, their worried expressions changing to smiles.

'My lady,' says the one closest to me. They move away before I can ask them anything, splitting up as they enter the crowd, trailing glittering temptation. I put my plate aside and get up, following in their wake, hoping to hear more.

Despite what Kyle told me, the rebellion still seems like nonsense. As if humans could do anything against the four families. But to hear our dancers talking about it… Again, I note the extra guards in the room, the feeling that something isn't quite right, the strangeness seeming to press at the walls. I can't just sit here and do nothing. I could ask my father, at least, though I don't want to get anyone in trouble.

I wander through the crowd, people dancing, feeding, talking in groups. But no one is saying anything interesting. Then I spot my father, broad-shouldered and lean in his usual gilt-edged black, talking with Mistral and another vampire. If I'm not mistaken, it's Stella's father, Artos Ravenna. I can't see my father's face, but Mistral looks serious.

I move closer. A few guests smile at me – they look vaguely familiar, so maybe I've seen them at Gatherings. I smile back, sipping my drink, trying not to seem as though I'm eavesdropping, though I'm sure my father knows I'm there. As does everyone else.

'… honestly, humans are becoming more and more difficult to control. It's like they don't want to be in Safe Zones anymore. If it wasn't going to cost so much, I'd be tempted to release them and let them take their chances. After all, stocks worldwide are heading back to record levels.' Mistral frowns, his arms folded.

'They're still nowhere near pre-Rising levels, though,' my father replies. 'And the unrest is getting worse. They're making incursions into our cities, and I've no idea how they're getting through the perimeters. I've had reports from all over the country.'

I sidle closer, as close as I dare.

'Yes, we've had similar problems, as you already know. I've had to double the guards on our UK estates. And their upkeep is becoming increasingly expensive – the amount of clean-up they require! Filthy creatures, really.' Artos Ravenna sounds annoyed.

Asshole. *I'm* human. I turn away, taking another sip of my drink.

'Not all of them, surely, Artos. Why, Emelia here is a rare beauty.' Cool fingers curl around my upper arm and I flinch, nearly dropping my drink. I turn to see Mistral close to me, his glorious face like something from an ancient coin.

'Emelia.' My father takes my hand, pulling me gently from Mistral's grasp, linking his arm with mine. 'Are you enjoying the evening?'

'Er, yes. Yes, I am.' I decide to go for it. 'Um, I keep hearing people talking about North Winds, though. What's that?' I smile, my eyes wide. My father's lips twitch. Artos Ravenna comes forward, taking my free hand and bringing it to his lips. His hair is darker gold than Mistral's, his features sharp in his lean face. He's taller than I am, though not as tall as Mistral or my father.

'Lovely Emelia! She is delicious, Aleksandr, truly so!' Ravenna cries. 'My dear,' he turns his attention to me, 'Stella told me she saw you the other week, at her Moon party. She flits about so much, one week a party here, another week there – I barely see her myself!' He's too jovial, as though he's covering up for something. I wonder what she told him.

I manage a smile. 'Um, yes, that's right. But anyway, what about—'

There's a sharp clapping noise and we all turn. My mother stands at the centre of the room, like a perfect jewel in a gleaming setting. 'Listen all,' she cries. 'Halloween is nigh, the moon rides high, so let the celebrations begin!'

A gold embroidered silk curtain hangs along one side of the room. Mother claps her hands again and it falls, revealing a band of musicians and a new group of dancers, glittering and lithe, wearing even fewer clothes than the previous group. There's a cry of excitement, moans as they enter the crowd, the musicians starting to play. The beat is wild, infectious, and the room starts to sway as one, couples twining around each other. I'm glad my father has hold of me.

'Lady, will you dance?' Mistral holds out his hand. I glance at my father. His brows draw together, a brief flicker, but he knows he can't really refuse. He may outrank Mistral, but there are courtesies to be observed. He brings my hand to his lips, kissing it under the guise of checking my anti-feed. He nods once, before handing me to Mistral.

And then I'm in Mistral's arms.

# Chapter Ten

## SUNRISE

**M**istral leans in close, his brilliant blue eyes crinkling at the corners. He's devastatingly handsome, and he knows it. He twirls me around the room, but goes too fast at first and I clutch at him as my feet leave the floor. He laughs.

'My dear Emelia, forgive me! You're so like your mother, I'd forgotten your, er… condition.'

'My condition?' I raise my eyebrows. Thankfully, he's slowed down, my feet touching the floor once more.

'Your sublime humanity.' He makes it sound like a caress. I don't give a shit. All at once he's not that attractive. I try to pull away from him.

'I would have thought it fairly obvious. I'm not that much like her.'

'Don't sell yourself short,' he says, his lips close to my ear, holding me so I can't move. 'You have more of Penelope in you than you think. I do think my son would like you.'

'I've already met them both.' I didn't care for either of them, both arrogant blonds like their father.

'I mean my other son, my third,' he says.

His third son? I frown.

'I don't believe you've met him.' He's still so close to me, his voice a purr. 'He's… away at the moment. I think you two would get along.'

The music changes, becoming slower, more sensuous. Uh-oh. All around us, couples are getting closer. My father appears, his hand on Mistral's shoulder. 'If I may,' he says. I make a face. I don't want to dance with Mistral to this music, but I don't in a million years want to dance to it with my *father*. Still, there's nothing either of us can do. Mistral releases me, bowing.

'It's been a pleasure, Emelia.'

'Thank you.' My father takes my hand but, thank darkness, instead of dancing he leads me through the crowd to the buffet table. Perfect. I do need wine, after all. I pick up a glass, pale golden in the candlelight.

My father grins. 'Are you all right?'

'I'm fine,' I say. 'Why?'

He raises his eyebrows and nods towards my glass. Shit. I don't drink in front of my parents. I'd grabbed the glass without thinking.

'I know you've been raiding the wine cellar since you were fourteen. At least you're old enough now.'

My mouth drops open. I take a breath, about to deny everything. Then I realise there's no point, if he already knows. I take a sip, then another. Mistral is still on the dance floor, wrapped around a blood dancer, his mouth at her throat. My father follows my gaze and his nostrils flare.

'You seemed annoyed, dancing with Mistral.'

'Oh, he was just being an idiot,' I say. 'He said he forgot I was human, then he was going on about how I looked like Mother, and how his son would like me.'

'His son?' My father's head is tilted, his voice soft.

'Yes, it was weird. I thought he only had two sons but he mentioned a third. He said he was away, that I wouldn't have met him.'

'Really.' It's not a question. 'Emelia, do not dance with Mistral again. I'll do my best to keep him occupied, and you do your best to stay partnered. Will you do this for me?'

I nod, surprised. 'Yes, of course. Father, what—'

'Don't worry for now. Just do as I ask.'

I pause. He looks at me. 'What is it?'

'The North Wind,' I whisper.

A curious expression crosses his face, his mouth curving, his eyes narrowing. He shakes his head, slowly, once. 'Later, Emelia.'

My mother arrives, leading a young vampire by the hand. His dark skin has a rosy tinge, his eyes bright. He's obviously well fed. I shoot her a look.

'Emelia, have you met Daniel? He's from Lion clan, visiting all this way! Daniel, this is my daughter, Emelia Raven.'

There's surprise in Daniel's eyes as he realises what I am. My parents, and their iron will, have contained the gossip about me well enough, I suppose, at least keeping it within our realm. Or maybe nobody cares enough to talk about it, figuring I won't last long enough to become Raven anyway. He recovers, though, and is perfectly courteous, bowing to me. 'It's a pleasure to meet you,' he says, holding out his hand. 'Shall we dance?'

And so it goes for the next few hours. I dance until my feet are sore, my parents taking turns to introduce me to partners, some willing, some not so, but not wishing to offend their hosts. Mistral doesn't get near me, our most luscious dancers trailed before him, an endless distraction of scented flesh. I keep my anti-feed topped up, keep my ears open for any more talk of rebellion, even going so far as to ask a couple of my dance partners, but no one else seems to know or even be interested in the idea of a human uprising. I suppose it's not surprising. I hadn't considered it myself.

*Until Kyle.*

Where in darkness is he? As I move from one set of arms to another, all I can think about is how it felt to dance with him, how I wish he was the one twirling me around the dance floor, even though I know it's not possible.

Finally, I excuse myself, needing a rest. I thank my latest partner and, when he releases me, head for the edge of the dance floor. I'm surprised to realise I've enjoyed the dancing after all. Or maybe I'm just drunk – I've had more wine since my dance with Mistral, possibly a little too much. Outside, the moon is low. Perhaps it's time to go, before the sun rises and the shutters fall, the guests retreating to the fortified rooms then resuming their dancing once the house is secured.

'Happy Halloween, my lady.'

My stomach lurches. I turn. Kyle is standing a couple of feet away, dressed in his Raven uniform, hands clasped behind his back. He bows.

'A-and to you.' I keep my voice cool, smoothing my hands down my dress. But my heart is pounding, a frantic beat.

'You look nice.' He inclines his head, his silver eyes bright.

'Thanks. You, too.' *You, too?* It must be the wine talking. *Pull it together, Emelia. He wears the same uniform every day.* However, I'm not lying. I'm desperate to kiss him.

He grins, like he knows what I'm thinking. 'Have you had fun?'

'It's been fine.' *Even though you weren't here.*

There's silence between us. I remember dark hallways, his mouth on mine. 'Where have you been?'

His grin widens. 'Did you miss me?'

Ass. 'I just wondered, that's all.' I try to think of ice and cold water, of frozen winter, wishing for a tenth of my mother's cool glamour.

'I was reassigned unexpectedly. Mistral's orders.' He inclines his head. 'I'm sorry I couldn't tell you.'

'Reassigned?' I don't care if Mistral ordered it. I thought he was my personal guard.

'Just something that needed sorting out.' He moves closer. 'I missed you,' he says, his voice lower.

HELEN GLYNN JONES

I stare at him. It's as though the entire ballroom is revolving around us, like we're at the eye of the storm. 'I'm glad you're back.'

He moves closer again, so I have to lift my chin to look at him. It feels like electricity sparks between us. If he touches me… Somebody bumps into me and I blink.

Kyle's eyes widen and he steps back. 'Can I get you anything, my lady?' His hands are clasped behind his back, but there's a gleam in his eye.

'Actually, I was just about to go back to my room.'

He raises an eyebrow. 'Shall I escort you?'

I nod, finding it hard to breathe. 'Yes. I just need to let my parents know I'm leaving.'

He steps aside, though he's still close enough I have to brush against him as I walk past. I spot my mother, dancing with my father, and make a beeline for them. I touch my mother's arm. She turns, pulling my father to a stop.

'Um, I'm tired and it's almost dawn, so I might go to my room. I'll come back down later, if that's all right?'

My mother's cheeks are flushed, her onyx eyes sparkling. My father looks well, too, colour on his high cheekbones. Good. They've been drinking.

'Of course,' my mother says. 'Off you go.' She caresses my cheek, languorous and smiling.

'Take care of her,' my father says, nodding to Kyle, who is just behind me. I daren't look at him.

'Good evening.' I curtsey to them both then leave the ballroom, taking the quickest route possible through the crowd, leaving the glitter and blood behind. The straps of my sandals are cutting into my feet, and I can't wait to take them off. I can't wait to be alone with Kyle, either. He follows me, two paces behind as we pass beneath the gleaming Halloween tree, lights swaying gently. The silk of my skirt slides against my legs, my cheeks heating up as we ascend the stairs. Upstairs, the hallway is dark and deserted. I stop. There's a bench against the wall, padded silk and carved wood. I sit down.

Kyle stops too. 'Are we still going to your room?'

I blush at how that sounds. 'Just a sec,' I wave my hand. 'I need to take off these damn shoes.'

He laughs. I take one off, kicking it under the bench.

There's a burst of laughter and two guests emerge from the room opposite, a blood dancer between them, her wrist to the mouth of the male vampire. All three glitter like fireflies in the dark. 'Oops, sorry!' the female vampire giggles. 'Don't let us stop you.'

'Raven have the best dancers,' says the male, removing his mouth from the girl's wrist. His lips gleam dark with her blood. 'Don't know what they put in them to make them taste so damn delicious. She looks a real treat, young man, you enjoy,' he goes on, clapping Kyle on the shoulder. 'Make the most of Halloween.'

All three laugh again, their heads going back. They disappear down the hallway, the blood dancer stumbling. My mouth has dropped open. The club was one thing, but this... I've been dancing all night, been talking to my parents, making the rounds. I am literally wearing the

Raven crest, in diamonds. Anyone with eyes should know who I am, surely?

'What the fuck? I'm in my own house and they think—'

'Don't worry about them.' Kyle slants his silver gaze my way. He's leaning against the wall, his arms folded. I try not to stare at the muscles visible through his guard's uniform, the lean hips, the long legs. 'Idiots, obviously. And drunk. I reckon that dancer had something extra added.'

'But my parents don't—'

'Your parents might not. Your guests are another matter. It's easy to do.' He comes closer, bending as though to sit next to me. I gaze up at him, my mouth dry with anticipation.

Then he straightens, standing to attention. Another vampire appears, his shirt collar undone, bowtie hanging loose. There are a couple of blood spots on his shirt. I guess he's been feeding as well. What the hell is with all these people wandering about up here? 'The ballroom this way?' he slurs.

'Er, yes, sir. To the end of the hallway, then down the stairs and left. You can't miss it.' Kyle holds out his hand. With a burst of speed, the vampire flashes along the hallway.

I bend to take off my other shoe. The buckle is stiff and I struggle with it for a second, until it comes open.

And the sharp metal slices the pad of my thumb, drawing blood.

Shit.

Kyle's head turns, silver eyes wide. 'Emelia?'

I stare at him, holding my injured thumb close to me. 'I'm fine.'

'Let me look.'

'What!? No!'

He's there before I can stop him, kneeling, his hands on mine uncurling my fingers. Blood pools on my palm, its coppery scent in the air. He takes in a breath. I hold mine. He puts my thumb to his lips, his mouth closing over it, and I think I'm going to black out. He licks at my blood, his tongue tingling rough, taking every last drop. No one has ever done this to me, not like this. I've had scratches healed, my parents' touch gentle. But this is something else, something that tugs at my very core, need building in me. It's unbearably intimate, my whole body responding. Kyle brings my other hand to his mouth as well, sucking at the vestiges of blood, then bites his lip, taking a single drop of his own blood on the tip of his tongue. He presses it to my cut, healing it.

'There.'

I can't breathe.

He moves closer still, his arms either side of me. Cool breath mists my lips. My heartbeat feels as large as the hallway, a thudding echo of noise. Forget control. I have none. He can have whatever he wants.

He smiles, his eyes a silver gleam. He says my name, the words dropping like stones into the deep pool of night. Sensation ripples from his touch, his breath cold fire on my skin. His eyes close and he inhales, breathing me in.

I gasp as his hand slides beneath the neckline of my

gown, caressing me briefly. The scent of violets is overpowering. He kisses me, a quicksilver touch of the lips.

'Perhaps we could,' he murmurs, his lips millimetres from mine, 'go somewhere more private. Just for a little while.' His fingers trail up the side of my neck. I curl into his touch, every nerve-ending alive, feeling as though I might fly, or explode, screaming into the night, dissolving like sparking embers, flickering gold against the dark. Every hair stands on end, an ache deep inside me. I reach up, his hair slipping like silk through my fingers as I pull him in for a kiss.

I feel him smile, diamond-sharp teeth nipping me, his lips moving across my cheek, past my jawline to my neck. I am gone. Caution thrown to whatever wind passed by. He can do anything in this moment and I'll let him. How would I stop him, anyway?

Somehow, we end up in my room. Whether Kyle carries me or I drag him there, I don't know. As the door closes it doesn't matter. Nothing matters except his touch.

Kyle unfastens my dress, pushing the straps down, the soft fabric crumpled beneath us on the bed. His mouth is on my throat, his hand closing on my breast. There's a sharp nip on my neck and I flinch. At once he pulls back, eyes wide. His fangs are dropped, and there's a faint tinge of blood on one pale tip. My blood.

'I'm sorry,' he whispers, sounding horrified. 'I didn't mean to—'

I reach a hand behind his head and pull him close, kissing him. 'It doesn't matter,' I say. Nothing does. Not in this moment. Besides, from what I've read, this is a normal part of vampire intimacy. But he's still hesitating, so I flick my tongue against his lips. The response is immediate. He snarls, deep in his throat, pushing against me as he kisses me back, his tongue flickering.

My dress is down around my waist but he's still fully dressed, which doesn't seem at all fair. I try to reach the buttons on his shirt, but can't get my hand in quite the right place. He lifts his head.

'Why are you wriggling so much?' There's laughter in the words and I giggle.

'Sorry,' I whisper, 'I was trying to undo your shirt.'

Both eyebrows go up. 'Oh really?' He pulls back from me, undoing his top buttons and pulling the shirt over his head in one smooth movement. Wow.

His torso is perfectly muscled, pecs and six-pack outlined by faint candlelight, a subtle gleam to his skin. Every inch of him is cool against my heated flesh, my hands tracing his back as he kisses me, stars bursting behind my eyelids. I'm drowning in sensation, my hands tracing the curve of his backside, my dress sliding further down.

'Emelia.' His kisses move lower and I think I might die. I lift my hips as he slides my dress away, his mouth soft on my stomach. There's a sharp knock on my chamber door and I jump, shaken from my passion. Kyle lifts his head, his hands still.

'My lady.'

Shit. It's Bertrand.

'J-just a minute,' I call out. Kyle is already up, moving in a blur as he gets dressed, shrugging on the silver and black jacket last of all. He goes to my mirror, running a hand through his hair, tugging his collar back into shape. I lie there, desire turning sour in my mouth, my breath returning to normal, sweat cooling on my skin. Eventually I sit up, pulling my dress back on, sliding the straps over my shoulders. Then Kyle is there, his arms around me, kissing me. He bites his finger and touches it to my throat, healing the small wound he made.

There's another knock at the door, this one harder than the last and we both jump. Shit. 'Go in the bathroom,' I hiss, giving him a push. He nods and is gone, the door closing with a soft click. I grab my blanket and wrap it around me, hoping I look sufficiently sleepy. I open the door a crack to see Bertrand's worried face. Dear Bertrand. I hate lying to him.

'Are you all right? Your mother said you came back to your room with Kyle, and I've been looking for him.'

I crinkle up my face. 'Er, I did. But I've been here, dozing.'

Bertrand pauses. 'I'm sorry to have disturbed you, my lady.' I feel awful. I open my door wider, so he can see in my room. He peers in over my shoulder, and I hope he thinks Kyle's violet scent is just anti-feed. He nods. 'I'll leave you to it,' he says. 'Let me know if you'd like to return to the ballroom later, though.'

'Er, thanks. Um, I might just stay in here for a while.' I close the door and lean on it, blowing out a breath. That was too close. Kyle reappears from my bathroom.

'I have to go,' he says, kissing me. 'I'm sorry.'

'S-sorry this happened?' My voice is raw.

'No, never.' He kisses me again, gentle. 'Trust me. I wish I didn't have to leave.'

I rest my forehead on his for a moment. 'You do, though. Go on.' I give him a little push.

One last kiss, and he's gone.

I stare at the closed door, as though I might will him back to me just by wishing it. There's a rumbling noise, and I jump. The shutters. I open my door. The hallway is deserted, light through the long windows growing pale. I don't want to stay in my room.

I have a couple of minutes. Which is enough.

I start to run, my skirt billowing like wings as I race through golden pools of dawn. Everyone else is gone, retreating to the fortified rooms at the heart of the house, in case some stray finger of light were to catch them.

I reach the library as the shutters finally close, sealing the house against daylight. I dart inside, closing the doors as quietly as I can. There's wine here, hidden among the shelves, and music, old songs, dead voices from before the Rising. Remnants of all my lonely days, all the time I've spent entertaining myself, educating myself about how humans live, dreaming of possibility. But that's not what I'm here for.

I scan the shelves filled with paperbacks. I've read every book in here, some more than once. But there's a specific one I need. *Interview with the Vampire*. Pulling it from the shelf, I reach between the books until I feel hard metal under my fingers. I tug, stepping back quickly. The bookcase slides silently to one side, releasing a small cloud of dust. I wave my hand, my eyes scrunched closed. Through an opening lies a narrow flight of stairs, curving upwards.

It's no surprise that a house as old as this would have secret passages. This is the one I use the most, though.

I step inside and pull another small lever. The bookcase closes again, sealing me in darkness. My hands on the walls to guide me, I make my way up the steps until my head bumps against something hard. I reach up, releasing the latch, and push.

Light falls all around me.

I ascend the final few stairs and step onto the roof.

It's glorious.

The sky is striped with colour, gold and red and orange and turquoise, the sun a ball of fire on the horizon. Mist wreathes the trees, the landscape spread out like a half-remembered dream, golden and beckoning, the dark mass of forest stretching towards the faint shimmer of the Safe Zone.

This section of the roof is flat, an ornate stone façade shielding me from below. I lean against it, resting my elbows on the edge, cool grit of stone against my skin. The little flame inside me, the one I felt in the ballroom, seems to respond, glowing as the light increases. My eyes fill with tears. It never fails to move me, whether sunrise or sunset, the turning of the world an endless wonder. Birds chirp in the woods as the sky brightens, ribbons of gold fading to blue. I shiver in the autumn chill, my bare feet curling against the stone. The distant Safe Zone is now a darker shadow, the lights that bound it in safety turning off as the sun rises. I can't believe it's a bad place to live, despite what Kyle says.

I sigh, my breath catching at the thought of him, of his hands and mouth on me. Of what might have happened if Bertrand hadn't come to the door when he did. I wonder where he is now, what he's doing, whether he's thinking of me. I don't care that he's a guard, that I'm the next Raven. I just want him. Not only to help me escape, but to stay with me, afterwards. I wonder whether we could make it work, a vampire and a human out in the real world. I wish he was here with me so I could tell him about my plan, ask him how he feels.

But he can't be. No one in the house can, other than the humans who live here as food. Even being out here feels wrong, my mother so cautious around light my entire life that, somehow, it's rubbed off on me. Even though I know daylight can't hurt me, there's part of me that wants to go back down, into the darkness. Yet a larger part of me rejoices in the feel of it on my skin, the strangeness of a sky not filled with stars. It's how things will be for me, every day, once I leave. My mouth twists, the landscape blurring. I cross my arms, rubbing my cold hands along them.

The party has started again, a faint thump of music coming from the now-shuttered ballroom. I should go back soon or I'll be missed, and I can't take that chance. No one knows I come up here, and I want to keep it that way. This is something just for me, and no one else. I make my way back down the stairs, closing the trapdoor, entering the cocoon of the library once more. I'm in a daze, swaying with lust and Kyle and the beauty of the morning. I'm about to sit down when there's a muffled booming noise followed by shouting, and the rapid thud of running feet. Then the library doors fly open and Bertrand's huge shape appears.

'Go to your room, my lady. Now.'

# Chapter Eleven

## LOYALTY

**M**y stomach lurches. 'What is it? What's happening?' There's a distant sound of screaming, which stops abruptly. I run to the door, but Bertrand won't let me pass. He stares at me with worried eyes.

'Bertrand.' I try to sound like my mother, cool and clear, even though my panic is rising. Bertrand blinks.

'There's been a disturbance, ah, in the ballroom.'

'Let me through.'

'My lady, you mustn't—'

'Please, Bertrand. Are my parents okay? I need to go...' My voice catches. I can see indecision in his face.

'But my lady, you're not wearing shoes.' There's silence now, even more ominous.

'Forget my shoes!' I push at his arm and he finally lets me pass. I run down the hallway, fear sharp within me. Bertrand is next to me, one hand on the small of my back. Halfway down the stairs I realise he hasn't answered me.

I cross the foyer, taking the turning to the ballroom. The hallway is deserted, which is odd. Then I realise I can see. And the lights aren't on...

I hear Bertrand hiss. 'My lady! I can go no further.'

'It's fine.' I keep running, leaving him behind. No vampire can get me now, anyway.

The double doors to the ballroom are splintered, half hanging from their hinges. I slow down, my hand to my mouth. Whatever happened here was quick, and violent. I enter the ballroom and my heart sinks. One of the shutters covering the long windows is bowed out of its frame, the window shattered, pale morning light coming in. The parquetry floor nearby is cracked and blackened, several piles of black ash drifting in the cool autumn air. I feel sick as I realise what they are. Vampires. *Or what's left of them.* What if one of them is my mother? Or my father? I cannot bear the thought.

'My lady.' The call comes from behind me and I turn. A group of blood dancers are huddled together, kneeling, in the furthest corner of the room. I can't understand why they're hiding from the light. Then I realise. They're shielding someone.

I start towards them, then stop. Oh darkness. Near to the wall, tumbled as though thrown, are the remains of a human. Blood pools on the floor, is spattered up the wall, a spray of crimson droplets. His head is on top of the pile of tangled body parts, mouth open for eternity. I try not to throw up. What in god and nightmares has happened here?

'My lady, please!' The call gets more urgent and I hear a groan. I think I recognise the voice. Please, no. I can't take any more shocks. I make my way to the huddled group in the corner.

'What… who is it?' I sniff despite myself. 'Are you hurt?'

'We're fine, my lady.' It's Elodie, her dark hair dishevelled, a smear of blood at her temple. She's closest to me, her body pressed tight with the others, their arms wrapped around each other creating a wall of flesh to shield whoever is behind them.

I bite my lip to stop from screaming. 'Who is it?' I ask again, my voice shaking.

'Emelia.'

My father. His voice is faded, old sounding, and I start to cry. The only reason he's still here, that he hasn't left the ballroom, is because he can't.

'Emelia, control yourself!'

I wipe my face, sniffing. 'Father, wh-what can I do? Where's Mother?'

'You have to fix the shutter, block the window. Do something. I can't move.'

'Uh, okay.' I can do that. I think. Spots of black ash swirl in the breeze, the gilt and mirrors silvered by the morning light. I avoid the piles of ash and blood spatters as I make my way to the broken window, feeling as though I'm in some horrible dream. The window frame is splintered beyond repair, the shutter bowed and blackened as though some force pushed it outwards. I still don't know where my mother is. My breath sobs in and out. I hope and pray she was among those who escaped. I put the thought away from me, unable to consider it any longer. I have a job to do here, and I need to focus.

Grabbing the edge of the shutter, I pull, the metal cutting my hands, black soot smearing my dress. It doesn't move. I groan with frustration, pulling again, but all I succeed in doing is hurting my hands, my palms red and scored with lines. 'I can't move it.'

'Try something else.' My father doesn't sound disappointed – rather, he sounds encouraging, like he knows I can do this. I look around and notice panelled inserts running either side of the recessed window frames. I pause, remembering an old video I once watched of a man playing piano as his dark-haired wife opened white wooden shutters, his song one of imagination, of a different world. The windows had been tall, the shutters set in panelled recesses like these. I run my fingers along the edge of the panels. There. A semi-circle indentation at the edge of the wood. I hook my finger in and pull. There's a creaking sound, and a cloud of dust appears. But the panel moves. I pull harder, managing to get more of my fingers around the wood and, gradually, the shutter opens, coming from the recess like a butterfly wing unfolding, hinges squeaking. It covers the window, not quite opening all the way, but enough to plunge the room into near darkness. The candle-lamps glow once more and there's a sigh from the corner. The blood dancers come apart, one dropping to all fours. I rush over to my father. Oh my god and darkness.

Daylight is the most devastating thing to a vampire, and it looks as though he was caught in it long enough to ignite. One side of his face is blackened, his clothing singed and torn. I glimpse charred flesh and cuts through the holes in the fabric. A blood dancer is curled up next to him, half fainting. He has her wrist to his mouth. Oh shit. That means he must have been much worse, if he's been feeding and yet still looks as he does.

'Father…' My voice breaks. I drop to my knees. He releases the dancer's wrist and I see him half smile.

'Good girl,' he says, his voice faint.

I hold out my arm. 'Take some from me.'

His brows come together and his smile fades. 'Don't be ridiculous.'

I am being ridiculous. But I don't know what else to do. 'Please, I want to help.' My voice cracks.

'You have helped. Here, take Danae.'

Danae is the fainting dancer. She's so pale, her freckled skin almost translucent. My father must have taken a lot of blood from her. The other dancers crowd around, silent. My eyes prickle with tears at their loyalty, at what they did to protect my father.

'Thank you, thank you so much,' I say. 'I just, um, thank you. Um, can anyone—'

'Here.' James, all lithe muscle and smooth dark skin, bends down next to Danae. He puts an arm under her and together we manage to get her to her feet. Her breathing is shallow though and, as James scoops her up, her eyes roll back in her head.

'Take her, get her well. I can manage from here. And thank you again, for everything.'

'This will not be forgotten,' my father adds. His voice is stronger, but he still hasn't stood up. As the dancers leave, I kneel beside him.

'Papa.' I haven't called him that since I was small. 'What happened here? Where's Mama?'

'It was a bomb.' His head rolls slightly to one side and I see the gleam of his eyes. 'She left. She had to... the light.' He gestures to the now-covered window. 'Mistral took her to the fortified rooms, along with the other guests. She didn't want to leave me, I told her to go.'

'A bomb?' I whisper. 'H-how is that possible?' Inside I'm melting with relief that my mother is okay. But my father... I sob, wiping my face with the back of my hand.

He pats my leg. 'You did well,' he says. 'I'll be fine.'

'But you're all burned, and...' I sob again, unable to control myself. 'I'm sorry,' I say, ashamed.

'It's all right,' he says, his voice gentle. 'Now, I need to get out of here.'

'Uh, of course.' I nod, sniffing. 'Can I... can you stand up? How badly are you hurt?'

My father grimaces, shifting his weight. 'Is Bertrand near?'

'Yes.' Of course. He can come in now. 'Bertrand!'

Bertrand arrives, knocking down the remains of the shattered doors. His hand comes to his mouth when he sees us. I want to cry again at his reaction. I stand up, my bare feet sticking to the floor. I don't want to know what's on them. My dress is ruined, smeared with dust and soot and blood. 'Um, Bertrand.' I swallow my tears. 'Father needs help. I can't lift him.'

Bertrand comes to lift my father in his arms. 'I'll take him to the sitting room, my lady.'

My father reaches for me, squeezing my hand. 'Find your mother,' he says.

I nod. There are no words. I leave the ballroom, heading towards the fortified rooms. Made of thick stone, half sunk into the ground and sealed against the light, they are the heart of the house. Built many centuries ago, they've since been strengthened with steel, floodlights installed on the outside controlled from the inside, with cameras on all sides. I press the intercom buzzer.

'Emelia!' My mother's voice sounds tinny, her usually smooth tones rough. She's sobbing, hoarse gasps coming through the speaker.

'Mother, he's all right, it's all right. I've sealed the ballroom.'

I hear my mother sigh. 'Aleks.' Then another voice comes over the intercom, deep and masculine.

'How do you know the threat is contained?'

'Who is this?' I frown, knowing the cameras can see me. But, seriously?

'It's Mistral, dear one. I don't think your mother should come out until it's safe.'

'I'm out here.' I don't add '*asshole*', but I want to. 'And so's Father. We're fine. Bertrand is here. Mama, I need you.'

That last bit slips out. I'm shaking, cold in my ruined

gown. I just want to hug her and know she's safe. Stupid Mistral isn't in charge here. Who the hell does he think he is?

With a hiss of steel, the great metal door opens. My mother is first out, shaking Mistral's hand off her arm. What the hell? Was he seriously trying to hold her back? When she sees me her face crumples and all at once she's curved around me, hugging me, kissing my hair. I hug her back, equilibrium returning to my world. Air rushes around us, but all I know is her. Thank darkness she's safe.

'Your lovely dress,' she mumbles. 'It's ruined.' I realise she's as shaken as I am. It's damp where her face is buried in my shoulder and I know she's crying. Mistral is standing nearby, his handsome head tilted, a look of sympathy on his face, though there's also a tightness, a slight frown. Blood is all over his crisp white shirt, fading red blotches on his golden skin.

'Mama,' I whisper. Childlike, again. 'Father, he'll want to see you.'

'Of course.' My mother sighs and releases me. Her silk dress is singed along the edges, red patches of burned skin on her pale neck and shoulders. Blood streaks her cheeks and she rubs at it, red flaking under her fingertips. There's more blood on my shoulder, to go with the mess on my gown. I almost want to laugh. What a pair we make. Other than Mistral and two guards, everyone else has gone – I suppose they've returned to their chambers.

'Come on.' I hold out my hand but to my annoyance Mistral takes her arm and they whoosh down the hallway, faster than I can go. I run along behind, the guards keeping pace with me easily.

When we reach the sitting room my mother is hugging my father, who is half-lying on the sofa. 'Oh, Aleksandr,' I hear her say. He's smiling, his eyes closed as he wraps his arms around her. Bertrand is standing nearby, hands clasped behind him, as are my parents' personal guards. Mistral is sprawled in one of the armchairs. He seems relaxed, but there's still something tense about him, something I can't quite put my finger on.

'What happened?' I ask. Two words, encompassing so much. The long night catches up with me and I collapse into a soft armchair, hugging a cushion close. 'Papa said it was a bomb.' I still can't believe this.

My mother turns to me. 'It was one of the blood dancers—'

'The one at the drinks table?'

My mother's eyebrows go up. 'Yes. Why do you ask?'

'I didn't recognise him. And...' *He smelled of violets.* 'I think he was wearing anti-feed. What in darkness did he do?'

My mother's expressive features seem to ripple. It's my father who answers.

'I was standing by the window when he came towards me, a jug in his hand. I waved him away, but he threw the jug at me. I sidestepped, and—'

'It blew out the window,' Mistral drawls. 'I ripped him apart, but the damage was already done.'

'And then he rushed me out of there.' My mother still sounds shaken.

I swallow. So Mistral is responsible for the pile of body parts. Fuck fuck fuck. How is this even happening? 'But, I don't understand—'

'He shouted something.' My mother's voice is rough. 'Before he threw the jug. "The North Wind will blow."'

# Chapter Twelve

## TWENTY LIVES

'The North Wind?' It's like a cold shock. 'B-but, they're humans!'

My mother grips my father, convulsive. 'Oh, Aleks, if he'd succeeded—' Her voice breaks and she buries her face in the curve where his neck meets his shoulder. He shifts, pulling my mother onto his lap. I look away. And catch Mistral frowning.

'How do you know of the North Wind?' he says.

Despite the fact that I'm shaking and cold, something about the way he asks puts my back up. 'I saw it written on a wall, when I was out the other night. And I asked Ky— er, one of the guards about it.' I pause to catch my breath. Everything feels strange, as though I'm in a dream. Or maybe like I just woke up. That little flame inside me flickers again. 'I thought they weren't a threat, though. I mean, they're just humans.'

As the words leave my mouth it's as though I can see

myself saying them. *Just humans.* Who in darkness do I think I am?

*Would you like it?*

I don't think I would.

'What do you know about it, Emelia?' My father is frowning, but one corner of his mouth curves.

'That they're rebels. And that—'

Mistral interrupts me. 'You don't need to worry about them, child.'

Screw him. I'm not a child. 'They just tried to kill my father – I think I do need to worry!'

He narrows his eyes. Then he smiles, once more flashing gold brilliance. 'They didn't succeed. And their agent is dead. Just another piece of human scum.' He snarls the last part.

'*I'm* human,' I hiss.

My mother leaves my father's lap and comes to sit with me, taking my hand. 'I'm sure Mistral didn't mean it like that.'

'Forgive me, dear one.' Mistral inclines his head in my direction. 'Now, Penelope, I think we need to—'

I cut in, my voice rising. 'But how did the bomber get in here? If he was "just another human".' I let scorn creep into my voice, hoping it will cover the shaking. 'And what do they want? For darkness' sake, people are dead! They nearly killed Father! I mean, is there something we're doing to humans, something we could change...' I trail off. Of course there's something we're doing. We *eat* them. And I don't see that changing any time soon.

'Who knows? Or cares, if I'm honest.' Mistral spreads his hands. 'They'll never win.'

I half-rise from my seat, my fists clenched, my control slipping.

My mother pulls me back. 'Your father will be fine,' she says, rubbing my arm. 'You needn't worry.'

'Yes, he was lucky, little one,' Mistral muses.

He really is a dick.

'Lucky?' I say, through gritted teeth. 'He was lucky only because of our blood dancers, who blocked the light to save him. Without them, he'd be dead. I doubt you'd care about them, though. They're just humans.'

'Actually, Emelia, you are right to question this.' All eyes turn to my father, who pushes himself up against the cushions, his movements stiff. 'No one should have been able to get in here tonight. The North Wind shouldn't be able to get past our perimeters, nor should they be able to get so deep into vampire territory. And yet they do. We receive reports daily and yet, maddeningly, we cannot find the source.'

'They are truly like the wind.' My mother's voice is rough. 'Impossible to catch.'

Mistral is staring at me, his eyes lazy slits of blue. I yawn, my eyelids starting to droop. I lean on my mother, hardly able to stay awake.

'Are you tired, dear one? I can take you to your room, if you like.'

I hear Mistral's voice as though from a distance. My lips part and it's that feeling again, as though I'm being drawn into a web of silk and gold. My mother's voice cuts through the strands.

'Bertrand will take her back later.' Her voice is sharp. She squeezes my hand, hard, the glittering fog in my mind dissipating. What the...? Was Mistral trying to *mesmerise* me?

Not all vampires can mesmerise and, for those who can, it's not something that's socially acceptable. It's used on prey, so to try it on a fellow vampire or, in my case, the human child of one, is the height of rudeness. What the hell is he thinking?

There's no chance to find out. Mistral's attention is back to my mother once more, his lapis-blue gaze a caress. 'Now, Penelope,' he says, all smoothness. 'Let us talk vengeance.'

'Vengeance?' My stomach twists.

'No.' The word falls, heavy, into the room. My father stares at Mistral, dark brows lowered over his golden eyes. 'I will not kill breeding stock to send a message. We need to get to the root of the matter, find out who's behind this. They came into my home, for darkness' sake, attacked me! The fact that they were able to do so speaks to an organisation with deeper, more complex roots than mere human rebellion.'

Mistral raises his eyebrows. 'Are you suggesting vampires are involved? A conspiracy against one of the great families? Who would dare?'

'Again, a good question.' My father holds Mistral's gaze and, interestingly, it's Mistral who breaks first. His gaze comes to rest on me, blue gold. I look away.

'What do you mean, kill them?' I ask. But no one answers. I feel like screaming.

'They tried to murder you, Aleks.' My mother's voice is softer, but there's steel in it. Everyone turns to her. Red is visible in her eyes. 'Came into the seat of Raven itself. Such a crime cannot go unpunished.' She is cold, now, like a sculpture of snow, glittering and beautiful. She's no longer holding my hand; instead, her fists are clenched, her back straight. Raven, in all her deadly glory. 'What if Emelia had been standing with you when the bomb went off?' There's silence. 'We *should* make an example. Show them the power of Raven.'

'They know about our power, beloved. It defines every moment of their existence. What use would killing a few humans be? A waste of good stock.' My father's voice is quieter, more reflective. He might argue with Mistral, but he'll do anything for my mother. And she's the true head of Raven. The decision lies with her as to what happens next.

Mistral knows it, too. He raises his hands, holding them wide. 'I am at your service, Penelope. Give the command and I'll do it.'

'Do what?' I whisper.

'A Moon Harvest,' says Mistral. He is like an avenging angel, all gold and fury.

'A Moon Harvest?' God and darkness. I've never heard of one happening, not since I was born. It's an old practice, from the old world, a night of blood-soaked feasting. Sacrifices, usually drugged in a pretence of consent. Jaguar made a whole religion from it, apparently. I cannot believe my mother is even considering this.

But then I look at my father, burned and broken, and there is rage again, for what could have happened to those I love. But it's tempered with sorrow – with the growing realisation of the many lives vampires have torn apart. It's a strange feeling, to hold such opposing ideas and know them both to be true. I feel like I might almost understand the rebels, while at the same time wanting to destroy them all. A headache is forming, pushing against the edges of my brain. Everything feels strange, as though the room might crack open and expose me to the world, the familiar walls tumbling down, my safety an illusion.

*You have no idea who you could be.*

My father is looking at me. But my mother is focused on Mistral, silver moon to his golden sun in the dimly lit room. 'Do it.' Her tone is decisive. 'But…' She holds up one pale hand. 'No children. And no one who cannot be proven to be a rebel. Twenty lives. Like the old tributes used to be.'

*Twenty lives?*

Mistral unfolds himself from the chair, lean and elegant, then kneels in front of my mother. She holds out her hand. He takes it, kissing her long fingers.

I feel sick. 'But the man, the man who did it – he's already dead.'

All heads turn to me. Mistral is frowning slightly. My father's golden eyes are soft, softer than I remember seeing them.

'What is it?' he says.

'I… just. I mean. Er…'

'Darling girl, these decisions are difficult.' My mother's voice is gentle. Mistral is still on one knee, golden light gleaming from his hair. 'As Raven you'll have to learn when to make them. Twenty lives are a fair exchange for the attack on your father, don't you see?'

Are they? I don't think I can make decisions like that. Decisions of life and death. Of *course* Father is important. Of *course* the people responsible need to pay. But this doesn't seem fair.

'How will you know?' I say, adrift in a tilted world.

'How will I know what?' My mother takes my hand. I hang onto her cool fingers as though they're a lifeline.

'That they're rebels.'

'I'll make sure of it.' Mistral, pushing in again. I really wish he would just fuck off.

'How?' I try to sound cool, like my mother. My father's lips twitch.

Mistral's slight frown deepens. 'We have intelligence forces, dear Emelia, agents who keep me apprised of such things. We are weeding them out, one by one, and—'

'Except for the one who attacked Father. Your agents missed him.'

My father coughs behind his hand.

'Mistral knows what he's doing.' My mother nods to him. 'So shall it be,' she says. 'Raven claw, blood and stone.'

He bows his head. 'Raven claw, blood and stone,' he replies. 'Your word is my command, as always, my Penelope. It shall be so, at the fireworks, five nights hence.'

The fireworks. I'd forgotten about those. They happen in the week following Halloween, and I love watching them. Usually.

'This is madness.' The words tumble from me.

'Emelia.' There is ice in my mother's cool tones, a warning.

'How can you even consider this? It will just make things worse!'

Mistral speaks. 'If you become Raven—'

'*If* I become Raven?' I'm on my feet, my hand slipping from my mother's grasp. 'I *am* the next Raven! I didn't realise it involved slaughtering people!'

Okay, I know. I'm going to run away. But it's not up to Mistral to make that decision.

'Are you questioning your mother's will?' Mistral's voice is hard, his blue eyes narrow slits of sapphire.

'I'm questioning *you*. Showing up here, acting like you own the place, leaving my father to burn while you took Mother and—'

'Enough!' My mother's voice is whip-sharp. 'Emelia, I realise this has been a long night, but you cannot speak to Mistral like this. You need to apologise.'

'What?' Embarrassment rushes through me, a prickling flush. My father seems about to speak, but she raises her hand.

'Emelia?'

I stare at her, breathing hard. But I will burn before I apologise to Mistral.

'Fine.' She folds her lips. 'You are confined to the house

for the next little while. For your own safety,' she adds. 'But also, perhaps you need some time to think about things, and about what becoming Raven will entail.'

Tears prickle my eyes, my breath hitching in my chest.

Mistral is smirking.

I run from the room, stumbling into the hallway. Bertrand follows, but even his familiar bulk feels more like an obstruction than protection, a stone wall I want to smash through. But I can't smash through anything, can't change anything, can't *do* anything.

'Can I help, my lady?' Bertrand cuts into my tangled thoughts. I take in a deep breath through my nose, rubbing my forehead. Then, to my deep shame, I burst into tears.

'Shall I carry you back to your room?'

'No.' I sniff, wiping my eyes, but the tears won't stop falling. Bertrand follows me as I stumble towards the stairs. When I bang into the wall for the second time he says nothing, scooping me up. I don't protest, leaning against his strong chest, turning my face into his familiar bulk. The air moves and I realise we're at my bedroom door.

'Emelia! Are you all right?'

Kyle. My heart leaps, despite all I've been through.

'My lady is tired. It has been a long day for her.' Bertrand's voice rumbles in his chest. I can't see his face, but I get the impression he might be frowning.

'Put me down, please,' I say, wiping my face, trying to be dignified. Bertrand sets me down. I walk as smoothly as I can into my room, but my foot catches in the rug. Before I can fall Kyle is there, holding me up. I wish I could stay in his arms. Was it only a few hours ago that I was there, my world filled with joy? We stare at each other, his touch like fire, despite how cool he is.

'Are your parents safe?'

'Um, yes, they are. I mean, it's all...' My face crumples and to my horror I start crying again.

'Don't worry. I'll be here to watch over you.'

I flush, despite myself, at the promise in his words.

Bertrand, disapproval in his voice, says, 'As will I, my lady. Guard cordons will be doubled, for the next little while.'

Kyle says nothing, but his eyes meet mine briefly, a flash of silver. Then he bows, as does Bertrand. They both leave the room, closing the door.

I'm finally alone. Except for my thoughts. Kyle, of course. But, also...

*Twenty people.*

Humans.

Like me.

I can't let this happen. I need to stop the Moon Harvest. If I can.

## Chapter Thirteen

### AFTERMATH

Three nights pass. The guests all depart, the Halloween decorations taken down. The house is strange and quiet. I'm confined inside, as per my mother's orders. It hasn't stopped me from going up to the roof, though, watching the guards patrol the perimeter fences. I wonder if Kyle is among them. He's been absent again, since the night of the ball, and my mind has played over a thousand scenarios as to why, and why he wouldn't tell me he was leaving again. I asked my mother, finally, but all she said was that he was on leave, and what did it matter anyway if I wasn't going anywhere. I hadn't pushed it, but it didn't mean I stopped thinking about him, lying awake during the long hours alone, reliving the sweetness of our last encounter, wanting it to happen again.

There's been one exception to my confinement. The ashes of the dead vampires were buried, with ceremony. One of them was Daniel, the young man from Lion clan. I'd thought it a sad thing, as I stood with my parents in the cold darkness under whispering trees, that he'd come all this way only to die here, caught up in a rebellion he was no part of.

My father was more badly injured than I'd realised, many of his bones broken as well as the burns. Vampires heal quickly, especially when they feed regularly. But burning is the most devastating injury to vampires – it's one of the only ways to kill them – and Father was alight for a second or so.

It hasn't stopped me from trying to prevent the Moon Harvest, though. At first, my mother was indulgent, listening to my concerns. But, as the nights pass, she's become less receptive to my pleas.

---

'There must be another way!'

My mother is kneeling next to my father, who is lying on the sofa in the living room. Two of my parents' personal guards, their livery featuring flecks of red among the silver, flank the double doors. More guards wait outside. Father's almost completely healed, but I suppose they're not taking any chances. James, the blood dancer who'd carried Danae from the ballroom, is sitting in a chair, head back and long limbs limp against the cushions, blood at his wrist. My mother is gently dabbing the last faint patches of red on Father's face with a white cloth, the sweet scent of rosewater filling the room.

She sighs, leaning back on her heels. 'This again?'

I frown. *Yes, this again.* 'How is sacrificing twenty lives the right thing to do? Won't it make the rebels angrier? If Mistral missed one of their agents, he could miss another! I just don't—'

'Enough!' My mother places the cloth into a nearby silver bowl. 'I've explained my decision. I don't wish to do so again. You see how your father is, what they did to him. We must be seen to respond, and to do so in such a way that it will dissuade others from trying again.'

'But you can't just… kill people like that! Can't you put them in prison or something?'

'You must listen to your mother. She is Raven, after all.' My father's expression is stern, but there's a tinge of sadness to his golden eyes. I get it. My mother's decree is now common knowledge, the attack on the seat of Raven fuelling news and gossip throughout the realm.

'I'm not saying there doesn't need to be a response from us. But isn't there another punishment we can use? One that isn't so… er… wasteful?'

'Mistral will ensure only rebels are selected. You don't need to worry. We don't need stock like that, anyway.'

'They're not *stock*. They're humans. Like me.'

And there it is. The thing that's been bothering me. For the first time in my life, I'm realising what it truly means to be human, in this world that my family has created. I might be Raven, daughter of vampires, heir to half the planet, but no matter how much I'm paraded at Gatherings, festooned with jewels, or dance with princes at private parties, *I'm human.* Just like the people who are farmed into Safe Zones, who live in cages so others can feed. Who will be sacrificed, whether or not they committed any crime.

My parents are both staring at me. Oh for fuck's sake. Did they not realise?

I turn and walk out. My mother calls my name, but I keep walking.

Two guards fall into step behind me. I wish I could shove them through the wall. There's an ache in my chest, my breathing uneven, the guards keeping their distance from my excess of emotion. The rebellion has broken into my mind as surely as it broke into our house, the explosion in the ballroom starting a chain reaction in me. Time is running out, though, taking with it any chance I might have to stop the Moon Harvest. My impotence infuriates me – trapped on the estate, with few resources. A cage indeed, no matter how golden.

But I'm not *entirely* without resources.

When I reach my room, Bertrand is there. I stop when I see him. 'Bertrand.' My voice cracks. 'Is Kyle back yet?'

Bertrand nods to the guards following me. They both salute and leave, whooshing down the hallway.

Bertrand tilts his head, a faint smile on his face. 'He is, my lady. He'll be feeding now, then on shift later. You'll see him when you wake, I believe.'

'When I wake?' My heart is beating faster and I hate its traitorous dance.

'Yes, my lady. It's near dawn, so I suppose you'll be sleeping soon. Unless you need to feed, of course.'

'Er, no, I don't.' I'd eaten earlier, a lonely meal in the kitchen downstairs, the lights on bright in an attempt to dispel my gloom.

'Well then. I'll be here until shift change, if you need anything further.'

'Thank you.' I stand there for a moment, but can't articulate what I need and don't think it's Bertrand I need to tell, anyway. I slip into my room, closing the door. I sit at my dressing table, pulling my laptop towards me. I'm too wound up to sleep, even though I know it's close to dawn. I open the laptop, typing three words into the search engine.

*The North Wind.*

A list of websites pops up. I've already been through most of them, mainly vampire-run news sites talking about the rebellion. It seems to be confined to the UK, for the time being. I scroll through the listings. An attack on a vampire nightclub in Watford. A riot in Oxford. Damage to Raven holdings in Edinburgh. And, of course, the attack on Father. The list goes on.

I'm desperate to know more about what's driving them. Oh, I have an idea, of course I do. But to be forced to a point where rebellion is their only option? Fighting vampires leads to only one thing, when you're human. Death.

I know. I'm still going to give away the whole Raven thing, the privilege, the darkness, the guards that constantly surround me, in exchange for a human life, lived in sunlight. But people can't just come into my house and try to blow up my family.

Again there's that feeling of holding two opposing

truths. Part of me is angry, angry at the threat to my family. While the other part of me understands, more and more, that being human is a death sentence in my world. My family name protects me, but that's all. Without that, I'd probably be long dead. It's an uncomfortable feeling, as though the walls of the house and all that protected me are gone, leaving me to navigate an unfamiliar space. My endless glittering nights feel like a dream. I'm awake now. I need to understand what I'm leaving to, what it's going to be like where I'm going. Perhaps I can still make a difference, somehow.

I scroll through the North Wind results again, but there's nothing new. Just more videos of vampires reading the news, images of fire and smoke drifting through the night. Sighing, I sit back, rubbing my eyes. I'd hoped to find something more, some way I could understand what was happening, or even contact them. I might not be able to stop the Moon Harvest, but perhaps there's a way to avoid further violence. I rest my head on my hand and go over the events of the ball again, in case I've missed anything. My gaze goes to the garden, dark trees swaying in the November breeze, a faint pale glow in the sky harbinger of dawn.

It comes to me then.

Oh my god and darkness.

*It's a nursery rhyme.*

That's what the blood dancer had said, on the night of the party. A *human* nursery rhyme. Very smart, when I think about it. Vampire children have their own rhymes. And, when my parents control everything, when our agents are no doubt scouring the internet for any clue that might lead them to the rebels, what better way to hide than behind something so innocuous?

I pull up the search engine bar and type again. *Popular Nursery Rhymes.*

Another list of results appears. I scroll through them, clicking occasionally when something looks promising, but most of the links are broken, or contain a few rhymes. Maybe I'm wrong.

I keep scrolling.

Then I see it. The subject reads *Popular Rhymes for Boys and Girls*. Underneath, there's a single line of text. 'And we shall have snow.'

My hand trembles as I click the link.

Fuck.

The Raven logo appears onscreen, black and silver on a white background. But it's been slashed with bloody red lines, a slogan written beneath in jagged black lettering. 'The North Wind Will Blow.' My stomach clenches. I click on the logo and a verse appears, replacing our tattered insignia.

> *The North wind will blow,*
> *and we shall have snow,*
> *and what will poor Raven do then?*

The words onscreen fade into a scattering of black dots, and a photograph appears. I gasp. It's my father. Once again, it's been slashed to red ribbons. Beneath it are his name, and the words '*Attack attempted: October 31st. More to come.*' His photo fades to be replaced by one of my mother, her beauty shredded by cruel red claws. I hold my breath, but there's nothing written beneath her image other than her name. It fades, and a third image appears. This one is a drawing, though, of a young girl with black hair in plaits, wearing a blue dress. Beneath it are the words. '*Emelia Raven. Photograph unavailable. Take on sight.*' What the fuck does that mean? Take my photo? Or take... me? The drawing doesn't look much like me, though. Which may work in my favour. It disappears, to be replaced by more Raven photographs, different members of the family. Including Mistral. Some images have dates beneath them, others just names. But that's it.

There's nothing else. No way of contacting the North Wind, or any more about what they want. Just the revolving carousel of photographs, both a threat and a message. I click on the page a few times, just in case, but nothing. Then a little spinning Raven logo appears – I click on it, and a box pops up, asking for password details. I slump back in my chair.

Onscreen, the images continue to revolve. All the Ravens listed, including Father, are still alive, as far as I know. I realise though, as the images turn, that they're all minor members of the family, other than Mistral and my parents. Some of them I haven't seen in years – they don't even come to the Gatherings.

I frown at the screen. Something doesn't seem quite

right, but I can't put my finger on it. If I want to know more about the North Wind, I need to find them. Yeah, I know. Mistral and his 'agents' are on it. But I don't trust Mistral as far as I can throw him. My plans haven't changed – I still don't want to be the next Raven – but I can't just stand by and do nothing, not when there's a chance I could make a difference. After all, I have one advantage that no other Raven has.

I'm human.

The shutters start to rumble, the pale square of garden disappearing behind dark metal with a final shuddering clang. My mind whirring, I get changed for bed, flopping onto the pillows. As I do there's a faint crackling noise. What the hell? I sit up and pull the pillow towards me. Beneath it is a single piece of paper, cream against the white linen sheet.

I pick it up. The writing is black, sharp, letters scratched into the paper.

*Emelia,*

*I've missed you. You smell like violets and taste of roses. I can't wait to see you again, and finish what we started. Will you have me, my lady?*

*Kyle*

Will I have him?

Well. Apart from the fact his timing is perfect, my heart is pounding so hard I'm surprised Bertrand can't hear it through the walls.

# Chapter Fourteen

## TO THE STARS

I wake from a restless sleep, Kyle's note still clutched in my hand. It was a bold move, on his part. I wonder how he even got in here without being seen. But I'm glad he did. For so many reasons. Not just because of what we did, or might do, even though my heart skips a beat at the thought. But also because he's the only person who has ever given me a choice, who offered me freedom at the edge of a waterfall. My plans might have changed slightly, but I still think he could be the only one brave enough, or mad enough, to help me. I just need to take him somewhere we can truly be alone.

And I know exactly the place.

I shower and dress, brushing my hair so it crackles with electricity. I choose a dress in deep burgundy velvet, silver leaves embroidered along the cuffs and hem, the neckline lower than I'd usually wear.

When I open my bedroom door, he's there. It's all I can

do not to fall into his arms, but the wide-eyed glance of the other guard with him, her hair pulled into a high silvery ponytail, stops me.

Still. I need to be alone with him.

'I'm going to the library,' I say. I pause, trying to remember the name of the other guard. 'Er, Giselle, is it? I'll be fine with just Kyle – I won't be going anywhere.'

Kyle looks down, but I can see he's grinning.

The other guard looks doubtful. 'But my lady, Bertrand ordered me to—'

'I'll speak with Bertrand,' I say, with as much authority as I can muster.

The guard frowns, a line between her silvery brows. But she can't disobey me. And with that comes a glimpse of the power waiting for me, once I put on the Raven robes. It's crushing in its intensity.

'My lady.' The guard nods her head, then whooshes away. As soon as she's gone I'm in Kyle's arms, his lips on mine.

'Wait,' I say, when he pulls back so I can breathe. 'Not here.'

'In your room?' He raises an eyebrow.

'No, not there either. I wasn't kidding about the library.'

'Okay?' He releases me. 'Lead on, my lady. I look forward to all the reading we'll do together.'

I laugh, my heart beginning to soar. Only he can do this to me. We race through the darkened hallways, hand in hand, until we reach the familiar arched doors. I open them, pulling Kyle inside. The library is quiet, moonlight coming through long windows to silver the bookshelves lining three walls, sliding across the carved wooden furniture and fine rugs.

'Are you going to tell me what's going on?'

I smile, shaking my head, feeling light as air. Outside, the night sky is bright with stars. I go to one of the padded window seats, kneeling to look up. When I'm living as a human, I'll be able to go outside whenever I like, day or night. All the pieces seem to finally be falling into place, freedom so close I can almost taste it.

Kyle sits next to me, his head back, silver eyes reflecting the sky. 'Are we looking at stars?'

'Yes,' I say. 'No. I mean, soon we'll have a better view.'

'Aren't you supposed to stay in the house?'

'Yes.' I hug my secret to me, stretching out the moment.

Kyle leans his head on my arm. 'In the pits, you can't see the sky.' He sounds reflective. 'It's all underground. No fresh air, no stars, no curving moon.'

My bright mood dims. I look down at him. 'It sounds awful.'

'It wasn't a nice place to be.' He lifts my hand to his lips, kissing it. 'So now, whenever I can, I look up at the sky. To remind myself that I'm free.'

'I'm sorry,' I say, wanting to ease the pain in his voice. The life of a pit champion can't have been an easy one. 'Were you always… um. I mean… in the pits. Were you born there?' It's kind of bad manners to ask someone whether they were blood borne, or changed. But I don't think Kyle will mind. It's not like we don't know each other.

144

'I wasn't always there, no. I had a life, outside, for a while.'

'As...'

'As a human.' He smiles, but his gaze is distant. 'A long time ago. I'm not blood borne, like you are. The memory is more like a dream than anything, vague flickers of images. But I've never forgotten the sky. It kept me going, when I was under there.'

'How long ago?'

'Long enough.' He reaches up, pulling me so I have to turn, sitting next to him. He leans in, his hand coming to my waist. All thought leaves me.

And the library doors open. Kyle is on his feet, the movement so quick it's a blur.

'Emelia. I thought I heard you in here.'

It's my mother, flanked by two of her personal guards, moonlight catching the flecks of red, like blood droplets, on their black and silver livery.

'Mother.' I stand up as well. Kyle's fingers brush against mine.

'Kyle.' She nods her head to him.

'My lady.' He bows.

'Emelia, what's this I hear about you dismissing one of your guards? They're here for your safety.' My mother frowns.

'I didn't think I needed two guards to come to the library,' I say. 'And it's not like I'm going anywhere else.'

Her eyes narrow, briefly, and flicker from Kyle back to me. I know she knows why I dismissed the other guard.

'Your father was attacked in this house. Please honour our wishes in this matter going forward.'

'Fine.' It is fine. I just need tonight, and a chance to speak to Kyle. There's a pause. 'I thought you'd be gone already.' My voice rises, like my hope that perhaps she's decided not to go through with the Moon Harvest after all.

My mother's smile fades. 'That's why I came to find you. Your father and I are leaving shortly. There are preparations we need to make… well.' She looks down for a moment. 'We'll be back tomorrow night, near sun-up. Kyle,' her onyx gaze moves to him, 'you are charged with Emelia's protection while we're gone.'

'My lady,' he says, bowing.

'So you're going through with it, then?' The magic of the night shatters, like a mirror falling from a wall.

'Emelia.' My mother pauses, looking away briefly. 'You know we have to.'

'I don't. I don't know that at all!' My voice echoes through the room. 'We have to do *something*, of course we do, but this… this *slaughter*, feels wrong! And it's not *you*! It wasn't that long ago you said violence wasn't the answer, but now you're going to murder twenty people to make a point!'

My mother draws herself up, her eyes glittering, arms crossed. She looks like a beautiful fierce statue. For the first time ever, I see her as Raven, the entity, an ancient predator, rather than my mother. It's a strange sensation.

Then she speaks and the moment passes. 'This is not up

for discussion. Your father was attacked! I cannot believe you're advocating mercy for those responsible.'

'The one who attacked Father is dead, thanks to Mistral. He's paid the price already. Why does there need to be more death? How do you know that Mistral is going to bring rebels to the Moon Harvest? He could show up with anyone!'

'I've known him for two centuries. He's our most faithful lieutenant, and a prince of Raven. If he can't be trusted, who can?'

'But—'

'*Enough!*' Her voice rings through the library.

I stand there, gasping, then turn away.

The air moves and Mother is there, catching me in her arms. I know she loves me. I know I love her. I'll miss her desperately when I'm gone. But this is bullshit. I can't deal with any of it right now.

'My darling girl, I wish I could make you understand.'

I'll never understand. My face is buried in her neck, her satin hair smooth against my cheek. 'Let go of me.' Torn between love and fury, I push at her. She lets go.

'We have to end this rebellion,' she says. 'And this is a step, a necessary step, towards doing so, towards making the realm safe again. If you'd been standing with your Father, when... I couldn't bear it if—' Blood tears are dark in her eyes.

I swallow, feeling as though bands of iron are suffocating me, and all I want to do is break through them and scream away the frustration at what I am, at what I put her through, simply by existing. She *cannot* make this about me, about making the realm safe for me.

'Please don't do this. There has to be another way.'

My mother's mouth is a perfect 'o', her brow creased. 'Emelia, I… it's just…'

'Talk to them, negotiate a ceasefire. Imprison the ringleaders, if that's who Mistral is bringing to the Moon Harvest.' I hate feeling this powerless, feel the twist of it in my stomach. She doesn't respond, so I keep going. 'Do I not get a say in this? I'm the next Raven, after all. And I'm human. Like they are.'

A single red tear spills from her eye, running down the porcelain curve of her cheek.

'I can't change this now.'

She's lying. She's Raven. She can change whatever she wants. Sadness rolls over me, heavy as though it might press me into the carpet. All I say is, 'Then go.'

My mother stares at me, her gaze blood and onyx in the moonlight. 'This is not as easy as you think.'

I say nothing. She waits a moment longer, then leaves, followed by her guards, her dress a flash of red in the darkness. I stand there, weighed down by the broken shards of the night, of what might have been.

'Emelia.' Kyle's arms come around me.

I sigh, sagging against him. Everything just feels huge and hopeless. I can't change a thing. I should just go back to my room and sit there until I crumble to dust, then everyone can get on with their lives and—

'Hey.' His hands come to my shoulders, setting me back

from him. His handsome face is serious. 'Are you really against the Moon Harvest?'

I nod. 'Not that it makes any difference,' I mutter.

'I think it does.'

I frown. 'How? How does it change anything?'

'Well, it won't save The Twenty but—'

'The Twenty?' He says it as though it has capital letters.

'The Moon Harvest is big news. Those twenty people, well – you don't know—'

'No, I don't know. I don't know anything, stuck in here. Other than there's some website that puts targets on me and my family.'

'A website?'

'Yeah. I found it last night. "The North Wind will blow" and all that.' I sigh. How could I have thought the rebels would want to meet me? I'm just a nobody. 'Anyway, what do you mean about The Twenty being big news?'

Kyle folds his arms. 'You have to understand, what they're about to do… it's going to make things worse. The Twenty will become martyrs, inflaming the rebels even more.'

'That's what I've been trying to tell them – I don't know why they can't see it!' It's infuriating that my parents, with all their centuries of experience, don't get this.

'Perhaps vampires have thought of humans as just food for too long.' A corner of Kyle's mouth curves in a half-smile. 'I think that's why you'll be a great Raven, when the time comes.'

'You do?'

'Yeah.' His grin widens. 'Who better to bridge the gap between humans and vampires than someone who sees both sides, like you?'

We both fall silent. It feels as though all that's important is here, in the space between us. Again I feel that urge, that flame of rebellion, the need to do *something*. To change… everything. I *can* do this. With him at my side.

'I need your help,' I say. Four words. But I hope they will change everything.

He takes my hands, pulling me to him. 'Tell me what you need.'

'Not here,' I say, glancing at the closed door. I'm sure my mother has stationed guards outside, and I don't want them hearing us.

'Then where?' There's laughter in his tone, now, and a deeper throb that sounds like anticipation. 'You did promise me a view of the stars.'

I put a finger to my lips. He stops talking, a smile in his silver eyes. I go to the bookcase and take *Interview with the Vampire* from the shelf, handing it to Kyle. I reach between the books and pull the metal lever, the shelf sliding back, silent as a dream.

The air moves as Kyle zips past me. He turns on the second step, his face lit up.

'This is so cool! What's up here?'

'The sky,' I say, my anticipation rising. 'The stars.'

'Then let's go and see.' He reaches out and grabs me.

'Wait.' I flick the little lever that pushes the bookcase back into place and it closes, leaving us in the dark.

'Hmmm, I like this.' Then Kyle's mouth is on mine and I cling to him, the stars behind my eyelids a match for any show the heavens might put on. He starts up the stairs, still carrying me.

'There's a trapdoor,' I say. 'Don't run into it.'

'I'm on it,' he says. I hear a clatter, then there's a rush of cool air and we're on the roof.

The sky is an uninterrupted curve of dark blue blazing with stars, the Safe Zone a distant glimmer, the dark mass of forest wrapping the estate like a blanket. Kyle puts me down, then speeds to each corner of the flat space, looking out across the chimneys and towers. It's chilly, and I wish I'd thought to bring up a blanket. Kyle turns back to me. His expression changes when he sees me hugging myself, rubbing my arms.

'I'll be right back.' There's the faint creak of the bookcase moving then, a few moments later, the same sound repeated. Kyle appears, his arms full of cushions and blankets.

He spreads one of the blankets flat, arranging the cushions at one end, then comes and tucks the other blanket around my shoulders, my hair lifting with the speed of his movement. Then he stands to the side, holding out his hand. I sit on the blanket, patting the cushion next to me. He sits beside me, shifting his weight to rummage in one of his pockets. 'One last thing.'

He pulls out a small candle in a glass holder, then retrieves a box of matches from another pocket and lights it, the flickering small flame protected by the fragile bubble of glass. There's something sweet about the small pool of golden light, a spot of warmth in the chill night. He smiles at me, and we stare at each other for a long moment.

'I missed you, when I was gone,' he murmurs. 'Did you get my note?'

I nod. 'Yes. Do I really taste like roses?' I blush as soon as I ask the question, but I don't try to control it. Not with him.

One corner of his mouth quirks up. 'Hmmm.' He leans in, brushing a kiss across my lips. Then his arms come around me, pulling me closer, and he bends his head once more. 'I can't quite remember. Perhaps I need to taste you again.' Then his lips are on mine, my mouth opening to his as we kiss, surrounded by the music of the wind and stars and our hearts, my sorrow sliding away into the night, lost in the beauty of the moment.

Then I push him away.

'What is it?' he says.

'I need your help,' I say again, wanting to get the words out before he can distract me again.

He takes my hand, bringing it to his lips. His eyes are a gleam of silver between smoke-dark lashes. His tongue flicks against my fingers, cold fire. 'You know I'll do whatever you want. But what can the heir to Raven possibly need my help with?'

'That's just it,' I say, struggling to keep focus. I want him, desperately. But I also want this. 'I might be the heir, but I'm powerless, mostly. A human. And—'

'Humans aren't powerless,' Kyle says. His arm slides behind me, lowering me onto the cushions, his weight delicious against me, his hands moving on me, distracting. It's difficult to concentrate on what he's saying, but I try. 'The fact they're still rebelling, more than fifty years after the Rising, is proof of that.'

And there it is. The perfect lead into my question. I take it, before I lose myself entirely. 'I want you to help me get off the estate.'

'What?' Kyle's hands stop moving. 'You... you want to leave?' There's a strange thread in his voice, like excitement.

'Yes,' I say. 'I want to see what it's like, for humans. Want to see how they live. It... it's what I've wanted for a long time. But now,' I take his hand in mine, threading our fingers together, 'after everything that's happened, with my father, and the bomb, I also want to understand.'

'Understand?'

'You said to me, in the woods... the thing is, I've seen how humans live, but not in real life. Yet here they are blowing things up and... and I just want to know what I can do to help. I can't stop the Moon Harvest, but if I can understand it, can speak to the North Wind, maybe I can stop the rebellion.'

He pulls back, staring at me. 'Are you serious?'

I nod. 'So will you take me to see it?'

His eyes widen further. 'To see... the Moon Harvest?'

I nod.

He rolls off me, sitting up. 'Are you mad? I can't take you anywhere near a Moon Harvest!'

I sit up as well. 'I need to do this. To bear witness.' My

voice shakes. 'If I can't stop it, I need to see it. They can't die alone.'

Kyle shakes his head, but there's something in his silver gaze. 'It will be a massacre. You won't be safe.'

'I'll cover myself with anti-feed! It'll be fine. Please. I swear, I'll do whatever you say.'

'Whatever I say?' One corner of his mouth curves, and he leans in, kissing me. 'I have to keep you safe, though. It's my job.'

I recoil. 'Your job?'

His hand goes behind my head, his lips on mine again. 'It's my job to look after you,' he murmurs, against my mouth. 'But you know it's more than that. I can't bear the thought of you being in danger.'

'You can't?' His hands move on me again, and it feels so good.

'I can't. You mean more to me than…' He is all violets and fire, his body against mine again as I lean back onto the cushions, his mouth descending on mine again.

'You mean a lot to me, as well,' I gasp against his mouth, his touch. 'So much.'

He pulls back again, his hand gentle on my face, his silver gaze soft, his body hard. 'Are you sure this is what you want?'

I'm not even sure what he's asking me anymore. I gather up the remnants of my focus. 'Yes. I need to do this. To see more. Of humans. See how they live. Live with them. Meet the rebels, if I can. Will you help me?' Each sentence is punctuated by a short breath, my heart pounding at his closeness.

'Yes, I'll help you, Emelia Raven, if that's what you want. Even though I think you're mad—' there's laughter in his voice now '—and we're bound to get caught, I'll get you off the estate.'

'H-how will you do it?'

'Leave it to me. We have until tomorrow night, so there's time enough.' His hands are under my dress now, sliding up my thighs, tracing me through my underwear. 'Do you really want to keep talking, though?'

I do not.

―――――――

A while later, I surface, my breath coming hard. His jacket and shirt are off, as is my dress, but I don't feel cold anymore. His hips are between my thighs, his hard length pressing into me, the sensation strange, my body responding on a deeper level. He kisses my throat, then lifts his head, stars bright behind him.

'Do you want me to stop?'

At that moment all the planets in the galaxy could put on a light show set to music and I wouldn't care less. What I really want is for Kyle to keep kissing me, for me to keep touching him, and for more, if not all, of our clothes to come off. It feels as though the ties that bind me to my life, that have held me in place for so long, are finally loosening. The realisation makes me blush, my skin getting hotter. I reach down between us, running my hand across him, fumbling with the button on his trousers. He takes a short breath. 'Emelia?'

'Kyle, I want to… er, I want you to…'

'What is it?' he says, so tender.

'Have you ever…'

He sighs, his breath violet scented. 'Of course I have. I'm older than I look. But—' he kisses me '—I've never felt about any of them the way I feel about you.'

Tears come to my eyes and I blink. 'It's just, I've never…'

'I know you haven't,' he says. 'Are you sure…?'

'Yes.' Such a weighted word. A word that can open doors, bring new realities into being. Such a small word, yet one that's about to change me forever. 'Yes, I'm sure.'

He stares at me a moment longer. 'If you want me to stop, just say, okay?'

I nod, trembling. His hands move once more. One on my back, unhooking my bra and removing it, while the other goes lower, between my legs, his fingers finding my sensitive core, sliding my underwear down. I gasp and sigh, my eyes closing as I pull at his clothes, moving them away. His mouth is on my throat as his hands work, the candle flickering in time with my breathing, my world all violet-scented sensation, flame and heat and unbearable sweetness all in one. He pulls back, his hand leaving me, and he licks his fingers, holding my gaze. He shifts again, and I feel something hard, nudging at my entrance. Kyle rolls his hips, carefully, and pushes in, just a little way.

There's pain.

'Oh!' I tense, unable to help it. He stills.

'Do you want me to stop?'

His fangs have dropped, his breath coming fast. I run my fingers down his back, his skin soft and cool, then lower, liking how he feels. 'Don't stop.' I squeeze him, gently, relaxing once more, opening to him. He gasps, then his hips move again, and he fills me, gradually, an inch at a time. He strokes my hair, kissing me as he thrusts deeper, his pace slow and tender. It's strange at first, but I soon find a rhythm to match his, both of us clinging to each other, our sighs drifting soft in the night air. He brings my wrist to his mouth, biting gently, a kiss of pain, a brief moment of suction. I whimper, then think for a second of the guards below before the thought is gone, overtaken by strange new sensations. He must have the same thought though, for he covers my mouth with his once more, his hand smoothing my hair as he moves faster, harder. Heat starts to build in me, coiling at my core, and I meet his hips with my own, wanting the friction, my breath coming faster. Then Kyle tenses, shuddering, before relaxing against me. There's heat and cold between my legs, a tingling sensation of fullness. He pulls back, and it feels like loss.

I sigh, my heart still singing. He kisses me, slow, his breath coming back to normal.

'I didn't hurt you, did I?' He kisses the inside of my wrist, his touch healing the tiny punctures there. 'Fuck, you taste so fucking good.' He licks my skin, another kiss.

I smile, everything feeling slow, as though I'm moving

through honey. 'No. I mean, just the first moment, then it was… fine.'

'Fine?' He raises an eyebrow and I try not to laugh. Seriously? Male pride is something not confined to humans, it seems.

A giggle escapes, I can't help it. His expression becomes more wounded. 'Well, it was my first time. What did you expect? Believe me,' I say, pulling him closer, 'I enjoyed it.'

'Hmmm.' He kisses me again. 'Well, you'll enjoy it even more next time.'

'Oh, and when will that be?'

'Whenever you're ready,' he says. I can feel he's telling the truth. Huh. That's different from the books I've read, human men seeming to need time—

'Oooh.' Kyle is moving against me, his hands exploring, and I find I don't want to think about books anymore. Behind him, stars streak the sky, silver and black. Then he thrusts into me again, and time disappears.

I must have fallen asleep afterwards because next thing I know Kyle's carrying me down the stairs, the blanket wrapped around me. There's the click of the lever, then the creak of the bookcase opening. He pauses.

'What is it?' I murmur.

'Well, Emelia—' I can hear the smile in his voice '— you're naked, I'm half dressed, and we've just come down from the roof together. Just making sure no one else is in the library.'

'Hmmm, I think they might notice the bookcase moving, somehow.' I'm too tired to care, though.

'Looks as though the coast is clear.' He steps into the library, depositing me on the sofa. My clothes are tangled in the blanket and I retrieve them, putting them on and wrapping the blanket around me again. The fire in the fireplace has burned low, candles guttering in their sconces. Kyle closes the bookcase, shrugging on his shirt and jacket.

'Come on, sleepyhead.' He grins. 'Let's get you back to your room before someone comes looking for you.'

I stand up slowly, clutching the blanket. I want him to carry me again, but that will mean far too many questions if anyone sees us. So I follow him along the corridors to my room, my feet dragging with tiredness. My heart is light, though, joy all through me. I feel different, on every level, as though what happened on the roof is a line drawn between the Emelia I was and the Emelia I am now. When we reach my room I turn to him. 'Will you come in, to check?'

He smiles, his head close to mine. 'Let me see you safe.' The words are innocent enough, but his eyes are molten silver. My heart leaps.

'Thank you,' I say, innocent words again but my hands touch him, staking their claim. He follows me into my room, closing the door. Then we're in each other's arms.

'I have to go,' he says, eventually, lifting his head. 'It must be close to sunrise.'

'Don't you know?' Vampires usually have a sense for it.

He grins. 'I'm not so good at it, especially when I'm distracted. And you are very distracting.' He leans in for a kiss, long and sweet. Then he gets up, running a hand through his hair. I straighten the collar on his jacket, brushing some dust from the sleeve. I don't want to stop touching him, or for him to leave.

'Until tomorrow,' he says, his hand on my cheek. 'Be ready, just after sundown.'

'Until then,' I say, slightly breathless. He kisses me, one last time.

'Go.' I push him, and he's gone.

## Chapter Fifteen

### SECRETS AND LIES

I rush to get dressed as soon as I wake, the deep blue silk of my shirt sliding against my skin as though my nerve endings are sensitised. My breath catches at the thought of Kyle, of his hands on me, his mouth. Of what we did on the roof. What I want to do again. I pull on black skinny jeans, looping several silver chains around my neck, though I leave my Raven necklace behind. I know I'm about to witness something awful as well as, potentially, meet the people who tried to kill my father. I hope, at least, to gain some understanding of what's really going on out there. And part of me, despite everything, is excited. If we succeed tonight, it means my plan to leave might actually work. I grab my navy leather jacket, making sure I have the vial of anti-feed.

When I leave my room Kyle is there, with another guard.

'I'm going outside,' I say. 'Just on the estate. Kyle, will

you take me?' I say this as though of course it will be allowed. Besides, my mother isn't here to stop us.

'Of course, my lady,' he says, bowing slightly.

He and the other guard flank me as we head down the curving golden stairs towards the front door. I hold my breath as it opens, hoping Bertrand won't be there. But our luck holds and a moment later we step into the cool dark, the other guard watching from the double doors. Stars burn overhead. Kyle adjusts his jacket collar, then turns to me. I'm buzzing with nerves.

'Ready?'

I squeal as he scoops me up in his arms. He starts to run, the night turning to flickers of silver and black. I turn my face into his neck, breathing in his scent, the world fading away so all that's left is him. All too soon we come to a stop, Kyle putting me down. We're outside one of the guardhouses stationed at each entrance to the estate. It's one of the smaller gates, the house a faint dark square in the distance. I think it's where deliveries come in.

'What are we doing?'

My question is lost as Kyle pulls me to him, kissing me. Mmmm.

A few minutes later he leans his forehead on mine. 'Are you sure you want to do this? The Moon Harvest... it's not going to be nice to see. Plus, I'm worried about your safety.'

'I know.' I don't, really. And my nerves are starting to get to me, my legs shaking. 'Are – are we going straight there?'

He shakes his head. 'It won't start till midnight, after the fireworks.'

'Midnight? It's barely nine-thirty – where are we going first? To meet the rebels?'

He laughs. 'I don't know. any rebels. But I do know where you can have an authentic human experience.'

'But—'

'Hush.' He kisses me again. 'This is what you want, isn't it?'

He starts towards the guardhouse and I grab his arm. 'What are you doing?'

'Trust me.'

I swallow, summoning my courage. And follow him to the guardhouse.

He knocks on the door three times. It opens a crack and I glimpse someone's eye. It opens further to reveal a guard in Raven livery. He shakes Kyle's hand.

'You made it, then?' He bows to me. 'My lady.'

I nod, but don't say anything, fear cold in my stomach. What the hell is going on? The guard turns his attention back to Kyle. 'Our deal holds?'

'It does. I'll keep your secret, if you keep mine.'

*His secret?*

As my eyes adjust I see a black shape further inside the room. It resolves into a young woman, with long black hair like mine. She's wearing a short sparkly dress, a leather jacket slung over one shoulder. Traces of glitter shimmer along her décolletage and arms.

Kyle touches my arm. 'Right. You two need to swap outfits.'

My mouth drops open. 'Are you mad? This is your plan? My parents—'

'Aren't here.'

'But Bertrand—'

'Is busy elsewhere. You made sure of that, right?' He addresses the other guard, who nods. Kyle puts his arm around me. 'I'll keep you safe, I promise.'

I bite my lip. This is madness. The girl is waiting, her dress glimmering like fireflies. The guard has his arms folded. Whatever happens next is up to me. I was the one who asked for this, after all. So, I can choose to trust Kyle, or I can go back to the velvet confines of the house. And then Kyle will probably never take me anywhere again, and all my plans will mean nothing. I gather up the last remnants of my courage. 'Okay.'

'Come with me.' The girl's voice is low and husky. She turns away, her long black hair swinging.

I follow her through the darkness into another room. There's a candle-lamp on the small table, a welcome glow of light. The girl closes the door, then drops her leather jacket on the single wooden chair. She slides down the straps of her dress, revealing a black lace bra.

I just stand there. This feels weird and wrong.

She stops what she's doing. 'Can I have your shirt?'

I swallow. 'Um, sure. Yeah.' I slide my arms out of my jacket. I'm keeping that, I don't care what Kyle says. It's my favourite.

'Is something wrong?' She tilts her head. There's more glitter on her, running down her bare stomach and, I see as she steps out of the dress, some on her inner thighs. A blood dancer. Not one of ours, though.

'It's fine.' I unbutton my shirt and slip it off, not looking at her. There's a rustle of fabric and the sparkly dress hits me on the arm. I fumble, managing to catch it before it drops.

'I couldn't believe it when Nick told me what we were doing tonight. Are you excited about going out?'

I don't know why she's being so chatty. 'Uh, yeah. I guess.' I slide the dress over me, pulling my jeans down underneath. The sparkly fabric is warm and smells faintly musky. I hand my jeans to the girl, who's standing in her underwear, arms folded.

'Sorry,' I say, though I'm not sure why.

'At least you can come back home, afterwards.' Her voice changes, a warning in her words, as well as bitterness. I don't know where she came from, but get the feeling that home, perhaps, isn't an option for her anymore.

'It's fine,' I say again. I tug at the hem of the dress. It's short and low cut, and I feel exposed, as though the glow of the candle-lamp is a spotlight. I shrug on my leather jacket, pulling it closed across my chest. The dancer, meanwhile, is in my clothes, her jacket over the top. We're similar enough in build, I suppose, that the guards won't be able to tell from a distance. And Nick, the other guard, has dark hair like Kyle. I remind myself why I'm doing this. To bear witness, and to test my plan. I don't want to be Raven, and this is my way out.

There's a knock at the door. 'Are you ready?'

# Chapter Sixteen

## DANCING GIRL

The club is dark and smoky, candles guttering in sconces, wax dripping down the walls to the floor. Kyle and I sit in a booth next to the small dance floor. The room is long and low-ceilinged, screens dividing it in half. I glimpse stacked chairs, grey with dust, beyond them. The bar has a mirrored backdrop with bottles lined up along it, stacks of glasses, and a fridge containing rows of white packets next to different coloured glass bottles. No caged humans here. I have a glass of wine, courtesy of Kyle. He has nothing. There are blood dancers and vampires, as well as quite a few humans, leaning against the bar. The blood dancers are sort of swaying and jumping, nothing like the sinuous movements of the dancers my parents use. The one closest to us, her shoulders bare above a black bustier, has a scar running from the base of her throat along one shoulder. Another dancer is wearing an eyepatch, her hair shaved short on one side.

'What is this place?'

Kyle grins. 'It's a bar.'

I frown. 'Well, that's obvious.'

'You said you wanted an authentic human experience. This is about as close as you're going to get.'

'Really?' I make a face, looking around. This is not at all how I imagined it would be, nothing like the old films I watched, nightclubs bright with neon and glossy people, cocktails poured from silver shakers. Perhaps things are different in the Safe Zones. 'But where are these humans from?' Humans stay in Safe Zones, as far as I know. Certainly at night. Yet they're here, mingling with vampires and blood dancers, smoking cigarettes, drinking, dancing.

'They're from your estate.'

My eyes and mouth stretch wide. 'What? What the hell – Kyle! What if one of them recognises me—'

He shakes his head. 'Look at them, Emelia. Do you recognise any of them?'

I glance quickly at the crowd. 'No. These aren't our dancers.'

'Who said they were? There are other humans on your estate. What do you think they do?'

I look down. 'They're food,' I say, my voice quiet.

'For whom?'

'For everyone. Except me.' My mouth twists. I don't like where this is going.

'That's right. They're food. For the guards, and for everyone else who works for your family. And when their shift is over, they go back to the Safe Zone and their families. Except maybe, on the way back, they might bribe their vampire drivers with a drink, or something more, to stop off here, earn a bit more money, or just forget, for a while, what they have to do to live.'

Well, fuck. I stare at the scratched surface of the table, ashamed. I don't want to look at anyone. I knew, of course, about the other humans on our estate. But my one and only visit to the guards' food hall, via the secret passages, made me determined to never see it again. I turned away from what I saw, instead of speaking up. Tried to put them out of my mind, convinced that they were somehow deserving of their fate, and that what I saw on TV was how humans really lived. How *I* was going to live. But this grotty bar, with its mix of humans and vampires, co-existing under the same roof, is just about the opposite of what I thought a human experience would be. I thought I'd changed, had opened my mind. But I can see now that I'm only at the beginning of what I need to learn.

'Hey.'

'What?' I look up. Candlelight gilds the planes of his face, the leather of his jacket.

'This is what you wanted, right? To understand?'

'I feel so stupid.' He's right, though. This is what I wanted. It's not his fault that things aren't quite as I thought they would be.

Kyle takes my hand, playing with my fingers. I don't look at him. 'How were you supposed to know?'

'Still.' I shake my head. 'I could have asked questions, tried to find out more, instead of just assuming. I mean, rebels attacked my home, tried to kill my father—' my voice is trembling '—and I still don't really understand their reasons, or why they think they can win.'

'Emelia.' His voice is gentle, as is his hand on mine. 'What don't you understand? Think about what they might want. What they would risk everything for.'

'I don't know.' My voice is small, and there's a pain in my chest. It's guilt, I realise, like a pebble-in-my-shoe pain, poking at me. Guilt at my ignorance, my lack of consideration. Of course I know what they want. It's the same thing I want.

Freedom.

I realise someone is staring at me. It's the blood dancer with the scar. When I turn to look, she curls her lip.

'Who's that?'

'What?'

'That girl. The dancer with the scar. She's staring at me.'

Kyle glances over and she turns away. 'Don't worry about her.' He puts his hand on my cheek, forcing my focus on him. 'This evening is going to be hard enough. Let's have some fun, shall we?'

'Fun?'

He jerks his head towards the dance floor. Music is playing, a pulsing beat. 'Shall we dance?'

I hesitate, but there's no smirking Stella here. And I need his arms around me, a moment of escape before whatever the rest of the night will bring. 'Sure.'

He leads me to the dance floor, pulling me into his arms. The scarred dancer is staring at us again. I curl my lip at her.

What the hell is her problem? Then Kyle kisses the side of my neck and I stop worrying. The dress I'm wearing is scratchy, and way shorter than anything I'd usually wear. But something about being here with him, wearing it, makes me feel more real than I've ever felt in my life.

The music changes and I lose myself in the moment, laughing as he spins me around until I'm breathless. My dress keeps riding up, so I have to yank at the hem.

Kyle pulls me close, resting his forehead on mine. 'Have I told you how much I like you in this outfit?'

I slide my hands under his jacket. 'You look pretty good, too.' He does. While I was getting changed, he discarded his guard uniform for jeans and leather jacket, a fitted black T-shirt underneath. He's still wearing his Raven badge, but it's subtle, an ebony gleam on his lapel. Still, enough to make a vampire think twice, I guess. 'I feel half naked, though. Was she a blood dancer?'

'She was. From here, actually. And, er, half naked is precisely why I like it.' He kisses me, his hands sliding low on the curve of my back.

Someone bangs into us, hard enough to break our embrace. Outraged, I open my eyes to see the blood dancer with the scar. She's shorter than I am, with shoulder-length dark hair, wearing black hot pants with her bustier, glitter smeared on her chest and arms.

Kyle snarls. 'What the hell?'

Her mouth drops open. She looks from him to me. 'Sorry.' She doesn't sound sorry, though, and her gaze is distinctly unfriendly.

'Well, you should be,' I say. 'Watch where you're going!'

'Yeah, I'm not the one who should be watching herself,' she snaps. I raise my eyebrows. Who the hell does she think she is? Why, I could call a guard and— Then I remember my only guard is the one pressed against me, his arms around my waist. He's tough, but there are a lot of vampires in here. And most of them are staring at us.

'Whatever.' I don't want to push things further. I turn my attention to Kyle. 'Where were we?'

She isn't finished. 'Dancing badly, I think.'

Bitch. 'I don't think you're anyone to give pointers on dancing.'

'That's enough.' Kyle's voice is low and hard. 'Just leave it.'

A couple of vampires move closer and I sniff my wrist, surreptitiously. Shit. The anti-feed is fading, and I don't need a repeat of what happened in the Dome. Dressed as I am, there's no way anyone would believe who I was if I told them.

'I'll be back in a sec,' I say. Kyle and the blood dancer are still staring at each other. I push through the crowd, heading for the ladies' room, making it unscathed apart from a few roaming hands I have to slap away.

The bathroom is deserted. There's a row of dingy pale green cubicles, all with their doors open. The mirror is cracked in several places, my reflection like a badly assembled jigsaw. I look wild, my hair dishevelled, my body sheathed in glittering black and dark leather. I run a hand through my hair, then pull out the vial of anti-feed and spritz myself, the reassuring scent of violets wafting around me. The little glass bottle rolls in my open hand, the silver Raven emblem etched on it glittering in the faint light, my initials, EIR, in entwined filigree below. My mother gave it to me when I was very young, teaching me how to apply it and why it was so important. With the thought comes sadness, once again, at how much I'll miss her, and a surging need to see her, to hug her again.

The bathroom door opens and someone comes in. It's the blood dancer with the scar. I tuck the bottle back in my pocket, heading for the door, but she puts her hand on my chest, stopping me. My mouth drops open.

'Let me pass.'

'Save it, Raven girl.'

What the fuck? My stomach drops.

She knows who I am.

## Chapter Seventeen

### FIREWORKS

**M**y mouth opens and shuts. I have no idea what to do. Then calm descends. I am Raven, just like she says. What could she possibly do? Tell my parents? It won't change the fact that I am who I am, and she is who she is.

Then I'm ashamed of myself.

All this runs through my mind in the few seconds it takes for the girl to cross the room to the sinks. She washes her hands, running her damp fingers through her hair. I'm still stunned. Then adrenaline kicks in. *What the hell are you doing, Emelia? Get out of here!* I reach for the door, but before my fingers make contact with the grubby paintwork the girl speaks.

'I wouldn't.'

'What?'

'Go out there.'

'*What?*'

'*What?*' she mimics me, making a face in the mirror, her

reflected gaze holding me in place as though she's a snake and I'm the mouse. She turns, leaning against the sinks, picking at her nails.

I swallow. 'What's your problem?' I mean it to come out tough-sounding, like girls I've seen in films. But it's more of a mouse squeak.

'You are,' she says, pushing herself off the sinks and strolling towards me. 'This is my territory. And I don't really like your kind.'

'My kind?'

'Ravens.' She draws out the 's', like a hiss.

My fists clench. 'I can't help who I am.'

'Kyle wasn't very smart, really, bringing you here.'

*Kyle?*

I reach for the door again. The girl puts her arm on the wall, stopping me.

I snarl at her.

Her eyes widen and she steps back, hands up. 'Your choice.' There's a faint tremor in her voice now. 'But, if I know who you are, how do you know I haven't told everyone else?'

'So what if you have?' I don't know where the snarl came from. It felt natural, though.

'There aren't many in here who are fans of Raven. It could be quite bad for you.'

'Have you? Told them?' Despite my bravado, I'm aware of being very, very alone.

She laughs. 'No. Not yet, anyway. I'm giving you a pass tonight.'

'A pass?'

'Yeah.' She narrows her eyes. 'A pass tonight and then —' she leans in close to me '—I don't see you here again.'

Screw her. 'Like I'd come back here anyway. Not really my scene.' I cast a derisive eye over the cracked sinks, the broken mirror. 'But if I want to, you can't stop me. I can have the whole fucking place burned down if I wanted to.' I know I sound like an entitled asshole, but it might be the only thing that gets me out of here in one piece. I draw myself up to my full height, looking down my nose at her, trying to channel my mother. The girl flinches. Actually fucking flinches. But my brief moment of elation passes when she grabs my shoulder, her fingers digging in as she pushes me up against the wall.

'Bitch! Take your stupid boyfriend and get out of here before I do something you'll regret.'

Her breath is hot on my face, her body uncomfortably close. No one has ever touched me like this in my life. The bathroom door flies open. It's Kyle, his nostrils flared, fangs dropped.

'Move away from her.'

The scarred dancer lifts her hands, stepping back from me. She's smirking, though, and takes her time with it. 'Sorry,' she drawls, not sounding it in the slightest. 'Come for your precious Raven?'

'Keep your voice down!' Kyle hisses, his shoulders raised, teeth bared, like a snake about to strike. The dancer seems unbothered, leaning against the sink once more and picking at her damn nails.

'Get out of here,' he says. I take a step. 'Not you, Emelia.' He's still glaring at the dancer. She huffs out a small breath, then pushes herself away from the sinks. Kyle steps in front of me.

'Oh, you're quite the tough guy, aren't you?' Reflected in the mirror, I see her run her fingers over the front of Kyle's jacket. My eyes widen. He's going to kill her, surely. But he just removes her hand, his expression hard to read.

'Enough,' he says, but his tone is calm. I frown.

'Okay, okay, I'm leaving. But hurry up, will you?'

*Hurry up?*

She walks past us to the door, still smirking. I wish I could rip her face off.

'You okay?' Kyle cups my face in his hands, kissing me. As soon as the kiss ends, I push him away.

'I want to go.'

'Don't let her get to you, Emelia, she's just—'

'She. Knows. Who. I. Am. You heard her. So we need to go.' What part of this doesn't he understand? If it's going to be bad for me, it'll be worse for him, when my parents find out he took me off the estate.

Kyle lets out a deep sigh, one hand on the wall next to my head. 'Fuck.'

Indeed.

'How does she know who I am?'

He takes in a deep breath. Which he doesn't need to do. There's a pause. 'She's my ex.'

*What. The Actual. Fuck.*

'Kyle.' I keep my voice low because I think I might scream if I don't. 'Get me out of here. *Now.*'

I'm going to kill him. Or her. Or someone. Or everyone. How could he put me in such an unsafe situation? I pull my phone out, but before I can dial Kyle scoops me up, holding me so tight I can't move. He rushes me out of the bathroom and through the crowd, taking me out of the club into the night. I struggle, furious, digging my nails into him.

'Ow! Emelia!' He skids to a stop and puts me down.

'What's going on?' I'm spitting fury. 'Why in darkness would you take me somewhere your ex works?'

We're under trees by the side of the road, Kyle a dark silhouette. He doesn't say anything and, as I can't see his face, I start to worry. I keep my expression fierce, knowing he can see me. I fold my arms.

He sighs. 'I didn't know she'd be there. And this is the closest place to your estate.'

Okay. I can buy that. I guess. 'What did she mean when she told you to hurry up?'

He becomes still, and I really wish I could see his face. He sighs again. 'I'm supposed to be helping her.'

'What?' My face scrunches up. 'With what? Why on earth would you help her with anything?'

'Her family. They were, er, they were good to me. When I was with her.'

I shrug, still frowning.

'They helped me get out of a bad situation. And, well, I'm supposed to be returning the favour. Her brother isn't well, and they want me to find a way to get them to a place where he can have treatment. She wanted to know if I'd arranged it.'

'Well, have you?'

'I just have to sort out a couple more things.'

He sounds sad when he says that, folding his arms, his head down. And, like an idiot, I feel sorry for him.

'Can I do anything?' God, I'm a sucker. But I can't help myself.

'What?'

I shrug again. 'If they're in the Safe Zone maybe I can talk to Father, arrange a doctor. After all, I know he'd want to—' I bite my tongue, then. I'd been about to say 'take care of the stock,' but realise how wrong that is.

'You are something else, Emelia.' Kyle shakes his head. 'No, though I appreciate your offer. There's nothing you can do.' He pauses. 'I'm sorry about tonight. About everything.'

*Everything?* I don't know what to do. I feel teary all of a sudden, and cold.

He moves closer, blotting out the stars. His lips trace my jaw to my neck and I breathe him in, hurt tangling with lust.

'Forgive me.'

The way he says it is like a question, and my heart clenches. With his arms around me in the darkness, there's no question. Tonight has already been strange and awful and wonderful at the same time, and it's all thanks to him. Of course I forgive him. I turn my head, kissing him, soft at first, then deeper. I feel him smile.

There's a series of loud bangs in the distance, and he lifts his head. 'Fireworks.'

*The Moon Harvest.*

'Do you still want to do this?' His breath is cool on my cheek. 'We can go home instead, if you want. And when we get back...' He nips me, gently, and I shiver.

'No,' I say. Just a breath. Still, he stops what he's doing. 'No,' I say again, louder. 'Let's see this through. But promise me one thing?'

'What's that?'

'Don't ever bring me here again.'

He laughs, soft, his forehead resting on mine. 'I promise,' he says. 'And now, pleasant as this is, we need to go. Once the fireworks finish, it'll be time. Are you ready?'

I nod and he lifts me into his arms. With a cacophony of bangs, the sky fills with light and colour. Fireworks above us like exploding stars, we start to run.

# Chapter Eighteen

## MOON HARVEST

We race through starlight and darkness, colours bursting overhead. I cling to Kyle, my face turned into the curve of his neck. He comes to a stop, and I lift my head.

We're among large rocks, embedded in the hillside like the ruins of an ancient temple. Kyle stops in the shadow of one of the largest – another, toppled like a fallen tower, lies on its side at an angle to us, shielding us from what lies below.

The Moon Harvest.

The night is clear, the moon bright, so there's enough light to see. We're overlooking a large clearing, a natural bowl in the hillside, more huge rocks tumbled around the edge. I realise it's where we usually hold our Gatherings. But this is no celebration, no coming together of Raven clans. There are people seated on the rocks, standing in groups in a semi-circle formation. Then, a line of silver and black. Raven guards. Beyond them, on a clear patch of grass, is a small cluster of humans, chained together. The Twenty. I'm faintly relieved to see that Mistral kept his word to my mother – there don't appear to be any children among them. There are also two large thrones, ebony black, silver details on the carved backs and sides touched by moonlight. Seated in them are my mother and father, cruel and implacable as statues. I take a shuddering breath. Mistral stands to one side, next to my mother. There are other vampires with them, too. One is wearing a large headdress and, as he moves, I realise what it is. A lion's mane. And I remember Daniel, how he'd smiled when we'd danced, how nice he was, only to become ash a few hours later. Shit. This is big. I can't see Jaguar or Scorpion, but still – if Lion are here, I can understand, a little more, why my mother couldn't change things once they were set in motion.

Kyle sets me down. His arms come around me, tucking me against his chest, his mouth near my ear. 'Stay very still,' he breathes. 'And no noise.'

I nod, just a very small movement. I get it. Once the feeding starts… well, I'm the only other human here. People will bite first and ask questions later.

The crowd is quiet, none of the usual hum of chatter you'd expect at a Gathering, or a regular fireworks night. There hasn't been a Moon Harvest for a very long time – during the Rising, they were used for both sport and punishment, until the Famine hit, and things had to change.

So tonight is significant. I notice a couple of vampires circling the crowd, cameras in hand. Oh darkness. They're going to record this?

There's a distant chiming sound, of hammer hitting bell. I count the chimes silently. Twelve. Midnight. Fuck. Here we go.

Kyle's arms tighten briefly. 'I'm here,' he says, feather quiet. 'I have you. Don't worry.'

My mother stands, moonlight turning her red dress to the colour of dried blood. The small group of humans cry out, the words unclear. The desperation is not. I'm shaking. The humans try to move back but the chains make it difficult, bound as they are in a group. Raven guards step forward, herding them towards my mother, who stands, waiting.

Maybe I can't watch this.

Her voice rings out, clear in the darkness. 'Five nights ago, at the height of our most sacred festival, an attack took place. In my own home, the ancient seat of Raven, targeting my beloved husband.'

There's a murmur from the crowd. The prisoners' wails grow louder. A Raven guard strikes one of them, who falls limp in his chains.

My mother continues. 'Fortunately, Aleksandr Raven survived the attack, and is whole once more. However, there were others—' the Lion clan representative steps forward, fists clenched at his side '—who were not so lucky. Such an attack, on my home, on the house of Raven, on those I love most, will not be borne.' She pauses, letting her words sink in. It's utterly silent, except for the whimpering humans. My heart is breaking.

'Therefore, we asked our most trusted lieutenant, a prince of the House of Raven, to act on our behalf. Mistral, are these the prisoners you promised?' She gestures with one graceful arm towards the shuffling mass of chained humans.

Well, of course they fucking are. Who else would they be? But her words have the ring of ritual and I guess they're part of what happens. Doesn't matter how they sugar-coat it with fancy phrases and thrones, though – this is going to be a slaughter. I blink back tears.

Mistral steps forward, his blond hair silvered by the moon. 'They are, my lady. Vicious rebels, every one of them, committed to the destruction of our house.'

There are hisses from the crowd. One of the humans shouts something, it sounds like a denial. But it's too late. My mother holds out her hand. My father, all in black, rises from his throne and comes to take it. My breath gasps in and out. My father appears to be frowning, but then he usually looks stern. Together, they approach the chained humans. My mother takes the arm of the human closest to her, an older, stocky man. My father does the same, taking the hand of a young woman. It's like a dance, the two of them so beautiful, so graceful, moving in tandem, counterpoint to the horror they're about to unleash. Both of them are gentle in their movements, in how they raise the arms to their lips. And bite down. The woman screams, the man struggling. But my parents are strong, so much

184

stronger than they could ever be. The crowd is dead silent, wind whispering around the stones. My father steps back first. There's blood around his mouth. He doesn't wipe it away. My mother steps back, blood smeared down her perfect chin. Both humans are still upright, though the woman is staggering. My parents return to their thrones. Still standing, my mother faces the crowd, raising both arms. Her voice rings through the silent night. 'First blood has been taken. Let it begin.'

Fuck. I think if Kyle let go of me, I'd fall.

Two Raven guards step forward. One is smiling. With deft movements they snap the chains holding the humans together. A final mockery of their weakness. Of *my* weakness. As the chains part, the one whom the guard struck falls to the ground, limbs askew. The others scatter. But where the hell are they supposed to go?

Oh, this is too cruel.

I guess I'm glad my mother didn't drug them, the way Jaguar used to in his stone temples, that at least they get to choose how to meet their deaths. But is this choice? As the humans run for the edges of the clearing, the group of vampires around the two thrones, including Mistral, move to capture them. The crowd isn't quiet anymore, shrieking and moaning as the bloodlust rises. Three of the humans, two women and a man, make it past the row of Raven guards. Or rather, the guards let them pass. The crowd surges forward, swallowing them up.

Mistral catches up to one woman, groping her before he takes her head between his hands and twists, holding her in a mockery of an embrace as he drains her dry. The other vampires have caught their first victims as well, their limbs flailing and jerking then, as life ebbs from them, becoming still. Their bodies are left where they fall.

I sob, raw sounds coming from my throat, my chest heaving. Kyle murmurs soothing words, his hands gentle on me as though trying to calm a wild creature. But I didn't know. How could I know? I've lived among vampires my whole life but never, *never* have I seen them hunt. It's horrific. The Lion clan member, roaring like his namesake, moves in a blur, pouncing upon his prey. Two other vampires each take an arm of another victim, and pull. Blood sprays, black against the silvery grass. Through all of this, my parents sit on their thrones, blood on their faces. My father turns to my mother and says something. She stares straight ahead.

There aren't many left now.

One, a young man, has made his way across the clearing. I realise it was the one who'd been struck by the guard. He must have been playing dead, hoping they wouldn't notice him in the frenzy. He's made it up onto one of the large boulders directly below us, curling himself into a ball, as though he can make himself so small he might disappear. My heart is in my mouth. I will him to escape, to make it. He looks up and sees me. His mouth and eyes open wide. So do mine. I recognise him.

It's the boy from the cage at the Dome.

What the hell? He's no rebel, surely. There's no way a rebel would sit in a cage, offering himself to vampires. So, either Mistral is full of shit and these people are no more rebels than I am, or… a frightened boy in a cage is some sort of terrorist. I know which theory I find more plausible.

I look up and see Mistral… coming towards the boy. Shitshitshit. 'Go!' I mouth silently. 'Go!' The boy stares at me a second longer, his dark eyes pools of fear, then tries to leap to the next rock. Mistral is too fast for him. The big vampire pounces, all muscle and fury, pulling the boy from mid-air and tearing him to pieces. Blood spatters up the hillside, almost to my feet. Kyle pulls me back, deeper into the shadows.

'Shit, that was close,' I hear him mutter.

I am lost. Kyle releases me and I crumple to the ground, curling up against the rock. I can't stop crying and retching. I don't care if we're found, I don't care about anything. All I see is the boy's face, the terror in his eyes as he faced death. And Mistral, that lying sack of shit, taking him from mid-air like a hawk with a sparrow.

'Hey, hey, Emelia.' Kyle crouches down, his touch gentle, wiping away my tears and snot and spit. 'I'm sorry, I'm so sorry.'

'The boy,' I hiccup the words. 'He was, he wasn't, he isn't…'

'Yeah, I recognised him too.' Kyle's tone is grim as he gathers me into his arms. I push my face into his chest, crying, utterly broken. 'C'mon. Let's get out of here.'

He puts his hands under my armpits, pulling me to my feet.

Then another voice speaks. 'Who have we here?'

Fuuuuckk.

Kyle tenses. Keeping me behind him, he turns. I rub my eyes, peering over his shoulder. A figure steps from the shadows. A moment later, I recognise who it is.

It's Ira.

# Chapter Nineteen

## CAUGHT OUT

The big vampire from the Dome is dressed in black, the tattoos on his arms covered, only a few curving lines visible at the neck of his shirt. He moves like a shadow, despite his size.

'Ira.' Kyle keeps his voice low. 'How are things?'

Ira spreads his hands wide. 'Things, my friend, are not so good.'

Kyle has his arm back, holding me against him. I manage to lean my head around. 'Hello,' I say, my voice cracked with emotion.

Ira pauses in his approach, his eyes widening. 'My lady! Is it so?'

'Er, yes. It's me.' I push against Kyle's arm and he lets me go. I pull the hem of my dress down, wiping my face with my other hand.

'What are you doing here? It's not safe for you.'

'I-I wanted to see. To… bear witness.' I gulp the words, stumbling on the long grass.

'It is a dark thing to witness, my lady. I salute your bravery.'

'I-I saw, the boy, the one who, he was—'

'Yes.' There is deep sorrow in Ira's voice. 'He should not have been here.'

'But, was he, I mean, how could he be a—'

'My lady, there is more happening here tonight than you know. In fact, it's best if you leave, as soon as you can.'

'We were just about to.' Kyle slides an arm around my waist.

Ira folds his massive arms. 'Taking her home?'

Kyle stares at Ira. Then he nods, once. 'Yes, home.' He scoops me into his arms.

Ira comes closer, laying one massive hand on my arm. 'I'd like to send you a gift, my lady. Will you be home tomorrow eve?'

'Er, yes?' I sniff again. 'I mean, thank you, that's very kind.' Odd, but kind.

'I'll deliver it myself, then.' He smiles, squeezing my arm briefly. It's surreal.

'We need to go.' Kyle steps back from Ira, who releases my arm.

'Safe travels, my lady,' he says. 'May darkness protect you.'

I nod. 'Th-thank you. And the same to you.'

Kyle starts to run but reaction has set in, a deep trembling through my whole body. I can't control it, try as I might, gasping for breath. Kyle slows again, coming to a stop.

Trees are tall around us, moon filtering through their branches to cast a lattice of shadow on the cold ground. Kyle sets me down and I slide like a jellyfish down the front of his body, curling into a ball, trying to pull all the shaking back inside myself.

Kyle kneels beside me, rubbing my back. I shake so much my teeth chatter, and I barely understand what he's saying. I suck in a breath, managing to control myself enough so I can hear him properly.

'—need to keep moving, Emelia. I'll keep you safe, I promise. It's all right, you're okay.' Is it all right? I think it's pretty fucking far from all right, to be honest. My world is upside down and I'm lying in a forest, shaking like the proverbial leaf. 'Please, my love, please.'

Did he just call me his love?

I know. I have bigger issues at the moment. But that… well. My shaking subsides and I roll over onto my back. When I open my eyes Kyle is leaning over me.

'S-sorry,' I croak.

'I'm sorry, too,' he says, sorrow in his silver eyes. 'Sorry you had to see that.'

I roll my head from side to side. 'I asked you to take me.' The image of the boy, the fear in his eyes and Mistral ripping him apart, flashes into my head and I start crying again, snuffling and huffing out breaths, my back arching against the cold leaves.

Kyle gathers me close, one hand stroking my hair. 'Hush

now,' he says, his lips soft on my cheek. 'Let me take you home.'

I clutch his jacket. 'I can't go back there,' I say.

'What?'

'Don't make me go back there.'

'What are you talking about? C'mon, Emelia, we need to get out of the woods. There could be Reaper gangs out tonight.'

I don't care. I'm drowning anyway. What's one death compared to another, compared to the twenty I just witnessed at the hands of my family.

'I don't want to be Raven.' The words spill from me.

Kyle's eyes widen. He shakes me, gently. 'What do you mean?'

'I don't want it!' My voice rises. 'All it seems to mean is death and sorrow and responsibility, choices I don't want to have to make, dealing with people like Mistral, that murdering bastard! I don't want any of it!' I'm sobbing again, my throat raw. 'You saw them, you saw what they just did! Those people weren't rebels, they were just humans, like me. How can I be part of something like that?'

Kyle's arms tighten around me. 'I know,' he says. 'I know.' There's a tinge of blood in his silver eyes, and I can feel tremors running through him. 'But I have to take you home tonight.'

I push at him. 'Aren't you listening to me? I can't go back there! I don't *want* that life anymore!' Sorrow rakes me, acid sharp, at the thought of my mother, my beautiful gentle mother, unleashing death. The hands that cradled me, killing some other woman's child. 'I had… I have a plan, I-I need y-your help to get away and we can just…'

'A plan?'

'To go to the Safe Zone. And then keep moving. Live my life as a human so I don't… so I'm not…' I choke up again.

'Shhh.' Kyle strokes my hair, staring into the night. I wonder what he can see.

'Where can we go?' I'm so tired. I just want to get into bed and stay there forever. I hope there's somewhere nearby.

'I have to take you home,' he says again. 'Wait—' he grabs my hand '—just listen to me. This isn't just about us.'

'Please,' I whisper. 'Please help me.'

He kisses me, gentle. 'Do you really not want it? To be Raven? Even with all you could be?' His gaze is intent on me, a line between his eyebrows.

I nod.

'I'll help you, then. But not tonight. Nick is still on the estate, as is Janine.'

I frown. Then I remember. Nick, the guard who helped us. And Janine must be the blood dancer whose dress I'm wearing. I look down.

'Yes,' Kyle says. 'Exactly. We have to go back tonight, before they get caught.' He touches my face, his hand trailing along my cheek.

I nod. 'All right. And then we leave. If you'll take me.'

'I'll take you,' he murmurs, kissing me again. 'But we have to do it properly. So let me take you home now, and then we can plan.'

'Y-you promise?' My teeth are chattering again, and I'm finding it hard to form the words. 'You'll help me escape?'

'If it's what you truly want.' He seems sad for a moment, his gaze dropping. 'Wherever you want to go, wherever you want to be, I'll go there and be there with you. But now, we need to go home.'

I don't have the energy to argue anymore. Kyle seems to take my silence as acquiescence. He stands, picking me up at the same time. 'C'mon, hold tight.'

I uncurl the fingers of one hand, snaking it around his neck. He starts to run. I hold on as best I can. We speed into the night, and there's a floating sensation as we clear the fence surrounding the estate. Home. I'm home.

I don't want to be here. Don't want to be any part of what Raven represents. I don't want to see my parents, either. I just want to go straight to my room, grab my bag, and head over the fence once more. Kyle is still running, moving swiftly between the trees. We're so close, I can see the walls of the house through the branches. Almost there.

Almost.

'Halt!'

Shitshitshit.

Panic thrums through me, a boost of adrenaline. There's a whooshing noise and a rattle of branches. Several guards appear. Kyle sets me down, then steps back, his arms raised. A guard grabs him, putting him in an arm lock. Double shit.

'My lady!' The other guards bow, realising who I am. Bertrand isn't among them, thank darkness – he'd see through me in a second.

'Let him go.'

The guard holding Kyle hesitates before releasing him. 'My lady, we've been searching for you.'

Shit. I'm trembling, close to dropping. But I need to get us through this.

'You have?' I hit just the tone I want, between surprised and slightly annoyed at their presumption. 'Was I missing?'

Kyle coughs. I try not to look at him.

'Your mother has asked for you.'

Oh my god and darkness, my parents are back already.

'I've only been for a run on the estate. With Kyle.' Shit. I don't need to justify myself.

'But none of us could find you, and—'

'Well, maybe you should have looked more thoroughly.' I fix the guard who spoke with a look. A look that says *do not question me*. It seems to work.

'Of course, my lady. I'm sorry.'

I relax slightly. 'As am I. I didn't mean to worry anyone. Kyle, if you will?' I'm all icy politeness, and hope he gets it.

'My lady.' Kyle picks me up again, reaching the looming bulk of the house in seconds, the open door a pale rectangular glow. Two guards are waiting there, more stationed in the shadows along the portico. Kyle puts me down at the top of the steps and we enter the foyer. Bertrand is waiting, his huge arms folded. I sigh.

'My lady.' He bows, then straightens, his gaze travelling over us both. His eyes narrow.

'I'm going to my room.' I start for the stairs.

'Your mother is waiting.'

I stop, my mouth trembling. I stare at Bertrand.

'For both of you,' he says, his voice gentle. 'In the library.' He pauses. 'Perhaps you'd like to get changed before seeing her?'

Shit. I realise I'm still wearing the borrowed dress. And Kyle isn't in his guard uniform. He realises at the same time as I do, his eyes widening slightly. 'If you'll excuse me,' he says, then is gone in a flash.

I turn to Bertrand, trying to seem dignified. His arms are still folded, concern on his face. But all I say is, 'Of course.'

I change quickly, throwing the borrowed dress in the bottom of my wardrobe. Bertrand, who's been waiting outside my door, escorts me to the library. I'm so weary I can barely put one foot in front of the other, but force myself to keep going. I need to get through this, then go. The large doors are ajar, my parents' personal guards standing either side. Anger rises. A black meadow and a boy on a rock flashes into my mind. I hold onto it as I step into the room.

Well, shit.

My mother *and* father are here.

# Chapter Twenty

## CAGED

'Emelia!' My mother rushes over, curving herself around me in a hug.

'I'm sorry, I'm sorry.' Despite my anger, guilt carves through me like a saw. Plus, I need to protect Kyle. 'I'm sorry you couldn't find me.'

Mother pulls back, blood tears in her eyes. 'Emelia, we've been so worried—'

'I will not have it!' My father's voice thunders through the room and I flinch. 'You *know* what's been happening, you *know* what happened to me, yet you disappear like this—'

'I didn't disappear!'

'We've had guards searching the entire estate for you!'

'If you'll forgive me, my lord and lady.' This is Kyle. He's in his uniform once more, immaculate in black and silver, his beautiful face serious. I half turn to him, my mouth opening. He *can't* take the blame. My parents are angry, but they'll forgive me. 'It was my fault,' he goes on. 'We were playing a game.'

'A game?' My father is very still, his eyes glittering. 'What sort of game?'

'Er, sort of an… evasion game. Which is why we were in the woods. I'm very fast, you see—'

I jump in. 'And I'd asked him to see, um, whether we could evade the guards, sort of, to see if he could do it. You know, to protect me, if I ever needed it.' Maybe we'll get away with this.

Or maybe not. My mother bites her lip. My father's nostrils flare and he takes a step closer to me. 'A *game*? Emelia, we have had half the estate mobilised looking for you, the guards on high alert and you tell me you were *playing a game*?' His voice gets progressively louder.

'I went for a run!' My anger rises, roaring like a furnace. I don't bank it down. 'How about you? Did you enjoy *your* evening? Have fun at the Moon Harvest? Kill a lot of humans?'

There's a moment of silence, as though time has stopped. Then I notice a spot of blood on my mother's top, near the neckline. And I lose it.

'How *could* you? You k-killed all those people, and for what? For *what*? Has it made things any better? Or will it just make things worse?' I stop, panting. My mother's mouth is open, tears red in her eyes. My father looks as though he's been carved from granite, the lines on his face deepening. Kyle is staring straight ahead, his hands clasped behind his back.

My father recovers first. 'Kyle, you are dismissed for the evening. Please return to quarters.'

'My lord.' Kyle clicks his heels together and bows, then leaves the room without looking at me. I am *raging*.

'*It's not his fault!*' I scream. 'You can't fire him—'

'I didn't fire him, Emelia. I sent him to quarters. Control yourself.' My father's voice is ice-cold. My mother still hasn't moved. 'If you're going to rule here, you need to learn self-control. Perhaps your human nature—'

'My human nature? I can't help what I am!' I'm still yelling. It's like I'm unable to speak at a lower volume. 'I *am* human! How am I any different from those you killed tonight? Maybe it's time you make another heir. It's not like anyone will take me seriously as their ruler, when all they see is food. Maybe it would have been better if you'd succeeded, when I was born.' I turn my gaze to my father, who has gone pale. 'Maybe it would have been better for everyone.'

My father is frozen, the way vampires do when overcome with emotion. I doubt it's for me.

My mother takes in a gasping breath. 'You… you were never meant to know…' A single tear, blood-red, slides down her cheek.

'Please. You think I don't know what a disappointment I've been, since the moment I was born?' I don't need to scream anymore. It's strange, but it's like I'm no longer in the room with my parents. All I see now is what they are. Vampires. Hunters. *Monsters.* I want no part of any of it.

'Emelia, my darling, how can you say that?' My

mother's voice cracks with emotion. 'All we've ever done is try to keep you safe. The world we live in – it's not—'

'Not safe for me? I know. I know it's not. So did the twenty humans you killed tonight, I guess.' The words fall, hard, into the room. 'It's the world you created, though. So maybe it's time for the world to change. If I'm to be Raven, maybe it's time for the world to suit me.'

I can't say any more or I'll start crying. My mother sways. My father snaps out of his trance, coming to put his arm around her waist, as though he's the only thing holding her up. He doesn't look at me, his mouth a sharp line.

Weariness rolls over me. I'm so tired. Tired of pretending, of holding back, of keeping my emotions, my body, my very nature, under control. Of trying to be something I'm not, nor will ever be.

I turn away, leaving the library. Bertrand is waiting outside. He seems smaller, his blue eyes turned down. I say nothing, heading towards my room. It's taking all I have to not start weeping. I feel a hand on the small of my back.

'You seem weary, my lady. Would you like to be carried?' Dear Bertrand. I shake my head, unable to stop my mouth twisting.

'No, I'm fine.'

'Of course, my lady.'

When we get there, I dismiss Bertrand. I don't care if anyone is in my room. Sitting on my bed, I take off my shoes, one by one, then flop back onto my pillow.

And I start to cry.

Huge, gasping sobs that catch and ache in my chest. My

mouth stretches wide, a noiseless scream, as I give in to my sorrow. The boy on the rock, the fear in his dark eyes. The cries of the prisoners. My parents, blood on their faces. The vicious fury of the hunt. The reality of what it means to be part of the house of Raven. And the fact that I cannot take over and continue the cycle of pain.

I'm ready to go. To leave this house of blood and velvet darkness, this glittering cage. To finally put my plan in motion. Leave the weight of responsibility, of my family name, of the crown that's waiting for me. Otherwise, I think it might crush me. I want to choose my future, and the person I am. I want to live.

And I know who I want to do it with.

Kyle.

# Chapter Twenty-One

## JUST A GAME

'My lady?'

There's a knock at my door. I look up from my laptop. I've not left my room since the confrontation with my parents – when my mother knocked, earlier, I told her to go away. It's easier that way. I don't want to see her, see the love and concern in her dark eyes, hear her try to change my mind. I don't want her to tell me I'm wrong, that I'm not a disappointment. That she is not a monster.

I'm leaving.

I've spent half the day checking my bag, repacking it, making sure I have all I need for my new life. I've spent the other half dozing, dreaming of a life with Kyle.

'My lady, are you there?' The knock comes again, the voice louder. It sounds like Bertrand. I close my laptop, rubbing my hands over my face and through my hair.

'I'm here.'

I open my door. Bertrand is there, holding a wrapped package.

'This just arrived for you.' Bertrand holds out the package. It's oblong, wrapped in pale lilac silk and tied with a blue satin bow. There's a small blue tag attached to the bow.

'Er, thanks?' I take the package. It's heavy, and sloshes when I turn it upright. I frown, turning over the tag. 'For my lady,' it reads. 'I trust you're safe at home.' I pull off the silk packaging to reveal a bottle of wine, encased in a fancy printed wooden crate.

'It's from the Dome.' Bertrand raises his eyebrows. 'Ira delivered it himself. He seemed... concerned, wanting to make sure you were here. I assured him you were fine, but not receiving visitors.'

Because I can't.

No visitors, not that I ever had any anyway. And no going outside the house. Basically, I'm grounded. Which is why I've not yet grabbed Kyle and had him jump me over the fence. My mother told me my sentence, after I told her to go away, her melodic tones sounding clipped through the wood and metal of my door. She and Father were leaving again, and I was to stay where I was.

Yeah, right.

She might shut me in my room, might surround me with guards, but I refuse to be a prisoner any longer. Refuse to be part of their rules, their violence and blood.

'Is Kyle on duty tonight?' I keep my tone light. 'I thought he'd be with you.'

Bertrand looks uncomfortable. 'Er, well, that is, he's busy. At the moment.'

'Busy?' Fear starts to curl, deep in my stomach.

'Yes.' Bertrand's frown deepens. 'In fact, your father sent me, my lady, before he left. There are some guard exercises taking place tonight, and he thought you might like to watch. You will, after all, be Raven soon, the guards yours to command.'

I will not be Raven soon. But I suppose I need to act as though I am, for tonight. I can do that.

'Fine.' I try to sound decisive, like my mother. There's a pang when I think of her. And I wonder at my father, wanting me to watch the guards.

---

A few minutes later I'm outside, standing at the top of the steps. Huge pillars stretch away either side of me, Bertrand standing at my shoulder. Another row of guards stands at the base of the steps, a wall of silver and black facing out to the silvery lawns. Where the games are in full play.

At first I don't understand what's going on. There's a vampire, shirtless, carrying someone, dodging and weaving as he evades a group of guards. Some of the guards are holding weapons, swords and long spiked things that glitter in the moonlight, and there are several cuts sliced into the running vampire's back, blood dark on his skin. I realise it's a woman he's carrying, a human. She's wearing dark jeans and a tattered blue shirt. It's *my* shirt, I suddenly realise. And I know who the woman is. Cold fear thrums through me. Then the running vampire turns, and I see his face.

It's Kyle.

I think I'm going to be sick. Bertrand's hand comes to my waist. 'Are you all right, my lady?' The words are murmured, meant for my ears.

It takes me a moment to answer. 'Wh-what are they doing?' I turn my head slightly. Bertrand leans in closer.

'Your father wanted Kyle to demonstrate how it was you evaded the guards until you were caught in the woods. He requested I reassign him, to train our other guards in his techniques. Useful skills, in these trying times.'

*Of course he did.* Not much gets past my father, courtesy of a long life and towering intellect. I knew he'd let me off too easy. And now, of course, he wants me to watch, to see how he knows of our lie. Kyle is very, very fast, and strong. But there are a dozen guards around him, who are also fast and strong. Even from here I can see he's straining, his muscles corded beneath his skin. The girl in his arms is screaming, the sharp blades only just missing her as they jab at Kyle, who shields her with his body as best he can.

Tears prickle my eyelids. I breathe in through my nose, trying to contain myself. The screaming woman, the darting vampires, bring back images of a dark meadow holding deeper darkness.

Bertrand's hand is on my back again, gentle. 'We can go back inside, if you wish, my lady.' My heart twists, then hardens with anger.

'If my father wants me to watch, then I suppose I'd better.' And remind myself what I'm giving up. The killing, the pain, the screaming humans. The blood and darkness.

Bertrand keeps his hand there a moment longer. 'He'll be all right, my lady. You see how fast he is.'

I turn my head, and I know Bertrand can see the glitter of tears in my eyes. 'He is, isn't he?' My voice shakes. Bertrand nods, his rugged face gentle. Oh, Bertrand. He's been part of my life since I can remember. And I wish, oh I wish he could come with us.

But he can't. And I'm going. I turn back to the games on the lawn, holding my breath as I count the minutes until this is over, and we can be gone.

I stand in the cold dark until the games are done. Kyle puts Janine down at one point and she staggers from him, crumpling into a dark shape on the grass. I step forward, but Bertrand puts a hand on my shoulder. 'The guards will take her, my lady.' As he speaks, two guards pick her up, taking her around the side of the house. Kyle keeps running, fresh wounds striping his back and arms. This is no game. It's punishment. And my father wants me to watch.

So I do. I bite the inside of my mouth hard whenever tears threaten and, when it's finally over, Kyle on his knees, arms braced against the dirt, head hanging, I go inside. To my room, and my bag, and my plan.

Now I'm sitting on my bed, watching the door. It's 5 a.m. My heart is cold within me, as though I am truly vampire, some icy beautiful thing waiting in the dark for prey. But I'm waiting for my future instead.

I thought my mother was my only regret, the one thing that held me here. That's before I knew what she really was. What they both are. And what it means to be Raven.

Now I regret nothing.

I've left my Raven necklace on my dressing table. Faint candlelight plays on the diamonds and silver, sparks deep within the jet. Slides, golden, across the folded paper lying beneath it.

I'm not going to cut myself off from my parents altogether, I've decided. Once I'm settled with Kyle I'll get in touch, letting them know I'm safe. And that they're not to follow me. I've written a note, telling them I can no longer be Raven, that they need to let me go and make a new heir. It's short and to the point because each word cost me. I hope they understand.

There's a scratching sound, then muffled knocking. 'Emelia?' Kyle's voice is faint.

I run to the door, pulling it open. He stumbles into my arms. I touch his face, his arms, making sure he's all right. Vampires heal quickly, are nearly impossible to kill. But that was a sustained attack by members of Raven guard, the most elite force in the realm.

'Come and rest.' I pull him to my bed.

He flops back, his arms curved above his head. 'Darkness, what an evening.'

I almost laugh. What an understatement. 'Just stay there, as long as you need to. Recover. Take your time.'

'We don't have time,' he says, slanting his silver gaze my way. 'If we're going to go, if you still want to leave, we need to do it now.'

'What?' I curl up next to him, my head on his shoulder, breathing in his violet scent. 'But you just got here. You need to recover first, and then—'

'Bertrand let me come up here, by myself. To say goodbye.'

It's as though the blood drains from my body. 'Goodbye?'

'Before he left, your father told me. He's sending me back to Mistral.'

I sit up. 'He can't! I won't let him!'

'Emelia.' Kyle takes my hand, his fingers playing with mine.

'I know.' Of course I do. I have no say here. Sorrow wells, deep and endless, at my weakness. 'Then let's do it. Let's go now. I-I can't lose you.'

He brings my hand to his lips. His silver eyes are so soft, his touch so gentle. 'I can't lose you, either.' He sits up, sliding closer to me. 'I never imagined, never dreamed I'd work somewhere like this, meet someone like you. Now that I have, well…' He pauses. 'I love you, Emelia.'

The world seems to stop, everything crystallising into one perfect moment of bliss. 'I love you, too.' The words tumble out, feeling strange, as though someone else is saying them. But it's my heart beating like a bird's wings, my lips he's kissing. The bars of my cage expand, my world growing larger.

Raven no more. Instead a bird set free.

'It's not going to be easy,' he says, a few minutes later. 'And it will be dangerous.'

'You'll keep me safe. I trust you.'

His head tilts to one side and he looks briefly sad, his silver eyes turning down. 'Are you sure you're ready to live a human life? You have more privilege here than you know.' He brushes my lips with his to sweeten the words.

'Can you help me do it?' I counter.

He smiles. 'For you, anything.'

'I love you,' I say again. I feel as though I could say it forever, over and over, and it still won't be enough to tell him how I feel.

'So,' he says, between kisses, 'how do you propose we get out of here? Bertrand won't let me stay much longer, but I was thinking you could meet me and—'

'Or,' I say, sliding from his embrace, from the bed. 'We could use this.' I walk over to the fireplace and press the carved leaf. The panel slides open.

Kyle's mouth drops open. 'Another passageway?'

'Yes. They're all connected. I can get to the library from here, then down to the basement.'

'And we can get out that way?'

'Well.' This is the bit of the plan I'm not sure about. 'I think there's another passageway, leading outside. Even if it doesn't, we could go from the basement. So I thought maybe—'

'—we could use it to leave?' He's smiling.

I nod. 'What do you think?'

'I think you're amazing.' He comes to me, picking me up and swinging me around. 'But we have to go now. We need an hour to reach the Safe Zone, especially with me like this. And dawn's coming.'

I leave his arms and pick up my bag. The idea of seeing the world, of being with Kyle, stretches out before me, unrolling like some wonderful carpet, lit with sunlight and colour. And possibility. I shrug on my jacket, then reach for my phone.

'Leave it,' says Kyle. 'They can track you if you have it. We'll get you a new one.'

I hesitate. Then I put it down, next to my necklace. 'I'm ready when you are.'

A smile curves across his face. 'Let's go, Raven girl.' He holds out his hand.

I take it, stepping into the passage. I look back at my room, at the neatly made bed, the velvet and silver and wood, the soft linen and luxury.

Then the panel closes, and I'm alone with Kyle in the dark.

# Chapter Twenty-Two

## FIFTEEN SECONDS

The darkness is absolute and, just for a moment, I'm afraid. I'm alone with a vampire, who could do anything to me and no one would ever find me. As soon as the thought comes it's gone. It's *Kyle*. He's sworn to protect me. And he loves me.

He takes my hand, pulling me gently to him. 'You all right? You looked sort of panicked.'

'Uh, no, I'm fine.' There are tears in my eyes though. I bury my face against him.

'Okay.' Kyle's voice is deep in the dark space. 'What do I need to do?'

'There's a couple of levers, quite high up,' I mumble, my face still pressed into him. 'I couldn't reach them. But you can.'

'Where… ah, I see.' I hear a click. There's a damp odour, the air cool.

'What is it?' I hope to darkness it's not a dead end.

'Stairs. Going up, though. And quite cobwebby. Don't think anyone's been up there for a while.'

'Not that one, then.'

'Don't think so. I'll try the other.' There's another click. 'Jackpot. Stairs again. Going down, this time. They're heading in the right direction, at least.' He scoops me up in his arms.

'Hey!'

'What? You can't see, and I don't want you to fall.'

'No cobwebs!' I squeal. Air whooshes around us.

'Not a one, I promise.'

I feel as though I'm falling, gripping him tightly. After a few moments, he comes to a stop.

'What is it?'

'A door.'

He puts me down and I lean on him. Metal rattles, then there's a cracking sound. A sliver of night sky appears, the air fresh and cold. Kyle's hand touches mine.

'Top up your anti-feed.'

I reach for the little vial and spritz myself, the violet scent filling the small passageway. Kyle pushes the door open further, sliding through the gap. His head turns, silhouetted against the sky.

'Come on,' he says. 'Quick.'

I slide through the gap, into the cold November night. Kyle picks me up again. 'Hold tight.'

I glimpse a dark mass of trees and realise where we are: at the foot of one of the towers, close to where the Great Forest enters our boundaries. Kyle heads straight for it, at top speed. I hold my breath, curling into him as he moves between the trees, leaves brushing us, the rattle of twigs. My whole body tenses, waiting for the guards to challenge us. Bertrand will figure out soon, if he hasn't already, that we're gone.

'Hold tight.' There's a moment of weightlessness and we're over the fence, still running. After a few minutes the thud of Kyle's feet becomes louder and I open my eyes. We're on a road, trees either side of us. I lift my head.

'Is this the road into town?'

'Yes. We'll be there in a few minutes. Just hold on, Emelia, I've got you.'

I relax as we speed through the night, the dark bank of trees giving way to buildings as we reach the outskirts of Dark Haven. We pass the burned-out restaurant, then the Dome, a line of people waiting outside as we flash past.

'Are we—'

'Shh.'

Hurt blooms, then I realise. We're still close enough to home that I could be recognised. And there's no way I'm going back. Behind me lies darkness and a weight of responsibility I don't want. Ahead, my future. And Kyle is carrying me towards it.

We pass through Dark Haven into darkened countryside. After a while Kyle slows to a stop, setting me down. We're on a road, plants pushing through the cracked tarmac, dark fields either side of us. Ahead is the glow of the Safe Zone, light pylons reaching high into the night sky.

'What happens now?' My voice shakes.

Kyle puts his arms around me, bringing me in for a kiss. 'I promise, you'll be fine,' he says, his mouth close to mine. 'We're going to some friends, a safe house I know.'

'Friends?'

'Friends,' he says, with another kiss. 'Here. Take this.' He presses a small roll of paper into my hand.

'What is it?'

'It's money.'

'It is?'

'Yes. Human currency. They don't carry gold like we do.'

I look at it, frowning. Despite his arms around me, I can't quite relax. 'Er, so what do you mean, a safe house?'

'A house where vamps can rest during the day, with an internal room. I'll stay there while they take you out for the day.'

'O-out for the day?'

'Yeah.' Kyle grins. 'This is the start of your human life. I thought you might like to see what you're in for.'

'But what if—'

'No one will recognise you. And we're not staying long, anyway.'

'We're not?'

'Emelia, my darling, you know they'll be looking for us. We must keep moving.'

Okay. That makes sense. Moving on was always part of the plan. But the reality of it, and how little I know, is giving me pause. I wanted to leave my home, my life, and live as a human. But it's starting to dawn on me what a big step this is.

'Where will we go next? I always thought I'd go to another Safe Zone, or maybe even travel somewhere, another country. But I'm not sure how—'

'Don't worry about that. We'll figure it out together.'

'And you know these people well?'

'I've known them for years.' He takes my face in his hands. 'Trust me, my love. I would never put you in harm's way.'

I cling to him, burying my face in his jacket and inhaling his violet scent, trying to relax. I have to trust him. I also know we can't linger. I step back, running my hands through my hair. 'Okay. Let's go.'

We start walking. I'm not used to lights so bright and it feels odd, as though I'm on a stage rather than outside. The lights are on tall poles connected by wires, their globes so bright I can't look at them directly. Kyle keeps to the shadows, while I walk through shimmering pools of silver and gold, fascinated. Then I notice a small square building up ahead. I stop. But everywhere else is fenced off and we can't avoid passing it. Kyle takes my hand.

'We're about to go through the checkpoint,' he murmurs. 'You're Emily Reynolds now. You cannot be Emelia Raven, not anymore.'

I try not to freak out. But as we near the building, a dark block against the grass, two vampires appear. Shit. Raven guards. I pray they don't recognise me. I squeeze Kyle's hand, my palm sweating.

'Don't worry, Emily,' he says. 'We just need to get you home.'

I know he's saying this for the benefit of the guards, who are well within hearing range. They whoosh over to us.

'Halt. You're entering a Raven Safe— Kyle!' One of the guards, stocky and dark-skinned, grins, his teeth white in his face. 'What are you doing here? Another day off?'

'Declan!' Kyle lets go of me to shake the guard's hand. 'Good to see you! Yes, another day off. Emily here has family in the Zone, so I said I'd take her in. You don't need to check her, do you?'

'We have to check every human who enters the Zone.' The other guard is tall, pale, his long blond hair tied back in a ponytail. 'To ensure they're disease free. It will only take a moment.'

Shit. Why didn't Kyle warn me?

'Well, make it a quick moment – dawn is coming, and I need to get inside.' Kyle's tone is light but his hand, gripping mine, is tense. The tall guard grabs my wrist, pulling me into the building.

It's dark inside; I can't see much. I suppress a squeal as my jacket is pulled from my shoulders, then my shirt, leaving me in only my bra. Then the guard's hands are on my body, the inside of my legs, turning one arm, then the other. He leans in to sniff my neck and I freeze. Shit. The anti-feed. It's expensive stuff, not many people wear it.

'Everything all right?' I can hear the strain in Kyle's voice.

'She's wearing anti-feed. And there's no blood port anywhere. Where did she come from?'

Blood port? What the fuck is a blood port? I'm trembling

with outrage and fear, outrage at his familiar touch, fear we'll be found out. I'll be fine, of course. But Kyle…

'She's a blood dancer. From the Raven estate. They don't have blood ports, you know that. Free range never does. They always douse them in anti-feed whenever they have a day off. C'mon, man, I just said I'd take her to see her family. Let us through, will you?'

I hold my breath. The blond vampire is still touching me. Declan, the other guard, is standing nearby. 'It'll cost you.'

'Fine.' We have no choice, and Kyle knows it. 'What do you want?'

'A taste of your pretty companion.'

I freeze. Holy shit. I pray to god and darkness and everyone else I can think of. There's a click and a small candle-lamp blooms on the desk.

'What's that for?' Kyle sounds furious.

'I want her to see me, while I feed from her.'

'Absolutely not.'

'Just a small bite. We rarely get to have free range. And your companion, despite the anti-feed, smells delicious.' He holds my wrist, his nose moving along my arm to the crease of my elbow. I'm freezing cold and trying not to cry. A blood dancer, after all, would be used to such attentions. So we're screwed.

Kyle's silver eyes flick to me. 'Five seconds.'

'Thirty.' Fuck.

'Fifteen, and I'll be timing you.'

'Done.' Before I can react the guard's fangs drop and he

bites down. I flinch, trying not to scream at the threading pull in my veins. How how *how* do blood dancers do this, day in and day out? A couple of tears escape and I try not to gasp. How the fuck long is fifteen seconds, anyway? It feels like fifteen hours.

'You're done. Let her go.' Kyle's fists are clenched, his face stone. But the guard doesn't release me, sucking harder. I groan at the pain, unable to help it.

'Let her fucking go!' Kyle roars. He lunges forward, but Declan grabs him, holding him back. 'She hasn't taken any painkillers!'

Oh. So that's how they do it. Or maybe they just get used to it. I'm starting to feel dizzy, and my eyes meet Declan's, pleading. The pull in my veins gets stronger, the guard's mouth locked onto my arm, his gulping swallows violent in their intensity. I don't think I can take much more of this.

'Please.' The word is a whisper, breath leaving me. Kyle is still roaring, pulling free of Declan. But before he can reach me Declan is there, his hand on James's throat, choking him.

'Let her go – you're taking too much. You don't need another report, James. And I'll fucking make one if you drain her dry here. You know Raven blood dancers are expensive – you damage this one and you'll be for the pits.' He shoves at the other guard who finally releases me, groaning, his lips dark with blood. My blood. Fucking hell. I feel sick.

'I don't care. It was worth it.' He sinks back into a chair.

'I've never tasted anything like it. Raven dancers really are the best.'

I'm half naked, cold and shaking. Blood runs from my elbow, pain radiating up to my shoulder.

Kyle catches me as I fall.

# Chapter Twenty-Three

## HAVEN

T hings are a bit blurry after that. I hear Kyle arguing with Declan. And Declan apologising. Someone touches my elbow and the pain lessens, as though it's healing. Then I hear birds chirping, the rustle of trees, a rush of cold air. I realise Kyle is talking to me. He's sitting down, cradling me close.

'I'm so sorry. I thought we'd be okay. Shit.' He shakes me. My eyelids flutter. I try to talk but only a small moan comes out. I'm freezing. Kyle pulls me closer. 'Wake up! Emelia, talk to me. Fuck. C'mon, Emelia, wake up.'

He sounds worried, so I make an effort. 'C-cold,' I manage to get out through my teeth, which have begun to chatter.

'God and darkness!' He almost sobs the words. I feel the satin tickle of his hair against my bare skin, then his hands as he slides my shirt and jacket onto me.

'I'm so sorry,' he says again, kissing me, cradling me to

him. 'I've arranged with Declan that we get passage straight through when we leave the Safe Zone. And that fucker, James – he's going on report.'

'S'okay.' My lips feel swollen and rubbery, the words mumbled. But I'm not lying. Someone almost drained me dry, I'm cold and weak – none of it matters, as long as I'm with Kyle.

'Can you stand?'

'Not sure.'

'I'll carry you. It's nearly dawn, so we need to hurry.'

In one smooth motion he's on his feet, holding me tight to his chest. We run through the last pale shadows of night, between low brick houses, the windows golden squares against the darkness. After a few minutes Kyle slows, turning up a driveway. The house at the end of it has metal shutters like the ones at home, plants in pots along the front veranda, small flowers and green leaves.

Kyle knocks on the front door. Once, twice, then a third time. A small window opens.

'Hello, Ruth. It's Kyle and a friend. Have you room?'

'Kyle!' I glimpse a face, pale and wrinkled. It disappears. A moment later the door opens. A woman is there, small and curvy, swathed in layers of knitted fabric. 'Come in, come in, it's near dawn,' she says, ushering us inside. She peers both ways before closing the door; I hear several locks engaging. The hallway is small, paved with tiles. I smell cooked food, vanilla, lemons, a tang of something chemical.

'Ruth, this is my friend Emily, Emily, this is Ruth. This is her home.'

'Lovely to meet you,' I say, though it's tough to lift my head. I'm so tired.

'Ruth, have you food for Emily? We ran into some trouble on the way here, one of the guards—'

'James?'

'Yes. Bastard! He had no right!'

'I've heard about him. Oh my dear, I am sorry.' She touches my arm. 'You do look unwell. Come on, bring her through.'

Kyle carries me through a doorway into a large room. It's like something out of a film. There's a sitting area with a brown padded sofa and chairs on a colourful rug, floral wallpaper on one wall. The other walls are all painted white. Next to the sitting area is a dining table and chairs, and beyond them a kitchen with brown wooden cupboards, separated from the dining area by a long countertop and two stools. Kyle carries me to the sofa and puts me down, wincing at the glow from two nearby lamps. Ruth turns them both down to candle strength, then pushes a button set into the wall. There's a faint rumble and shutters start to slide down the windows, obscuring the rapidly brightening sky.

Kyle kneels at my feet, easing my boots off, his silver gaze so soft and tender I feel like crying. Meanwhile, Ruth is bustling around in the kitchen – there's the clatter of a saucepan, the smell of something delicious, a hissing noise, and a crackling plastic sound.

She brings over a tray holding a bowl with steam coming off it, a spoon and a fabric napkin, the edges slightly frayed. There's also a plastic packet of some dark liquid and a straw. She sets it on a low wooden table, the tiles on top worn smooth.

'Can you sit up, dear? I have some bone broth for you. It'll have you feeling better in no time.'

Bone broth? I've never tried it, but it smells delicious. 'Y-yes, I think I can.' With Kyle's help I sit up. I'm not so dizzy anymore, which is good. The bowl is filled with beige liquid, green leaves floating in it. I dip the spoon in and bring it to my mouth. Flavours explode on my tongue, garlic and herbs and salt and meat, hot and delicious.

'How is it, dear?' Ruth stands nearby, her hands twisting together.

'Mmm, lovely. Thanks.'

Ruth smiles. It changes her face, the careworn look lifting. She reaches forward to pass my napkin and her sleeve falls back, revealing a round mark cut into the skin on the inside of her elbow, a clear plaster over it.

'You're welcome,' she says. 'Will you be staying long?'

'Just today,' says Kyle. 'Would you mind showing Emily around while I rest? She hasn't been here before. She, er, lives in night, mostly.'

'Oh?' Ruth's head tilts, her brown eyes fixed on me. 'Of course. I don't have much planned today though – I hope it won't be too boring for you.'

'It's fine,' I say, somewhat absentmindedly. Kyle has picked up the plastic pouch and I've just realised it's filled with blood. The plastic is opaque, milky coloured, the liquid dark inside. He's drinking it through the straw and I've never seen anything like it in my life. I frown, opening my mouth to ask him. He widens his eyes slightly, shaking his head. I stop. This must be something I should know.

Ruth, thankfully, hasn't noticed. She's gone back to the kitchen and returns, holding another bowl of broth. 'May as well join you two,' she says. 'It's almost breakfast time.'

It is? It's time for me to sleep, usually. I drink more of the delicious broth, feeling the goodness all through me. I yawn, putting my spoon down, my hand covering my mouth.

'I'll take you to the safe room in a moment,' Ruth says. 'Do you need a rest, dear? Or would you like to go out straight away?'

'Um, a rest, I think. If that's okay?' I'm sleepy. I also need some time alone with Kyle. Not just to be with him, but also because I'm realising how unprepared I am.

'Of course. Give me a minute to get the bed made up.' Ruth gets up, heading into the hallway. Kyle puts his arm around me.

'You feeling okay?'

I nod. 'Much better.'

'Good.' He kisses me. 'You had me worried.'

Ruth comes back in. 'All ready for you.'

Kyle gets up, offering me his hand. I take it and stand, pleased to realise I can. We follow Ruth into the hallway. A heavy-looking door at one end is ajar, the room beyond dark except for the faint glimmer of a candle-lamp.

'I put the light on for you,' says Ruth, smiling at me. 'We'll go out, once you've had a rest. Kyle—' she takes his arm, leading him away from me '—do you have a minute? I just need to ask you something.'

I enter the room, the door closing behind me with a heavy thud. The space is small and square, no windows, the walls painted blue. There's a double bed against one wall, made up with white bedding, spotlessly clean. Next to it on one side is a small table with a single candle-lamp, a jug of water and a bowl. On the other side are two wooden caskets. There isn't room for anything else. I slip my jacket off, hanging it on one of several hooks on the wall. Sitting on the bed, I lie back, sighing in relief. There's a murmur of voices from the hallway, but I'm too tired to listen to what they're saying. The voices stop and the door opens, letting in Kyle. He hangs up his jacket, then lies on the bed next to me. I turn to him and, to my horror, start crying.

What the hell?

Here I am, alone in a room with my impossibly sexy vampire boyfriend at the start of our new life together, and all I can do is cry. A part of me is shouting *What are you doing? Make the most of this!* But I can't seem to stop. I realise it must be reaction, the combination of tiredness and leaving home and the horrible events at the border station overwhelming me. Kyle is great, cuddling me until my tears become sniffles, stroking my hair.

'You okay?'

I huff out a laugh because I'm really not. 'I hate being human.' Shit. Where did that come from?

'What? I thought this was what you wanted, to live a human life.'

'I hate it. I hate it so much. I wish I was like you.' More words, tumbling out of me. It's like a wall has broken down. I've never told anyone this, other than my parents. It's unbearably intimate, being alone in this dark room with him, the gleam of his silver eyes watching as I unburden myself, his hands stroking me. 'I wish I was stronger, faster, could do... all the things you do! Fuck.'

'Hey.' Kyle shifts and I roll onto my back, his weight half on me. He kisses me. 'I love you just how you are, Emelia Raven. If you weren't human, you wouldn't be you.'

'But,' I say between kisses, 'if I were vampire we could run together, we could do everything! We wouldn't have had to leave. And you wouldn't have to protect me.'

'And then we would never have met.' He smiles, his hair falling forward to tickle my forehead.

Well. That's a pretty solid argument. I'm unable to think of anything to refute it, his kisses distracting.

He lifts his head. 'Emelia, I get it, believe me. But you've lived a life of privilege beyond any human I've ever met. Did anyone ever try to, um, change you?'

I nod. He pulls back, eyebrows raised.

'Really? What happened?'

What happened? Ugh. It was awful. My mother's blood-streaked visage still shows up occasionally in nightmares. I'd begged her to work the blood magic on me, hating my soft pink body with its monthly blood and embarrassment, its weakness and emotion. My father had refused any part in it, his disdain almost as tough to take as my mother's tears. It was a disaster from start to blood-soaked finish. I turn my wrist, the glow from the candle-lamp catching the faint scar shimmering on my wrist. It's almost invisible, only seen from the right angle. But the scars inside me are still there. I feel their tug, can pick at them, on my darkest days. I never asked her to change me again.

'Um, well, it turns out I'm immune,' I mutter. 'Because my parents are vampires. I already have the blood magic within me.' I tense. Maybe he won't want to stay with me now he knows I'll never be like him.

He kisses my brow. 'Well, I did wonder…'

'About what?'

'You heal quite fast, you know.'

'I do?'

'Yep. I mean, the night when we went to the waterfall, when we came out of the woods, I dropped you. And the speed I was going at… well, you should have been hurt. But you weren't. And today,' he goes on, his hand under my shirt, fingers moving on my skin, 'James took a lot of blood from you. Like, a lot. I wanted to rip him to pieces.' His expression darkens. 'You shouldn't be awake right now, let alone be able to stand.'

I remember Danae, fainting as my father fed from her after the attack in the ballroom, how limp she'd been when she was carried away. Okay, maybe he has a point.

'And finally—' his hand slides lower, moving with more intent '—who says I like vampire girls, anyway?'

Oh.

Kissing resumes, Kyle's hands, his body, erasing the touch of the guard, the horrid intimacy of him feeding from me. After, we lie curled together, his skin cool against mine. I'm almost asleep when a thought hits me.

'Kyle?'

'Hmm?

'What's a blood port?'

He shifts against me. 'Did you see the mark, on Ruth's elbow?'

'Mm.' The round scar, covered with a clear plaster.

'That's a blood port. Humans have to give blood every month. That's how the Safe Zone works.'

'It is?' I mean, I knew that they somehow involved blood, and getting it from humans. But I guess I thought it was done with needles or something, like when people gave blood on the shows I watched.

'Yep. Your family… er… you have to realise, Emelia, things aren't like that for most vampires. Raven have livestock… er… humans, on demand, for everyone. Even the guards. That's not how it is, usually.'

'Right.' The desire to sleep is gone from me. I stare into the darkness, considering. I'd watched old films, read books, learned about the human past in my lessons. I thought I knew what I was getting into, what living a human life would mean. Thought I knew what to expect when I got to the Safe Zones. But now, meeting Ruth, seeing the mark on her arm, and the way the guard treated me, makes me realise how wrong I was. I can't go back home. But I'm also realising that things might not be quite how I thought they'd be. I wrap my fingers around Kyle's muscled forearm as though he's a lifebelt, keeping me safe. I wanted a life in his arms. But I wonder, now, how it will be when I'm out of them.

'You sleepy?'

I can feel he's ready again, hard against me.

'Hmmm.' I'm not. I just need to think without Kyle, lovely as he is, distracting me. I snuggle into his arms and slow my breathing. But he knows me too well. A predator, as I've said, misses no nuance in his prey.

'What's wrong?'

'Nothing.' He squeezes me gently. 'Okay, well, will I have to get one of those?'

'One of what?'

'A blood port.'

Kyle kisses me. 'No. We won't be staying long enough for that.'

'Right, of course.' We can't stay in this Safe Zone. It's one of the first places my parents will look for me. My plan had always been to keep moving, to go to other human settlements, further away. But I'd only had a vague sort of idea as to how to do that, my recent thoughts consumed by my dream of a future with Kyle, one free of the weight of being Raven. 'Where will we go next?'

'Don't worry about that.' He kisses me again. 'We're here, together. Isn't that all that matters?'

I don't answer.

He pulls me, gently, so I roll onto my back. He lowers himself onto me, heat and coolness, soft and hard. 'What else is bothering you?'

His kisses are soft, but I can't relax. 'I just… I didn't like it. How the guard treated me.'

The kisses stop. 'He nearly killed you.' Anger threads his tone.

'Oh, not that. I mean, yes that, but also…' I think about how to put it into words. 'The way he stripped me. And sniffed me. The way he wouldn't talk to me, only to you. Is that how it is, for humans? Is that all we are?' The words tumble into the blue-tinted darkness. It's as though we're underwater, in a silent place just for us.

Kyle is quiet for a moment. 'It's how most humans are treated, yes.' His voice is flat. 'But there can be love, between human and vampire, despite their rules!' He sounds fiercer, his voice deepening.

'Rules?'

Kyle is silent for a moment. 'Emelia, what we're doing together, this life you want to live with me, it's frowned upon. Oh, not because of who you are, although—' he laughs '—that would be a problem for me, I think. It's because of *what* you are.'

I'm silent, my mouth twisting.

'Humans and vampires… well. They can't stop us from loving each other, but what they've been doing in recent years is forbidding us from creating any more vampires. Humans are too valuable, you see, as blood stock. And vampires, well, there are enough of us. So, if you were a different human, and I wanted to change you so we could be together forever—' his voice roughens '—it wouldn't be allowed. You would be killed, and I would be sent to the pits.'

'But you can't change me anyway.' God, I can't even be human correctly. 'I didn't realise…'

'I don't *want* to change you! You're perfect as you are.' He kisses my cheek, then rolls onto his side, pulling me into his arms. 'Don't worry about what's going to happen next. I'll take care of you.'

He falls silent. I stare into the blue shadows, thinking.

# Chapter Twenty-Four

## THE SAFE ZONE

I wake to Kyle shaking me. 'Hey, sleepyhead. You'll miss the day if you don't get up soon.'

The fog of sleep clears and I remember where I am, what's happening. I sit up, running a hand through my hair.

'How do you feel?' Kyle's hand slides along my back.

'Fine.' I do. Whether it's the sleep or the bone broth or my supposed healing powers, I feel good as new. Or maybe it's Kyle. I give him a fond glance as I wash using the jug and bowl, drying myself with the soft white towel folded on the small shelf underneath. I get dressed then go back to the bed and lie down again.

'Having second thoughts?'

I shake my head, even though I'm scared. I've never been anywhere without a guard, never been anywhere during the daytime, and now I'm about to do both, in a world I have no idea how to navigate.

'I wish you could come with me.' I nestle into his shoulder, breathing his violet scent.

'You know I can't.' He holds onto me, though, as though he doesn't want me to go.

'What if I slip up?'

'You won't. You're too smart for that.' He strokes my hair. 'But if you do, tell them you're free range, wild. That you live with me in the night.'

'B-but Ruth knows you.'

'She does, but she hasn't seen me for a while. Things change.'

I say nothing.

'Hey, Emelia. You'll be fine. This is an adventure, remember? The start of a new life. Daylight awaits.' He's right. I might be scared, but there's excitement as well. I *want* to see it. I just wish he could, too. He nips my neck and I jump. 'I have to stay here, you know that. So go, enjoy yourself.'

'I wish you could see the sun.'

He half smiles. 'I remember,' he says. 'And I'll be here when you get back.' He kisses me, intense. My eyes squeeze shut as though to capture every ounce of essence, my lips on his until the last moment. Then he lies back, and his silver eyes close. There's a knock on the door.

'Morning, Emily. Are you ready?'

I am. Despite the fact that this could go wrong in so many ways, I'm ready.

'I'm coming out.' Opening the door, I slide through the smallest gap possible, though the hallway is still dark. I make sure the door is shut, then follow Ruth into her living room.

Where the shutters are open.

My hand goes up involuntarily, my eyes dazzled. I've seen the sun rise, but this is different. This is the blazing light of morning. I resist the urge to hide, to retreat to the shadows. I am not my mother.

'Here, try these.' Something hard is thrust into my hand. I squint to see a pair of glasses, the lenses tinted dark. I put them on and the relief is instant.

'Thanks.'

Ruth is regarding me curiously. 'You never seen this before?'

I shake my head, careful not to dislodge the glasses. 'No. I er… I live in the night.'

'With Kyle? You been together long?'

'A little while.' For a second I want to be back with Kyle in the darkness of the safe room. It feels as if the brilliant white light is laying me bare, that Ruth, kind as she is, can see to the heart of me. 'He looks after me.'

Ruth's face crinkles up. 'Just be careful.' She lays a gentle hand on my arm. 'If he tires of you, come here. Be safe.'

I frown. 'Uh, thank you.'

She stares at me a moment longer, then her face splits in a grin. 'Shall we go? There's a lot to see, if you've never been here.'

I follow her back into the hallway. She opens her front door, standing silhouetted in the frame. I can *feel* the light now, warm on my skin despite the November cold. For the first time in my life, I can't smell violets.

Outside, on the small veranda, the flowers on the potted plants are open, soft purple and yellow petals bright. Light is everywhere, turning the red bricks a glowing orange, sparking off the windows, the silver buckles on my jacket. My skin is blinding white, gleaming, almost how my mother looks. Despite how I feel about her there's a pang, that she's never known, will never know, what this looks like or how it feels. I slide the glasses down, but it's too bright and I hastily poke them back up to the bridge of my nose.

'You have pretty eyes, Emily.' Ruth is smiling. 'Shimmery. Quite unusual.'

I go cold. Perhaps there's enough vampire in me that my eyes are different. Perhaps I smell different. I start to panic, then realise that there's no chance any other vampire will see me, not until I'm back with Kyle and under his protection.

So I shrug one shoulder and half smile. 'Thanks.'

We walk along a street with houses either side, some with pretty gardens edged with small hedges, others with smooth paving. There aren't many cars, and the ones I do see look old and weathered – some with rust or paint peeling, nothing like my family's sleek black Mercedes. One goes past, moving slowly, the engine rumbling and coughing. I watch it pass.

'Emily?'

'Oh! Sorry. It's just…' I don't know how to finish. Ruth's

head is slightly tilted, her arms folded. 'Oh, well, the cars. They're… a bit different.'

'To what you're used to?'

I take in a short breath. How can she know what I'm used to? 'Uh, well, we don't really drive much.'

'Neither do we, anymore. You know how it is. Petrol is in such short supply, and the vamps tend to keep what there is for their own use. And of course, we're not really making much of it anymore.'

'Right.' I fold my lips tight over my other questions, trying not to stare at everything. But the sky! It's wide and high and blue, but not the dark navy of night. This blue is brilliant, shading to white gold where the sun shines. And the sun is another wonder – far brighter than the moon, so bright I can't really look at it, even with glasses on. White clouds drift like puffs of smoke and it feels limitless, as though I could push off from the ground and float up, surrounded by blue light, spinning in the bright fresh air.

'You're really not used to this, are you?'

'Er, no, I guess not.' I pause. 'Is that weird?' I'm glad of the dark glasses covering my eyes.

Ruth shrugs. 'Well, it's unusual, to meet someone who lives in darkness all the time. Though I suppose there must be other humans like you. We need sunlight, you know? Didn't your parents ever take you out during the day?'

'No.' I try to think of a plausible lie. 'They, um, they were blood dancers. So, they were up mostly at night. And I guess I was, too. Then I met Kyle and it seemed easier, to just keep going with that.'

Ruth nods, the sun glinting gold off her mousy hair. 'So your parents aren't around anymore?'

'No.' I silently beg my parents' forgiveness for the lie. 'However, they asked Kyle to look after me.' That's true, at least.

'Hm.' She doesn't look at me. 'And he's good to you?'

'Yes.' Another truth.

'Good.'

We reach an intersection, Ruth taking the left turn, the road widening. Another car passes, string holding the door closed, cardboard covering one of the side windows. I think of the deserted dark roads I used to travel, soft leather and curving glass keeping me safe, of the cars I've seen in movies, shiny and bright, filled with laughing people.

*We need sunlight.* Ruth's words roll through my mind, along with anger. My mother tried her best, I suppose. But the fact is that I've been kept in the dark my entire life, in more ways than one.

'Where are we going?' The buildings are becoming larger, like square boxes with large windows. Some of the windows are cracked. Behind one, a group sits around a large table while a man stands at the head, his arms out as he addresses them. I can barely take it all in. It's as though the films I used to watch, alone in the library, have come to life. Sunlight dapples through bare branches, the buildings with their signs and people moving to and fro, even the cars, old and worn as they are, adding to the illusion.

For that's what it is. I'm becoming uncomfortably aware that these people are trapped, that this isn't the sunny life of freedom I'd imagined. Where else can they go? With each step I take, my anger builds. I feel as though I understand their desire for rebellion a little more.

'I thought I'd take you to the beach,' says Ruth, cutting into my thoughts.

I stare. 'The beach?'

The road has been rising as we walk, the blue sky arcing above. We reach the crest of the rise and I gasp. The sea.

I saw the sea, once, on the way home from a Gathering. My parents had stopped the car, letting me out to see. It was dark, of course, only a sliver of moon, the sea like lace and velvet, endlessly moving. I still remember the smell of salt, the way the wind stung my face and tangled in my hair, the pull of water in my own blood, echoed in my heartbeat.

Standing at the top of the hill, I feel that same pull again. Houses cluster along the seafront, coloured dots of people moving along the streets and on the golden curve of sand. I push my glasses back on my head, taking it all in. Nothing has prepared me for the vastness, the blue stretching to the horizon, sprinkled with a thousand moving points of glitter. I smell the salt-tang again, freshness on my face. My eyes fill with tears.

Why has this been kept from me? Resentment blooms, twining around my anger, snaking beneath my joy to be here.

'Are you all right?' Ruth touches my arm.

'I've just never seen it like this,' I whisper.

'Well, then,' she says. 'Let's take a closer look. If you're lucky, I might even get you an ice cream. Doesn't matter what time of year it is, you always have ice cream at the seaside.' She laughs. I smile. I've tried ice cream, of course. But a wandering human, tied to a vampire, probably would never have.

We start down the hill, white and grey birds circling above us, their cries plaintive in the cold salty air. The large square buildings give way to a row of smaller shops. I pause at one, taken by a brightly coloured dress hanging in the window.

'That's nice.' I turn to Ruth.

She smiles. 'Geneva's clothes are about the nicest around here. She's very good at making the most of what she gets in.'

'What she gets in?'

'Well, it's like everything. We just get bits and pieces, you know? Nothing like it used to be. Clothes used to be made all over the world, right? Big factories, lots of shops. I hear in Old London some still remain, though they only open at night, of course.'

I nod, slowly, as it dawns on me. 'Because the—'

'Vamps keep everything for themselves. Oh, I'm sorry,' she goes on, twisting her mouth. 'I know you care for him.' She jerks her head back the way we came.

I bite my lip, anger an ache in my chest. My family. They're the reason why humans, like this nice lady, live the way they do. Why nothing is like it's supposed to be.

'Perhaps we could ask them—'

'Huh!' Ruth barks out a laugh. 'What – our high lords of

Raven? No—' she shakes her head '—we're lucky to have what we have.'

I don't say anything, moving along to the next shop. This one has toys and children's books in the window, colours bright against crumpled tissue paper. On closer inspection it's obvious the toys aren't new. They're clean, but the stickers decorating one small car are worn, while the books are tattered along their cardboard edges, obviously having been through many small hands. My throat closes and the ache in my chest grows stronger.

A small voice says, 'I like that one.' I look down to see a little girl standing next to me, a young woman nearby.

'Wh-which one?' My vision is blurry.

'The pink one.' She smiles up at me, her teeth like rice grains, her cheeks rosy and her brown eyes bright. I look in the window again. There's a book near the front, a girl in a pink dress on the cover. *Posey Prefers Pink*, reads the title.

I swallow. 'It does look very good.' I think of my library, of the piles of children's books put to one side once I grew out of them, discarded and gathering dust.

'Yes, I want to have it.'

'Amber!' The young woman comes up, smiling apologetically. 'I'm sorry,' she says, taking the little girl by the hand as if to pull her away.

'No, it's fine,' I say. Seized by a sudden impulse, I reach into my pocket, pulling out the roll of bills Kyle gave me. The young woman's eyes widen. I pull a bill loose, tucking the rest back in my pocket. 'Please.' I hold it out. 'Please, if this is enough, buy it for her.'

'Oh, I couldn't possibly accept.'

'Please please please, Mummy!' The little girl hugs my legs. It's all I can do not to burst out crying. I keep holding out the money and the young woman, looking uncertain, finally takes it.

'It's too much,' she says, her voice soft. 'I'll bring you the change.'

'No.' I shake my head, a tear escaping. 'Please. Keep it.'

The little girl lets go of my legs. Ruth touches my arm. 'You ready to go?'

I nod.

The little girl tugs her mother's hand, pulling her towards the shop. I wave, wiping my eyes as I walk away, following Ruth towards the water. The air is wonderfully fresh and cold, filled with the sounds of people talking, laughing, living life. I barely register any of it. I've been so naïve, I realise. So sheltered. 'Your family farm,' Kyle had called it, a distant mirage under a starlit sky. I'd thought it would be so different, just like the lives I'd seen on screen, a shining dream. But now I see it's nothing like that at all.

And how, but for an accident of birth, it would have been my lot as well.

Ruth stops, joining a small queue leading to a window. The faded sign depicts ice cream in cones. I stand with her, not knowing what else to do.

## Chapter Twenty-Five

### THE SCENT OF VIOLETS

'Y ou hungry?'
The words cut through my thoughts. I'm lying on my side, running my fingers through cold sand, marvelling at the colours in the tiny grains, polished pearl and gold and brown. I sit up, wrapping my arms around my knees.

'A little.' The sea is a glittering line in the distance, the sun high. A round tower stands on the edge of the shore, not too far away. The walls are smooth and brown with no windows, only a door in the base. Just below the crenellated top is the glint, silver and black, of my family insignia. Further along the curving coastline is another tower, squat and round like a troll guarding the shore.

'What are the towers for?' I ask.

Ruth takes in a long breath, blowing it out of her nose. 'I guess you wouldn't know, not having seen the sea before. They're guard towers.'

'Guard towers?' I grow cold. What if they have cameras?

What if they're watching me, right now? There's movement along the top wall, someone's head and shoulders silhouetted against the sky. Shit. 'Er… who, what…?'

Ruth glances over at the tower and her lip curls. 'Vamps at night, human guards during the day. The great lords of Raven like to keep us safe.'

I feel sick. 'Guarding against people… coming here?'

Ruth laughs without humour. 'Why would anyone come here? No, they're to stop us leaving. Don't know where they think we'd go. Europe is no better than here, if not worse. Out of the frying pan into the fire.'

'But can't you visit other Safe Zones? And, aren't there islands, out there? In the Channel?' This I did know. I'd seen the maps in our library, studied them in my lessons. Maybe Kyle and I will go there, if we can.

Ruth frowns at me, taking a moment to answer. 'There are. They used to be free folk, living there. Some of the last places. But the vamps found them all, eventually. Can't even let us have that, a couple of tiny islands.' She huffs out a laugh, humourless. 'And forget about going to any other Safe Zones. They like to keep us where they can see us. Besides, how are we supposed to get there?'

She sounds more resigned than bitter, but her words fall like stones into my stomach. Fuck. I know I have Kyle, and he can run as fast as any car. But I'm worried, now. What if we can't get to the next Safe Zone?

Ruth touches my arm. 'C'mon. It's getting cold. I'll get you lunch.'

I think of the roll of money in my pocket, the way the

little girl's mother's eyes had widened when she saw it. Of towers filled with darkness that border her world. 'Let me pay. You've been so good to me already.'

Ruth smiles her transforming smile. 'That sounds lovely. There's a café along here. Shall we go?'

A café. I've never been to a café. This day is one revelation after another, not all of them bad. I feel a thousand miles away from Emelia Raven, from her world of velvet and blood, of guards and golden staircases. Even Kyle, waiting in his dark room, seems distant, a link to a half-forgotten life. It's hard to believe I've only been here a few hours.

Getting up, I follow Ruth to the stairs leading up from the beach to the road. The iron railings, once painted blue, are now peeling and rusted. I slide my hand along them, taken by the light bouncing from the metal.

'C'mon.' Ruth waits at the top of the stair, her head tilted, eyes slightly narrowed.

'Sorry.' I laugh, trying to cover my confusion. But everywhere I turn there's something to see. The buildings along the seafront are a mix of tall houses painted different colours, and one that looks like a wedding cake, white and tiered. Letters on the front spell 'rand Hotel' – I realise the G is missing. There are several smaller buildings in a row, single storey, with bright striped awnings. All of the awnings are folded away except one, below a painted sign reading 'Café', a couple of white plastic tables and chairs set outside, optimistic in the November sunshine. As we draw closer there's a delicious smell. My stomach growls.

Ruth pushes open the glass door and I follow her, trying not to stare at everything. But I can't help it. The colours are so bright, the shadows so different to what I'm used to. I notice a small crack in one corner of the door windowpane, a piece of paper taped over it. Inside, the chrome and glass display case is gleaming. And it's filled with food. Not people in cages, not strange plastic packages, but real food. Sandwiches, a few round buns with raisins. A big bowl of salad. Not a huge variety, but I remember what Ruth said, about how hard it is to get things. My own diet was as rich as I'd wanted it to be, my mother happy to indulge any whim I had, anything I saw in a film or read about and wanted to try, found and brought to the house. I bite my lip, looking again at the small display.

'What will you have? There's soup today, chicken and vegetable, if you'd prefer something warm. And they do lovely chips. I know I'm chilly after sitting on that beach.'

The man at the counter, an apron over his shirt, smiles at us. Behind him on the wall is a menu, written in chalk on a blackboard. The soup is on there, plus several types of sandwiches, salad, something called a pasty, and chips. Tea, milk and water look to be the only drinks on offer. I'm not that cold, though, and I think again about what Kyle said, as I look at Ruth in her padded coat, while I wear silk and leather, my jacket open to catch the sunshine. Still, soup sounds good.

'I'll have the soup, please,' I say. 'And some tea. Oh, and chips, too.'

Ruth orders and, when it's time to pay, I peel off several

bills, handing them to the man. He seems surprised, handing one back to me straight away. 'That's too much,' he says. I watch, fascinated, as he puts the notes in the till, counting out my change. He hands it to me. A jar, a few coins in the bottom, stands on the counter. A faded sign on it reads 'Really good-looking people leave tips.' I drop my coins in before following Ruth to a table by the window, looking out at the sea.

Ruth is right. The chips are good. So is the soup, flavourful with herbs and meat. I dip my chips in it, enjoying the combination.

Ruth raises her eyebrows. 'That's a different way to eat chips.'

'It is?' I sort of smile, feeling awkward. I've never eaten with anyone before. Maybe I'm doing it all wrong.

Ruth grins. 'Might try it myself.' She takes a chip and dips it in her soup, then eats it. She laughs. 'Not bad, actually.'

I laugh too, more from relief than anything.

Once I've finished, wiping my mouth with a rough paper napkin, I realise I need the loo. A sign above a doorway at the back, black lettering on white, points the way.

'Back in a minute.' I get up. The doorway leads to a small hallway, tiled white like the rest of the place. A boy is there, leaning against the wall. He's waiting, just as I am, the white painted door closed with the lock flicked to engaged. He nods at me, a flash of grey eyes, chin-length shaggy blond hair pushed back from a strong jaw, high cheekbones. He's tall and broad-shouldered, wearing black jeans and an oversized dark grey jumper, the long sleeves frayed at the wrists.

I nod back and lean on the wall, not too close to him, my arms folded. Then I realise something. I can smell violets.

I gasp, unable to help it. The boy turns to me.

'You all right?'

'Uh, fine.' I look down, not sure what else to say.

There's a pause. 'So, hey. I'm Michael.'

I look up, surprised. 'I'm Emel— er, Emily.'

'Nice to meet you, Emily.' He holds out his hand. As he moves, the light catches his eyes so they shimmer, iridescent for a moment.

I take his hand and shake it, like I've seen on TV. He laughs. So do I. The bathroom door unlocks, the door swinging open. A woman steps out, dark hair in a puffy cloud around her wrinkled face, bright pink lipstick smeared on her lips. She looks surprised to see us. I realise we're still holding hands. Michael must realise at the same moment, because he lets go.

'Ladies first.' He indicates the empty room.

'But you were waiting.'

'It's fine. I can wait.' I bite my lip, unsure what to do. 'Go on.' He grins.

'Well, thanks.' I step into the small cubicle.

'You're welcome. It was nice to meet you, Emily.'

'You too,' I say, closing the door. When I come out a few minutes later, he's gone. So is the scent of violets.

After lunch we head back up the hill, Ruth taking a different street than we did coming down. There's a building on one side of the road, a large square place with a blue metal roof, people lined up outside.

'What's that place? Is it a club?'

Ruth sort of curls her lip, her brow furrowing. 'It's a harvesting plant, of course.'

'A what?'

Ruth shakes her head. 'Surely you know about them, I mean…' She's really frowning at me, and I know I've slipped up.

'Oh, is that what it is?' I say, trying to cover my error. 'Of course, I didn't realise. I guess the one near us is different. So it's where everyone goes to, er…'

'Be harvested? I know you don't have a blood port.' She gestures to her elbow. 'So your parents must have been part of a great house, for you to have avoided that fate. Where's your mark?'

I'm frozen. Of course I'm part of a great house. One of the greatest. Fuck. And what does she mean by a mark?

Ruth rolls up her other sleeve, turning her arm to reveal the pale underside. I feel sick. Burned into her skin, red scar against white, is my family mark. Raven.

'Um, my mark, it's um, well, it's under my clothes,' I whisper, because I can't trust myself not to start crying.

Ruth's face creases with what looks like sympathy. 'Oh my dear,' she says. 'Mistral, then, is it? I hear he likes to

brand his dancers, especially the young women, in more...
intimate places.'

I nod, feeling even worse. Fucking Mistral. That sounds
like him, sleazy bastard. The ache of anger returns to my
chest, like a flame inside me.

'I'm sorry I asked, dear.' Ruth takes my hand, squeezing
it, her face still crumpled with concern. 'Come on, shall we
go along here? I have some shopping to do.'

'Wait.' I'm mesmerised by the shuffling line of people
making their way into the building, as though they're being
slowly sucked inside. Ruth says nothing, still holding my
hand. 'That little girl today, the one we saw. She... she
doesn't, surely she doesn't have to...' I'm going to throw
up, I know it. Or scream.

Ruth tilts her head, eyes shrewd on me. 'No, she
doesn't. Not yet. But she'll be thirteen soon enough, taken
to be assessed. If she's lucky, she might get chosen as free-
range, a blood dancer. If not...' Her eyes go to the shuffling
line.

'If not?' I whisper the words.

Ruth's gaze comes back to me. 'She'll be branded, have
her blood port cut in, then be sent to the plant for her first
harvesting. And so on, every month for the rest of her life.'

Tears fill my eyes. 'That's awful.' I'm still whispering,
my throat feeling thick and sore. What the fuck. I'm trying
to recover from everything I've seen, everything I've been
told, and how different it is from what I imagined. But *this*. I
swallow down bile. This is who my family are. Who *Raven*
are. To these people, anyway.

'It's life.' Ruth shrugs. 'At least, it is now. It's the deal we made.'

'The deal?'

'With the vamps, of course. They let us have electricity, water, warmth and light, live a semblance of a normal life. In return, we give them our blood. It seemed the best option, at the time. But now…' Her gaze becomes distant, then fixes on me once more. 'Surely you learned this at school? The Red Rising, then the Famine, and the Blood Agreement?'

I shake my head. 'No. I mean, I learned some of it. I guess, just not… I was tutored at home.' Shit. That slipped out. But I'm shaken to my core. I knew about the Blood Agreement, of course. But it had always been told to me as a happy ending, that everyone was safe. Not this… this trap of an existence. The desire to tear it all apart washes over me, fierce and strong.

Ruth says nothing, her dark eyes on me. I meet her gaze, my lips trembling. 'Come on then,' she says. 'Let's get to the market before all the good things are gone.' But she's still watching me. I shrug, like it's no big deal, and start walking again.

As we continue past the harvesting plant I notice something daubed in black paint on the rear wall, like a scar on the pale painted metal. At first I can't figure out what it is. Then I realise. It's a raven. In a noose. Underneath are five familiar words. *The North Wind will blow*. Ruth stops again.

'Don't you worry about that.'

My lips press tight together against sickness. I'm not worried. I understand, now. More than she can know.

'It's just nonsense,' Ruth says.

'But—'

Ruth shakes her head slowly, her eyes fixed on me. 'Just nonsense.'

We start up the hill again. I'm reeling. I think of my father, broken and charred on the ballroom floor, my fear for him and my mother. I hadn't been able to understand why anyone would want to hurt us, the benevolent lords of Raven, with our nice Safe Zones and well-fed dancers. But now it all starts to make a terrible sort of sense, how people wouldn't want to live like this, how they wouldn't want their children to live like this. Trapped, and forced to give up their blood each month, simply to get something which should be a basic right. To be safe.

And I begin to doubt my decision to leave.

In Kyle's arms it had been easy, his embrace a haven from the weight of my old life. After the Moon Harvest it had been easier still, to walk away from death and pain, from what my people were revealed to be. But there was also a dance under moonlit windows, the collected memories of my ancestors reminding me where I came from. And what I could be.

*You'll be a great Raven*, Kyle had said. Bridging the gap between vampire and human, fostering understanding. I'd wanted to meet with the rebels, tried to force my mother to negotiate with them. But all my resolve had broken in a single night, in a field filled with blood. And I'd forgotten one thing. *I* was the next Raven. If I chose to do it, to take on the title after all, maybe I could stand for something different.

Maybe I *could* change things. Tear it down, just like I want to.

'We're going along here.' Ruth is waiting, her head tilted to one side.

I blink, shaken out of my disquiet. 'Oh! Right.' I follow Ruth across the road to another street, running parallel to the water. It's a market street, stalls along the centre facing both ways and shaded by awnings, colourful in the sunshine, people walking up and down. As we draw closer the illusion starts to break down again. The goods on the stalls aren't new, the clothing worn, books with tattered covers, mismatched plates and trinkets. There's food, but not a lot – one woman is cooking meat over a charcoal grill, fragrant smoke billowing, while a man and woman stand behind a small array of vegetables – potatoes, carrots, onions and turnips – plus a basket of apples. The stalls, on closer inspection, have been mended many times, the cloth patched and frayed in places. And the people… Their clothing is colourful, there's laughter and chatter, all of them walking free in the sunshine. But I see them now for what they are, what I've heard them being described as: breeding stock, cattle, meat. Food.

There's a building on the other side of the street, burgundy tiles on the front facade, the front door still with fragments of stained glass in the dark wooden frame. There are several rough wooden tables and benches outside, all full. Men and women, their hands curved around tall glasses of reddish-brown liquid, all drinking and talking loudly. They look as though they're having a good time, until I notice the dark circles under their eyes, the strained manner of their smiles.

And I'm the same as they are.

Slightly enhanced abilities (*if* Kyle is right) aside, I'm human, just as they are. Last night I'd been food for a hungry guard, his touch impersonal and intimate at the same time, my comfort of no concern to him. And these people, if I understand it right, have to bleed into plastic bags so my people can eat. I suppose it's a kinder way of doing things; at least they get some semblance of life, rather than simply being slaughtered. But is this living? They're as trapped as I was, inside my world of gilt and mirrors. At least in my cage, no one was feeding from me.

'D'you fancy some apple crumble tonight?'

I come back to earth with a start, realising we've stopped at the stall with the apples. Ruth is selecting several, inspecting them carefully before placing them on the counter. Six green globes, gleaming in the sunlight, their sides smooth.

'Sounds lovely – I mean, I don't know if I'll be staying though. Um, Kyle and I, we're supposed to be going…' I stop, remembering I have no idea where we're going. Or if we can even leave. Once again, I wonder whether home is an option.

'We'll eat early.' Ruth pats me on the arm. 'My husband

will be home, and I'd like you to meet him. I'll take six, please,' she goes on, turning to the stallholder.

'Let me.' I pull out my roll of bills. 'Please,' I say as Ruth protests. 'My contribution to dinner.'

'Oh, go on then. Thank you.'

I pay, and Ruth carefully places the apples in a string bag. We wander past the other stalls, stopping every so often so Ruth can buy something. Each time, I insist on paying. Each time, she lets me. As we round the last two in the row of stalls, I glimpse someone watching me. It's the boy from the café, the sleeves of his jumper pushed up, hands in his pockets. I meet his gaze and he grins. Then someone walks between us. When they pass, he's gone.

# Chapter Twenty-Six

## WE ARE THE MEAT

I help Ruth carry her shopping back to the house. It feels like afternoon but I'm finding it tough to know what time it is, not used to the way the light shifts as the day wanes. I'm so tired, the night's events and lack of sleep catching up with me.

Ruth seems to know how I'm feeling. 'You just sit, now.' I protest, but she shakes her head, waving her hand at the long countertop.

I sit on one of the stools as Ruth bustles around, chopping vegetables and throwing them into a pot, the scent of onion and garlic and herbs curling around us. I watch, fascinated, as she slices the apples, layering them in a glass dish and shaking oats and spices over the top. She puts the dish in the oven, straightening up with her hands at her lower back. Another pot, standing on the countertop, beeps. Ruth lifts the lid, taking a spoon and poking the contents. 'Ooh, that's done nicely,' she says. She goes back to the stove, stirring the vegetables before putting a lid on, turning the heat down low. Then she comes to sit with me, pulling the other stool around the counter so we're facing each other.

'So, what did you think of today?' She smiles, her eyes creased at the corners, shining in the fading light.

I shake my head. 'Uh, I mean, there were things that were just… and I…' The words stick, emotion choking me. I place my hands flat on the counter, the cool feel of it anchoring me. 'Thank you. For showing me. I have a lot to think about.'

Ruth pats my hand. Her skin feels warm and powdery. 'It was a pleasure. Nice for me to have some company on my errands.' She smiles again. 'You ready for some stew?'

'Oh! Yes please.' My stomach is growling again.

Ruth gets up, opening a cupboard and taking out three reddish bowls. They're shiny, the edges chipped. She places them in a row on the counter, then picks up and fills two of them in turn from the beeping pot, ladling some of the cooked vegetables on top.

'Come on,' she says. 'We'll sit at the table. Not often we have company for dinner.'

I get off my stool, following Ruth to the dining area. There's a small pile of placemats in the middle of the table and Ruth reaches for one of them. I realise what she's doing. 'Oh, let me, please.' I take the mat from her, placing it in front of one of the chairs. She pauses.

'Well, thank you, Emily. That's very kind.' While I lay out the mats, she bustles off back to the kitchen and returns with the two bowls, which she sets down on the mats.

I take a seat and, after a glance at Ruth, start to eat. The stew is hot and fragrant, the meat rich and chewy in my mouth. It's strange and wonderful, sitting at a table with light outside, eating food with another human.

Finished, I sit back, comfortably full. 'Thank you, that was delicious.'

Ruth has finished as well, her spoon clattering as she drops it in her bowl. 'I'm glad you liked it.'

There's silence for a few moments, but it's comfortable. Outside, the sky turns from blue to gold. 'I guess Kyle will be up soon.'

Ruth shrugs. 'There's a bit of time yet.'

'Have you known him long?' Kyle said he'd known Ruth for years, but something makes me want to ask her.

'A while.' She pauses, frowning. 'I'm curious, though. Where did you meet him?'

Shit. Where did we meet? I chew my lips before answering. 'I, er, we met at a club.'

'Ah.' She nods her head. 'It's a tough road, loving a vampire. So I hear, anyway.'

I raise my eyebrows. 'It's not so bad.'

Ruth puts out her hand. 'Oh, I mean no offence. I only mean because of how things are, how different we are to them. It must be strange, growing old while they stay the same.'

'Er, I guess? I mean, I haven't really thought about it—'

'The young never do.' She laughs, again without

humour. 'Do you want him to change you? Do you want to change?'

I take in a sharp breath.

Ruth's face changes. 'I'm sorry, I shouldn't pry—'

'Why wouldn't she want to change?'

I turn to see a man standing in the doorway. He's tall, his shirt straining over the curve of his stomach, feathers of dark hair clinging to his pate.

'Emily – this is my husband, Andrew. Andrew, this is Emily. Remember I told you she'd come to stay, with Kyle?' She shoots him a look that's clearly a warning. He ignores it, putting down the bag he's carrying and coming over to the table, clapping me on the shoulder before taking a seat.

'Why wouldn't you want to be changed?' He jerks his chin at me, though his eyes are kind. I don't know how to answer.

Ruth gets to her feet, going to the stove and ladling him a bowl of the stew. She brings it back to the table, putting the bowl down with a thump. 'Ignore him, Emily. Are you ready for some crumble?'

'Er, yes please,' I say, holding out my bowl. Then I realise this is rude and stand up, pushing my chair back.

'Become the hunter, rather than the hunted,' Andrew goes on, as though I've answered him.

Ruth takes my bowl and I sit down again, feeling awkward. She shoots her husband another glance. 'She doesn't need to hear this.'

'Doesn't she? Not all of us agree with the deal our grandparents made. Maybe Emily is one of them.' He holds up his spoon, a large chunk of meat on it, and glances at me. 'For thousands of years, *we* were the hunters. Taking meat, eating it, farming it, giving no thought, really, to the animals, to how they might feel.' He puts the spoon in his mouth, chewing, his dark eyes on me. He swallows. 'And now we are the meat. We are the cattle, kept in our pens, our meadows. No matter how big the farm, do you think we don't know, we don't always remember? Your protector in there—' he jerks his head towards the hallway '—could eat any of us, at any time. Even you.' He jabs his spoon at me, then dips it in the stew. 'So, enjoy eating meat while you can, Emily, because one day, like it or not, you'll be the meal.' He laughs, long and loud, as though he's told some wonderful joke. I stare at him, the hot burn of tears at the back of my throat.

Ruth returns with two smaller bowls, glass this time, both filled with apples, crumble and cream. She gives one to me and sits down with the other, shooting her husband a glance. The crumble smells delicious, but my appetite is gone.

'And so we work and bring children into the world, and for what?' Andrew continues. 'What's the point, when we're nothing but cattle? Safe Zones? There are no safe zones, not when we are meat. We can pretend all we like, but that's what humans have become, and—'

'Andrew, that's enough!' Ruth slams her hand on the table, causing the glasses to shake. 'Emily, I'm so sorry.'

'No, it's fine. I mean, it's true, isn't it?' My face is hot with anger. Anger at what he's saying, at the truth behind it, at my parents, at this stupid world I live in where being human is a life-long prison sentence. My dream of a human life is crumbling, right before my eyes. We are the fucking meat. And I can't bear it.

'And another thing—'

'Andrew, eat your stew.' There's more steel to Ruth's tone. She tilts her head meaningfully towards the window.

The sun is setting. Andrew fixes me with a watery stare. 'Just remember,' he says, as though he knows who I am, that telling me would mean something. The three of us sit in silence as the sun sinks, its golden light filling the room in one last glorious burst.

There's a faint noise from the hallway. The room is purple, the light in the west nearly gone, only a faint gleam of gold on the horizon. Lights come on in the nearby houses. Ruth gets to her feet, lighting several candles in wall sconces.

The door opens. Kyle appears, stretching his arms, smiling a sleepy smile at me. 'Did you have a good day?'

There's a gleam of pity in Andrew's eyes, gentle sorrow in Ruth's. I swallow, then smile. 'I did. It was the best, really.' My voice breaks on the last few words.

'Would you like something to eat, Kyle?'

'That would be wonderful.' He takes Ruth's hand, bringing it to his lips. Her eyes widen and she blushes. Andrew snorts, looking away. Ruth goes to the kitchen, bending to pull a metal case from under the counter. There's a hiss as it opens, the crackle of plastic. Then Kyle's arms are around me, his lips on mine. I close my eyes, an ache in my heart.

'You caught the sun.' His fingertip touches my nose. I open my eyes.

'What do you mean?'

He grins, releasing me. 'Go and look at yourself.'

I walk over to a nearby mirror, hung above the long sideboard. And I see what he means.

'Oh!' My skin is rosy, as rosy as the blood dancers' at my parents' party. My cheek feels warm, as though holding a piece of the sun inside.

'It will fade, dear.' Ruth comes up behind me, her hands gentle on my shoulders. 'It's just a touch of sun, no burn.'

A touch of sun. I close my eyes, remembering how it felt to have the sun touch me. There's a melancholy in me, wild and sweet. Despite all I saw, my illusions shattered, I would go through it all again, just to have that experience, to learn what I've learned. My heart hurts, as though it's breaking. I hear a clatter, then a tube of something is pressed into my hand.

I look at it. 'Aloe Gel.' The writing is faded, the text partly rubbed away, the tube half compressed.

'Just a little will help.' Ruth nods at me. I unscrew the lid. A clear gel with a fresh smell squirts onto my hand. I take some on my fingertip and rub it across my cheeks, feeling it dissolve like water, cooling my flush. Ruth looks at me curiously.

'What?' I half smile, unsure if I've done something wrong.

'Oh, nothing.' She shakes her head, but she's frowning again. 'It's just, I've never seen it work so fast.'

I take another look in the mirror. My skin is moon-pale once more. My eyes widen.

'Oh!' I panic, because this obviously isn't normal. I remember what Kyle said, about my healing. 'Um, maybe it's because I live at night?'

I glance at Kyle, trying not to seem freaked out. He's drinking from another of the plastic pouches. When he catches my look, he coughs.

'Right, Eme— Emily. We should probably get going, hey?'

He jerks his head towards the window. It's dark outside. And I've no doubt my family will be sending guards after us.

'Er, yes. That would be good.' Ruth and Andrew, meanwhile, are watching us, Ruth with a knowing look in her eye. I feel terrible for deceiving them. 'Ruth, thanks so much for today.'

I hold out my hand but she surprises me with a hug, her small body soft. She smells of cinnamon and bone broth, a comforting scent. 'Be safe,' she says, her voice low. 'And remember, you're welcome any time.'

She lets go and Andrew comes to hug me. It feels strange, his male scent different from the violets I'm used to. 'Lovely to meet you, Emily. Don't worry about me, I just like to go on about things sometimes. I didn't mean to upset you.'

I catch Kyle's eye and he raises his eyebrows. I shake my head. There's no way I can explain it to him.

'Thank you both, again. It's been... great.' I yawn, clapping a hand over my mouth. It feels strange to yawn as the night begins, but on some level it feels normal as well, that after a day in the light I might want to relax into the dark.

'C'mon, sleepy, let's go.' Kyle puts his arm around me then, without warning, scoops me up, heading into the cool dark outside. We race into the night, but there's pressure in my chest, as though something is building, wanting to get out.

'Wait. Stop.'

Kyle slows, but doesn't come to a complete stop. 'We need to keep moving. We have passage through the checkpoint, but there's a way to go before we reach the next place.' We're on the same road Ruth and I took earlier, golden lights in the town below, the sea a dark shifting mass beyond.

'Just for a minute,' I say, pushing at him. 'We need to talk.'

# Chapter Twenty-Seven

## GIVE ME TONIGHT

This time, he does stop. 'What is it?' His tone is gentle, but there's a thread of something else running through it, like the tension I feel in his body. He releases me, though.

'I, er…' Crap. How do I say this? For the first time I consider he's also ruined his career, at least once my parents find out he was the one who took me away from them. He's done everything for me. I'm ashamed I haven't thought of this before. And now I'm going to tell him it's not what I want, after all. I clear my throat. 'I think I might want to go back. Home.'

There's silence, like a breath drawn in. I brace myself.

'Are you serious?'

His voice is quiet, though, not the shout of anger I'd expected. Maybe that's worse.

'I-I… just, the things I saw today, the way people live, it's just not—'

'—not what you expected?' Again, that dangerous quiet. It's as though the world has stopped, absolute stillness.

'No! I mean, yes, partly. But also… You said, once, you thought I'd be a good Raven.'

'I did.'

His arms are folded. I pause before continuing, knowing it's important I get this right. I also want to get a handle on myself, on the anger blooming inside me again, threatening to well up in my eyes, my throat. 'Well, maybe I should do it, then. Maybe I can change things for everyone, so humans get a better deal, more opportunity.' I think about the little girl again, her future, bleeding into a bag, tied to the same place until she dies. 'I think with the Moon Harvest and the upcoming coronation and… everything, it was reaction. I just wanted to get away. I'm sorry I involved you.'

Kyle's mouth is tight. He looks away, a muscle flexing in his jaw. There's pain in my chest, at what I've done, at how I've dragged him along in my plans.

'We can go back now, you can drop me at the gates and then go to Mistral, like you were supposed to – no one needs to know you were with me, I won't say anything. I can handle my parents punishing me, as long as you're all right.' It's the best plan I can come up with. I hope he goes for it. And forgives me.

The muscle in his jaw stops flexing. He turns back to me. Moonlight catches the silver of his eyes, carves shadows along his cheekbones. His arms are still folded. 'What about us?'

'Wh-what about us?' Oh god. This is it. It's over. The pain in my heart increases.

'What about the life we wanted? Together?' He unfolds his arms, takes a step closer. 'I was going to show you the world, Raven girl.'

'You still can!'

'What, as your guard?' He shakes his head. For the first time, he sounds angry. 'Be realistic. You're the heir to Raven. If I take you back there, you'll find someone else, someone more suited to your station. Or your parents will marry you off.'

'Not if I don't let them.'

'Do you think you'll have a choice? Once you put those robes on, take the sceptre, that's it. You'll be Raven.'

'And then I'll change things.'

'Change things. Ha!' He huffs out the sound. 'Do you think it will be that easy?' He turns away, hands on hips.

The pain moves up to my throat, the ache of unshed tears. 'No. I don't. But I'm the only one who can do it. You said it yourself, a bridge between humans and vampires! I can help people. Like your ex and her brother. Like Ruth. Like... all the people I saw today.'

'This is just one town, Emelia. You're talking about changing the world.' He's turned back to me, hands in pockets.

'I know.' I do know. I mean, I'm just realising it, how big the task will be. 'You could help me.'

'Me? I'm just a guard.'

'Not if I promote you. I don't want Mistral as my first

lieutenant.' I don't want anything to do with Mistral, my skin crawling at the thought of him.

'Mistral is a prince of Raven.'

'And a lying asshole.'

Kyle grins, a flash of white in the dark. 'There is that, I guess.'

I breathe easier, the pain in me starting to subside. 'So will you do it? Will you take me home?'

He comes closer, finally, tucking a strand of my hair behind my ear. 'Will you give me tonight?'

'What?'

'If I agree to take you back, will you give me tonight? Just the two of us, like we wanted.'

His touch awakens tingles in me. 'One night?'

'For now. But one where you make sure this is what you truly want. And one where we can be together, truly together.'

He hugs me and I melt into him. One night? I'd give him all my nights, if I could.

But this, this is a beginning.

# Chapter Twenty-Eight

REBEL YELL

The market street bustles with people, lights strung between the stalls like small hanging moons, the smell of roasting meat drifting on the cold night air. There are more traders than I remember seeing when I was there earlier with Ruth, the pub with the long tables full, people spilling into the street. A woman in a short skirt catches her high heel on the cobbles and stumbles, spilling her drink, laughing as she's steadied by her friends, men whooping their approval.

There are shadows, too, the shops along one side of the street shuttered for the night, awnings out over the front of them. And, in the darkness, keeping away from the moon lights and bright stalls, are small groups of people, couples kissing, others talking. With a lurch of shock I realise that some of them are vampires. What the hell? Instinctively I duck my head into Kyle's shoulder. What if one of them recognises me? His arm tightens around me. 'You okay?'

I keep my face turned in as we pass another vampire, who is with... a human. What? 'There are vampires here,' I whisper.

'So? C'mon. Enjoy yourself.'

'What if someone recognises me?' I mutter, my hand twisting in the front of his jacket. I can give him a night, no problem. A lifetime, if he wants it. But I can't give him anything if we get caught.

'No one knows who you are, remember?' There's laughter in his voice. I grin, despite myself. Anonymity has its upside, it seems.

'Right. That's right. I'm plain old Emily Reynolds.' I untwist my hand, turning my face forward once more. 'And you're sure they won't send guards here?'

'As sure as I can be.' He squeezes me, his lips brushing my ear.

I'd been so worried about that, had wanted to keep moving. But when I asked Kyle, on our way back to the town centre, he'd laughed. 'This is the last place they'll look for you,' he'd said. 'They'll search the vampire towns first.' Of course they would.

I'd wondered how it was that Kyle had known the Safe Zone so well, had spent time there. But the rule is that no vampire can *hunt* within the Zone. Not that they can't spend time there. And it seems that, for many, spending time among humans is what they want to do. The more I see of life beyond the estate, the more I realise how little I know about anything. But tonight I'm not going to worry about that. Tonight is for me, and Kyle.

We wander beneath the awning, the lights of the market to our left. To the right, more entwined couples, vampire and human. Vampires in small groups, talking. Several have the plastic packs I'd seen Kyle drink from, sipping human blood casually through a straw. And no one seems bothered. There are voices everywhere, talking, laughing, singing. And music, rising above it all, a skirl of flute and drum and violin, an irresistible dancing beat.

Keeping to the shadows, we follow the music to an open square, large trees surrounding a statue in the middle. There are more lanterns, hanging in glittering lines among the bare branches of the trees. The musicians are at one end of the square on a small stage, humans dancing in the open space in front of them, their breath puffing in the night air. Vampires watch from the darkness, some dancing, others tapping their feet. The beat is catching my feet, too. I hop and sway on the spot, Kyle's hand at my waist. I turn to see him smiling, lanterns reflecting specks of light into his eyes. He bends his head to kiss me, and it's bliss, this moment, anonymous, just part of the crowd. I wonder whether I'm right to go home, after all.

'What is it?' He lifts his head, his cool breath on my lips.

'It's just… I love you. And I love… this.' I wave my arm at the crowd, which is getting larger, more and more people dancing.

'I love you too,' he murmurs, gazing into my eyes. 'So dance, and then later…' One corner of his mouth curves, and he presses his hips against mine, his silver gaze hooded.

I sigh, reaching up for another kiss, my hands tangling in his satin hair. After a moment he sets me back from him, turning me around so I'm leaning against him, his arms around me. 'Patience, Raven girl.' There's laughter in his tone. 'Just a little longer, then we'll go.'

'We could go now,' I say, tilting my head to look at him.

But instead of smiling he's serious, something in his gaze that worries me. 'Not yet,' he says. 'I want you to have this, enjoy this moment. Because after this, everything will change.'

I gaze up at him. Our eyes meet, and there's this moment of deep connection. And for a moment I'm scared. Scared of what he means to me, scared of what's going to happen next. He's right. Everything will change after tonight. I have to go back to my parents, to a world of blood and violence and beauty where I am nothing more than prey, no matter how they dress me up. And I'm going to try and change it.

I turn back to the crowd, leaning against Kyle, breathing in his scent, enjoying the feel of his arms around me. This is my last night of freedom. He's right. I need to enjoy it.

I jig against him, my feet becoming restless as I get caught up in the scene once more. The dancers swirl, people changing partners, moving around each other, arms waving. It looks like so much fun, so different from the sinuous moves of the blood dancers and vampires. A girl reaches out and grabs my hand. 'Come on!' she cries over the music, her face bright with the joy of the dance. I look back at Kyle, unsure. He grins, and gives me a gentle push.

'Have fun.'

Then I'm bouncing along with everyone else, my feet flying over the pavement stones. It's amazing, and I can't stop laughing, my worries drifting away with the dance. The girl who grabbed me twirls me, and I spin away from her to be caught by an older man with a curling moustache, who pulls me against the curve of his belly, holding one of my arms straight out as he swings me through the crowd. I glance back, helpless with giggles, and glimpse Kyle, the flash of his teeth as he laughs as well. The moustachioed man swings me around once more, then lets me go. I twirl into the arms of another dancer, and the pattern continues, as though I'm a bead travelling along a chain, my feet light as if they have wings. I've never felt so free. I twirl again, into the arms of another dancer.

And catch the scent of violets.

'Hey, it's you!'

It's the blond boy from the café. He's even more handsome, close up.

'Emily, right?'

'Uh, yeah... um, Michael?' He grins, his blue eyes twinkling. He twirls me around the square, lanterns swaying above.

'I haven't seen you here before,' he says.

'It's my first time,' I say. Which is true. Something about him makes me not want to lie, as much as possible.

'Fun, hey?'

'Yeah!' I squeal as he lifts me, both of us laughing.

'So, do you wanna—'

The lanterns go out, suddenly, as do the rest of the lights in the square. The music stops, and there's the sound of screaming. It takes a second for my eyes to adjust. When they do, I realise I'm on the other side of the square from where I left Kyle. The crowd is surging towards us, and there are more screams. Then I see a tall vampire in black livery, silver glinting from his badge and epaulets, and realise what's happening.

The square is full of Raven guards.

'Shit.' This is possibly an understatement. I can't see Kyle anywhere. I hope to darkness he's been able to get away.

Because that's why the guards are here. Despite Kyle's assurances, it has to be. *They're looking for me.* Michael's arms are around me, the crowd shoving and jostling.

'Don't worry,' he murmurs, close to my ear. 'They won't hurt us.'

I know they won't. I hope and pray Bertrand isn't here, because then it will all be over.

'I need to get out of here,' I whisper.

'Just keep moving,' he says, his feet shuffling with mine as the crowd presses into us. Above us I see a break in the shops surrounding the square, a narrow alleyway with high brick walls. And we're being swept, like leaves in a stream, towards it.

Michael grabs me tighter around the waist as we reach the mouth of the alleyway. 'This way.' He pulls me sharply to the side, up a small flight of steps into a covered walkway. There are lanterns hanging from the vaulted ceiling, so there are no vampires here. Only a few humans, huddling in the shadow of the pillars framing the openings to the square. Michael pulls me into an alcove, his arms still around my waist, the intimacy disturbing and comforting at the same time. He smells of spice and violets, his hands warm through the silk of my shirt.

'You all right?' His head is close to mine, as close as anyone's has ever been. I nod, the movement slight. I'm not really all right – if anything, I'm terrified of being found, of being exposed in front of everyone. And I'm desperate to find Kyle. I turn my head slightly. Guards fan out across the square, calling 'Raven one, Raven two,' as they move through the crowd. They don't talk to any of the humans, though, simply moving them out of the way whenever they need to, as though they're herding them. *Like cattle*, my mind offers, an image of Andrew with meat on his fork.

My heart is pounding. So, I realise, is Michael's. I've never felt anyone else's heartbeat like this, or this encompassing warmth. The wool of his jumper is soft against my cheek, and I can feel tension in his stomach and chest, the hard muscles there. My own body responds, despite myself. It's almost as though I'm cheating on Kyle, and I try to move back.

He shifts his weight slightly, so there's more space between us. 'Sorry,' he says, his breath warm against my ear. 'I know we've just met, and this is a bit… We need to keep still. Hopefully, they'll find whatever they're looking for and move on.'

But they won't. Maybe I should give myself up, end all

this. Because people are scared. There are children crying, a woman cowering in a doorway, all the light and joy of the evening gone. Because of me.

The Raven guards cross to the other side of the square, disappearing beneath the shadowed awnings. Where the vampires are. Shit. I strain my eyes but can't see much other than flickers of movement, the occasional glint of moonlit silver. My heart sinks. Whatever happens, I need to make sure I absolve Kyle of any involvement. Once I find him.

But I've no chance of doing that from here. 'I need to—' My words are cut off by a furious burst of shouting, a woman's wail rising eerily above it, a howl of pure pain. Another group of humans surge into the square, but these ones hold flags and placards. Some carry lit torches. Others have scarves tied over the lower half of their faces, or black balaclavas on. The howling woman has a megaphone, as does another man, who shouts slogans, similar to those on the placards.

'For The Twenty.'

'And we shall have snow.'

And my family crest, slashed with three bloody red lines.

It's the North Wind.

Michael's hands tighten on my waist. 'We need to move. Now.'

I don't need to be told twice. If I don't want Raven guards to find me, I sure as hell don't want the rebels to find me.

Yeah, I know. I thought I wanted to talk to them. And I

still do. But not like this. With that, my decision is easy. I'll return home, take up the weight of Raven, and start to make change. Meet them as an equal. The last few sparks of freedom inside me sputter out. My rebellion needs to start from within. Kyle and I will work things out, I know we will.

Michael moves back and it's as though heat has been pulled from me. He grabs my hand – oh, welcome warmth – pulling me along the walkway towards a side street, the humans in the square already rushing to fill it as panic strikes. The howling woman is even louder. I make out two words among her desperate cries.

*My son.*

I stop, turning back. 'C'mon,' Michael hisses, pulling at my hand.

But I need to see. On several of the placards is a photo of a young man. It takes a moment to recognise him. The boy from the Dome. And I realise who it is that screams, and why she would do so.

Most of the crowd has left the square. Raven guards appear from the shadows, whooshing into formation, a line of silver and black blocking everyone in, including the rebels – who don't stop their march forward, still shouting. The crowd starts to join in. There's a smash of glass and a guard ducks, crystal shards flying up from his shoulder, dark liquid on the pavement. Someone throws another glass, then another, the crowd baying with the screaming woman, the night ugly with noise. It reminds me of another crowd, this one of vampires, shrieking their bloodlust as three defenceless humans disappear beneath them. It becomes clear to me that this is a cycle of violence that will keep repeating. Unless somebody puts an end to it.

A man pulls a torch from his jacket, switching it on so a powerful beam of white light cuts through the crowd. There are screams, the guards flinching and stumbling away as it touches them. Shit. More Raven guards have arrived, another line of silver and black curving to the rear of the rebels.

And all hell breaks loose.

Dark uniforms flash through the crowd, knocking people to the ground. The torch is swiftly extinguished, the holder dragged away, his legs kicking as he disappears into the melee. There's more screaming, some of the humans scattering down alleyways, others a surging shoving mass surrounded by an ever-smaller ring of guards. Guards flash along the edge of the square, dragging people into the centre. More torch beams appear, extinguished as soon as they're lit. Then a young man, his clothes tattered, races forward, carrying a bottle with a rag stuffed into it, flames licking up the fabric illuminating his face as he throws it at the guards. It catches one of them, exploding into fire. The line of guards breaks, humans pouring through, trampling the burning guard to the ground.

I'm frozen. Michael tugs at my hand, flames reflecting in his eyes, gilding his panicked expression.

'Come on!' he yells over the noise. 'Now!'

I take one last look at the mayhem below, and make my decision. I can't change anything if I'm dead.

So I run.

Michael holds me to his side as we battle through the throng. I'm knocked and jostled, people screaming in my ear, projectiles flying overhead. I curl instinctively into Michael, his arm strong around me, trying to block it all out. Then there's a thud. I feel him jerk, his hold on me falling away. He staggers back, his hand to his head, which is bleeding heavily from a cut over his eye. He reaches out but the crowd takes me. I see his face, a mask of blood as he calls my name.

Then he's gone.

# Chapter Twenty-Nine

## TIMING

The only thing keeping me moving is the crush of people. I'm gasping, scanning the crowd for Kyle, for Michael, for anyone who might help me. But I don't know who are rebels and who aren't, and I can't take the risk. I'm swept in a river of people along one street, then another, elbows digging into me, feet trampling mine. We pour into another square, this one colonnaded along the side closest to me, a large building in the centre. The crowd parts around it. I manage to break free, stumbling to the nearest pillar and sinking to the ground.

The noise picks up again, a thud of running feet, and a surge of new people appear in the square. I huddle further back. Then an arm comes around the pillar, grabbing at me. I squeal and roll away, kicking out and connecting with something solid.

I roll again onto all fours, pushing myself upright before I'm trampled by the running crowd. A dark shape huddles next to the pillar where I was sitting, arms wrapped around their middle. They must be human, thank darkness – I'd have had no chance against a vampire.

I start to sob, unable to help it. I want Kyle, desperately. I turn my head one way, then another. *Come on, Emelia. You're stronger than this.* I gasp in a shuddering breath. Then a hand grabs my ankle. I shriek, stamping my foot. The dark figure is lying on the ground next to me, their bony fingers around my ankle.

'Please.' The word is stretched, grotesque, like the squeak of a rusty gate. The face turned up to me is battered, teeth missing, dirt on their cheeks. And human. I stare in horror. 'Please, pretty, help an old fella out with some cash.'

I manage to shake my foot free of his grasp, backing away as he grabs at me again. I pull the roll of bills from my pocket and throw them. He catches them, surprisingly deft, hugging them to him, and I hear him gurgling as I turn and run.

I shove through the people coming the other way, gasping and sobbing, not caring anymore if I'm found. I just want this nightmare to end. I fight my way back along the street, against the flow of the crowd, towards the clock tower poking its moon-face over the dark buildings. There's more shouting up ahead, the noise getting louder. I head towards it.

Then arms catch me, and I collapse.

A familiar scent of violets and something fresher twines around me. 'Emelia. Thank darkness.'

*Kyle.*

Relief floods through me. He pulls me back, away from the crowd and noise. We're next to a shop, the large glass window dark. Kyle puts my back against it, keeping his body between me and the rioting humans.

'Are you all right?' He cups my face in his hands. I can't speak, sobbing. He gathers me close and my hands twist into his jacket, melding myself to him as though I could disappear inside him. He strokes my hair and lets me cry it out, the noise from the square a swelling soundtrack to my sorrow.

When my tears slow he wipes my cheeks with his thumbs, his touch gentle. He's a dark silhouette, the glow of fire behind him. It's this surreal sort of quiet moment where the rest of the world doesn't seem to matter, as long as we're together. As though we're in a bubble of our own.

It bursts, quickly. There's a booming noise and Kyle's head turns. Quick as a flash, he scoops me up, holding me tight. 'We need to go. Now.' He starts to run, the night becoming a blur. I hold tight. Then there's another loud boom, the ground shifting. Kyle skids to a halt. Things start hitting me on my head and shoulders, as though it's hailing. Kyle twists his body, trying to protect me, and I feel sharp pricks and scratches where the strange hail hits me. My hearing seems to have gone, as though I'm underwater. Time stretches out, everything happening in slow-motion. Then it speeds up again, my hearing gradually coming back. I hear screaming.

Kyle swears.

'What's happening?' I whisper.

'Quiet.'

I try to lift my head, but Kyle stops me. 'What?'

'You're bleeding.'

He murmurs the words, but I stiffen. Shit. I realise what the strange hail was. A shop window has blown out, shards of glass everywhere. My hand is covered with little puncture wounds and scratches, glass splinters glinting on my skin. My scalp feels sore, warm wetness on my cheek. Double shit. Kyle's strong, but it's mayhem out here. Humans are everywhere, some caught up in the stampede, others with fabric tied over the lower part of their faces, their clothing tattered. There are more vampires too, not all of them Raven guards, flashing through the crowd with no regard for anyone in their way. A young man is thrown to the ground, and there's a crack as a vampire steps on his arm, the bone poking through his skin. As more blood is spilled, vampires are starting to turn on the vulnerable humans. Across the square a cordon of Raven guards are roaring commands, fire blazing from several buildings turning the night golden red. There's no way Kyle can protect me in this. I feel his muscles bunch as he prepares to run. Then a voice says my name.

'Emelia?'

It's my mother.

# Chapter Thirty

## BREAK OUT

'Is she hurt?'

Oh my god and darkness, my father is here as well. Kyle is frozen, overcome, his arms like iron bars. I manage to poke my head out from his protective stance.

'Oh, thank goddess we found you. But you're bleeding!' Mother rushes to me, her hands on my face, smoothing my hair, red gleaming in her eyes.

'Hush.' My father sounds worried – I guess the fewer people who know who I am, the better.

Mother turns to him. 'We have to get her out of here.' The background glow is becoming fiercer and there's crying, a high keening sound. Raven guards are everywhere, silver and black in the night.

'I agree,' Father says. 'Take her home. Then she can explain herself.' His stern gaze moves to me and my stomach drops. This couldn't be any worse.

'Father, I'm the one who—'

'Later, Emelia. Penelope, take her, take both of you to safety.'

'I have to stay. You know that I need to be seen. The North Wind need to know Raven is here.'

My father's lips tighten, then he nods. 'Fine. Help me break her out.'

'Wait, *what*?! No, no, you can't hurt him, just wait! He'll come out of it.' I'm crying, trying to wriggle my way free of Kyle's frozen embrace, so my parents don't have to break his bones. But my father takes one of Kyle's arms. My mother, after a moment's hesitation, takes the other. I scream, I can't help it then. And Kyle snaps out of it.

'My lord! My lady! Forgive me.' He lets me go so quickly I fall. He drops to one knee, his head bowed. My father catches me, his nose wrinkling. I guess I smell like blood and fear, not the best thing right now. No anti-feed spray will cover that. There's another loud boom, a flare of light, the ground moving. I stumble, bumping into Kyle. He steadies me, but when I look at him he doesn't seem to see me. My mother's beautiful face twists with what looks like pity. My father's lips are pulled back from his teeth, his fangs dropped. Uh-oh.

'It was all my idea,' I say, quickly.

'What?' My father doesn't look at me, his hazel eyes fixed on Kyle. My mother does, though.

'To leave. I-I made him do it. I-He's not to blame.' I daren't touch Kyle. I think my father would rip him apart. My mother tilts her head.

'Is that true?' She takes a step closer to me. 'We've been so worried. When I found your note I…'

'It is. I promise.' I feel terrible.

'I'm taking you home,' my father says, all stern lines and darkness.

'What? No, Kyle—'

'*Kyle*—' he fixes him with a glare '—can stay here and protect my wife while I'm gone. That is your job, after all, isn't it? Protection?'

'My lord.' Kyle bows, then steps into a guard position by my mother. He doesn't look at me. I know it's because he can't, not because he doesn't want to. Tears well in my eyes; I'm too tired to stop them.

My father hisses. 'Emelia, control yourself!'

Oh, yeah, like that's going to help. I give him an injured look yet when I do I'm surprised by his expression: a gentleness I've only seen rarely, and fear in his eyes. Fear for me. Raven guards have formed a square around the four of us, but it's getting more dangerous here with every second that passes.

'Aleks, take her now!' My mother's voice is urgent. 'Take two of the guards, too. Kyle will look after me.'

'He'd better.' My father shoots him a dark look before moving swiftly to kiss my mother, caressing her cheek. He murmurs something to her, but I can't hear what. Then he has me in his arms. 'Hold on.' And we're gone.

He's careful, holding me tight but not too tight, protecting me from the wind as we rush through the night, leaving the Safe Zone behind. I try not to think of Kyle, or my mother, back there in the madness, or my guilt that I've taken my father and two guards away from the scene. But I'm scared. Scared of what I've done, and of what's going to happen. I wanted to help humans, not make things worse. The scratches on my arms and scalp sting, my head aching. The only sounds are the air moving, the thud of running feet.

We run for a while, my father tense – it's like being held by a statue. I think desperately of something to say, some way to defend my actions, but I have nothing. As we move through the night, I'm conscious of a glow up ahead, getting brighter. It can't be sunrise yet, surely. Both guards draw level with my father and we slow. There's the pad of running feet coming from the direction of the glow. Two more Raven guards appear. They stop, saluting.

'My lord. It is as you feared. The rebels have entered Dark Haven.'

Dark Haven? Shit.

'Father, I—'

'Be quiet.' The words are stern, but his tone calm, that of someone assessing the situation. 'Your report, Captain?'

The guard nods. 'Sir, this is not the only area under attack tonight. There are reports coming in from across the realm. Human rebels, targeting Raven holdings.'

My father swears. 'It is imperative we get my daughter home safe. Send word that she has been found. Then take as many more guards out as you can and get this under control. Are other units being mobilised?'

'They are, sir.'

My mind is whirring. This is happening across the realm? There's a selfish relief, that it wasn't just my actions that caused Raven to descend on the Safe Zone after all. I push the thought away as soon as it comes. Me being there just made a complicated situation even worse. How stupid I was, to leave during the middle of a rebellion. Perhaps my parents grounding me wasn't punishment as much as it was protection.

'Good. Let's go. We'll take the forest route.'

The guard salutes. 'Sir.'

We take off into the night once more, the glow from Dark Haven disappearing as we enter the Great Forest. The last time I came through here was with Kyle. I wonder if I'll ever get to run with him again. Or go anywhere. I've been such an idiot.

But it doesn't change what I've learned, or what I want to do.

We emerge from the forest onto the road running up to the gates, raven statues dark against the sky. My father calls out and the gates swing open. We race through them, my father skidding to a halt.

'Close them immediately!' he snaps. 'And beware. The rebels are close. Watch for my lady when she returns, and make sure the perimeter is well guarded.'

'My lord!' The guards scramble into action, darker blurs against the night. My father runs us the last few steps up the curving drive, depositing me on the steps at the front door. I'm home. And it's a relief. A stupid, ridiculous relief. I start to sniffle, unable to help it. I try to control myself, rubbing my nose with my hand and blinking.

'Thank you,' I mumble, my head down. I brace myself for whatever Father is going to say. But he surprises me.

'Are you all right?' His hand comes to my shoulder.

'I'm fine,' I say, my head still down. 'Just sore. You'd better go, help Mother—'

'Your mother will be fine for the moment, especially with that fighter from the pits.' I look up. His head is tilted to the side. I can't see his face but know he can see mine. He holds out his hand. 'Come, sit with me.'

'Er, okay?' My voice goes up. I swallow. This is not going to be good. I take his hand and let him lead me to the edge of the steps, next to one of the great pillars. I clasp my hands over my bent legs, and I wait.

My father clears his throat. Well, shit. Vampires don't need to do that, so this is going to be something big.

'I think, Emelia, we might have made some mistakes, your mother and I. With you.'

My mouth drops open. *What the hell?* 'It's fine.' My voice catches.

'It's not fine.' He takes my hand, playing with my fingers, putting his other hand to his lips. He touches my scratches, one after the other, healing them with his blood. My distant, beautiful father. I can't breathe for sorrow.

'You know how I felt, when you were born.' I nod. There's no apology in his tone, but his touch is oh-so-gentle. 'And you know how your mother felt, and what she did.' I nod again. 'I cannot tell you how glad I am that she did. That she succeeded. For you are most precious to me, Emelia.' His cool tones become rougher, his hand clenching briefly on mine.

I can't speak, a giant lump forming in my throat. He turns his head, kissing my hair, and I want to cry.

'We shouldn't have kept you hidden away,' he says. 'We should have given you more freedom. But you understand how hard it was…'

I find my voice. 'I get it. I mean, I'm pretty vulnerable, I guess, being what I am.' My voice gets very quiet on the last words. He lets go of my hand, putting his arm around my shoulder and hugging me to him.

'What you are,' he says, 'is my beautiful, brave, intelligent daughter. You're also heir to Raven, and should have been treated as such. Does it help if I tell you I'm sorry?'

'Father…' I choke up, not knowing what to say. I lean my head on his shoulder.

'We should have brought you into society more,' he goes on. 'But we wanted to protect you, so much. You don't know…'

'I can guess.' My mouth twists, hating the reminder of what a disappointment it is that I'm human. Then he surprises me.

'From cruelty, as much as anything else. I couldn't bear it, that anyone should think that you, my wonderful daughter, be anything less, simply because of what you are. You cannot help it, nor should you be made to pay for it.

There's nothing wrong with you, as far as your mother and I are concerned.'

'But…'

'No.' He pats my hand, then sighs. 'Perhaps there needs to be change in our society, in the way we do things. That's the trouble when you live so long; you become set in your ways.'

There's a buzzing noise. My father pulls out his phone. 'Your mother is on her way back.' He puts his phone back in his pocket and pauses. 'About tonight.'

I feel a lurch of apprehension. Shit. This is all very nice, but the fact is I ran away, almost got killed and put both of my parents in danger.

'Father, I know I shouldn't have—'

'No, you shouldn't have.' His voice is gentle. 'So, why did you?'

I pause. I know why I ran, of course. But then I would have to admit… more things. My hands to my mouth, I consider what to say. Then I decide to come clean.

'I didn't want to be Raven anymore.'

'I know,' he says, still quiet. 'I saw your note. What your mother and I don't understand, is why?'

Tears come to my eyes. I stare into the glimmering darkness, to the distant glow of Dark Haven. It blurs and shakes. I take in a shuddering breath.

'I saw the Moon Harvest.' I brace myself.

'What?' My father shakes his head. 'You shouldn't be looking at that sort of thing online—'

'Not online.' There. I wait for my world to come crashing down.

'What?' The word is sharp, whispered. 'How?'

'I wanted to see it. If I couldn't stop it, I wanted to b-bear witness. So they wouldn't be alone.' My voice catches on the last word. 'So I made Kyle take me. And I saw it all.'

'Oh my dear.' My father's other arm comes around me. I turn into him, my head on his shoulder, breathing in his violet scent, laced with wood and moss. It's comforting, bringing back a hazy memory of being held this way when I was very small. It feels like home. 'I'm so sorry,' he says. 'You should never have had to—'

'Yes. Yes I should.' I lift my head. 'If I'm going to be Raven, and make decisions like that, I need to know what I'm agreeing to. I need to know what being Raven truly means. And now I do.'

My father says nothing.

'And-and, when I saw it, wh-when I saw you and m-mother, how you were, I wanted no part of it. I'd rather be human, and live with them than have to see something like that, do something like that... I don't want to be Raven if that's what it means.'

'That's why you'll be such a good Raven,' my father says.

I shake my head. 'How can I be? I'm weak, need constant protection. And I don't want to kill any humans.'

'Neither do I. Not unless I absolutely have to.'

'But it's part of who we are.'

'It can be. But it doesn't have to be. You could be the one to change things, you know. Really, while I could shake you for putting yourself in danger, at the same time I'm proud of you.'

'You are?' I wonder if perhaps he's been hit in the head, or something. But vampire super healing would take care of anything like that. So, he must really mean it.

'Yes.' He hugs me again. 'I wish you'd told me how you felt.'

'I tried! I tried to talk to Mother, but she didn't want to stop it, and you seemed to agree, and… after the Moon Harvest I just…' I thought my parents were monsters. But I can't say that. 'I guess I felt I had no other option than to leave. I don't know how you can be proud of me, after all I've done.' I drop my head.

'I am, though,' he says. I look up. 'Because this is what I want for you. That you feel confident enough to speak your mind. To fight for what you believe. And to go after it. That you see there's more to ruling than robes and parties. Although, while I remember…' He pulls something from his pocket. My Raven necklace. It unspools from his fingers, glittering faintly. 'Here. You really should wear this.'

I take it from him with shaking fingers and put it on. 'Kyle said the same thing, you know. That I'd be a good Raven. So, maybe I will be.' I speak without thinking.

'Kyle.' My father's voice changes. 'Yes, the young guard. Emelia, I don't want to tell you what to do. But you do need to remember who you are.'

'I know.'

'And don't assume you can't get pregnant.'

'Whoa! What? *Father!*' I squeal, pushing at him. Oh. My. God. He starts laughing. In the distance Dark Haven is aglow, buildings aflame. It seems completely surreal to be sitting here on cold stone with my father, in an oasis of darkness and quiet, and to hear him laughing.

'Emelia, forgive me, I have to tell you this—'

'I don't need the sex talk!'

He laughs even harder, his whole body shaking. Perhaps he's embarrassed, too. God knows. I feel as though I'm about to dissolve with shame. Seriously, I don't need this.

'All I'm saying is that you can have fun, but you need to be careful. With him, with any vampire. You're human, true, but you're also full-blooded Raven. Your blood is different. You could have a vampire child, should you choose to fall pregnant. You carry the magic in you.' He grows serious. 'You are the future of this house, you know.'

I'm silent for a moment. Then I ask the question I've been wondering for a long time, wandering the hallways alone. 'Why didn't you and mother have another child? Was it because of me? Because of… how I am?'

'Oh, my child.' He hugs me again, all hilarity gone. 'Yes… and no.' I tense. 'No, not because of how you are. You're perfect, Emelia, just as you are. If we'd had another child like you, I would have been happy. But if we'd had another child that was vampire, they could have seen you as a threat to their position.'

He pauses. I don't say anything, letting it sink in. Because this is beyond huge.

'We didn't want to shut you away any more than we

already had.' His voice goes quiet. There's an ache in my chest again, love and pain mingling like acid. My father continues, ancient sorrow in his words. 'You would not have been safe. So, we decided to wait.'

Until I'm dead, I guess. Humans born of vampires live human-length lives. I don't say it, but I know my father is thinking it from the way he hugs me close, his breath catching. I hug him back, my heart brimming with love for him and my mother, for all they've done for me, all that I'm realising now.

It's a perfect moment in the cool dark. I close my eyes, wanting to take it in. Then there's a muffled boom, and I open my eyes, startled, to see a flare of bright light.

My father freezes for a moment. Then he says my mother's name.

# Chapter Thirty-One

## DON'T SAY A WORD

'Go!' I push at my father. He kisses my forehead then is gone, a dark blur down the drive. There's another blur and Bertrand arrives.

'I think you should go inside, my lady.'

His tone is grim. My worry flares into full-blown panic, and I get to my feet. Bertrand places both hands on my arms and fixes me with his ice-blue gaze. 'You know where to go, don't you, if…'

My eyes widen. 'Do you think…?'

He shakes his head, his mouth tightening. 'I don't know, Emelia.'

My fear increases at the use of my name. 'The fortified rooms. I know.'

He nods, squeezing my arms gently before letting go and turning away.

'Bertrand!'

He pauses. 'I have to go to the gates, my lady.'

My hands twist together, my voice trembling. 'Be safe.'

He nods again, then disappears. I go inside, quickly. More guards close the door, locking it.

'Don't do that!' The guard with the key hesitates, turning to me in surprise. 'My father, my mother, the, er, other guards. They're still out there. They'll need to get in when they come back.'

'But, my lady…'

I stare in disbelief. 'A locked door won't keep them out anyway, so what's the point of locking it?'

The guard nods. 'Of course, my lady.' He unlocks the door again then turns, standing with his back to it. The second guard comes to join him, the two of them linking arms to create a barrier. There are guards at each of the long windows as well, both inside and out, a wall of silver and black against whatever might be coming.

I go over to a long bench and lie down, but can't get comfortable. I'm desperately tired, but can't sleep, not with my parents and Kyle out there. Giving up, I get up and go to one of the windows. I gasp. It looks as though half of Dark Haven is ablaze. There's another explosion, lights winking on and off. I sob, squeezing my eyes shut, praying to everyone and everything I can think of to keep them safe.

There's muffled shouting from outside and I run to the front door, trying to push past the guards. One holds me back, and I struggle. There's a sharp knock, a shouted command, and the other guard opens the door.

'Let me go!'

Two figures race up the drive, a blur of black. One seems

strangely bulky. As they reach the steps, I realise it's my father and Kyle, who is carrying…

'Mother!' I scream, lunging against the guard's iron embrace. He releases me, finally. I run down the steps. There's dirt on my father's face, one shoulder of his jacket torn. Kyle's jacket is gone, his shirt ripped across the back. But my mother… She's slumped against Kyle, her clothing shredded and singed, her long black hair covering her face. 'Mama…?'

'Emelia, inside.' My father's voice is curt, miles away from the laughing closeness we shared less than an hour ago.

'She's alive.' Kyle's face is smeared with soot and blood, black in the moonlight.

'Then why isn't she moving?'

My mother lifts one pale hand, brushing the hair from her eyes. I gasp. Her face is cut, a slash down one cheek healing slowly. Whatever happened to her must have been serious.

'Emelia.' She breathes the word, a whisper on the wind.

'Inside! She needs to feed.' My father takes my arm, pulling me up the stone steps. Kyle and my mother follow. My father calls out. 'Food, for my lady! Now!' The waiting guards, their faces drawn with concern, snap to attention, two of them racing off in a blur. My father throws open the doors to the sitting room, beckoning Kyle through. I follow them, hurrying to catch up, to see him gently laying my mother on the sofa. My father stands behind it, his hands clenched so tight on the carved wooden frame I can hear it splintering. And my mother, my world, is crumpled and burned, like a rose crushed by a careless fist. She sees me and smiles, though it's a weary smile, her onyx eyes dark.

'Beloved girl,' she says, 'I am fine.'

'You are not!'

'I will be.'

There's a sound and I turn to see a guard leading a young woman into the room. It's one of the blood dancers, just roused from sleep, her hair tousled, her face pale and soft without the usual make-up and glitter. When she sees my mother her eyes widen.

'Oh, my lady!' Shaking her arm free, she runs to kneel next to the sofa, holding out her wrist. My mother takes it. I turn away, hearing the snap as my mother bites down, the lapping noises.

Kyle leans against the wall, his tattered shirt half-hanging from him.

'What happened?' I wish I could go to him.

'It was an ambush. We left the Safe Zone, the worst of it under control, we thought. Then they blew the petrol stores as we passed through.' Kyle's voice is rough, dry sounding. There are dark red patches on his skin, visible through the rips in his shirt.

'But how – I mean, how did you…'

'Survive? It was close. The blast almost got us and took out some of the humans. I grabbed one of them, forced his blood for your mother, so that she'd heal enough to get back here.'

'Oh, Kyle.' I ignore the faint thread of disquiet. It doesn't matter what he did, or how he did it. He saved my mother. If I didn't love him already, I would love him for that alone. I want to go to him, to kiss him and give him my blood so he can heal. I turn to my father.

'Can we... isn't there someone we can get, for Kyle? He's hurt...'

My father's head snaps up, his eyes narrowing. Fuck. He walks over to Kyle. 'We need to talk.'

Kyle drops to one knee, his head down. 'My lord, I shouldn't have taken Emelia off the estate without—'

'You should not.' My father folds his arms, his legs apart as he stands over Kyle. 'Yet you did. Not once, but twice, it seems. However—' he glances at me '—I doubt very much you could have done so without her co-operation.'

'Father, please, he's hurt.'

'Injured because he was somewhere he wasn't supposed to be.'

'Injured because he saved Mother!'

'Who wouldn't have been there if not for him.'

'That's crazy! You were already out—'

'Because we'd heard there was going to be trouble tonight and we wanted to stop it before it began! We did not need the added complication of having to look after you!' my father snaps at me, the words becoming a growl.

'It was all my idea. And he did save Mother. You'd both have been hurt if he wasn't... if I hadn't... um.'

'She's right.' My mother's voice is stronger. She sits up, one delicate hand to her mouth wiping the last traces of her meal away, the slash on her cheek almost healed. The blood dancer kneels next to her, my mother's other hand resting on her shoulder. 'If we'd both been there, Aleks, we'd have been killed. Kyle called a warning just before the petrol went up – it saved most of the guards. As well as me.'

My father goes to my mother. The blood dancer moves out of the way, staggering as she gets to her feet. Father kneels, biting his finger, using his blood to heal the last of the slash across Mother's cheek, the gesture intimate. I look away. Kyle still kneels, his head down. I rest my hand on his shoulder. He turns his head, silver eyes bright in the half-light, and kisses my wrist. I take in a breath.

'Let me help you up,' I say.

'I'm fine,' he says, his voice faint. He pushes himself to standing. It's all I can do not to hug him.

'Emelia, move away from him.'

Oh, no.

'Father—'

He's sitting on the sofa with Mother. She isn't looking at me. I swallow and step away from Kyle, who has gone very still.

'Kyle, you are relieved of duty at this time. As to what the future will bring, that is to be decided. Perhaps a stint at one of the towers?'

'Father!' I try not to shriek, rage burning my throat. 'It was all my idea, all my fault, you can't—'

'Silence!'

I take in a shuddering breath. Kyle hasn't moved. The blood dancer is wide-eyed in the corner of the room. Her wrist is still red where my mother fed, and my hand goes to my elbow, remembering the threading pain of the guard feeding from me. Two of the guards have moved closer. Shitshitshit.

'The facts are this.' My father turns his attention to Kyle. 'You were supposed to be gone to Mistral by now, but for some reason,' his gaze flicks to me, 'you are still here. Then you took Emilia off the estate. I don't care how much she begged you, or what she promised you. You have disobeyed my direct orders. You were employed—' his voice rises '—to keep her safe. You answer to me, and to her mother, in that regard. Do you understand?'

Kyle nods. 'Yes, my lord.'

He looks so beaten; my heart bleeds for him. I hold my breath, though I'm screaming inside. I can't believe this is happening.

'However—' my father's voice softens a touch '—there is the circumstance of you saving my wife, and several of our guards. Tell me, how was it you were able to warn them?'

I go cold. What the fuck?

'I caught a glimpse,' Kyle says, his voice monotone. 'One of the humans, behind a silo. An error on their part, my lord. So I called out a warning.'

'Lucky for you that you did,' says my father. 'It might save you from being sent back to the pits, at least.'

Kyle's head comes up, his eyes wide. 'I'm sorry, my lord. Truly. I do not wish, I mean, I can't—'

'No! You can't send him back there!' The words tumble out, despite my father's warning. I know I'm supposed to be Emelia Raven, daughter of a great house, expected to mate well and continue our line. But I'm human, and I love him.

My mother's mouth twists. In one swift movement, my father is standing in front of me. He's all ash and gold and granite, fury in his eyes.

'I will not ask you to be quiet again. Do not make things worse.'

I can hardly breathe. Was it only an hour ago that he'd hugged me, that we'd laughed together on the steps? Tears spill down my face. I don't wipe them away, a small act of defiance as my existence closes around me like a velvet shroud. I will *never* forgive him.

'Penelope, take her out of here.'

My father doesn't look at me. Kyle does, though, his silver eyes holding mine as my mother takes my arm. Her grip firm, she leads me from the room, two guards falling into step behind us. I'm too shocked to cry out, my breath heaving in my chest as I stagger along the hallway, my mother's pace unrelenting.

'Mama, stop,' I sob. 'Please.'

My mother stops. She takes in a deep breath. 'How could you?'

'What?'

'*How could you?*' She turns on me, her hair flying, the shreds of her dress swirling. There's a streak of red on her perfect cheek, more in her eyes. 'Leaving us like that! What if something had happened? If we'd lost you, we wouldn't have even *known* what happened to you. Our precious daughter, lost forever.'

'What about all the others who've been "lost"?' Hurt lances my chest; anger bubbles up, spewing out of me. 'They're all someone's daughter, son, husband, wife. Not just casualties, not just food.' I spit the last word.

'Emelia—'

'They're people! No wonder they're rebelling!' Snot clogs my nose, my breath hitching. 'Do you even know what their lives are like? I know you know what their deaths are like, though. I saw you, at the Moon Harvest. I saw what you did. What you *are*.' I spit the words, gulping another sob, rubbing at my face with the back of my hand. '*That's* why I left. Because I don't want to be Raven if that's what it means!' My mother's hand goes slack, dropping from my arm.

'Emelia. I-I'm sorry. I—'

'That's what Father said earlier, when we were talking, he said that you'd made mistakes with me. But now you're sending Kyle away and I'll never get to see him again!' The guards are standing to one side, studiously ignoring us. My mother's mouth is a perfect 'o', her dark eyes brimming with red.

'He has to do this.'

'Who? Father? *You* are Raven, not him! *You* should decide! Decide what's best for *me!*' I jab my chest with my hand. 'Why does he have to be sent away?'

'Because he disobeyed us and put you in danger! Whatever Kyle is to you, Emelia, he's a Raven guard first and foremost. He's lucky to escape death for what he did. Believe me when I tell you your father is being lenient, and that he is being so for both our sakes.'

I stare at her. Darkness pools around us, her words fallen into it like ripples in an endless pond of night. If I could burst into flames, I would, burning my pain and anger away. I can't lose Kyle, not like this.

But there's nothing more I can do.

'I'm going to my room.'

She touches my arm, her hand cool. 'Will you come and sit with me a while? I think we should talk.'

'I don't want to talk.'

Her hand drops from my arm. I turn away, heading for my room. She doesn't follow.

# Chapter Thirty-Two

## ONE LAST KISS

My pillow is soaked. I don't think I can cry any more. But every time I think about losing Kyle there's a fresh bout of tears. I remember how his face twisted when Father mentioned the pits, and can't bear the thought of him being sent back there to die.

There's guilt, too. I'm the one who asked him to run away with me. I hadn't thought it through. He's going to be sent away, and then it will be over. He probably hates me now, anyway.

It's been about an hour since my outburst, since Kyle was taken from me. I can't lie here any longer. I don't know where he's being held, and I can't just wander the house looking for him, but I need to do *something*. He would fight for me. I need to do the same for him. I sit up and wipe my face, drag fingers through the tangle of my hair. My gaze falls on the fireplace, an idea taking shape. I need to move fast, though. I've wasted enough time already.

I pull my boots towards me and put them on. Then I go to the fireplace, pressing on the carved leaf. Stepping through the opening, I flick the torch on my phone as the panel closes. The stone wall is cool beneath my fingers as I descend, heading for the library.

At the small landing I shine my torch around, looking for the lever that opens the basement passage. I swore I would never go down there again, not after the screaming I heard. But my need to find Kyle is stronger than any fear. I flick the lever, a section of stone swinging back to reveal more stairs. I start down them, my hand on the wall for support, until I reach a wooden panel. I put my ear to it, holding my breath, but can't hear a thing. I push the panel until there's a click and it opens, revealing a hallway. My torch throws circles of light across the dark blue-grey painted walls, the slate tiled floor. There's no one here, thank darkness. Directly opposite me is another door. Looking both ways, I step out of the passage and open it.

Shit. It's the feed hall. The room is large, wooden benches scattered across the black and white tiled floor. It's also deserted, thank darkness. Except for the food. There are cages suspended from the ceiling, in each one a human either sitting or lying down. The bases of the cages are padded, and there's water and food for them. I suppose my parents think that makes it comfortable. My elbow aches at the memory of the guard feeding from me, the pull in my veins.

Most of the occupants of the cages are sleeping, except

for a man who's lying on his side, reading a book by the glow of a candle-lamp, and a woman, who's sitting with her knees drawn up to her chest, her arms wrapped around them. Her head turns as I creep past, her dark eyes watching me. I put my finger to my lips. I have no idea if she knows who I am. She doesn't speak; whether it's due to my gesture or because she simply has nothing to say, I don't know. I want to do more, wildness in my chest at the thought of setting them free. But where would they go, in the darkness, alone? I suppose they're safe here, but I see now how wrong it is, how fucked up everything is.

I cross the room to another set of double doors. I pause to listen. Nothing. Carefully, I turn one of the handles. The door opens noiselessly... to reveal a room filled with rows of bunks. Shit. I close the door as quickly as I can, then lean with my back to it, gasping, my heart pounding. Guard quarters. But where the hell do I look now?

'Psst!'

I jump. Turning, I notice two more doors in the far wall. One is part-way open, revealing a small metal-lined room containing a casket. The other is closed. There's a small grille set into the metal. Someone's face is pressed up against it.

'Kyle!' I run across the room, almost skidding into the door.

'Steady on.' He's laughing. After all he's been through, all I've put him through, he's laughing. My heart clenches with love.

'Are you all right? I'm so sorry.' I thread my fingers through the grate and feel the touch of his lips.

'It's not your fault. I shouldn't have taken you.'

'I shouldn't have asked you to!' I'm half sobbing, half laughing with relief that I've found him.

'Emelia, my love?'

'Yes?'

'You need to get me out of here. Your father wasn't joking about the pits. I can't go back there. Please. Let me go. I'll take the passage and escape that way, through the woods. Please.'

There's such yearning in his voice that I swear I can feel it, his distress my own. There's pain, too, because I know what this means. Once I let him go, I'll never see him again. I have to give him this chance, though. He's already saved me.

'Kyle, I—' My voice breaks. 'It – it's why I'm here, to save you.' My world is shaking upon its foundations, bitter salt in my eyes. I feel his lips on my fingers again, his cool breath. Then he releases me.

'Be quick, my love,' he whispers. 'They'll come for me soon.'

'How... um...' I stop, gulping. 'How do I open this?'

'It's the wheel lock, on your side.'

I step back. The door is solid metal with three bars running horizontally, two more running vertically, locking into the metal door frame. It's magnetically sealed. No point simply locking a door against a vampire – they'd be out in seconds. But magnets and metal will hold them for longer, long enough for any escape attempts to be overheard. There's a wheel set at the centre of the door, the bars running through a central locking system. I put both hands on it, straining. It doesn't move.

I groan, twisting harder, my hands slipping on the metal. There are noises behind me, rustling and faint metallic clangs. I turn to see that more of the caged humans are awake. They're all watching me. 'Please, don't say anything,' I whisper. There's no response.

'Emelia, try again. You can do this.' Kyle sounds frantic, and it spurs me on. I brace myself, my teeth clenching as I push and twist at the metal wheel. It gives slightly. I stop, panting.

'Are you okay?' Kyle stretches his fingers through the grating.

'I'm fine. Just need a moment.' I give it one more try, the muscles in my arms and shoulders protesting. Finally, it turns, a dull thud as the bars disengage. The door swings open and Kyle is out in a flash.

'Oh, my love.' He buries his face in my neck as I cling to him. I want to stay like this forever, but we need to keep moving. I take his hand, leading him past the cages, trying not to look at the faces watching me. Faces like mine, human. Yet I am here and they are there, a world between us. Something I'm going to change. But for now I need to get Kyle to safety. I pull him into the hallway, where the passage is still open. He blows out a breath.

'Genius.'

'C'mon.' I pull him through the opening with me. The

panel closes and we're together in the darkness. He lifts me off my feet, kissing me over and over. My hands are in his hair as I kiss him back, tasting salt and blood. My heart is breaking.

'Where do we go from here?' he says, once he can speak.

'We go up, to the library passage, then to my room. And you know there's a passage from there to the outside. Will you… are you going to be okay?'

'I think so.' His arms are still around me.

'Where will you go?' I ask between kisses.

'I have a place I can hide out for a while.' He runs his hand along my cheek. I sigh, curving into his touch even though my heart is snapping in two, tears leaking from my closed eyes. I can't stop touching him, because I know this is the last time.

'I'll come and find you, once I'm Raven, I promise.'

'One last kiss, before I go.' His lips touch mine and it feels as though I'm flying, his body curving around mine, his arms lifting me. I close my eyes, enjoying the sensation, as though I'm at the centre of a storm.

When we stop, we're still in darkness. He releases me. I can't see a thing.

'Kyle?'

'Emelia?'

Oh, thank darkness. But he doesn't come closer. I hear his voice again.

'Do you still trust me?'

'Yes.' Of course I do. It's *Kyle*. He loves me and I love him and—

A cool hand comes around my neck and I hear him sigh. 'Well, you shouldn't have.'

'Kyle.' My voice is strangled by his grip. It tightens, and everything goes black.

And my world shatters.

# Chapter Thirty-Three

## LOVE HURTS

I wake. Something heavy is pinning me down. I can't see anything.

'Where—'

A hand comes over my mouth. I realise the weight is Kyle, lying on me.

'Be quiet!' He whispers the words, close to my ear. 'We're under the pits. If anyone finds you—'

He doesn't need to say any more. I stiffen. The pits? Is he fucking insane? His hand leaves my mouth. I shift slightly and feel the hard vial of anti-feed spray in my pocket.

'Spray. Pocket.' I breathe the words, knowing he'll hear them. There's a faint sigh. Then his hand is in my pocket. I still don't understand what's happening. Is he taking me away with him? I hear a faint hiss, feel cool mist on my skin. Then I hear a cracking sound and the scent of violets becomes eye-wateringly strong. I realise he's broken the vial.

Revelation rolls over me like a wave, cold as ice, bitter as heartbreak. His hand closes around my throat again. Blackness descends. Fuck. I'm going to die here.

---

When I wake a second time I'm lying on something soft, cushions around me, smooth fabric beneath my hand. My throat aches and I want to rub it, but my arms are so heavy. There are voices, echoing at first, then resolving into words.

'So you'll keep your promise?'

*Kyle.*

The pain of his betrayal crashes over me, the horror of that moment in the darkness. I daren't move.

Another voice answers. 'Yes. You've brought me the key to my own happiness. It only seems fair you have yours as well.' Fuck. I'd recognise that elegant drawl anywhere. *Mistral.*

'Thank you.' Kyle sounds pleased. 'The rebellion seems to be going well.'

*What?*

'It certainly is, though it's almost out of my hands at this point. It's bigger than I ever imagined it could be.' Mistral laughs and I wish I could punch him in his stupid perfect face. 'I'll shut it down once I'm Raven, I suppose, but it's serving its purpose for now.'

*Serving its purpose? When he's Raven?*

Kyle snorts. 'You sure? Raven can't shut it down at the moment. What makes you think you'll be able to?'

'The fact that I don't care how many of them I have to kill to do it,' Mistral snarls. He laughs again, a short sound devoid of mirth. 'Who knew that humans still had so much fight in them?'

'I suppose any animal will fight, if cornered. And humans have been cornered for a long time.'

'If it were up to you I'm sure we'd all be living together, vamps and humans, like one big happy family.' The scorn is evident in Mistral's voice.

'Would that be so bad?'

'They're food, Kyle. Blind, foolish cattle. How anyone can think otherwise—'

'Yet here we are, with a full-blown rebellion on our hands. Tell me, did you think the seeds you planted would grow so strong?'

There's a pause. Tension crackles through the room. I don't want them to know I'm awake, but it's tough when I want to scream. I cannot fucking believe what I'm hearing. *Mistral* is behind the North Wind?

Kyle speaks again. 'What are you going to do with her?'

*With me?*

'I need you to keep her with you for now, but don't hurt her. It's taken you long enough to get her to me, for darkness' sake. Third time lucky, I suppose.'

*Third time?* And it hits me. When Kyle took me to the waterfall, he must have been testing whether or not he could take me somewhere else without me protesting too much. I'd not only gone along with it, I'd begged him to do it again. First to the Moon Harvest, then running away with

314

him. All the while thinking he loved me. My fingernails dig into the palms of my hands.

'She's well-guarded. And your rebels got in my way, if you remember.' Kyle sounds irritated.

But he also offered me a night. Would have given it to me, as well, if Raven hadn't shown up when they did.

Mistral snarls. 'Aren't you one of my rebels? Remember who you're working for.'

I'm reeling. Kyle is a rebel. I remember our conversation at the waterfall, how he'd tried to tell me what humans wanted.

'I'm only working with you because you can give me what I want.'

'Oh I know.' Mistral laughs again, a dry sound, no humour in it. 'Just remember – I got you out of the pits. I can put you back there.'

'But you won't.' Kyle's voice is hard.

'No, I won't. You've delivered the girl and I'll honour my bargain.' He's silent for a moment. 'Honestly, these damn human throwbacks! Abominations, each and every one of them! Once I have her mother, maybe I'll kill her myself. After all, Penelope and I will create the most wonderful children. She'll have no need of this one once I'm lord of Raven.'

*What. The. Actual. Fuck?*

Mistral must be out of his mind. Lord of Raven? He can fuck right off. What about my father? I remember the bomb in the ballroom, the way Mistral had stepped in so neatly, ripping apart the blood dancer to protect his lord... or protect himself, more likely, so that his plans wouldn't be revealed. Shit. I don't care what he thinks, he'll never have Mother, not in a million years. There's no way she'd let him kill me. I mean, I know I'm human and weak, but I also know she loves me. Unlike Kyle. At that thought there's pain, like a crack across my mind, as though I'm a shield holding all the pieces of me together.

'This hasn't been easy, you know.'

Oh, I'm so sorry, *Kyle*, that betraying me has been so hard on you. If I wasn't trying to keep still, I'd roll my eyes.

'I'm sure. If the bomber had done his job properly, we wouldn't have had to go to quite these extremes. You could have ended it much earlier.'

'So, once you're in power, I can change her?'

*Change me?*

Kyle knows I can't be changed. Maybe he *had* to knock me out, to trick Mistral that he's on his side, but really he still loves me, and we'll be together. Maybe he's just pretending, to protect me, and he'll take me back to my parents. Maybe I'm clutching at straws.

'Yes, yes.' Mistral sounds even more irritated. 'You can change her now, for all I care. A fighter from the pits and his little dancing girl. A love story for the ages, I'm sure.' He snorts.

'I'll take Emelia to the safe house, then.'

A safe house. My heart lifts. Oh, thank darkness. He's going to keep me safe, after all. I'm still puzzling about why he thinks he can change me, though. And why is Mistral calling me a dancing girl?

'Keep her there until the trap is sprung. I can't keep her here, as much as I'd like to – too obvious, really.'

The trap? I strain to hear more, but one of the cushions by my legs falls away. There's a soft thud as it hits the floor.

I feel a rush of cool air. I daren't open my eyes, and stay as still as I can. But my heart is racing. I'm in a room with at least two predators, both of whom will be able to tell I'm faking unconsciousness. Fabric covers my mouth, an acrid scent in my nostrils. And I'm gone once more.

## Chapter Thirty-Four

### THE FINAL BLOW

I wake again, lying face-down on a carpet. It's grey with dust, and it smells. I roll onto my side, coughing, my throat feeling bruised inside and out.

'We've woken up, have we, my lady?'

The words are scornful, the voice oddly familiar. I look up to see a girl standing over me. She's slender, wearing baggy trousers and a cropped T-shirt, her dark hair pulled back messily from her face. A scar snakes up from the neck of her T-shirt. I recognise her. It's the blood dancer from the bar, the one who threatened me. Kyle's ex. What the hell is she doing here?

I push myself into a sitting position, hugging my knees. 'Where am I? Tell me.'

'I give the orders here, Raven. Not you.'

'Here' appears to be a bedroom. Quite a big room, the windows covered with long wooden shutters. There's a large bed against one wall, a dusty small table either side holding guttering candles, melted wax spilling in rivulets. There are holes in the bedspread, the fabric stained. A faded photograph hanging on one wall shows a family – two parents, two children. This girl is none of them.

But she is human. Which means that, as far as getting out of here goes, she and I are equals. I wonder where Kyle is, and when he's going to arrive, though I've no idea what time it is, whether it's day or night. I'm also not sure what's going on, but I'm still clinging to the hope I had at Mistral's, that Kyle was faking and he'll keep me safe, that he still loves me. The presence of his ex is making the fantasy harder to maintain, though.

I scoot back to the wall, using it to push myself to my feet. 'Fuck you.'

She smirks. 'Really? Is that what you think is going to happen?'

Bitch. I straighten my shoulders. 'I wouldn't touch you with a ten-foot pole.'

Her grin gets wider. 'Too bad your boyfriend doesn't feel the same way. Kyle!'

He comes through the door, locking it behind him, slipping the keys in his jacket pocket. He's beautiful as always, clad in black denim and leather, his satin dark hair brushed back.

'Kyle!' My heart leaps. I just know he still loves me, even if he is working for Mistral. This is all some weird misunderstanding, a plot to expose Mistral and his stupid rebellion. Kyle *had* to do what he did, to keep me safe, so he can get me back home and we can tell my parents. I reach for him.

But, to my horror, he ignores me, going to his ex and sweeping her into his arms. She turns her head, smirking at me, her arms around his neck. He bends his head to kiss her.

And my heart breaks.

Just snaps.

I remember him in a blue room, telling me about the rules that prohibit humans and vampires from being together. I'd thought he meant us. Shock rolls over me, cold and dark, along with the realisation that he didn't. The fantasy that he still loves me, that he'll keep me safe, dissipates like morning mist, leaving cold agony in its wake. He wasn't talking about me. He was talking about his dancing girl.

Oh god. Pain is everywhere. I control it, tamping it down into a ball, hot and heavy inside me, not wanting to give them the satisfaction of seeing how hurt I am. I fold my arms and look away. There's a whoosh of air and Kyle is in front of me.

'I'm sorry, Emelia.' I swear I see a flash of pity in his eyes.

'Yeah. I bet you are.'

'You have to understand – we had no choice—'

'I don't understand *anything* about this.' I bare my teeth at him.

'Why would you?' The girl comes closer. 'You have no idea how things really are for us out here.'

'Jessie, leave it.' *So that's her name.*

'Oh, yes,' she goes on, avid eyes shining, 'poor little Raven, all alone in her tower. No wonder you fell for the first one to show you any affection.'

My gaze moves to Kyle. He meets it, silver eyes bright, one hand rubbing the back of his neck. A tear escapes, warm on my cheek. 'Why?'

'Because I had to,' says Kyle. 'There was no other way, believe me, to get what I want.'

'I thought I was what you wanted.' It's taking everything I have to stay so calm, to speak this way. I feel as though I'm having an out-of-body experience. This cannot be happening.

Kyle looks down.

'You... you looked after me. You told me you loved me, that we would have a life together. You saved me from the Reaper gang, at the waterfall.' My voice cracks, like my heart.

'Did I save you?' One corner of Kyle's mouth tugs up. 'Or did I call them? When I left you alone for a moment? What better way to gain your trust than by saving your life?'

My mouth drops open. Cold ripples through me. 'Y-you... how would you...?'

'You never asked me, did you, why I was in the pits. Not that I would have told you. That's where they send the Reaper gangs, if they catch them.' Pain flickers across his face. 'To die.'

'You're a Reaper?' I curse my own stupidity, that I've

been so dazzled, thinking him some champion of the pits, feeling sorry for him.

'I was. The last of my gang, when Mistral found me.'

'Mistral.'

Kyle nods. 'Do you really think your parents would have hired me to watch you, their most precious daughter, without his recommendation? Too easy, really.'

'Why?' My voice rises. 'Why would he do this? He's family!'

'It doesn't matter why.' Kyle's expression shuts down.

'It does to me! He's behind the fucking North Wind! My father almost died! When I tell them—'

'When you tell who, Emelia?' Kyle shouts at me, his fangs bared. 'You're not going to ruin this for us, and you're not going to tell anyone anything. When Mistral is with your mother, he'll see to that.' He snarls at me, and I shrink away, my heart broken.

'Kyle, enough.' Jessie pulls him from me, stroking him as though she's soothing him, their heads close together. It's too much. I turn away, heading for the window. Maybe I can throw myself out of it.

'Not so fast, my lady.' Kyle's arms come around me. I struggle, screaming, not wanting him to touch me while at the same time in agony that he never will again. He turns me to face him, his hands tight on my shoulders.

'Be quiet!'

'Fuck you!'

He slaps me, hard, my head snapping to the side. I stop screaming, my cheek stinging.

'I don't want to hurt you.'

'Too late for that,' I snarl.

'I'm sorry—' he says. I stare at him in disbelief.

'Kyle.' Jessie sounds worried, which is weird.

'—but I'll do what it takes to keep you quiet. Are you going to be quiet?'

If he wants me to be quiet, that must mean there are people nearby. People who can help me. I scream again. Kyle grabs my throat and squeezes. Black spots form in front of my eyes. Jessie protests, telling him he's squeezing too hard. Kyle says he's not going to hurt me, that I'm just harder to knock out than most people.

'Time to sleep again, my lady.' Scorn colours his words.

And I'm gone.

# Chapter Thirty-Five

## INTO THE LIGHT

'I don't like this.'

I blink. I'm still lying on the carpet. My eyes feel full of grit, my cheek sore where Kyle slapped me. But not as sore as my heart.

'I don't like it either. But it's the only way, Jess.' Kyle. I remember when the tenderness in his tone was directed towards me. 'We have to keep going, for your family, for us. For what we believe in. Mistral promised, he promised that at the end of this we'd be free, that your brother would get his treatment.'

'It doesn't seem right.' Huh. That's a surprise, seeing what a complete bitch Jessie's been. I keep my eyes closed and try not to move. I want to hear this. 'What's he going to do to her?'

'Mistral? I don't know. I mean, he says he wants to kill her, but there's no way he can, not if he wants her mother to be with him. She dotes on her.'

But he will kill me. He doesn't care. All he wants is to be Lord of Raven. It's so clear to me now. As is the fact that Kyle, despite what he says, is no rebel. He's just a Reaper vamp with a human girlfriend, making a deal with the devil. After all, why would any vampire support a human rebellion? Why would they want things to change?

'What? I mean, I kind of hate her for being with you, plus she's a fucking Raven, but really, she's just a kid—'

'I know.' Kyle sounds sad. 'I know. But there's no other way. I really don't think he'll hurt her. He'll probably just shut her away again.'

Screw that. There's no way anyone is putting me back in my cage.

'It doesn't seem fair.'

'I know. I hated deceiving her. She's more than I'd expected her to be.' Another surprise. It doesn't change anything, though. A tear slides down the side of my face. I hear rustling noises. Jessie speaks again.

'I wonder why they didn't change her.'

'They tried. But she's immune. She may be human, but she has vampire blood.'

'Really?' Jessie sounds intrigued. 'I didn't even know vamps could have human kids, you know? Not until we found out about her.'

Yeah. Emelia Raven. The big fucking secret. When I become Raven, one of the first things I'm going to do is tackle the stigma surrounding us. Well, me, I guess. I suppose I'm the only one. But then, how would I know?

'Vamps aren't so different from us, really.' Jessie sounds reflective. 'So why do they treat us like they do?'

'You know why.'

'Because of our blood.' Jessie's voice is teary. 'That's all we are to them. And my brother—' her voice breaks '—is going to die because of it.'

Oh. That's sad. I remind myself what a bitch she is. And the fact that she's basically condemned me to death. Actually, you know what? Fuck her. I'm sorry for her brother, but that's as far as it goes.

'That's why we're doing this, why we *have* to do this. So he won't.' Kyle sounds fierce.

'I don't know why we have to look after her. What if her family tracks her down? This whole thing is such a mess.'

*Yes, Jessie. It is. A big fucking mess. Just like you'll be, when my family catches up to you.*

Kyle speaks again. 'You know Ruth told me not to hand her over? She refused to help me, once she figured out who she was.'

'Maybe you should have listened to her.'

Wait, *Ruth* knew who I was? It's becoming more and more apparent how little I know about anything. I hate myself for being so naïve. But what else could I be, brought up in darkness and solitude, surrounded by guards, watching old films and reading books? I feel sorry for the girl I was, who knew so little. She's gone, now.

There's silence, then more rustling, a creaking noise. 'You cared for her, didn't you? I could tell. I hated seeing you together.'

More silence. I hold my breath. Whatever Kyle says, it's going to hurt. I hear him sigh. 'I didn't know you'd be at the bar, the night of the Moon Harvest. I thought you were going to meet me afterwards, when I took her to Mistral—'

'But of course you had to run into Ira! Mistral was raging, you know.' Jessie is sobbing. 'I tell you, Kyle, he'd better keep his word.'

Ira? I remember the strange delivery of wine. And realise what he was trying to do. He must have suspected Kyle; I remember his insistence that Kyle take me home, how annoyed Kyle had seemed. And Ira, dear Ira, had let him know he'd be checking I made it back there. Sadness at Ira's kindness, at the thought I probably won't ever get to thank him, washes over me.

'Well, he's already come through with one thing.'

There's more rustling, a soft sigh. 'He has?'

'Yes. I can change you. Finally. We can be together and protect your family, get them out of the Safe Zone.'

'Oh.' It's just a small word, a sound, really. But there's yearning in it, a deep sighing sorrow. I almost feel sorry for her again. Almost. But the fact they both feel bad doesn't change the fact that they're going to hand me over to Mistral.

The sounds in the room change to creaking and sighs. My moment of sympathy passes, replaced by surging anger as Jessie's moans become more rhythmic, the bed squeaking. I squeeze my eyes shut, trying to block out the memory of Kyle's mouth on my body, how it felt when he ran his hands through my hair, across my skin…

I grimace, trying not to cry out.

Asshole. *Assholes.*

There's a snapping sound and Jessie gasps, high-pitched. Is he…? Would he *dare*, while I'm right fucking *here*? I gasp, too, as though the breath has been punched from me.

He's changing her.

I hear lapping noises, her moans muffled as she sucks from him, the choked groans he makes. I start to cry, then.

For my mother, my father, for the disappointment I am, endangering them all. I cry for love, gone from me forever. Because this is it. I'm fucked. This is how it's going to end for me, here, in this shitty room. I think about home, the costumes waiting in the darkness, the robes I'm never going to wear. The last fucking Raven – at least, until my parents have another child.

Something occurs to me, cutting through my agony. If he turns Jessie, she'll be out of it for the next little while. Meaning it will be just me and Kyle, alone here. I shrink into myself, wondering what he's going to do to me.

Then it's as though someone shakes me. A tendril of fire starts low in my stomach. I *am* Raven, and Ravens don't give up easily. While there's breath, there's life, right? And I'm still breathing.

I open one eye. They're both naked on the bed, their bodies twined together, Jessie's mouth a red stain against Kyle's neck, his head back, eyes closed in ecstasy as he drinks from her wrist. I scan the room for something, anything I can use to fight my way out of here.

Then I realise something. I shouldn't be able to see them. The candles have burned down to nothing, and the room should be in darkness. I turn my head, ever so slightly. But I could probably have done a dance. They're oblivious to me. And I see light around the old shutters, a thin line of gold.

I tuck my legs under me, sliding up the wall to standing. I keep my eyes on them the whole time, no matter how it hurts to see them locked together. I run my hand along the shutters, feeling for the catch. It's locked.

But the key is in the lock.

I turn it. It clicks.

Kyle snarls. 'Emelia!'

Fuck him. The catch is stuck, but I work at it. Kyle tries to extricate himself from Jessie, but the blood magic has taken hold and she's stiffening, her limbs wrapped around him.

'Emelia, stop!' His face is distorted, angry, yet he's still beautiful, his muscles shadowed perfection. I swallow. But I know what I have to do. It's the only way I'll get out of here.

His voice changes, to how it used to be when he spoke to me. 'Please, Emelia – don't.' He manages to untangle himself. But it's too late. For him, for us, for everything. I step aside, and the shutters come open.

Sunrise.

Light, golden and terrible, pours in, catching Kyle in its blaze. And he burns. Oh, it's horrible. His skin blisters, great red bumps appearing where the light touches him. He screams, writhing in agony on the dusty carpet. Jessie is whimpering, but I can't take my eyes from Kyle. His black hair crinkles and shrinks, his body curling and cracking as the ligaments catch and burn. The last thing to go are his eyes, silver in his blackened face, staring at me.

Then he's gone.

# Chapter Thirty-Six

## SOMETIMES, THERE REALLY ARE MONSTERS IN THE WOODS

All that's left is a pile of black ash.

I hang onto the windowsill, sobbing great gulping sobs. Jessie stares at me, her eyes the only part of her that seem alive. She's terrified; I can see it, the way her gaze swivels, the whites of her eyes. She's also frozen, the blood in her, Kyle's blood, taking over. She can fucking stay that way, as far as I'm concerned.

Screw her.

If the blood magic takes over completely before nightfall, she'll burn. If it doesn't, well, she might live, if the Raven guards don't find her. I imagine they've been tracking me all night, anyway. But I need to get out of here.

I push myself away from the window. Kyle's jacket hangs over a chair and I put it on, rummaging in the pockets. There's pain, for a second, as I touch the smooth leather, remembering how it felt on him. I pull the keys out, flipping Jessie my middle finger as I unlock the bedroom door.

Downstairs there's a long hallway, the coloured tiled floor now dull, remnants of stained glass around a wooden front door. The door is locked from the inside. I fumble with the keys until I find one that fits. The door opens with a cracking sound, dust motes dancing in the bright cold air. I step outside onto a small brick porch, pulling the door closed. The street is deserted, but I stay in the shadow of the porch, conscious of being alone, in a strange place, with no idea where home is from here. My legs shake, my breath uneven, but I have to keep moving. I force myself to take a step. Then another, until I reach the small front gate.

The house I'm in is part of a terrace stretching in an unbroken line down the hill towards a distant smudge of blue. I realise it's the sea. The houses look bright, their faded colours lit by the rising sun, like a piece of the past come to life.

Rust flakes under my hand as I push the gate open, the hinges protesting. I start down the hill, my eyes creased against the light, wishing I had the dark glasses Ruth lent me. It's cold, frost silvering the low garden walls. I zip my jacket and pick up the pace, wanting distance between me and the house where I left Jessie. And Kyle.

When I close my eyes I see him, his silver eyes staring at me as he burned.

Perhaps, if I head towards the water, I'll be able to orient myself. If this is the Safe Zone, I can work my way back to Ruth's house, maybe ask her for help. It's not much of a plan, but it's something. I try not to consider the possibility that I'm somewhere else, much further from home.

As I near the water the houses become larger, some with ornate carved wooden porches. On the corner of a side street are several shops, most of them still closed. One, however, has the shutter raised, the scent of fresh bread floating on the air. I realise I'm ravenous. I check my pockets, and Kyle's jacket, but I have nothing. I unzip the jacket, feeling in the neck of my shirt. My Raven necklace is gone, and there's a moment of sorrow for its loss. But I'm still wearing a silver chain. I pull it over my head, untangling it from my hair.

The glass door to the bakery is locked. There's someone inside, moving around in golden light, wiping their hands on their apron. They look up when I knock, coming out from behind the counter to the door. It's a woman, her hair tucked under a white cap, her brown apron sprinkled with flour and tied tight around her ample waist. Her mouth is pursed tight, a line between her eyebrows. She twists the lock and the door comes ajar.

'Yes?'

'Please.' I hold out the silver chain. 'I'm so hungry. This is all I have—'

'I can't let you in.'

'I don't want to come in. I just need food. Some bread, anything. Please, take this. It's silver.'

'How do I know that?'

'Er, I don't know.'

The door opens further. Her hand comes out. 'Give it to me.'

I drop the chain in her hand and the door closes. The woman examines the chain, running the links through her fingers, squinting at the clasp, then goes behind the counter and takes a fresh loaf from the shelf. She hesitates, looking back at me. I smile, trying to seem as though this is something I do all the time. She reaches for another loaf, this one speckled dark with fruit, and puts it in a bag. Dropping the chain in her pocket, she comes back to the door. She unlocks it again and thrusts the bag out.

'Here.'

'Thank you, thanks so much. Can you tell me where—'

The woman closes the door, locking it, and goes back to her work, ignoring me. I stand there a moment longer. Huh.

The bag in my hands is warm and smells amazing, yeast and fruit and spice. I uncurl the paper top, pulling out a handful of fruit loaf, jamming it in my mouth, my eyes closing as I chew. It's the most delicious thing I've ever eaten.

I start walking, pulling more bread from the bag and eating it as I head towards the ocean. At the end of the road I stop, looking both ways. Oh, thank darkness, I'm in the Safe Zone. There are the blue painted railings, the squat brown towers guarding the shoreline, the large wedding cake hotel I saw on my first visit. I sigh with relief.

I turn right, heading past the big hotel, trailing my hand along the ornate railings. Ahead is the small café where Ruth and I had lunch. It's closed, the striped awning rolled up, blinds covering the windows. Along the seashore people are walking, some hand-in-hand, some with dogs who gambol through the waves, racing for thrown sticks. It's beautiful and peaceful, and makes me sad. I cross the street where the harvesting plant is, a metal square looming against the sky. My mind whirls with tiredness and sorrow. I could stay here, I suppose, and beg to borrow someone's phone. But no one will be able to come and get me until nightfall, and I don't want to take the chance that Mistral might get to me first. It's better to keep moving while I can, during the daylight, and hope to make it home.

I pass a row of shops, some shuttered, some empty, and reach a road leading uphill. I take it, hoping for the best. And I'm rewarded. There's Geneva's clothing shop – her window display has changed, jumpers in autumn colours interspersed with sparkly garlands and snowflakes. Next to it is the toy shop, little cars and worn books grouped together with more garlands, red bows and tags on them.

My eyes blur, the food in my mouth hard to swallow. I roll the top of the loaf bag tight, tucking it under my arm. The breeze is strong and cold, and carries the scent of ash. Tears streak my face, my hair blowing back. It reminds me of running with Kyle, how he would hold me close, my body curled against his.

*Don't think about Kyle.*

My breath hitches and I walk faster. The road rises, large buildings giving way to houses. I look for the turning leading to Ruth's house, the thought of the bed in her blue room comforting. But, as I near her house, my steps slow. I remember how well she seemed to know Kyle. How he said he'd known her for years. How, despite her kindness, she seemed to have other agendas. And the fact she knew who I was but said nothing. Even though she'd refused to hand me over to Mistral, what would stop her from doing so when I showed up alone, asking for help? I also remember Andrew's anger at my family. How would he react if I asked to call home? For I know when I do, a battalion of guards and probably my parents will descend upon their house once darkness falls. I'm not sure he'll welcome that.

All at once it feels as though eyes are everywhere. A bang makes me jump, but it's only the sound of someone closing their front door, a man in a dark suit. He nods to me and I nod back, my breath coming fast. I need to go home. Even if I can just reach Dark Haven by nightfall, Ira at least knows who I am, and I'm sure he'll help me.

I take in a deep breath and blow it out, feeling better. I've passed Ruth's house, the streets giving way to overgrown scrubland, bits of litter caught in bare brambles and trodden into the mud. Beyond the scrubland is a small copse of trees, then the light towers, their metal frames gilded by sunlight. Okay. If I'm in the right place, I should come out by the guard huts, and from there be able to pick up the road towards Dark Haven.

Fuck. The guard huts. I need to go that way, but I also need to avoid being seen, especially if it's the same guards. I start to panic, remembering how it had felt to be treated like meat, the pain of the guard drinking from me.

Hang on a second.

It's daylight. Even if they can see me, they can't exactly do anything.

I start across the scrubland, stumbling on the frozen mud. I'm cold and thirsty, but it's bearable. There's a path trodden in the grass and I take it, winding between huge mounds of brambles, densely woven and thorned like something from a fairy tale. I eat more bread, then wish I hadn't, the doughy mass sticking to the roof of my mouth. The path leads into the trees and I stay on it, reasoning that, if there's a path, it must be because people come this way. Tangled branches curve above me, painted green with moss and yellow with winter, a few dead leaves still clinging to them. It's peaceful and I relax a little more, proud of myself for getting this far. I can do this. I can make it home. And when I do, I'm going to apologise to my parents and—

'Where d'you think you're goin', sunshine?'

A man, dressed in clothing patterned with greens and browns, steps out from a tangle of trees, blocking my path. His hair and short beard are grey, his eyes blue, his cheeks pale above the beard. He's smiling, but he's also holding a gun.

Fuck.

# Chapter Thirty-Seven

## RAVEN CLAW

I'm such an idiot. Of *course* the Safe Zone borders would be manned during the day – otherwise, what would stop humans leaving? *The fact they have nowhere to go*, my mind whispers, recalling Ruth on the beach, looking out at the waves.

The man on the path moves closer. He's not smiling anymore, and has raised his gun.

'I asked you a question.'

'Er.' I swallow the last vestiges of bread, clearing my throat. 'Um, I'm going to… er… the Raven estate.'

There's a glimmer of silver on the man's jacket. As he comes closer, I see it's the Raven emblem. Oh, thank darkness.

'Oh, yes? What's your name?'

'Emelia Raven.' I smile, expecting him to do the same. *Of course* my parents would have sent word that I was gone. I'm sure all the guards will be looking for me.

There's no answering smile. Instead, he tugs on a small black box attached to the front of his jacket, bringing it to his mouth.

'We've got a live one here,' he says. My heart sinks. 'Thinks she's a vampire. Lady of Raven, no less.' He laughs. A moment later there's an answering squawk of noise. He speaks again, then lets go of the box, returning his attention to me.

'Right. You going to tell me who you really are?'

*I just did.* My mouth opens and closes. Why doesn't he believe me? *Because he doesn't know who you are*, my mind replies. Just like everyone else.

'Right then. Come with me.' He jerks his gun at me, then turns and starts along the path. I have no choice but to follow. If I try to run he'll shoot me. I can't help sniffing. I'm so fucking tired, my throat hurts and I'm desperately thirsty. The pain of Kyle's betrayal is held behind a dam in my mind. I cannot release it. If I do, I'll break.

We emerge from the trees, and there's the guard hut. It looks different in daylight, mostly because there's a large gun mounted on the flat roof. An open-topped vehicle is parked next to the hut, painted the same greens and browns as the clothes the guard is wearing, the Raven emblem silvered on the side door.

My captor comes to a halt. 'Right,' he says. 'You need to tell me who you really are. Or are you still going with the whole "lady of Raven" thing?' He snorts. 'That's a laugh, if I ever heard one. The only vampire who ever came out during the day.'

'But it's true,' I say. 'I *am* Emelia Raven. I'm just… human…' My voice trails off because I know how stupid it sounds. What had Jessie said, that she hadn't even known vamps could have children? If she didn't know, I doubt this guard would, either.

He walks around me, his gun still pointed at me. 'Tell you what, I bet you're a blood dancer. Maybe got it on with one of our high lords and now have ideas above your station.'

'That's not true! I'm telling you, my family are expecting me.'

'Is that so?' He stops, putting his face close to mine. 'Because Bill says he's no mention of you on the pass list. And Ravens, as far as I know, are vampires. So tell me, pretty girl, who do you dance for? Maybe you'd like to entertain me. Or maybe,' his expression hardens and he raises his gun so it almost touches my chin, 'you're one of those rebels, trying to trick your way onto the estate.'

'I'm not,' I manage to say, trembling from head to toe. 'I swear it. You have to let me pass.'

'Oh? Who says?'

*Raven says.* I remember Kyle on our first night out together, holding a vampire by the neck. I grit my teeth. No. Not here. Not now. I push the pain of his loss back once more.

'That's enough!' Another voice rings out.

My captor tenses, glancing to the side. 'But sir—'

'Lower your weapon! That's an order!'

My captor's throat works visibly. He obeys, lowering his gun and stepping back from me, standing to attention.

'What's all this?' My rescuer is dressed similarly to the other guard, though he's also wearing a black beret with a flash of silver at the crest. He's taller than I am, with a brown beard and golden-brown eyes set in a reddish weathered face. 'Who are you?'

I clear my throat. 'Emelia Raven.' I try to sound like my mother, but it's hard when my voice is shaking. However, I stand straight, looking him in the eye.

His eyes narrow, then he turns his attention to the other guard. 'Is there a reason for detaining her?'

'Sir! She is not on the list, sir.'

'So you decided to stick your gun in her face? You know how this works. That list is never fucking up-to-date, anyway.'

The other guard's jaw clenches. He salutes. 'Sir!'

'Right, young lady.' He turns his attention to me. 'Where are you going?'

'To the Raven estate. Er, sir.'

'Who's meeting you?'

'Meeting me?' I shake my head. 'I told you, I'm Emelia Raven. Surely my family have put the order out, that I'm missing? I just need to get home.'

He presses his lips together, frowning. 'Raven don't share their concerns with us.' He folds his arms, considering me, then sighs. He jerks his head towards his vehicle. 'Hop in. I'll take you as far as the town. I have business that way.'

'Oh, thank you.' Relief floods through me. I run to the vehicle, opening the door and sliding into the front passenger seat. My rescuer gets in as well, pulling the side door shut and starting the engine. The other guard still stands to attention as we pull away. I resist the urge to give him the finger, huddling in my seat instead, thanking my lucky stars to be in a car rather than on foot. I'd have been lucky to make it to Dark Haven by nightfall, the short winter days working against me. I'd have done my best, though, because there's no way I'm going back. Not to the girl I was. Not to the dusty room where Jessie is waiting to change, where ash blows in the breeze. Nor to Mistral, and whatever he had planned. I'm going home. And when I get there, I am going to be the next Raven.

The road curves through dense forest, a mix of evergreens and bare branches on either side of us. In some places they meet overhead, like we're in a tunnel. The wind whips through my hair and I scrape it off my face.

'This was all farmland once,' says my driver, shouting over the noise of the road.

'Really?' I blink, peering through the tangle of trees. There are darker shapes back there, humped buildings, a flash of red brick. I wonder whether anyone ever goes back to them.

'Yes, so my father told me. There are houses in there, too, you know. Whole villages swallowed up. And other things. You'd know that, I guess, if you are who you are.'

But I don't know. The Rising is a proud part of my people's history. I'd never considered how much had been lost.

'You still don't believe me?'

My driver glances at me. 'About who you are?' He shakes his head, half-smiling. 'Well, you seem pretty convinced.'

'My parents really haven't alerted the guards that I'm missing?' I find this hard to believe.

His smile slides away. 'They could have. But not us.'

Realisation dawns. Another shitty, shitty realisation. 'B-because you're…'

'Human.'

This is crazy – why the hell would my parents not have told all the Raven guards to look out for me? *Because their world is a world of night.* Another thing I want to change.

There's a bottle in the centre console, dark green with a narrow top, liquid sloshing in it. My mouth prickles with thirst.

'Please, can I have some of your drink?'

'What's that?' He leans closer to me and I notice a small red pin on his collar, a flower.

I shout louder. 'Your drink. Can I have some?'

'Help yourself,' he says, with a nod.

I do, relieved to find it's water. I drink too much at first, coughing so hard he takes a hand off the steering wheel and bangs me on the back. My bread is gone, lost at the guard hut, but the water is like cool heaven trickling down my throat.

'Thanks.' I pop the lid back on, replacing the bottle in the console.

We drive for a while longer, neither of us saying

anything. I relax, everything blurring slightly. The trees give way to houses, shuttered against the day, then businesses, shops and bars and cafés, all of them closed, the face of the town covered as though with a veil.

My rescuer pulls the vehicle to a halt next to the kerb, the engine grinding, gravel crunching. We're outside the Dome. Strange to be back here, where it all began.

'This is your stop,' he says.

There's so much I want to ask him. But all I say is, 'Thank you. So much. For everything.'

He smiles. 'You make sure you wait here. Ira, who owns this place—' he jabs a thumb towards the Dome '—well, he's pretty sympathetic to humans. Raven are often here. Don't go anywhere else, though – after nightfall it'll be suicide.'

I don't want to wait. I want to go home. By nightfall I'm sure the place will be crawling with Raven guards, but there's no guarantee they'll find me first.

I open the door and climb out. 'How far is it?'

'How far is what?' He's about to drive away.

'The estate. Raven.'

'Oh, not too far. Ten miles or so up the road.' He points. 'Just stay here, though.'

'Can you take me?'

'Sorry. I'm already late. Just do as I say and you'll be fine.' He raises his hand, gravel shrieking under the wheels as he drives away. I watch him go until I can no longer see him. Then all is silent.

I close my eyes, trying to banish the thought of being

here with Kyle, of how safe I'd felt in his arms, the magic and beauty of running with him under the stars. Pain waits, like a raw wound inside me. I push it down once more, though it's getting harder to hold back. I have no idea what time it is, the sun directly overhead. Ten miles, my rescuer said. I think I can make it. I have to make it.

But I'm so tired. My feet hurt, boots chafing my toes and heels, my neck is aching and I'm starving. It's all I can do to put one foot in front of the other. But I have to. I *have* to. If I can get to the gates, I can figure it out from there.

There's damage to a lot of the buildings in the town centre, shop fronts blown out and blackened, signage torn down. I pass the burned-out ice cream parlour, the North Wind graffiti still visible on the wall. A couple of small black flakes float past me as the wind lifts. To think it was Mistral, all along. I cannot *wait* to tell my father.

The thought spurs me on as I wind through the streets leading out of Dark Haven, past shuttered homes with manicured gardens, shining cars in some of the driveways. The comparison to the Safe Zone isn't lost on me. I realise, again, as I pass the last of the houses, that I need to do something about it. That I'm possibly the only one who can. I can't believe I considered leaving it all behind. And for what? *For who?* my mind whispers. I grit my teeth, pushing forward.

I'm back among trees once more, the road a smooth ribbon of asphalt. Of course it's well maintained. It's the approach to my house. Things I've taken for granted my whole life now appear in a new light, and I wonder at the injustice of it all as I stumble along the verge.

After a while I need to stop. I'm so tired, plus the water has gone through me and I need to pee. I step into the bushes and relieve myself, then sit beneath a large tree. My neck aches, my feet throbbing. I daren't take my boots off, though – I'll never get them back on again. I lean my head against the rough bark. My eyes close.

I wake with a start. Where the hell am I? I'm freezing cold, lying on my side in dead leaves. The shadows are long, and there's rustling among the trees. I push myself up to sitting, my hand to my head. It all comes back to me. Kyle, and the need to get home. Home. Oh shit. What time is it? It's dark beneath the trees, though not pitch-black. I get to my feet and push through the bushes to the road. It's lit by fading sun, tree shadows striping the tarmac, the sky turning to rose gold. Shitshitshit. The sun is starting to set.

I don't know how far I have to go, but I know I need to move, and quickly. I gather the last of my energy and start to run, tears cold on my cheeks, my muscles protesting as I force myself onwards. The road curves, then curves again. My chest feels banded in iron, but I keep going, fear driving me as the light fades. And there they are. The gates of home. I sob in earnest when I see the raven-topped pillars, the long curving drive. I stagger and stumble the last few yards, reaching for the ornate ironwork.

But the gates are locked. Fuck. Of course they are. I rattle them, but they barely move. Disappointment overwhelms me. I sink down, my legs folding beneath me. Wrapping my arms around the wrought iron, I rest my head, waiting. I only hope the guards realise who I am before they attack. The sky is a flaming bowl above me, the trees shading to purple. It's completely glorious, yet I feel nothing. It's as though everything is gone from me, drained by the night's events and the day's walk. I stare at the clouds, but see nothing. Gradually, my head droops, and I slip into a doze.

A hand grabs my arm, squeezing tight so I wake up. 'Ow!' My squeal becomes a scream as I'm yanked upwards, my shoulder twisting painfully.

'Human!' The guard on the other side of the gate snarls, his fingers digging into me.

'Emelia Raven,' I shout, my face pressed painfully into the scrolled iron. 'You have to let me in. Raven claw, blood, and stone.' The last bit is muffled, but all of a sudden my arm is released. There's a rattle of keys, then the gate moves and I collapse, sprawling across the gravel. Hands turn me over, and I hear the rapid thuds of vampires running towards me.

'My lady!' I recognise that voice. It's Bertrand. 'Get her to the house, now!' The last command is barked out. I'm gathered into strong arms, feel wind rush around me, hear the clank of the gates closing. I'm home.

## Chapter Thirty-Eight

### SANCTUARY

A few minutes later I'm lying on a sofa, a blanket tucked around me. My mother leans over me, blood tears in her onyx eyes. She strokes my hair, my face, murmuring soft words. It's tempting to give in to her caresses, to let tiredness take over, but I can't.

'Mother! Mistral—'

'Hush, lovely girl. You are safe now.'

'What about Mistral?'

My father. I turn my head to see him standing on the other side of the sofa. His voice is gentle, and I swear I see a tinge of blood in his eyes.

'Aleks, surely she can tell us later, when she's rested.'

'No, I need to tell you now.' I try to push myself up. My mother helps, sliding a pillow behind me. Her arms come around me and I lean on her smooth shoulder. My father comes closer, his arms folded.

'He… er…' My voice falters and I try not to cry. 'He

kidnapped me. Or, rather, he had someone, someone I trusted, someone I thought loved me—' I sob, unable to finish, ashamed at what I've put my parents through. My mother rubs my arm, kissing my brow. I wipe my eyes, taking a breath. 'Mistral is behind the rebellion. He's the North Wind.'

'What?' Both my parents cry out at the same time.

'He was going to kill me. He thinks he's going to be with Mother, make babies with her. He called me an abomination.'

My father turns away then smashes an ornate wooden box, crushing it, growling in fury.

'I'm so sorry,' I whisper, tears in my eyes. 'I'm so sorry.'

'But Aleks—' my mother is looking at my father '—he's on his way here…'

I stiffen. 'He what? No, no! You can't let him in, he's the one, he was the one who tried to kill you, Papa, you can't!' I struggle against my mother's arms. She's frozen, vampire still. My father comes over and kneels. His handsome face seems more lined than usual, his golden eyes gleaming. He takes something from his pocket and puts it on my lap. It's my Raven necklace.

'What… how did you—'

'It arrived last night. With a note.'

'A note?' My voice is hoarse.

My father nods. 'Asking for something, in return for your life.'

'Wh-what did they want?'

'Me.'

I can't speak, tears spilling down my face.

'I was to go to them tonight, to a meeting place. They would hand you over, and I was to go with them in return.'

'Papa, I—'

'I was getting ready to leave when they found you at the gates.'

'You were?'

His head tilts slightly, his mouth curving. 'Of course, dear one. How could I do any different, when your life was at stake?'

My mother gasps, her arms tightening convulsively. I can't stop crying. I reach for my father, pulling him to us, my mother's arms opening so we tangle together, a perfect shield of love as I weep.

When we come apart there's blood on both their faces, my mother dabbing her eyes with a lace handkerchief, then wiping my father's. He kisses her, then me, his lips cool and soft on my cheek.

'Come, my loves,' he says. 'We must get you safe before Mistral arrives.'

'What? You're still going to let him in?'

'Don't worry. I know what I'm doing.' He picks me up, my blanket trailing as he carries me from the room, my mother at his side. Two guards fall into step behind us as we speed through the corridors to the fortified rooms.

'Aleks, do you think this is necessary?' My mother is even more pale than usual.

'It is, beloved. I don't want him anywhere near either of you.' Father punches in the code and the magnetic locks disengage, the door swinging open. Inside, the fortified rooms look like any other room in the house, stone walls lined with polished wood the colour of flame, soft sofas resting on embroidered carpets. Against one wall is a four-poster bed piled with cushions and made up with white damask, illuminated by the soft glow of candle-lamps.

My mother pulls back the bedcovers and my father places me on the bed, tucking the blanket around me. He kisses me on the brow, then kisses my mother.

'Stay here. I'll be back soon.'

'But Father—'

'Don't worry, Emelia. Mistral will be very sorry he chose this path.' The lean lines of his face tighten, his eyes glittering. He goes to the door and opens it. 'Keep them safe,' I hear him tell the guards. The door closes, a dull thudding as the locks engage.

My mother sits next to me, leaning back on the pillows. I snuggle into her. She strokes my hair, her cool fingers soothing.

'Mama?'

'Yes?'

'I'm sorry.'

'For what?'

'For… everything. For leaving. For arguing with you. For not being… what I'm supposed to be.'

'Oh my darling girl.' She hugs me to her. I smell her comforting scent, violets mixed with spice. 'Do you want to talk?'

'Er, sort of. I mean, yes. You know about Kyle, don't you?'

'That you had feelings for him? I'd guessed.'

I swallow. 'Yeah, that. Well, he's dead. I killed him.'

And it all pours out of me. The betrayal, my ordeal at Kyle's hands, Mistral, even the border guards. And more. The Safe Zone and what I'd seen there, how I'd felt. My mother holds me as waves of sorrow crash through me, my tears marking the silk of her gown, her own tears mingling in spots of red, bright on the white bedding.

Once I'm spent, there's silence. It wraps around us, soft as the blanket covering my legs, comforting as my mother's embrace. We lie there together, mother and daughter, heart to heart, awaiting my father's return.

# Chapter Thirty-Nine

## A PLACE TO START

'Are you sure?'

'I'll be fine, honestly.' I smile, but my mother's brow creases, her hands twisting together. Then I get it. 'I'm not going anywhere. Just to the library, that's all. I don't know why I can't watch, anyway.'

'You know your father doesn't want you anywhere near Mistral.'

I'm still in the fortified rooms, my parents not wanting to take any chances with my safety until Mistral was dealt with. My father had met him when he'd arrived at the house two nights ago, a cordon of guards taking hold of him the minute he'd crossed the threshold. He'd struggled, of course, but when my father told him what he knew, that his plans had been exposed, he gave in. He hadn't even known I'd escaped.

Now the house is full of high-ranking vampires, Raven affiliates from everywhere travelling in for the trial. It hadn't taken long – once word got out that Mistral had been behind the North Wind, the other Raven families turned on him. He's being held in one of the basement cells, awaiting his execution. Which I really, really want to watch.

But Father has forbidden it, despite my insistence that I need to see Mistral gone. He says the threat isn't over. The seeds Mistral planted have grown into fully-fledged rebellion, disturbances still being reported throughout the realm.

'So can I go? Bertrand can take me.' My mother's mouth twists. I know she won't deny me for long. 'Pleeeaase?'

'Fine.' She sighs out the word. 'But take another guard too. And lock the door. And—'

'Mama.' I hug her. 'I'll be fine. The house is crawling with guards. If I'm not safe here, where will I be? I'm sorry I left, more than I can ever say. I won't do anything to worry you like that again, I promise.'

Her cool hands cup my face. 'You'd better not,' she says. 'Now go. I'll come to you when it's over.'

'Okay.' I kiss her, her cheek smooth and firm. 'I'll see you then.'

My mother told me how Mistral had done it, what he'd initially promised the humans to convince them to work with him. Apparently, he'd told them that, once he'd taken over as head of Raven, he would set up a new Safe Zone. One where humans could be free, rather than tied to our blood machines and factories. Where they could bring up their children in peace. Where they would have a future. All lies, of course. I think I cried the most when she told me that.

I can see, though, how they would have gone for it. Taken any chance for things to change. For them to have a future beyond being farmed, beyond watching their children suffer the same fate. The world is a big place, yet we've taken that freedom from them. No wonder they want it back. And Mistral can be charming, when he wants to be. When there's something he wants. But his charm won't help him now.

Because it's time. I don't care what my father says. I need to watch Mistral burn, the same way Kyle did. And I'm the only one in the house who can. I go to the door and punch the code into the keypad. It opens. There are several guards outside, including Bertrand. They all turn to look at me. I run my hand through my hair, putting my shoulders back. 'I'd like to go to the library.'

'My lady.' Bertrand signals to another guard, and together they escort me through the corridors until we reach the carved wooden doors. The other guard opens the door, while Bertrand flashes around the room. He comes back to me. 'All is well, my lady.'

I told Bertrand what happened, though not all of it. I asked him about the Safe Zone, too, and what he thought of humans. His response surprised me. Apparently, until I was born, he hadn't thought of humans as anything but food. Now he feels that, if anyone can change things, it'll be me.

I smile. 'Thank you. I'm going to put the light on. Mother said I should lock the door, too.'

'I'll set guards outside. You understand, I cannot stay, I have to attend—'

I nod. 'It's fine. I'll see you afterwards.'

He bows and leaves, closing and locking the doors. I'm alone. Through the long windows I see the moon, a curving silver gleam hanging low in the sky. I feel strange, vulnerable while at the same time cocooned, the house like a blanket around me, the guards a shield, and me a soft raw thing in the middle. The carpet is soft under my bare feet as I wander over to the bookcase. I pull *Interview with the Vampire* from the shelf. My mouth twists. I take a deep breath, blowing it out my nose. I need to do this. I reach for the metal lever, pulling it. There's a rush of cold air.

Taking a blanket from the sofa, I start up the staircase to the roof.

---

It's cold, the night clear, dawn not yet visible on the horizon. Frost lines the crenellated edges, the ornate chimneys, bites at my bare feet. I hug the blanket as I get my bearings, hearing muffled voices from below. I start across the roof and, as I do, catch my foot on something. The small candle globe Kyle brought up when we were here. It's cold and dead, half filled with water, fragments of old leaves clinging to the glass.

I grit my teeth, blinking, hugging the blanket around me as I near the low wall that borders the roof. I don't bother to hide. No one will be looking up here. I don't care if they are, anyway. I am Raven, and this is my home. I hold onto that thought, pushing the others away.

I peer over the edge, my hands gripping the cold stone. Mistral is directly below. They're fixing the last of the restraints around his arms and legs. The metal chair in which he sits is spiked and cruel, his blood already pooling on the frosted grass. His golden hair gleams, silvered by the last pale moonlight. He isn't struggling, which surprises me.

I want him to see me.

Asshole.

I try not to think of Kyle.

My parents are down there, as is Artos Ravenna and several other Raven nobles, all of them standing in a loose semi-circle. Bertrand steps out of the shadows, holding a metal ring with spikes on the inside. I hold my breath. He puts the ring around Mistral's neck, pulling it tight. I hear Mistral groan.

Good.

The shadows are changing from black to purple, a golden tinge to the blue-frosted lawn. The moon is gone. My mother steps forward.

'For your crimes, Mistral, you are sentenced to go into the light. Raven claw, blood, and stone. So be it.'

'So be it,' the others intone. Light is glinting off the metal chair. There's a hiss, and everyone is gone. Mistral is alone, exposed. Just like I was. And the sun is about to rise.

With a rattling clang, the shutters begin to fall. Mistral writhes, straining against the metal and spikes. But he's too weakened by blood loss, the chair at the centre of a spreading red stain, like a poppy on a field of frosted white. His head tilts back, his eyes open wide. He sees me.

I do nothing, except watch.

His teeth clench, his clothing starting to smoke. There's red on his skin. The sun gets brighter, rays cutting through the morning haze. I can't feel my feet, my fingers cramped and stiff as I hang onto the stone.

There's a whoosh, and Mistral catches fire. He screams, still staring at me as flames rage across his body and out over the grass, igniting the rivulets of blood. His body twists and blackens, his back arching, blue eyes open wide.

Then he's gone.

Black ash drifts with the dawn.

I uncurl my fingers and stumble away from the roof edge, climbing through the trapdoor and down the stairs. There's a hard hot ball of something choking me. I swallow it down.

I emerge from the passage, closing the bookcase, and rub my hands together, stamping my feet to thaw them out. I go to the row of cupboards beneath the bookcases, opening the first two doors. Inside are old exercise books, piles of them. I guess they're mine, but they're not what I'm looking for. I open the next two, and there they are. Children's books. Stacked on the shelves, their colours still bright. Some of them I've read only once. I pull them out, pile after pile, until the cupboard is empty, then sit in the midst of them.

I pick up the book nearest to me. The cover shows a woman and a little girl, the pair of them holding a white kitten, illustrated beautifully against a moonlit sky. It's in pretty good condition and I put it to one side. Then I pick up the next one. It has a picture of a princess on the cover in a pink-frilled dress, her brown hair topped with a golden crown. My fingers run over the flat painted frills and I think of the little girl, of the joy she found in a second-hand book, her soft rosy cheeks and the way she'd hugged me.

And I break.

I cry and cry, tears hot on my face, falling onto the cover of the book. I hear the door creak, but I don't care. Let them deal with it, for once. I'm human, and humans cry warm tears of salt and silver, not blood and onyx. Footsteps come in, then retreat. I cry it all out. Kyle, the little girl, the people I'd met in the Safe Zone, the blood dancers, the Moon Harvest, the caged humans at the bar, my sheltered existence, everything in my life. I roll onto my back, the book hugged to my chest, tears running into my ears. As I cry an idea forms. I know what I need to do.

There's a knock at the door. I sit up, putting the book to one side and wiping my face.

'Come in.'

It's my mother. Her red velvet gown shimmers in the glow from the candle-lamps. 'How are you feeling?' She sits on the floor next to me, her skirts settling like the centre of a rose, her lovely face creased with worry.

'I'm fine. I feel fine. I mean, physically. The other stuff…' I look down. 'That might take a while.'

'I'm so sorry,' she says. 'We should have checked him more carefully. But we were so pleased to see you happy.'

'I need to ask you something.'

'Of course.' My mother becomes still. I reach for her hand, playing with her alabaster fingers, the silky-smooth skin reminding me of my childhood. I take a breath, then I say it.

'I want to live in the Safe Zone. For a while. Until my coronation, at least. Wait.' I can see she wants to say something, but I need to explain. 'Mistral was able to get to me, to us, because of how things are there. Because of how things are for humans. It needs to change, if we're to be in this world together. And I think that's a good place to start.'

My mother frowns slightly. I press on. 'I'm human, aren't I?' She nods. 'So, am I food?' Her mouth makes an 'o' of surprise, her eyes widening.

'No! Of course not! You're my daughter. You are Raven.'

'An accident of birth, though, right? If I'd been born in the Safe Zone, to human parents, all I could look forward to was living and dying in the same place and, possibly, being meat for some hungry vampire. There's no difference between me and them. Yet you want me to have an education, to travel, to be your heir, while all they can do is drink and read second-hand books and p-pretend that they have a life—' I'm trying not to cry '—and I think they should have more. That Raven should set an example.'

'So, what do you want to do?'

'I want to live there for a while, and see how it works. How we can make change, perhaps offer humans a different way of living, where they have a choice. There are islands, you know, not too far out. Perhaps we could even set up a proper Safe Zone there, one where humans can be truly free again. It's time, I think, to try and build a world that works for us both.'

'A good idea.' My mother and I both turn to see my father leaning against the doorframe, his arms folded. 'It won't happen overnight, though, Emelia. There will be hard work involved.'

'I'm ready,' I say. I don't just mean for the work. I mean for all of it. The crown, the mantle of Raven and all that it means. I've been through the fire and come out the other side, harder, stronger than I was before. 'And it's what I want to do.'

'You might fail.' My father is still serious, but there's light in his golden eyes. 'Are you prepared for that?'

'Better I fail than don't try at all.'

He pushes off from the doorframe, coming towards me. 'Spoken like a ruler.' One corner of his mouth curves. 'You are right. It is time for change. But it won't be easy.'

'Because I'm human. I get that. But my weakness is also my strength.' I see this now, so clearly. *You have no idea who you could be.* Words spoken in a darkened hallway, what feels like a lifetime ago. He was right. I had no idea. But now I do.

'Are you sure this is what you want?'

I know my mother won't want me to go. Almost losing me frightened her, and I know she'll worry. But I'm determined. It's time for the work to begin. 'I'll come back and see you, every week,' I say. 'I'd miss you too much, otherwise.'

She stands, holding out her hand. I take it, and she pulls me to her feet. We're the same height and, for the first time, I feel I might live up to her. She smiles. 'Well then, my beautiful girl, let's make this happen.' She takes my other hand and we dance, my bare feet twirling on the soft rug, my spirit rising at the potential of what's to come.

# Chapter Forty

## SECRETS

It's early morning and I'm walking through the Safe Zone. I've been here for just over a week. This time of day suits me – there aren't too many people around, and I'm still adjusting to sleeping at night. I have a small house near the beach, which I share with one of our blood dancers, sworn to secrecy. Mother insisted I take a guard as well – I refused at first, but knew she was right. After all, there's still a rebellion going on. They keep themselves scarce, a gleam of silver and black in the night. The house has been modified, too – oh, nothing too opulent. Let's just say I have a very effective security system.

I reach the small café I visited with Ruth. The awning is up, someone setting up tables and chairs on the pavement. I realise who it is.

'Michael?'

He stops, putting the chair he's unfolding down. When he turns I see a faint red line curving above one eyebrow.

'You're all right!' We both say it at the same time, then laugh.

'Oh, thank darkness,' he says. 'I was so worried about you.'

'Worried about me? You were *bleeding*.'

'Oh, that? Just a scratch.' He grins, lifting a hand to the scar. It's fainter than I would have expected, considering how much he'd been bleeding. His fingers are long, his hands beautifully shaped. 'You made it home, then?'

'Eventually.' I put my hands in my pockets, all at once self-conscious, remembering our closeness in a dark alcove.

'I'm glad,' he says. Morning sun turns his hair to gold, his smile wide. 'So, what brings you out so early?'

'Oh, I just like it.'

'I don't mind early,' he says.

'Me either. It's peaceful.' I try to think of something else to say. 'Well, it was nice seeing you again.'

'You too, Emily. Hope to see you around.'

---

For the next couple of weeks, whenever I take my morning walks, he's outside. Almost as if he's waiting for me. We talk, and sometimes I buy a coffee to take away, though I enjoy the aroma more than the taste. One morning, as he makes my coffee, I notice something. His shirtsleeves are rolled up past his elbows, his muscular forearms bare. He has no Raven mark. He doesn't have a blood port, either. Like me.

'Here it is.' He puts my finished coffee on the counter. 'Your usual, mademoiselle.' I like how he looks when he smiles. I like how he looks all the time, really, but my heart, still bruised, cannot take it any further.

'Thank you.' I dig in my pocket for coins.

'This one's on me.' He slides the cup forward.

'Really? I mean, thank you.'

'On one condition,' he goes on. I raise my eyebrows. 'Will you go out with me? For a walk, one morning?'

My mouth drops open. His cheeks are pink and he looks down.

'Sure. I mean, that would be nice.' It would be nice, actually. I ignore the butterflies in my stomach.

'Really?' His face lights up. 'How would tomorrow be? I can pick you up at seven?'

I frown. 'I thought you said morning.'

'I did – 7 a.m., if that's okay with you. I mean, you did say you liked early, didn't you?' He sounds worried. I don't want him to be.

'Seven is fine. I'm, er, just around the corner. The little white house.'

'See you then.' He hands my coffee to me. Our fingers touch and I blush.

———

The next morning I'm up early. I call my mother and speak to her, telling her I'm going for a walk with a friend. 'Be careful,' she says, her cool voice chiming down the phone. I can tell she's pleased, though. I dress warmly, in fleecy leggings and a long jumper, my leather jacket over the top. I feel queasy, for some reason – it must be nerves, though I don't know why I'm nervous. Still, I can't seem to shake the feeling, even once I've had peppermint tea.

Just past seven there's a knock at the door. I open it to see Michael. He's wearing a jumper too – black, the sleeves and neckline frayed – over dark jeans with chunky leather boots. His blond hair is pushed back, a faint scruff of stubble on his jawline. He looks… hot. I don't know if I'm ready for this.

'Morning,' he says.

'Morning.' I step outside, locking the door, my phone tucked in my jacket pocket with my keys. We start walking, our footsteps echoing in the pre-dawn quiet.

'So where are we going?'

'I thought we could walk on the beach.' He takes my hand.

I flinch, then feel stupid. 'Sorry.'

'D'you want me to let go?'

I shake my head.

We turn the corner onto the promenade. The streetlights are still on, though a faint gleam on the horizon tells me dawn is coming soon. I'm still not used to the fact that I can be outside when it changes, the magic of night turning to day.

'Do you think this is what it was like, back in the old days?'

'Before the Rising?' He grins, one eyebrow raised. 'Maybe. It's pretty peaceful, isn't it?'

'It's lovely.' It is.

We cross the road, taking the stairs down to the sand. It's smooth and damp, our feet leaving faint indents as we walk towards the water, still holding hands. I like it, the warmth and roughness of his skin different. Waves crash and whisper against the shore, the endless song of the sea.

'I love the sound of the ocean,' I say. 'I've never really spent much time near it.'

'You haven't?'

'Uh, no.' I fall silent, wondering if I've given away too much. Our hands swing between us as we wander along the edge of the waves, the sky getting lighter.

'Shall we get a coffee soon,' he says, 'once the café opens?'

'That sounds nice.'

'But first, will you tell me something?'

I glance at him. His profile is silhouetted dark against the sea, like the back of a coin. 'Okay?'

He pauses. 'Who are you really?'

'What?' I frown, then laugh, though I've gone cold inside. 'I told you, my name's Emily.'

'What's your last name?'

I stop walking. So does he, letting go of my hand. I swallow. 'Uh, it's Reynolds. Emily Reynolds.' I give him the last name Kyle once gave me, as I can't think of anything else.

His brow creases. 'So why, *Emily Reynolds*, can I smell violets all around you?'

The way he says my name, I know he knows I'm lying. What I don't know is how. He holds my gaze a moment longer, then rolls his eyes, sighing. He holds out his arm, the inside of his wrist turned upwards, his fist clenched. 'Smell me.'

'What? No!' I make a face. But he keeps holding out his arm and, as I take a breath, I catch it. Violets. I bend closer to his outstretched wrist. His skin is pale, smooth, the muscles strongly defined. I sniff.

'Is it… anti-feed?' I know it isn't. He shakes his head, taking his arm back.

'No. It's me. My bloodline. Like yours. You know humans can't usually smell it, don't you?'

I stare at him. I hadn't known that.

'So tell me again, Emily. Who are you?'

'Who are *you*?' I whisper.

'You first,' he says, starting to smile. The sun is red gold on the horizon, the cool morning breeze blowing softly from the ocean. I shake my head.

'I can't,' I whisper. The amusement leaves his face.

'Okay.' He leans forward. His voice becomes lower, quieter. 'I'll go first. But you have to promise not to tell.'

'I promise.'

'I'm Mistral.' His voice is pitched so low I have to strain to hear him. My eyes widen. 'No one knows,' he goes on. 'I'm just Michael, here. Another orphan among so many.'

I stare at him, open-mouthed. 'B-but, I don't understand—'

'No one does. It's not a known thing, is it? That vamps can have human children. I haven't even met one like me. My father tried to turn me, several times, after my mother died—' his eyes flicker with remembered pain '—but it didn't work. So he threw me out. And I came here.'

'I'm so sorry,' I say. It's all I can manage, my mind reeling. I remember his father, burning in a metal chair. And my mother, sitting on my bed. *I did hear there might be one other*, she said. And here he is. Tears fill my eyes at the thought of her, of my old life.

'Hey, I didn't mean to upset you.' He touches my hand. 'It's ancient history, no need to worry. So—' he shrugs '—hit me with it. Your secret can't be as big as mine. Trust me.'

I take in a breath, blowing it out, then another. He starts to look worried. But my secret is so much bigger than he knows. Can I trust him? My trust is a fragile thing, still, Kyle's betrayal like a mark on my soul.

Then I realise. It doesn't matter. This isn't about Michael. It's about me, and who I really am. The world is turning to gold, the sky a blue-streaked bowl. Waves murmur, the breeze ruffling our hair. Everything feels as though it's waiting, the world poised between night and day. When I decide it feels like release, as though I'm unfurling. The words come out in a rush of breath.

'I am Raven.'

# Acknowledgments

Writing a book is a journey. *The Last Raven* is one that began many years ago as a small piece of flash fiction, written as a blog post. But the story kept growing, and I'm amazed to be at this point, and for you to be reading all about Emelia and the world of Raven. Thank you so much for choosing to do so.

Just like many journeys, I didn't get here alone. A huge thank you to my lovely agent, Laura Bennett, for taking a chance on me and my stories. I'm so grateful to be working with you.

An equally huge thank you to Charlotte Ledger and the wonderful team at One More Chapter, HarperCollins UK. You have all championed my book so beautifully, and I'm thrilled to have it in such safe hands. From editing to promotion and sales, you've helped to make *The Last Raven* the book it is today, and I am full of appreciation for you all.

I've been writing for a long time, and have been lucky enough to make some wonderful friends along the way.

Sacha, you got behind Raven from the very beginning, badgering me for more instalments, keeping me going when I felt like giving up, and adding your considerable insight as a beta reader (how many versions of this have you read?). You are a dear friend, one of the best, and I couldn't have got here without you.

Michelle, you came late to my Raven world, but your friendship and encouragement through all of this has been invaluable, as has your appreciation of haunted dolls. Louise, Lynn, Suzie, and Dianne, thank you so much for all your love and support; you are truly friends to treasure as we navigate this crazy writing world together.

To my family, thank you for believing in me, and for giving me the space to fly.

To my husband, thank you for flying with me all of these years, and for always championing my art.

And finally, to my daughter, thank you for being a joy and an inspiration. When I started writing this book, I knew it would be about a mother and daughter, and the love between them. The story has grown as you have and, when it came to the dedication, I knew it could only be for you.

**ONE MORE CHAPTER**

The author and One More Chapter would like to thank everyone
who contributed to the publication of this story...

**Analytics**
James Brackin
Abigail Fryer
Maria Osa

**Audio**
Fionnuala Barrett
Ciara Briggs

**Contracts**
Sasha Duszynska
Lewis

**Design**
Lucy Bennett
Fiona Greenway
Liane Payne
Dean Russell

**Digital Sales**
Lydia Grainge
Hannah Lismore
Emily Scorer

**Editorial**
Simon Fox
Arsalan Isa
Charlotte Ledger
Bonnie Macleod
Jennie Rothwell

**Harper360**
Emily Gerbner
Jean Marie Kelly
emma sullivan
Sophia Wilhelm

**International Sales**
Peter Borcsok
Bethan Moore

**Marketing & Publicity**
Chloe Cummings
Emma Petfield

**Operations**
Melissa Okusanya
Hannah Stamp

**Production**
Denis Manson
Simon Moore
Francesca Tuzzeo

**Rights**
Vasiliki Machaira
Rachel McCarron
Hany Sheikh
Mohamed
Zoe Shine

**The HarperCollins
Distribution Team**

**The HarperCollins
Finance & Royalties
Team**

**The HarperCollins
Legal Team**

**The HarperCollins
Technology Team**

**Trade Marketing**
Ben Hurd

**UK Sales**
Laura Carpenter
Isabel Coburn
Jay Cochrane
Sabina Lewis
Holly Martin
Erin White
Harriet Williams
Leah Woods

**And every other
essential link in the
chain from delivery
drivers to booksellers
to librarians and
beyond!**

YOUR NUMBER ONE STOP

## ONE MORE CHAPTER

FOR PAGETURNING BOOKS

One More Chapter is an
award-winning global
division of HarperCollins.

Sign up to our newsletter to get our
latest eBook deals and stay up to date
with our weekly Book Club!
<u>Subscribe here.</u>

Meet the team at
<u>www.onemorechapter.com</u>

Follow us!

 <u>@OneMoreChapter_</u>
 <u>@OneMoreChapter</u>
 <u>@onemorechapterhc</u>

Do you write unputdownable fiction?
We love to hear from new voices.
Find out how to submit your novel at
<u>www.onemorechapter.com/submissions</u>